RUNNING TO YOU

THE WRIGHT HEROES OF MAINE

ROBIN PATCHEN

JDO PUBLISHING

Cover by Lynnette Bonner.

Ebook ISBN: 979-8223522492

Print ISBN: 978-1950029372

Large Print Edition: 978-1950029365

Hardcover ISBN: 978-1950029341

CHAPTER ONE

SAM WRIGHT LIKED BEING ALONE. He'd built an empire alone, and he wouldn't apologize for that.

But maybe he should be a little more hospitable when he had houseguests.

Daniel stood in his office doorway, a container of nuts in his hand. "I guess if you won't come out, I'll have to come in."

"Sorry." Sam closed his laptop. "I had a couple of details to hammer out."

"Big deal?"

"Yeah, pretty big." The biggest of Sam's career, though he didn't tell Daniel that. His oldest brother was still getting his feet under him after coming back from the dead. Not literally, but close enough.

Considering what Daniel and his family had been through, Sam's financial success seemed trivial. But putting together an eight-figure deal was not nothing. His cut would set him up for life.

As if he needed more money.

Daniel settled in the chair on the other side of the desk and held out the can of nuts.

"I'm good."

Daniel pulled it back and ate a few, staring out at the dark night. Lights glittered on boats in the harbor below. "You always work so late?"

Though it was after ten o'clock on a Friday night, it wasn't unusual that Sam was still in his office. "I lost track of time. Where's Camilla?"

"Getting ready for bed." Tearing his gaze away from the view, his brother leveled that intense gaze on Sam, the one Daniel had so often worn when they were growing up, though it was different now on his mature face. He seemed happy and healthy, more so than before he'd disappeared. "Why aren't you on a date or something?"

"I have company."

"Otherwise, you would be? Because we wouldn't have noticed one way or another. You've hardly left your office all day."

"Like I said—"

"Business. I get it. I spent my life at the hospital as if my work were the most important thing in the world. I've since learned that nothing trumps family."

"I don't have one of those," Sam snapped.

His brother's look—chin lowered, eyebrows lifted—told him Daniel hadn't missed his sharp tone.

And...fine. Sam did have a family. Two parents and five brothers, most of whom lived nearby. None of them needed him hanging around, though.

"Maybe it's time—"

The doorbell rang, loud in the quiet room.

"You expecting someone?"

Sam stood. "It's probably a delivery driver. The houses aren't well marked around here." He passed his brother, thankful to have an excuse to escape the conversation.

The doorbell rang again, followed by pounding.

Sam picked up speed down the hall and around the corner, his brother on his heels. The entryway was dark, though enough light came from the lamp in the living room to illuminate the way. He reached the door and opened it, ready to give whoever was on the other side a piece of his mind.

The words stuck in his throat.

A woman stood on the stoop in the glow of the porch lights. He barely took in the sight of her before she spoke.

"Thank God I found you." Then she stepped inside and slid her arms around his waist, hanging on like she might never let him go.

On the street, a man—no, a teenager—stood beside a white pickup. He called, "You got her, dude? She was lost."

Before Sam could think of a response, the kid hopped into the truck and took off.

Sam held her, breathing in dirt and bracken and the scent of coconut shampoo and something else, something elusive and familiar. He didn't move, didn't dare.

If he moved, she'd disappear again.

He'd be left alone.

So he held very, very still and allowed himself to enjoy the moment. The perfect rightness of the moment.

And then he came to his senses.

He gripped her arms and stepped back.

She wore a thin red windbreaker two sizes too big over a wrinkled blue plaid button-down shirt, ugly navy work pants, and black sneakers.

Nothing like the high fashion she used to wear.

But other things were the same. Her shiny, sable-colored hair. High cheekbones, full lips. He'd once heard someone refer to her as *sort of girl-next-door pretty*. That guy was an idiot.

Not that Sam wanted her. Not anymore. "Who was that?"

"Who was what?"

"The guy who dropped you off."

"Oh. Um..."

She didn't seem to know how to explain. Had she been hitchhiking? More importantly, "What are you doing here?"

She blinked up at him, her hazel eyes filled with confusion. She raised her hand and stroked his beard. "Where did this come from?"

He backed out of her reach. "Why are you here?"

"What do you mean?"

The overhead light flicked on.

She winced and lifted a hand to shield her face.

And he saw what he'd missed before.

There were dead leaves in her hair, which hung far longer than the shoulder-length it'd once been. She had a scrape on her cheek. Her hazel eyes were red-rimmed. Her lip was swollen.

"What happened?" Sam demanded.

"I don't..." Voice small, almost frightened. "Are you mad at me?"

Before he could formulate a response—because this made no sense at all—Dan's hand clamped on his shoulder. "Hi. I'm Sam's brother, Daniel."

Her gaze shifted to him. "I'm..." There was a pause. A long pause. And then, "Um, Eliza?"

Daniel glanced his way. "Why don't we go sit down?" He reached toward her, but she ducked and raised an arm as if to ward off a blow.

Daniel dropped his hand and stepped back. "That's all right." He spoke in an *everything's going to be okay* voice. "Sam, why don't you and Eliza join me in the living room?" He swiveled and walked out, pulling his phone from his pocket and tapping the screen.

Something was seriously wrong.

Trying to emulate his brother's soothing tone, Sam said, "Is that all right with you, Eliza?"

She seemed to relax at the use of her name. "Okay." She took a step but seemed to lose her balance.

"Whoa." He caught her and kept her from falling. She held on as if he were the only thing keeping her from tumbling over. He scooped her into his arms.

"Oh."

She didn't seem alarmed, just surprised, as he carried her into his living room toward the sofa.

Again, her fingers found his whiskers. "I like it. It makes you look fierce."

"Hold up." Daniel grabbed a fleece throw from a basket and laid it over the white upholstery. As if Sam cared about stains.

At that moment, all he could think was *Please, let her be all right.*

He'd spent five years trying not to think about Eliza. Apparently, not time well spent.

He settled her on the blanket and sat on the coffee table across from her. "What happened?"

"I don't..."

Her words faded when Daniel pressed the button that closed the curtains. She watched them slowly cover the wall of windows and the darkness beyond.

"Eliza." Sam tried to maintain the calm tone as he pulled her focus back. "What's going on?"

Daniel hit a switch, and the overhead lights came on.

She winced and closed her eyes.

What was she hiding? "You show up here after—"

"Sam." Dan's voice was still low, but now it held an edge of warning. "Would you let me, please?"

"Fine." He stood and stepped away, running a hand through his hair, not sure what to do.

Daniel took his place.

Eliza's eyes opened, and she shrank back at the sight of him so close.

"It's okay," Sam said. "Daniel's my brother. You remember I told you about him? He's a doctor."

She nodded, keeping her head down.

The lights were bothering her. He turned on a table lamp beside them and flicked off the overheads. The room dimmed considerably.

"Is that better?" Daniel asked.

"Uh-huh."

"Does your head hurt?"

Sam watched from a few feet away as Eliza nodded, squinting as if even that pained her.

"Can you tell me where exactly it hurts?"

She probed the back of her skull. "It's all over, but this is the worst."

"Would you mind if I take a look at it?" He didn't move toward her, just remained steady, giving her the opportunity to refuse.

She looked to Sam, and when he nodded, she said, "Okay."

Daniel touched the sides of her head, then inched his fingers back toward where she'd indicated. "Ah. You have quite a bump back here. I bet that's painful." He sat back on the coffee table. "Can you do something for me? Can you try to think past that pain for a second and tell me what else hurts? I know the head injury is the worst, so close your eyes and breathe through the pain for a few moments. Let the rest of your body speak to you."

She did as he asked, taking a few deep breaths. Lifting a palm to her cheek, she said, "Here." And then, she rubbed her opposite wrist. "And here."

Her arms dropped to her sides.

"Good." His voice lowered further, taking on a rhythmic cadence, almost meditative. "Take your time. Is there anything else that hurts?"

She opened her eyes. "I can't think past the headache. I'm sorry."

"No need to apologize. I noticed you stumbled. Do your legs hurt? Or your feet?"

"I was just dizzy."

"Do you feel sick to your stomach? Any pain in your chest? Your ribs?"

She considered the questions. Then, "No."

"Okay, good. If something else starts to hurt, or if you start to feel sick, you need to tell me, okay?" At her nod, he said, "Sam, grab me another blanket."

He did and laid it over Eliza. She snuggled beneath it. It wasn't cold in the room, but she was shivering. Was she in shock?

Thank God Daniel was here.

Camilla stepped into the space wearing yoga pants and a T-shirt. No shoes. Daniel must have texted her. She stopped beside Sam and addressed Eliza. "Hi. I'm Camilla."

"Hi." Eliza's voice was low, but she smiled. She'd always been like that—kind, welcoming.

Daniel spoke to Sam. "Go get a warm, wet washcloth and a glass of water. And you might start some tea, if you have some."

"I'll stay. Maybe Camilla—"

"You'll go." Again, Daniel's voice was gentle but firm.

Eliza hadn't asked him to leave. But then, Eliza seemed very confused.

He hurried to the kitchen and shoved a mug of water into the microwave. While it warmed, he searched for tea bags. He had to have some somewhere. His housekeeper kept the pantry stocked. Weren't tea bags a staple?

There. A box of herbals right beside the coffee. He chose one at random.

Three minutes later, he carried both drinks back to the living room, a wet towel draped over his arm, his pockets filled with antibacterial cream, bandages, and a bottle of ibuprofen.

Daniel was giving Eliza simple commands, which she was responding to.

Camilla met him at the door and took the two cups and the wash cloth, whispering, "Daniel wants you to wait in the kitchen."

No chance.

But he stayed at the threshold, watching his brother work. Daniel was confident and competent, but it was his soothing tone that impressed Sam. Eliza had gone from fearing him—though why had she?—to trusting him in a matter of minutes.

He examined her wrist, asking her questions as he did. After a moment, he said, "It's just a sprain. We'll get something to wrap it."

Camilla touched Sam's arm. "In the other room?"

Sam kept his voice as low as his sister-in-law's. "Has she said anything? Why she's here?"

Camilla shook her head. "She doesn't seem to remember."

"This is my house. I'm not leaving."

Camilla didn't argue. She approached Eliza with the two drink choices outstretched. Eliza chose the mug and sipped, and Camilla took the space on the table beside her husband. "You've got a little dirt on your face. Do you mind if I clean it?"

Eliza pressed back, looking around. She found Sam and held his gaze with wide eyes, blinking rapidly.

What was she afraid of? Not Sam, obviously.

This was ridiculous. He crossed the space. "I'll do it."

Daniel and Camilla shared a look, but they moved out of his way. He took the washcloth, sat on the table, and leaned close. "Tell me if I hurt you, okay?"

She nodded, the movement barely perceptible, and he dabbed at a smudge on her forehead as gently as he could.

She closed her eyes, her shoulders falling. Relaxing. Trusting him.

That wouldn't last.

He continued down to her cheeks, careful of the cut. By the time he'd gotten most of the dirt cleared, the towel had cooled.

It was too dark to see if there were bruises, and maybe too soon. He still had no idea what had happened to her. But the cut on her cheek didn't look deep. He dug into his pocket and set the things he'd brought on the table beside him.

"Good thinking," Dan said.

If he hadn't thought of it, no doubt his brother would've sent him to fetch the items. And he didn't want to be away from Eliza now. Not when she so obviously needed him.

He'd analyze that later.

"Can I ask you some questions?" Daniel shifted closer, and Sam slid off the table to kneel beside the sofa. Daniel dabbed a bit of antibiotic ointment onto her cut.

"Okay."

"Can you tell me your whole name?"

"Elizabeth Marie Pelletier."

"That's a beautiful name," Daniel said. "When's your birthday?"

"January seventeenth."

"And you're how old?"

"Twenty-three."

The wrong answer was delivered with such confidence.

The anxiety humming on Sam's skin ramped up.

"Okay." Daniel's voice gave away no worry. "And what year is it?"

She sipped the tea, then lowered it to her lap. "Twenty seventeen."

Wrong by five years.

Five years ago, Sam and Eliza had been together. Five years ago, they'd been in love.

"Do you remember what happened before you came here tonight?"

"Um..." She found Sam with her eyes. "I don't know. I probably went to work?"

She voiced it as if he'd be able to confirm or deny.

Daniel asked, "Where do you work?"

"At an investment firm in Portsmouth."

She had, once upon a time.

"Do you have any drug allergies?"

"No."

Daniel looked at Sam as if he should know. He didn't remember drug allergies. He did remember her taking over-the-counter pain meds.

He nodded to the bottle of pills. "She can take those."

Daniel took the mug from her and poured four pills into her palm. "These'll help with the headache."

She put them in her mouth, then drank from the glass Sam held out.

"You've got a head injury," Dan said, "and it's affecting your memory. We're going to get you to a hospital—"

"No!" Her eyes widened, then found Sam again. "I can't go to the hospital. I can't."

"Okay." In response to the terror radiating off her, Sam's body tensed as if preparing for a fight. "Nobody's going to make you do anything."

"You need tests." Daniel ignored Sam's interjection. "We need to find out why you can't remember—"

"I can't go to the hospital."

"Why?" Sam asked. "What will happen?"

She looked from him to Daniel, then to Camilla, who stood behind the table. "Please, don't make me go. I can't go."

"Okay, that's okay." Camilla spoke as if to a small, frightened child. "We'll talk about it tomorrow. Maybe things will be clearer in the morning."

In the morning.

Which meant she'd have to stay somewhere tonight. Sam had no idea where she lived. After she'd left him, she'd blocked his number. He hadn't heard from her—or about her, or even seen her on social media—in five years. He had seen her in person once, six months before.

In Salt Lake City. A long, long way from his house in coastal Maine.

Apparently, Eliza would be staying here tonight. Under his roof, in a room just down the hall.

So different from when they'd been together. Five years before, she'd have stayed not only in his house but in his bed.

He wasn't going there again, not with any woman, and certainly not *this* woman. She'd ripped his heart out. No way was he handing it over again.

Sam liked being alone. And yet his stomach did a stupid little flip at the idea of her staying. As if it could last.

As if there might be a chance.

Sam leaned against the wall outside the guest room. Since Daniel and Camilla were occupying the larger guest suite on the other side of the house, Eliza would need to stay in this one, right down the hall from the master bedroom. It had a full bath, and Camilla was in there now with Eliza, helping her get cleaned up and ready for bed.

The shower had gone off thirty minutes before. He thought he'd heard the hum of a hair dryer. How long could it possibly take her to get ready for bed? He'd need to get her proper clothes. Maybe Camilla could loan her something to get through the next day. They were about the same height, though Eliza was thinner than Sam's sister-in-law. Too thin, in his opinion. She'd lost some of the curves he'd liked so much.

Finally, the door opened.

"Oh." Camilla startled at the sight of him. "I didn't realize you were waiting." She stepped into the hallway and closed the door.

"Just want to make sure she doesn't need anything." After Daniel had finished examining her, Sam had offered her food—which she'd refused—and then found an old, soft T-shirt for her to sleep in. "Did she remember anything else?"

"Not that she said. She wants to talk to you."

Why...why did his pulse race at those words? "Is she dressed?"

"She's under the covers. I'm sure it's weird for you, but she wouldn't be put off. And since her jeans are covered in dirt... I could give her my yoga pants so she can come out here, if you'd prefer. It'll just take me a sec to change."

"I think I can handle it." He knocked on the door. "It's me."

"Come in."

He pushed inside and closed the door before he looked toward the bed. The only light came from the bathroom, illuminating her just enough for him to know she was sitting up, his gray UNH T-shirt hanging from her narrow shoulders.

Images flashed in his memory—Eliza in his bed. Eliza in a

towel. Eliza making eggs, his favorite sweatshirt hanging nearly to her bare knees.

He squeezed his eyes closed. The woman in his guest bed wasn't his and never should have been. He'd repented and chosen to make better choices, but his body didn't seem to remember that.

I'm gonna need Your help here.

"Are you just going to stand there?" She patted the bed beside her with her good hand. The other wrist was wrapped in a bandage Sam had found among his first aid supplies. "I can hardly see you."

He crossed the room but stopped a few feet away. Eliza had folded the comforter at her feet. The sheet and a thin blanket outlined her legs and hips.

He was grateful the light wasn't on. He didn't need a clearer view. "Feel better after your bath?"

"Much. Thank you." She looked around the space. "I don't remember this room. Or this house. Your brother said I've lost some of my memory. Did you just move in?"

Daniel had gotten right on his laptop after Eliza and Camilla had walked away, researching. Sam had sat on a barstool in the kitchen waiting for him to explain what was going on. And tell him she'd be all right. But he hadn't spoken until Sam stood to leave.

"Don't tell her anything." Daniel's words halted Sam's retreat. "At least not tonight. We want her to rest, not to worry. The most important thing for her is sleep."

"So I'm supposed to pretend to be her boyfriend? What happens when she remembers? She'll hate me." More than she already did.

Daniel's lips slipped into a smirk. "I feel like you can find a happy medium. Be kind. Be wise. Be holy."

Three things he definitely hadn't been when he and Eliza had dated.

Now, he tried to figure out how to take his brother's advice as he answered Eliza. "You haven't seen the whole place." There. That was both true and vague.

"How come? Have I been out of town? It looks like you're completely moved in."

"It's just a house, Eliza. It doesn't matter. How do you feel?"

"My headache is fading, but whenever I try to remember where I was tonight, it starts to pound. It's so strange. It's like my brain hurts. Do you know where I was?"

"I'm sorry. I don't."

"How come? Are you and I... Are we okay? You've been acting weird all night."

"You took me off guard, that's all. Showing up, obviously hurt. Memory...off."

She patted the bed again. "Why won't you sit with me?"

"You need to rest. We'll talk tomorrow."

Everything about her attracted him, but it was her eyes he loved the most. Big, expressive hazel eyes that now filled with hurt.

"I wish you'd stay with me."

He stepped closer. He couldn't help it. How was he supposed to be kind and...? What had Daniel said? Three minutes with Eliza, and Sam had already forgotten.

He leaned down, brushed her hair back, and kissed her forehead. "You need to rest. Let me know if you need anything. I'm just down the hall on the right."

"Okay."

He swiveled and escaped.

Headed back to the kitchen, where Daniel was still focused on his laptop screen.

Camilla was sitting beside him, sipping from a mug. She looked up when Sam walked in. "How is she?"

"The same." He shoved out a barstool on Daniel's other side but didn't sit. He was too restless. He paced across the hardwood floor and opened the refrigerator.

He wasn't hungry or thirsty.

He slammed it shut and crossed to the opposite side of his kitchen island from his brother. "Have you learned anything?"

Daniel looked up, blinked. "She has amnesia."

"Amnesia? Eight years of med school, an hour behind that stupid screen, and that's what you came up with?"

Daniel didn't rise to Sam's bait. "Amnesia isn't uncommon with head injuries. The extent of it—losing five years of her life —that's less common, but not unheard of."

"What should we do?"

"She needs rest. I'd like her to go to a hospital for a CT scan, but"—he tipped his head side to side—"honestly, there's no reason to believe she has a brain bleed or clot. She isn't sick. Her headache isn't getting worse. Her speech and motor skills haven't been affected." He turned to Camilla. "She had no problem getting cleaned up and dressed?"

"Right. She can take care of herself. She was moving slowly. I think she's in more pain than she said."

"It's hard to think past a pounding headache." Daniel didn't seem concerned. Which was really starting to tick Sam off. "She has no broken bones. My guess is she was in a car accident. Did you see who brought her here?"

"A white pickup truck. It left as soon as I opened the door."

Dan pushed the laptop away. "You didn't recognize it?"

"How would I?"

Camilla recoiled from his raised voice.

Daniel barely reacted. "Let's not wake her. She needs her rest."

His house was big enough that Eliza wouldn't hear him. But that wasn't really the point. To Camilla, he said, "Sorry. I didn't mean to yell."

"You're understandably concerned." She was kinder to him than he deserved. She dumped the rest of her tea in the sink and slipped the mug into the dishwasher. "I'll leave some clothes outside her door for tomorrow." She gave Sam a quick side hug. It's going to be okay." She rounded the island, kissed Daniel, and said, "Don't stay up too late."

He held her hand until she was out of reach and watched until she disappeared. They were like newlyweds, those two, despite the fact that they'd been married twenty-something years.

Finally, Daniel turned back to him. "You want to tell me what's going on?"

"Uh... An ex with amnesia is sleeping in my guest room?"

"You're acting weird."

Irritation surged. "A woman who disappeared five years ago shows up on my doorstep and throws herself into my arms—a woman who clearly thinks we're still together—and *I'm* acting weird. How's a person supposed to behave in that situation? Is there a manual?"

Daniel fished something from his pocket and dropped it on the island between them.

Sam looked at it but didn't pick it up. He didn't need to. He knew what it was. "Where'd you get that?" His voice, too loud before, was now unnaturally low.

"It was in her hand. I found it when I examined her wrist."

The business card was crumpled and worn, as if she'd held onto it for a long time. It explained one question Sam had yet to vocalize—how she'd found him.

"You gave that to her in Salt Lake City, right?"

Sam's gaze snapped up. "How did you know that?"

"When Camilla and I went to dinner that night, we saw you talking to a woman. You wrote something down and gave it to her. Your address, apparently."

Sam's hasty scrawl was smeared in blue.

"You looked..." Dan shrugged. "I would say worried, but I couldn't see your face, just your body language. I thought you'd tell us about it, but you never did. I forgot about it until I saw the card in her hand."

Sam didn't like that his brother had seen. He didn't like that he had to explain himself. He didn't like any of this. He wanted to tell Daniel to mind his own business.

But Eliza was Daniel's business now. He'd examined her, after all. He was concerned for her health. And he was Sam's big brother. He could be trusted.

"After we broke up, she disappeared. She blocked my number."

"Did you deserve that?"

"Probably."

He wasn't about to share the details. He would have tried to win her back if she'd given him any opportunity. But she didn't want to hear from him. She didn't care enough to listen.

"The point is, she didn't just disappear from *my* life. She disappeared completely. Quit her job. Moved out of her place. She blocked me on social media, but I'm still in contact with her mother and some of her friends. I'll admit, for a while"—the first two years, but Daniel didn't need specifics—"I looked for her. Photos, mentions of her on other people's pages." He'd even hired a PI, though he didn't want to sound too pathetic. "I wanted to know she was okay. I mean, we were together for a long time, and then... There was nothing. Not a single mention of her. No photographs. Nothing."

"What do you think happened?"

"I have no idea." There went his volume again. He tamped

it down. "That's why, when I saw her in Utah... It's not that I wanted her back. I just wanted to know she was all right. But I got the opposite sense. I thought she looked scared, like she was afraid somebody might see us talking. The way she acted—"

"I know what you mean. She looked nervous."

As much as he hated knowing his brother had witnessed him practically begging her to talk to him, he was glad to have his impression confirmed.

"Did she tell you anything?"

"Nothing. And she never contacted me." Which had told him everything he needed to know. Not that he'd dreamed they'd reconcile, marry, and live happily ever after. But the way she'd so thoroughly cut him out of her life as if he hadn't mattered...and then rejected him that day in Salt Lake six months before. It had hurt.

And yet there was the business card he'd given her, its hard edges softened and curling. She hadn't tossed it away. Maybe she hadn't completely tossed him away.

"You loved her." Daniel's words held no question.

Sam didn't bother responding. He had loved her. But it wasn't enough. *He* wasn't enough.

And he wasn't going there again. Only an idiot would restart a story he knew ended in tragedy. "We'll take her to the hospital tomorrow."

If Daniel was surprised by the subject shift, he didn't let on. "You told her you wouldn't take her if she didn't want to go. And she definitely doesn't want to go."

"Something happened to her. Somebody needs to figure out what. If not the hospital, then the police. She must've been in some kind of accident, right? For all we know, somebody's looking for her."

"The people in the white pickup know where she is."

"That kid? He couldn't squeal out of here fast enough."

Who would do that? Who would dump an injured woman with no memories and not even walk her to the door? A stupid teenager, but still...

Not just that, but Eliza had carried no phone, no purse, no anything except the business card crumpled in her hand. Where were her things? Where was her wallet?

What was she doing in Shadow Cove? Her mother lived an hour down the coast. Eliza's apartment had been even farther, just over the border from Portsmouth.

Why Shadow Cove? To see him?

It didn't make sense.

"If she doesn't need the hospital," Sam said, "we'll just take her to the police station tomorrow. They'll figure out what's going on, contact her family, get her—"

"You should contact her family."

Right. He should have done that already.

Eliza's mother had never liked Sam, and frankly, the feeling was mutual. They were still connected on social media, but only because he'd wanted information on Eliza. And Linda Pelletier had probably wanted to stalk him, prove to herself he was the playboy she'd always suspected.

But Daniel was right. Eliza's mother needed to know what was going on. She'd take care of Eliza.

Sam stalked out of the kitchen, through the living area, and into his office, where he sat at his desk and opened his laptop.

He navigated to Facebook.

Daniel stood in the doorway, arms crossed, as Sam typed in the woman's name.

A number of profile pages came up, but none of them belonged to the Linda Pelletier he was looking for.

Had she finally severed their connection? What unfortunate timing. Except... Even if they weren't friends, her profile would come up, wouldn't it? They had friends in common.

Weird.

Daniel stepped around Sam's desk and peered at his over-size monitor. "What's going on?"

"I guess she got off Facebook."

Sam checked other social media sites but got the same results.

"You have her phone number?"

Did he? Sam pulled his phone from his pocket and searched his contacts. Sure enough, there she was. Not shocking, considering he'd dated her daughter for a year. He hated to wake her in the middle of the night, but maybe she was frantic with worry.

He pressed the number.

And got a computer-generated voice. *"The number called has been disconnected..."*

"What in the world?" He tossed the cell phone on his desk. "She changed her number? Why would she do that?"

Daniel clamped a hand on his shoulder. "Let's just get some rest tonight. We can regroup in the morning."

"Yeah. Okay." Much as he wanted to argue, he had no more ideas.

At the top of the stairs, he was about to tell his brother good-night when he saw him headed toward Eliza's room. Daniel stepped inside and closed the door.

A moment later, he came back out. "She's asleep," he whispered. "Barely stirred when I checked her pulse. She should be okay until morning."

"But she has a concussion, right?" He matched his brother's volume. "Aren't we supposed to wake her every hour or something?"

Daniel smiled. "We don't do that anymore. She'll be fine." He squeezed Sam's arm, then headed toward the other end of the house.

Sam went to his room and prepared for bed. If Daniel said she'd be all right, then she would be. Who was he to second-guess a physician's opinion? Everything he knew about concussion protocol he'd learned watching football games.

But, despite his fatigue, despite the late hour, after he clicked off the light he stared at the ceiling. Praying for Eliza. Trying not to think about her sleeping in the next room.

And that she thought they were still in love.

CHAPTER TWO

THEY FOUND HER.

Eliza ran, ran as fast as she could. But the ground was squishy like dry sand. Branches gripped her ankles, pulled her down.

She could hear them. They were closing in. It was over. Everything she'd done, everything she'd tried, and it was all over.

Terror started deep inside. It clawed its way up from her stomach to her throat and choked her until she couldn't breathe.

She sat up, gasping for breath.

A nightmare. Only a nightmare.

But...where was she? This wasn't her bed. This wasn't her room.

She propelled herself off the mattress, stumbled. Caught herself with her hand. Pain stabbed her wrist, and she sucked in a breath and reached for something to steady herself.

A crash broke through the silence. What was that? Where did—?

A door opened.

A man rushed inside. "Eliza? Are you all right?" He moved toward her.

She backed away, bumped the mattress. Climbed on and scrambled to the far side, away from the stranger.

"Hey, hey. It's me. You're safe. It's Sam."

Sam.

It was Sam.

He came toward the bed, hands up, palms out. He froze and, after a glance at the floor, headed for the other side of the bed. Toward her.

Her heart pounded with fear, but she didn't know why. She didn't know anything.

"It's just me, Eliza." His voice was soothing. "I heard a crash. I didn't mean to scare you. Are you all right?"

With the hallway light behind him, she could barely make out his face. But his voice calmed her. Yes, she could trust that voice.

"What happened?"

"A nightmare. That's all. Just a stupid nightmare."

"You're okay, then? How's your head?"

Oh. It ached, now that he mentioned it. Right. She'd hurt it. She touched the bump on the back of her skull. It seemed bigger than before.

"Is it all right if I turn on the light?" he asked. "I want to get these pieces picked up so you don't cut your foot."

"What pieces?"

"The lamp. Lie down and close your eyes so the light doesn't make your headache worse."

She shouldn't let him clean up after her. But her wrist throbbed—because in her panic, she'd stupidly put her weight on it. Her head pounded, and her heart raced.

She did as he suggested, snuggling beneath the covers on the comfortable mattress.

The light came on, and the room filled with the clink-clink of lamp fragments falling into a trash can. It was quiet for a few moments, and then the swish-swish of a broom. The tinkling of tiny pieces.

"I think I got it all." Sam spoke in barely more than a whisper. "I'm leaving your shoes beside the bed. Please put them on when you get up. I'd hate for you to step on a piece and cut yourself. Okay?"

"Thank you. Sorry."

"It's just a lamp." He fell silent, but she felt him there. Then, his fingers brushed the exposed skin on her upper arm. "Does it hurt here?"

Did it? Once she concentrated on it... "A little. Why?"

"You have a bruise." His voice was still low, but anger hummed on the words.

Why, though? She wanted to open her eyes and look at him, but the light was too bright.

"Do you remember how you got it?"

She tried to think back, but concentrating made her head pulse with pain.

After a minute, he said, "How about your nightmare? Do you remember that?"

"Just that I was scared. Running."

"Scared of what?"

She shrugged. "It's gone now."

He tugged the T-shirt down over her arm, then brought the blanket up to cover her. The light flicked off.

She opened her eyes.

Sam stood beside the bed. "Do you need anything?"

"I'm all right. Sorry I woke you."

"Camilla brought you some clothes. I put them in the bathroom. And Daniel left more tablets on your nightstand beside a glass of water. You can take them at five o'clock. It's three thirty now." He removed his watch and set it there. "So you can check the time."

"Thank you." She knew how much he loved that watch. "I'll try not to break it."

She expected a chuckle, but he made no sound as he closed the door.

Definitely angry. At her? For what?

More concerning. He hadn't kissed her, not even a light peck on her temple like he'd done earlier. In fact, he'd barely touched her at all.

The house felt wrong. The world felt wrong. She didn't know what was going on. She did know that the man she trusted more than anyone else was treating her like a stranger.

Worse than that. A niggling in the back of her mind told her she'd forgotten something.

Something incredibly important.

CHAPTER THREE

"HEY, BRO."

The whisper reached Sam as someone jostled his shoulder.

He opened his eyes and sat up, stretching his aching limbs.

His brother was crouching over him in the hallway. He pressed a finger over his lips, then held out a hand.

Sam gripped it and allowed himself to be pulled up, then followed Daniel down the stairs. Dim light shone through the windows beside his front door, illuminating the house as they made their way into the kitchen.

"What happened?" Dan sounded concerned. "Did she get sick? You should have woken me."

It was too early to talk, especially after spending the bulk of the night outside Eliza's door. He started the coffee brewing, then opened the blinds to let in the day. A glow above the sea on the eastern horizon promised a pretty sunrise.

"Sam."

He turned to see his brother watching him, impatience etched on his features.

"If she was sick—"

"She had a nightmare. Panicked and broke a lamp." Which

didn't explain why Sam was sleeping outside her door. "I was worried she'd wake up again and... She was scared. I didn't want her to be afraid. But I didn't think I should stay in there with her, so..."

"Did she? Wake up again?"

"I heard her cry out a couple of times and peeked in on her, but she went right back to sleep."

"From pain, you think, or...?"

How would he know?

He didn't answer the question, just stood in the kitchen, the only sounds coming from the gurgling coffee maker. Finally, it beeped, and he pulled clean mugs from the dishwasher and poured his brother a cup, then himself. They sipped silently.

The coffee warmed him. The caffeine awakened him.

"I saw something last night." Sam set the mug on the counter as the memory of it raised bile in his throat. "Her sleeve had slid up. She has bruises on her upper arm. They look like..." He didn't know how to explain it. He reached across his body and grabbed his opposite arm just below the shoulder. And squeezed. "It's a handprint. I think. I need you to confirm it."

Daniel's lips tightened, and he nodded once.

"Not a car accident," Sam said. "Not an *accident* at all. Somebody did that to her. Somebody..." He couldn't voice it.

But he could picture it. A man grabbing her, shaking her. Banging her head into whatever left that lump. Her getting away, running through the forest, based on the leaves in her hair.

He turned away from his brother, squeezed his hands into fists to contain the anger. The idea that somebody would hurt her like that.

That she would leave Sam and run into the arms of an abusive...

And never reach out. Never ask for help. Just...live with it.

Suffer. Was a man who physically hurt her really better than he was? He would never have hurt her.

Physically, anyway.

"We don't know what happened," Dan said.

"Mmm-hmm."

"Let's not jump to conclusions."

He swallowed a retort. His brother was right. Maybe the attack had been random. Maybe she had left the abuser, and he'd found her. Maybe...

There were too many unknowns to formulate any real theories, though his mind seemed intent on trying.

"We should get the police involved," Daniel said.

Sam turned back to him. "If she wants to. The thing is, she had a nightmare. I think, deep down, she remembers. So... I mean, you're the doctor, but that's a thing, right? Stuffing memories into your subconscious?"

"It is."

"She didn't want to go to the hospital. Maybe she knows instinctively that whoever did that to her will track her down if she does."

"Maybe."

Sam rubbed the back of his aching neck. What kind of idiot slept on the floor?

Outside the room of a woman who didn't want him?

"It's not my problem." After worrying and praying and worrying some more, Sam had finally reached that obvious conclusion. "I'll take her home today. Her mother will take care of her."

Daniel nodded. "They're close, her and her mom?"

He sipped his coffee. "Her mother's..." Controlling. Manipulative. Judgmental. "She has a very strong personality. But she loves Eliza. I'm sure she'll be able to fill in the blanks about what's been going on in her life. Eliza could barely sneeze without consulting her mother." Bitterness tinged those last few words.

"Did she have something to do with you two—?"

"We need to tell Eliza the truth today, right? I mean, she can't go on thinking I'm her boyfriend. And thinking it's twenty seventeen." He needed to get Eliza to people who could take care of her.

Daniel didn't press his question. "Assuming she wakes up feeling refreshed—and hasn't remembered everything already, which she might. Yeah, we need to tell her."

That she'd lost five years of her life. Her memories.

That she no longer loved the man she'd run to the night before.

CHAPTER FOUR

SUNSHINE PEEKED between the curtains and the window jamb, lighting the room Eliza had barely seen the night before.

After a stretch cut short by unexpected aches—wow, what *didn't* hurt?—she sat up in bed and took the space in. It was large enough to easily accommodate the queen-sized bed, two nightstands, and an oversize bureau beside the door. Between narrow bookshelves that faced each other, a little built-in bench sat beneath a bay window, covered with an upholstered cushion and throw pillows. The perfect place to recline, read, and enjoy the view. Not that she knew what that view showed, with the blinds closed. Her headache warned her that she wasn't ready for quite that much brightness.

The space was beautiful, light and airy and welcoming. There were no personal items. No photographs. Nothing to indicate that anybody stayed in this room. Apparently, it was for guests.

How was this Sam's house? How could she not remember it?

She swung her feet to the floor and caught sight of shoes

there. Right. She'd broken a lamp. Sam had come in and cleaned it up.

The memories of the night were fuzzy. Memories of how she got here were nonexistent.

She had memories, though. Her and Sam walking on the beach. Seated on her sofa, watching TV. Flying across the waves on a jet ski. But they felt distant and...off.

And also right there, as if she could touch them.

Her stomach growled. When was the last time she'd eaten?

She and Sam had gone to dinner...not last night. At some point. *Italian*, she thought.

She pressed her palms to her temple. It was no use. Her own brain was fighting her. Despite the ibuprofen she'd taken a couple hours before, the ache remained, more acute when she tried to think back.

She shoved her feet into sneakers she didn't recognize and headed for the bathroom.

It was beautiful and modern. The pale blue walls matched the bedroom. White countertops. Gold fixtures. A chandelier hung in the center of the space. Fluffy white towels were perfectly arranged on open shelves. Beside them, a basket filled with travel-sized soaps and lotions and deodorant and toothpaste, along with unopened packages of toothbrushes. Sam's sister-in-law's hairbrush still sat on the counter, left for her use. She pulled it through her hair, which hung straight and flat and far too long.

She stared at her reflection, horrified at what stared back. She had dark smudges around her puffy eyes. Wait. One was worse than the other. Not just dark from lack of sleep, but... Was that a bruise? She touched the swollen spot and felt a dull pain.

She had a black eye?

Yup. And beneath it, a small bandage on her cheek. Daniel

had dabbed ointment on it the night before. How could she remember that so clearly but not remember how she'd gotten the cut in the first place?

What in the world had happened?

After she dressed in Camilla's clothes— clean yoga pants, T-shirt, and zipper sweatshirt—she grabbed Sam's watch... Not the Rolex he loved but a make she'd never heard of before. Patek Philippe? Looked expensive.

Whoa. It was nine-thirty? Was she late for work?

What day was it?

Watch in hand, she opened the bedroom door.

A low rumble of voices told her everyone was awake. Her stomach growled at the scents of bacon and coffee rising from below.

She closed the door and made her way to the walkway that overlooked the first floor. On one side, the living room she'd seen the night before, the back wall covered with blinds she vaguely remembered closing the night before.

On the other side, a sweeping staircase led to the foyer. This house was so grand, so much bigger than his last. An impressive chandelier hung beneath her, its tiny crystals sparkling in the light coming through two-story windows that surrounded the front door. Outside, familiar Maine landscape—bright green grass that led to thick forest on both sides. She glimpsed a narrow road at the end of the driveway and the roofs of neighboring homes.

The sight brought a weird nostalgia, as if she hadn't seen anything like it in a long time.

Strange.

She descended quietly, then followed the sound of voices through a fancy dining room and into a kitchen.

Where she froze.

She barely noticed the room itself, enthralled by the view.

Beyond the wall of windows, a wide porch overlooked an amazing vista.

White clouds hovered low over the gray waters of the Atlantic. Boats bobbed in a harbor a couple hundred yards below. It was somehow both expansive and charming.

"Wow."

She didn't realize she'd said the word aloud until the conversation stopped.

Camilla and Daniel were seated on the far side of a huge kitchen island.

Sam was leaning against this side of it and turned. She expected him to rush to her, to hold her and make sure she was all right. But he regarded her warily from where he stood. "Good morning."

Anxiety bubbled in her empty stomach.

She pressed on a smile. "Sorry to interrupt." She held out the watch. "Thought you'd want this back."

Sam got just close enough to take it.

"Good morning." Camilla rounded the island. "Did you sleep all right?"

"Eventually, yeah." Her gaze flicked past the sweet woman to Sam, who was snapping the silver watch onto his wrist. Not looking her way.

"Thanks for the clothes."

"You're swimming in them." Camilla ushered her through the kitchen to a round table in front of the windows. It was set with plates and utensils and condiments. "We'll need to get you clothes that fit, but those work for now."

Daniel pressed a button, and the blinds closed, hiding the pretty view. In the dimmer light, her headache abated a little.

"How do you feel this morning?" he asked.

She sat and looked up at the two concerned faces. Daniel's hair was graying at the temples, and a few wrinkles were etched on his skin. But, if memory served, he was the oldest of the Wright brothers, so that made sense. He was handsome, though not as handsome as Sam, not even close.

But his eyes were kind, his expression patient as he waited for her to answer.

She didn't know how to describe how she felt and settled for, "All right."

Camilla rested a hand on her husband's arm but spoke to Eliza. "We have breakfast made. Are you hungry?"

"Starving."

The three of them worked together on breakfast while she sat at the table like the Queen of Sheba.

She offered to help, even standing, before Sam shot her a look. "Don't get up, Eliza." His voice was...emotionless. "You're hurt."

Not that badly, but she felt like she'd used her daily energy stores just getting down the stairs. Maybe she'd feel better after she ate.

Sam set a mug of coffee in front of her. By the look of it, he'd already added the cream she loved. Probably the sugar too. He knew how she liked it.

He didn't linger or give her a good-morning kiss. Just scurried back into the kitchen.

She sipped. "It's perfect. Thanks, babe."

He nodded, not meeting her eyes, and opened the refrigerator.

Within minutes, an egg casserole, a basket of biscuits, a plate of bacon dripping onto paper towels, and a bowl of fruit were on the table. Not to mention butter, honey, ketchup, and salsa.

What else could a body want?

Before anybody reached for the food, Daniel and Camilla held their hands out.

"Let's pray," Daniel said.

He held her fingers, careful not to hurt her wrist.

Sam took her other hand, his warm palm covering hers completely. The touch, gentle and familiar, brought a tingle to her eyes that had her bowing her head, thankful the prayer gave her an excuse to hide her face.

Daniel spoke simple words of blessing over the food and thanked God for protecting Eliza and bringing her there the night before. She'd never been comfortable with prayer in the past, but this one made her feel safe and welcome.

The prayer ended, and everybody dug in.

She took a tiny portion of eggs, a single slice of bacon, one biscuit, and a spoonful of fruit. At the first bite of eggs, she realized exactly how hungry she was.

Famished.

The others talked about nothing important—the weather, the leaves, which were starting to change. Which meant it was... September? October?

Okay, that felt right.

They talked about Zoë and Jeremy, Daniel and Camilla's kids. Jeremy was starting at UNH in the fall, Sam's alma mater. They were in town looking for a house but apparently lived in Oklahoma City.

Occasionally, one of them would try to draw her into the conversation, but she couldn't add much. Nothing she wanted to say felt right, as if the three of them were living in one world, and she was living in a different one. A different world with different rules and different history, and...

What was wrong with her?

They seemed to realize her confusion and didn't push.

Though the biscuit had looked delicious, her one bite felt heavy and uncomfortable on her stomach. She set it aside and finished everything else on her plate.

At a break in the conversation, she asked, "May I have more eggs?" Her voice sounded strangely small, like a little girl's.

The three of them looked at her as if she were crazy.

"That's okay," she said quickly. "I'm full."

"You can have as much as you want, Eliza."

She squirmed under Sam's scrutiny.

"You need me to scoop it out for you?"

"I can do it. I just didn't want to... I mean, it's not polite to just help myself. Every bite I take is food out of someone else's mouth."

His brown eyes narrowed, crinkling at the corners. She didn't remember those tiny wrinkles. But she liked them. Not the way he was looking at her, though. What had she said wrong?

Before Sam could voice whatever was forming on his lips, Daniel said, "What other mouths, Eliza?"

She looked his way, started to speak. Stopped herself. "I don't...I don't know. Just..." What she'd said made no sense. Where had the words come from?

Daniel scooped a giant portion of eggs and plopped it on her plate. "Bacon?"

She shook her head, staring down. Avoiding looking at them. Feeling like a fool.

"It's okay." At Sam's gentle tone, she looked up. He smiled and nodded to her food. "Eat as much as you want. Or as little as you want. There's no pressure." He leaned in and added, very low, "You're safe here."

A lump formed in her throat. She swallowed it back and lifted her fork, though she wasn't sure she'd be able to eat with all of them looking at her.

After a moment, their conversation resumed, as carefree as it had been before.

But a dark and forbidding memory niggled on the edge of

her consciousness. She'd forgotten something. Something vital. Something that would change everything.

~

When breakfast was over, Eliza stood and lifted her plate to take to the kitchen. But Camilla whisked it out of her hands. "You need to learn to be served." She delivered the flippant words with a wink and a smile, then snatched the other plates and set them on the island.

"I can help."

"While Sam cleans," Daniel said, "I'd like to have a look at that wrist and the bump on your head, if that's all right." He gestured toward a doorway. "Shall we?"

She looked into the kitchen, where Sam was transferring leftovers into plastic containers.

Camilla dried her hands on a towel and approached. "I'll come too."

Leaving Sam to do the work alone. Which felt wrong. Not just wrong, but...almost frightening.

Daniel stood by the door, reading her as if her strange thoughts were written on her forehead.

She passed him, entering the living room. It looked different in the daytime. A white couch was flanked by two chairs on each side, all oriented toward a stone fireplace, which rose two stories. Like the rest of the house, it was beautifully decorated. And unfamiliar. And it didn't seem like...Sam.

Eliza sat where she'd been the night before, and Daniel sat on the coffee table opposite her.

Camilla settled on a chair, out of the way.

Daniel unwound the bandage from her wrist and had her move it this way and that. "How's it feel?"

"It aches, but it's not bad. Better than last night."

"Good, good. It's not swollen. Let's keep this on for now. Hopefully, it'll be even better tomorrow." He rewrapped it, then felt the bump at the back of her head. "That's a doozie." He sat back. "How's the pain on a scale of one to ten?"

"Most of the time, six."

"When is it worse?"

"In bright lights, though that's better than it was last night. Mostly, when I try to remember what happened." Just saying the words made her brain throb. She pressed her fingertips against her temples until it passed.

"Hmm. Okay." He touched the bruise beneath her eye, not enough to hurt, though. "I'm afraid this is going to look worse before it looks better."

"I'll need to come up with a good story."

He smiled. "We should see the other guy?"

She attempted a smile but didn't think she quite managed it. "Something like that."

He lifted the bandage from her face and dabbed more antibiotic cream there before putting a clean one on. "That should heal fast. I doubt it'll scar. Just keep it covered." He dropped his hands to his lap but didn't sit back. "Sam said he saw some bruises on your upper arm. Does that hurt?"

There had been some pain in her arms when she slept, but it was nothing compared to the headache.

"A little."

"Do you mind if I look?"

She slipped out of the sweatshirt and turned so he could see. He slid back her T-shirt and studied the front of her arm, then stood to get a look at the back. "Can I see the other one?"

She shifted to give him access, and he did the same, studying both the back and the front.

"You have bruises on both arms. No memory of how you got them?"

She shook her head.

He sat back, and she pulled on the cozy sweatshirt.

"Do you mind if Sam comes in?"

"Of course not."

He stood and scooted away, calling, "Sam," toward the other room.

Sam came in seconds later as if he'd been waiting for the summons. Maybe he had. He looked from Daniel to Camilla before finally meeting her eyes. "There are a few things we need to tell you."

She expected him to sit beside her, but he chose the chair opposite Camilla. Daniel had settled beside his wife, leaving Eliza on the sofa alone. Feeling very exposed.

She focused on Sam. "What is it? Do you know where I was last night?"

"No."

"You must have some idea. Did I go to work yesterday? What day is it?"

Everything was so confusing.

Sam rested his forearms on his knees. "It's Saturday. I don't know if you went to work yesterday, Eliza. I don't know what you've been up to lately because..." His gaze flicked to Daniel.

Who gave him a go-ahead nod.

Sam's Adam's apple bobbed. "You and I aren't together anymore."

"What? No, that can't be. I don't..." Fear dripped down her spine, set her skin tingling and raised goose bumps. Everything was off. Wrong.

He'd broken up with her.

Of course he had. Mom was right. Mom was always right.

But when? And how could Eliza not remember?

She lowered her face into her hands, pressing against her temples. Her head throbbed, a low but steady drum beat.

They weren't together.

That explained his strange reaction to her. His distance.

How embarrassing. What must he think of her, throwing herself into his arms? Staying the night in his house.

"Hey, hey." Sam's voice was low, closer than she'd expected. Then, his fingers wrapped around her wrist. "Come on, sweetheart. It's okay. Look at me."

Sweetheart. But she wasn't his sweetheart. Not anymore,

"What happened?" Her voice was shaky, but she forced herself to look at him. She needed to see his face. "Why would you—?"

"You ended it," he said. "Not me."

"That can't be true. I would never... I love you."

"I think maybe you *loved* me. But like a bad virus, you got over it." His lips quirked at the corners, but she didn't see amusement in his eyes.

"That doesn't make sense. Is that why I didn't recognize your house? You moved here after? I'm so confused."

"I know. I know you are. You've lost... You have amnesia."

It sounded so bizarre, but it must be true. If she and Sam had broken up, and she didn't remember...

Was that the dark thing hovering at the edge of her consciousness? She tested the idea, tried to make it fit. But it didn't.

There was something else. Though what could be darker than losing the man of her dreams?

"Tell me what happened." She had to know.

He returned to his chair. "We don't need to get into that. You'll remember when—"

"But maybe it explains what happened last night. Maybe you broke up with me, and I freaked out or something. And maybe that's why..." Her voice trailed when Sam looked at Daniel and Camilla. "What?"

Daniel cleared his throat. "It's been a while since you two broke up. I can't see how what happened last night could be related."

"How long?"

Daniel let Sam answer that.

He met her eyes and held her gaze. "Five years."

"Five...?" No. No. That couldn't be.

Five years?

Five *years*?

How? Where had she been? What...?

Her head pounded. She squeezed it, trying to make it stop, swallowing against the nausea that churned her stomach.

The words floated around in there, trying to find a place to land. But there was no place that made sense.

Five years.

Gone. Just like that.

The sofa shifted, and arms snaked around her and pulled her close. Not the strong arms she craved.

Camilla said, "It's okay, honey. It's going to be okay."

But how could it be?

She allowed herself to be comforted, breathing through the pain in her skull. When it faded enough for her to open her eyes again, she looked at Sam. She wanted to demand that he explain what happened.

But he looked so...sad.

He shuttered his expression. Lifted his chin. As if waiting for a blow. As if she might hurt him.

Which, apparently, she had.

"Okay." Not that it was, but... "Okay, so we broke up five years ago. Then what happened? We stayed friends? I obviously knew where you lived, so we must've."

Daniel fielded that. "I don't think you did. You remember that piece of paper I took out of your hand last night?"

She did, now that he mentioned it.

"It was a business card with Sam's address written on it." Again, Daniel nodded to Sam to explain.

"I hadn't seen you or spoken to you since you ended things," Sam said. "I have no idea what you did after our breakup. But last spring, I ran into you in Salt Lake City."

"Utah? I've never been there."

"You have." His words were calm, not demanding but confident. "We talked."

That didn't make sense at all. But when she looked at Daniel and Camilla, they were watching her with sympathetic expressions. As if they believed his story. His crazy story.

"We saw you too," Camilla said. "We didn't know who you were, but we saw you."

"And we saw Sam give you the business card." Daniel fished something from his pocket and handed it to her.

She studied the wrinkled card stock with Sam's name and business on it. He'd written his address on the back.

Shadow Cove, Maine.

She'd never heard of it. Except, obviously she had. She was there now.

"Is it familiar to you?" Daniel asked.

She shook her head. "I've never... I don't remember any of this." To Sam, she said, "Why was I in Utah? Did I say?"

"You wouldn't tell me anything. You kept looking around as if you thought somebody might see you talking to me. That's why I gave you the card. I thought you were in trouble. I should've... I shouldn't have let you walk away. I should've demanded to know what was going on." A muscle in his jaw worked. "But you weren't... You didn't seem to want my help. You told me you were waiting for friends, and before I could stop you, you took off and jumped in a car that pulled over at the curb."

She couldn't imagine any version of herself rejecting Sam.

She had a million questions, but apparently, Sam wouldn't have the answers she sought.

"I tried to call your mother last night," Sam said, "but her number's been disconnected. Any idea why?"

"No. Why would she do that?"

Sam ignored the question. "Any chance you remember another number for her?" At her quick head shake, he continued. "I thought we'd drive over there. She's probably frantic with worry. She'll take care of you."

She would. Mom would take over, manage whatever needed to be managed.

But the thought of going to Mom's house brought a strange sensation. A...warning. "I don't think that's a good idea."

"Why?"

"I don't know. It just feels wrong."

Sam and his brother shared a look.

Camilla squeezed her hand. "Are you and your mother close?"

"I guess." She looked at Sam as if he could fill in the blanks. Not that he knew better, but he knew enough. Or used to.

Sam's smirk told her he remembered her mother well. "If you don't want to go there, then we can take you to the police. They'll figure out—"

"No. No police." The idea of it raised panic and sent her heart racing. She pressed her fingers to her temples and kneaded, waited for the pain to pass.

"Okay, then." There was an edge to Sam's voice, despite his attempt at soothing. "Then your mother. Or maybe Jeanette?"

Of course.

They weren't together, and Sam wanted to get rid of her. But he'd always been kind. She could trust him to make the right decision. She needed to, since she had no idea what to do. And it was so much easier to let somebody take the lead.

Even though it felt like the wrong idea, she nodded. "Let's go to Mom's house. We'll figure out...Mom and I will figure out where to go from there."

"Good." Sam spoke to his brother. "You saw the bruises?"

"I did. We should tell her."

Sam's eyes darkened, and his lips tightened at the corners. "Go ahead."

The brothers shared a long look, and then Daniel spoke. "Sam said you had a nightmare last night. You remember that?"

"I think I was running from something. I don't remember the details."

"When he was in your room, cleaning up...was it a lamp?"

Eliza turned to Sam. "Sorry about that. I can replace—"

"It's just a lamp." His words were low, nearly a growl. And there was that anger again. "It doesn't matter."

Daniel said, "He saw some bruises on your upper arm. The ones I looked at just now."

"Okay." She was bruised all over. Which was weird, but obviously she'd been in some sort of accident.

"There's one on the front of each arm," Daniel explained. "Three on the back."

She was nodding, trying to figure out what he was saying.

Sam stood suddenly, scooted past Camilla between the sofa and the coffee table, and plopped down. He reached toward her, then stopped. "Is it okay if I just show you? Demonstrate?"

"I guess."

He placed his hands on her upper arms. One on each. He didn't squeeze, though, just left his hands there. And watched her reaction.

A million memories came. Dancing. Gazing into his warm eyes. Kissing that strong neck.

He had a line of hair down the middle of his chest and moaned with delight when she skimmed her fingers over it.

She remembered tickling his ribs, eliciting a very girly giggle. And then being tickled into submission.

She loved him. With everything in her, she loved him.

Had loved him.

Now, his brows lowered, his mouth pressed tight. And she forced herself to stay in the moment, even if the past was preferable. The past where she knew who she was, knew Sam loved her.

Now, he was holding her because of bruises...

And she got it.

One bruise in front of each arm. Where the thumb goes.

Three in back.

Apparently, the pinky wasn't strong enough to leave a bruise. But the other fingers...

"Somebody..." She started, confused. "Are you saying...? What are you saying?"

"Whatever happened to you last night, it wasn't an accident." His hands dropped. "Somebody grabbed you. Maybe shook you. Maybe bashed your head against—"

"We don't need that much detail." Daniel's voice silenced him.

Sam returned to his chair and sat heavily. "The point is, somebody hurt you. On purpose. Until you know who it was, you need to be on your guard."

She watched his face, waiting for him to say something else. Something that made sense. Because she would never be with a man who abused her. Would she?

How far had she fallen?

What could possibly have happened to bring her...here?

CHAPTER FIVE

THE TRAFFIC WASN'T terrible for the last weekend of September. Still, the drive from Shadow Cove to York, where Eliza's mother lived, would take nearly an hour. He'd started an old playlist Eliza used to like, hoping she'd settle in and enjoy the music. And not want to talk.

But she lowered the volume after a few minutes. "I don't remember this car."

"I bought it a couple of years ago."

"It's an Audi, right? It's really smooth."

Should be for what he'd paid for it. Technically, his business had paid for it. This was his impress-the-clients car—and it worked. Once the snow came, he'd leave it in the garage and drive his pickup. The salt from the ocean was bad enough without adding the junk they dumped on the roads all winter long.

"Your house is beautiful," she said. "When did you buy it?"

"A while back."

"You live there alone?"

Was she fishing for information? Wanting to know if he was with anyone? Probably.

"Yup." He reached for the volume.

"Who decorated it for you?"

He dropped his hand. "I hired someone."

"I thought so."

That had him glancing her way. "Figured I didn't have the talent, huh?"

"It's not that. It's just...not really your style. It's nice, don't get me wrong. But... I don't know. It feels sort of feminine."

A woman he'd been dating had helped him pick out the house. Back then, he'd still held out hope that he'd find someone to share his life with. But it turned out she'd loved his money a lot more than she'd loved him.

He was left with the house. Not that he minded, really. It was a nice place. Great view.

Just really...big for one person.

"I hired a decorator," he said. "Told her to do whatever she wanted in most of the spaces."

"And the others?"

Did they have to do this? "The other rooms are more my style." He reached for the volume again.

"Business is good, obviously."

Again, he dropped his hand. "Very good."

This questioning would be fair if he could reciprocate, grill her about her life. Maybe he should claim amnesia.

"What are you working on right now?"

"It's confidential." His business deals always were.

"Come on. A hint." The teasing words brought to mind a million memories he didn't want to revisit. Eliza had always been able to needle information out of him. He never betrayed his secrets, but she was always able to get him to say more than he'd planned to. Back then, he'd trusted her completely.

She didn't push the question, just waited.

"A computer chip manufacturer is looking to sell. If the

buyer can come up with the funds, we'll sign the papers in the next couple of weeks."

"Big deal?"

He shrugged, fighting the urge to tell her just how big, how much he was worth. A petty little space inside him wanted her to know what she'd lost when she left him. But Eliza had never cared about money. Her mother had, and five years earlier, Sam's balance sheet hadn't impressed her. His charm had only raised her hackles. Sam hadn't given a whit about impressing the venerable Linda Pelletier.

Tactical error on his part.

He was not looking forward to seeing the woman who'd never forgiven him for botching the sale of her husband's business. Not that he had. He'd put the deal together. He'd told them the risks. They'd chosen to take it.

It wasn't Sam's fault it went the way it did.

"How's your family?" Eliza asked. "It was nice to meet Daniel and Camilla. They're sweet. Didn't they use to live in... was it St. Louis?"

How could she remember that but not where she was last night?

"They did. Now they're in Oklahoma, but they're planning to move here. They're staying with me while they look for a house. Dan's joining Dad's practice." At least he would, when he got his medical license back.

"You must be looking forward to that."

"Yup."

"And your other brothers?"

He stifled a sigh. How long could she keep this up? They still had forty-five minutes left. "All good." He was tempted to leave it at that, but she'd always had a soft spot for Sam's little brother. "Grant got married."

"Oh, I'm glad to hear it. He's such a nice guy. Have he and Bryan mended fences?"

"I guess so. Grant comes around more than he used to. His wife, Summer, is already like a sister to us." Before she could ask another question, he said, "What about you? Any fresh memories?"

She said nothing. From the corner of his eye, he saw her shaking her head. Real helpful while he was driving.

"What's the last thing you remember?"

She pressed her hands to her temples as if the memory hurt. "You and I were dancing. That might not be the most recent, but it's the clearest. We were at a party of some kind—super glittery and fancy. We danced all night, and you were... Well, obviously we were still together then."

He remembered. It was a Christmas party put on by one of the businesses he was working with back then. Grand ballroom, tuxes and ballgowns. Eliza had worn a green shimmery dress that showed off all her curves. He could still feel her in his arms, swaying to the music, looking up at him with those big hazel eyes, flecks of emerald and gold glinting. She gazed at him as if he were her knight and she his princess.

He'd been head-over-heels. A fool for love.

That was what he got for asking. Brought to mind that old adage—don't ask a question if you can't stand the answer.

He cranked up the music.

CHAPTER SIX

OBVIOUSLY, Sam didn't want to talk.

Fine, then, Eliza could be quiet. Even though the silence was pressing in on her, raising her anxiety.

Or maybe it wasn't the silence. The closer they got to Mom's house, the faster her pulse raced. Like they were driving into...danger.

Which made no sense at all. Not that any of this did.

If she had her phone, she could search her calendar and find out where she'd been and what she'd been up to.

If she had her purse, she could dig through it, see if any clues could be found.

But she'd arrived at Sam's with nothing.

He exited the highway and wound along familiar roads. Some things were different—a building here, a new housing development there. But for the most part, this was the York she'd known most of her life. The York she'd grown up in.

It should feel comfortable, but fear thrummed.

"Do you really think we should do this?"

He lowered the stereo volume. "What's the problem?"

"I don't know. It feels like a bad idea."

She didn't miss the huff of breath. "Then where do you want me to take you? Jeanette's?"

Jeanette was Eliza's best friend. Maybe that was a better idea. At least that idea didn't scare her.

"Does she still live in the same place?" He sounded annoyed.

Eliza shrugged, not that he could see.

"Right." The word was clipped. "You don't remember."

"I can't help that I have—"

"I know. I'm sorry." He offered her a quick smile. "It's a frustrating situation." After a moment he added, "Much more so for you, I realize. I know you're nervous, but your mother loves you. I can't think of anybody who'll take better care of you than she will. I really think this is the right play."

"If you're sure."

He hit his turn signal, pulled into a lot, and parked. "What is it?"

"What is what?"

"Why don't you want to go to your mother's?"

"I don't know. I can't..."

"I know she can be...hard to get along with. Is that it?"

Was that it? It didn't feel right, but nothing made sense. "Maybe. But if you think this is the best idea, then I believe you."

Frustration crossed his features, reminding her of an old argument. She could almost hear his voice.

You trust everyone's judgment but your own.

Only because her judgment had proved wrong so many times.

When she said nothing, Sam resumed the drive.

Eliza watched the world pass by outside the window. It was familiar, but also...different. Like she'd just been there the day before. And yet, overnight, everything had changed.

Like Sam. She couldn't help the feelings she still had for him, even though he looked different now, hiding behind a beard, not that it didn't look good.

Everything was wrong.

The world. Herself. Sam, most of all. He'd always been sweet and charming. Quick with a smile or a joke. Today, he was tense, almost nervous. Distant. And right on the edge of angry.

Which made sense, she supposed, if she'd ended things with him. Maybe he hadn't forgiven her. Maybe she didn't deserve his forgiveness.

Finally, he turned into the driveway of her childhood home, a two-story colonial. Green siding, mature bushes, annuals blooming beside the porch steps.

She could almost see Dad kneeling in front of the flowerbeds, showing Eliza how to plant the trunkful of flowers Mom had bought at the nursery. Dad's weathered face and easy smile were clear in her memory. His gentle voice instructing an awkward preteen in exactly how deep to dig the hole, how wide. She could feel the brush of his hand against hers.

Your turn. One of these days, you'll have your own house to pretty up.

But Dad wasn't there. He'd been gone two years... No, seven.

She'd never get used to living life without him. Or...maybe she had. Maybe the wound had scabbed over.

Now, the grief was fresh and tender.

"Here."

She snagged the handkerchief Sam held out and dabbed at her tears. He was the only man she knew who carried one—like Dad had. The first time Sam had handed it to her, she'd fallen a little bit in love with him.

Who'd planted Mom's flowers? Had Eliza? Had she put Dad's instructions to good use?

The effort to remember only made her head hurt.

No memories came, only fresh nervousness.

"Park on the street, please."

Sam had already turned into the driveway. He shot her a look but didn't ask, just backed out and pulled over, half on the grass, half on the asphalt. Mom would hate that, but Sam probably didn't care.

It seemed wise to park where they could leave fast. She didn't say that because she couldn't explain it.

The houses on this street each sat on one-acre lots, leaving plenty of room between them. The neighborhood looked lived in and loved, cozy and familiar.

"You ready?"

She handed him back his handkerchief, which he took without a word, and climbed out of his sedan. She had to hurry to keep up with Sam's long steps, down the driveway and up the walk. Puffy clouds were low and thick, the sky bright blue behind them. The breeze, a constant this close to the ocean, carried air tinged with the scent of rain.

A lawnmower buzzed in the distance. Children's laughter came from the other direction. A typical Saturday afternoon in suburbia. A van was parked in front of the house next door, a good fifty yards away. She'd once known the people who lived there, but maybe they'd moved.

She should feel relaxed here. She should feel at home.

She should look forward to seeing her mother.

They reached the front door, and she tried it. Locked. She pressed the doorbell. Then knocked.

Sam knocked louder. When there no answer, he knocked again. Eager to be rid of her, obviously.

"Hey!"

They turned at the voice.

The seventy-something neighbor across the street raised a hand to block the sun. "Eliza?"

Sam and Eliza met her in the driveway. "Hey, Mrs. Jensen," Eliza said. "How are you?"

"Confused." She looked from Eliza to Sam and back. "Not that I'm not glad to see you. What's it been? Five years? What are you doing here?"

"Uh..." The gray-haired woman's words had Eliza stumbling over her own. Five years since she'd been to her mother's house? That couldn't be right. "I came to see Mom. You know where she is?"

"What happened to you?" The woman's sharp gaze hit Sam. "He do that?" She grabbed Eliza's arm and tugged. "You come home with me. You don't need that piece of garbage."

Eliza pried herself away, then rubbed her wrist. She'd taken the bandage off earlier, not wanting to alarm Mom, but it still ached. "What's going on?"

"You're asking me that? You're the one with the bruises. The one who hasn't been home in ages. You're supposed to be with your mother."

"I am?"

"What do you mean?" The woman's gaze flicked to Sam as if it were all his fault. "He keep you from going?"

"Going where, exactly?" she asked.

"Florida, of course."

Florida?

"I don't remember..." Eliza started over. "I was in an accident." Seemed easier to say that than explain what she didn't know.

"Is that what you call it when some guy roughs you up?" Again, the woman glared at Sam.

"Hold up, now." Sam lifted his hands. "I had nothing to do with what happened to Eliza. I'm just trying to help."

The woman opened her mouth to retort.

"Sam's a friend," Eliza said quickly. "My memory's got a few holes in it. Why is Mom in Florida?"

Mrs. Jensen's head tilted to the side. "She said she was going with you. She asked me to keep an eye on her place, which is why I came over. Saw you two on the stoop."

If Eliza was supposed to be in Florida with Mom, then how had she ended up in Shadow Cove?

"For how long?" Sam asked. "Did she say when she'd be back?"

"Just said her daughter needed her."

"Huh. That's..." Eliza turned to Sam. "It doesn't make sense." Fear and confusion pitched her words high.

"We'll figure it out. It's okay." To Mrs. Jensen, he said, "Thanks for your help."

The woman turned to leave, but Sam asked, "Do you have a key? Eliza lost hers, and we need to get inside."

The older woman fished a set of keys from her pocket. She took her time removing one, then handed it to Eliza. "Leave it under the mat at the back door when you're finished. I'll pick it up later. Unless you plan to stay, in which case—"

"No." Just being here swirled anxiety in her stomach. "I'll leave it for you. Thanks."

"Mmm-hmm. You let me know if you need anything." She marched across the street toward her split-level.

"I've still got my charm, obviously."

Sam's words almost elicited a smile. "Why would she assume I've been abused? Unless... Would Mom have told her that?"

He nodded toward the front door, and they walked that

direction. "I don't know your mom like you do. What do you think?"

"I think... I think, even if Mom thought that, she wouldn't tell the neighbor."

"Which means she was guessing. But that black eye... It's not a bad guess." They climbed the steps. He took the key from her hand and unlocked the door, but before it opened, he faced her. "You haven't seen that woman for five years. Wouldn't you have, if you'd been here?"

"Nothing makes sense, Sam. None of this. I mean, even Florida. My mother hates Florida."

Sam pushed the door open and then stood aside for her to enter.

She did, and froze.

It was the entry she'd walked into since she was nine years old, but different. Nothing obvious, but... In the living room, there were new throw pillows on the couch. The TV was larger. Dad's old recliner was gone, replaced by a wingback chair.

"What's wrong?" Sam asked.

She shook her head. Of course things looked different. It was just disconcerting.

"I don't think you should stay here. Do you think you left any clothes?" Sam stood beside her in the entry, taking up far more space than a man had a right to.

With his height—over six feet—and those broad shoulders, with his strong personality, his confidence, his...power. He'd always seemed too big for her modest house. For her life. No wonder they hadn't made it. She had no idea why he'd ever wanted her to begin with.

"Maybe you could pack a bag," he suggested.

"I will, after. First, let's see if we can learn anything." She walked through the living room toward the antique roll top desk against the wall. She glanced toward the kitchen down the back hallway. It looked wrong too. Everything looked wrong.

She pushed up the desk cover.

A day planner. A cup with different colored pens sticking out. A stack of pink sticky notes. A glass paperweight. Otherwise, the space was cleared off.

Before she could reach for the day-planner, Sam reached past her and snagged it, so she opened one of the drawers and dug through it instead.

A second later, he said, "Here we go." He laid it on the surface and tapped on a date.

But her gaze caught on the year printed in bold letters at the top.

They'd told her that five years had passed, but it hadn't seemed real. Still didn't.

"Eliza?" He was back to his soothing *I'm dealing with a crazy person* voice. "You with me?"

"Yeah."

He tapped the calendar. "I bet that's a flight number."

"Huh? Oh." On the column marked Friday, September twenty-third, Mom had written a four-digit number and a time —four p.m.

"What time did I get to your house last night?"

"A little after ten." Sam tapped his cell phone screen. "This must've been your incoming flight. It goes Newark to Manchester." He lowered the phone. "You probably just changed planes there, but you weren't living in New Jersey. As far as I know, anyway."

She turned and looked up at him. He was so close, just inches away.

He stepped back, putting space between them. "We know you'd been in Salt Lake. Maybe you came from—"

A crash had her looking behind.

A man barreled down the hall from the kitchen, coming straight at them.

Sam pushed her out of the way, and she stumbled, bumped against the back of the couch.

Turned to see Sam throw a punch at the guy, who backed up, swung toward him.

Something glinted in the man's hand.

"Knife!"

Sam spun, squeezed the arm with the weapon between his upper arm and his rib cage, and elbowed the attacker in the face. The guy seemed about to go down, then levered back, trying to pull Sam off-balance.

From behind her, a hand slipped around her neck and yanked her off her feet.

"Sam!"

He looked, eyes wide with terror. The distraction had him stumbling back. He fell onto his attacker.

Eliza fought as the second man dragged her backward. Toward the door. She grabbed a table leg, but it slid, banging into the sofa.

He punched the side of her head.

Everything spun. The world grew dark at the edges.

No. No, she couldn't pass out. She had to fight. She reached for something, anything, to stop herself from being taken away.

Sam was disappearing in the darkness.

And then, he turned her way. Launched himself across the space.

The arm around her neck loosened and was gone.

But everything was gray and fuzzy. The bangs and grunts faded. She fought the darkness, but the darkness was winning.

CHAPTER SEVEN

"RUN!" Sam dodged a punch as he shouted the word.

But Eliza wasn't moving. *Dear God, please...*

The first man—chubby face with a goatee—was still down. Sam had seen the second attacker coming, seen him grab Eliza.

Felt his heart stop.

Focus.

He heard his martial arts coach in his head, instructing him. He couldn't save Eliza until he saved himself.

He'd allowed himself to be dragged down. On his way, he'd grabbed the paperweight off the desk.

Flipped himself over. Bashed Goatee's head with it.

The guy went limp, allowing Sam to scramble off him. He dove at the second attacker—this one smaller with spiked blond hair—from the side. He got the guy away from Eliza.

She was free, but she didn't run.

Which meant he had to defeat Spike. Fast, before the other one got to his feet.

This one was smaller than Goatee, scrappier. Fought dirty. Sam could fight dirty too. Spike came at him from the right. Sam moved to protect that side, feigned a stumble, flipped around.

Kicked him in the chest. Pushed him off-balance, then swept his feet out from under him.

Spike went down, flat on his back. Gasping for breath.

That wouldn't last.

Eliza had crawled to the storm door and was halfway outside. Sam slid an arm beneath her chest and lifted her to her feet, propelling her outside.

She stumbled and would've fallen down the steps if he hadn't caught her.

What did that guy do to her?

He scooped her up and carried her to the car. Tossed her in the front seat. Bolted around to the driver's side as one of the men pushed out the door—Goatee. He limped toward the street.

Sam should've hit him harder.

Goatee made for a white van parked in front of the neighbor's house.

Sam pressed the ignition on his Audi and gunned the engine.

Reached the end of the street. "Which way do I go!"

Nothing.

"Eliza! Which way—?"

"Left." Her voice was low, like she was fighting to focus.

He turned the wheel and floored it again. "Stay with me. You need to navigate me out of here. I don't know the neighborhood. We need other people. Cars. Crowds."

"Okay." Her voice was weak, but she directed him.

He kept one eye on the rearview. The van was back there, never too far behind.

He careened down residential streets, praying no children or pets would run into his path. It felt like Eliza was leading him farther and farther from the main road.

The van spun around a curve behind him, closing in.

"Where are we going?" he shouted. "We need—"

"It's right ahead."

What was? But...there. A wider road. He barely paused at the stop sign, spinning into the right turn, earning a blaring horn from the guy he'd cut off.

He angled into the turn lane, passed a truck in front of him, jerked back into the lane in front of the guy.

That earned a honk and a hand gesture.

But the truck shielded his Audi from the guy pursuing them.

Sam accelerated, desperate to put space between them. Traffic kept him from getting too far.

Think.

They had to get off this road. Hide. Wait for the goons to give up and go away.

Ahead, he saw only open space—the ocean. There'd be fewer places to hide once they hit the coastal road.

He needed a packed lot. A seafood restaurant on a corner. The lot was full.

At the last second, he yanked the wheel to the right, moving them into the parking lot, praying the truck blocked the attacker's view. Barreled to the back. No outlet. He stifled a curse word as he maneuvered the car between two pickups on the edge of a forest.

And stopped. Breathed. Prayed.

If the goon found them, they'd be trapped. "We gotta hide."

Eliza's eyes were closed.

His heart, already racing, dropped to the floor. "What is it? What can I do?"

She opened the car door and vomited.

Okay. Nausea he could handle. He knew how she felt.

Everything in him was itching to leave. Abandon the car. Take off into the woods. Get Eliza away from those men, as far and as fast as possible.

But could she run? She'd seemed barely conscious at the house. Would running make her injuries worse? Would she even be able to?

What should they do?

Something told him to just...wait.

He got out of the car and moved into the shadow of the truck beside him. Watched the entry to the parking lot. If they came, he'd...what? Climb into the car, try to ram the van? Maybe. What else could he do?

He should've brought a gun. Why hadn't he grabbed one of his handguns? Why hadn't it occurred to him?

Stupid. Stupid, arrogant, boneheaded... He'd known someone had hurt her. It hadn't occurred to him that anybody would attack when Sam was with her. Certainly not two people.

Sam wasn't going to let them take Eliza. They'd have to kill him first.

Which, considering the blade Goatee had wielded, was probably the plan.

Still, no van.

He watched for another few moments, letting the adrenaline drain. Breathing. Trying to think.

The goon wasn't coming. They'd lost him. For now.

He climbed back in the car and closed the door.

Eliza's eyes were shut, her head leaning against the window.

"Are you with me?"

"Yeah." But she didn't open her eyes.

"Who were they?"

"I don't know."

Of course not. That'd be way too easy.

"Not even an inkling?"

Her closed eyes scrunched up. She rubbed her temples. "I

don't know, Sam. Maybe. Maybe, but..." Her voice trailed. Then, "I knew we shouldn't have gone there."

"What?" His blood pressure spiked again. She'd said that, but... "What are you saying?"

"It just...it felt like the wrong move. Dangerous. But you said we should, so—"

"I don't know what you know!" His words reverberated in the small car, and she shrank away, covering her head with her hands. "Sorry. I didn't mean to..." He forced himself to speak at a normal level. "Why didn't you tell me?"

"I did, didn't I? I said it felt like a bad idea."

"I thought you were nervous about seeing your mother. You never said anything about danger."

"It didn't make sense. I didn't understand, and your logic was sound."

"My logic was based on the information I had. I didn't realize..."

Getting angry with her wasn't going to help. They'd survived, somehow. She hadn't been hurt too badly. She hadn't been taken. Thank God.

Eliza obviously hadn't known what would happen. Except she'd had a feeling, which he definitely should have heeded.

He worked kindness into his tone. "If you get another feeling like that, will you please tell me?"

"Sorry. I will."

"You need to trust your instincts. Your wisdom."

Words he'd said to her plenty during their relationship. Words she'd rarely heeded.

"Are you hurt? More than before?"

"He punched me in the head. It...I nearly passed out. But I made myself stay awake."

He'd always marveled at Eliza. Once she made a decision, she had a stone will. She'd follow it through, and nobody could stop her. Getting to the decision was hard for her, but once she did, she was unmovable. So different from how he lived, making snap decisions based on the information he had. Not always the best decisions, but he kept moving forward.

Eliza was a ruminator. Sometimes, that drove him nuts. Other times, her thoughtfulness, her desire to seek counsel, brought him fresh insights. They'd been a good team, once upon a time.

"Do you need a hospital?"

"I think I'm all right." Her eyes opened, and she turned to him. "How about you? Are you hurt?"

The adrenaline had drained now, and he felt the bruises. "Nothing I can't handle."

"I didn't know you could fight like that."

"It's my workout. Martial arts. I train every day, just to stay in shape. I've never had to use it in real life." Of course, back in the day, he and his brothers had gone at it more than once. Never to hurt, just to see who could best the others. Sam liked to think he could take any of his brothers. He liked to think it, but Grant had been a Green Beret. Suffice it to say, he wouldn't be challenging his little brother to a fight anytime soon.

Her eyes drifted closed again. "It works."

It had, this time.

He stared at her, this woman he'd loved so much. She looked small in his passenger seat. Bruise darkening beneath her eye. Tiny bandage on her cheek.

Someone had done that to her.

The men who'd just come after her?

Was she in a relationship with one of them? Or had she been? But why would the other man help him?

Abusive boyfriends didn't recruit abusive friends, did they?

And they hadn't seemed emotionally involved. It hadn't felt like a crime of passion. They'd been calculating. Their attack had come from two directions. One to distract, maybe kill him while the other dragged her away.

She'd almost been taken. Maybe murdered.

The thought had his stomach wanting to expel breakfast.

He itched to question her. Demand answers. Demand she tell him everything.

Which would do no good at all.

Tears leaked out between her closed lids, dripped down her cheeks.

"Hey, it's okay." He took his handkerchief from his pocket and held it out to her, tapping her arm so she'd open her eyes. "We're okay."

"You could have been killed. It would've been my fault." Her voice was high and squeaky. She looked his way, eyes filled with fear and pain. "What is going on, Sam? I don't understand."

He shouldn't do it. Told himself not to. But when she didn't take his handkerchief, he reached across the space and brushed the tears from her face with his fingers. Her skin was soft and warm.

She blinked those large eyes. So vulnerable. So beautiful.

He pulled his hand back. "We should go to the police."

"No!" The word came out loud as she jerked up, then pressed her hands to her skull. "Ow, ow, ow."

He waited until she settled again. "Why not?"

"They'll find us if we go to the police."

"How do you know?"

"I don't... I don't know how I know, but I do. We can't."

He squeezed the steering wheel, trying to tame his frustration. "Can we call them at least, tell them what happened?"

"Um... Maybe? Yeah, but we can't tell anybody where we're going. That is, if you're... If we're..."

"Fine." He knew what she was asking. He opened his navigation system and reversed out of the space, aiming for the interstate. The goons were surely gone now. *Please, let them be gone.*

Somehow, they'd gotten out of that. *Lord, direct me. Direct us.*

Sam was trying to get into the habit of praying. He knew God, he'd trusted Him for salvation, he tried to follow the rules —something he hadn't done with Eliza but was careful about now—but he'd been managing the day-to-day operations of his own life. He'd asked God to help him rely on Him, and apparently, God was answering that request in a big way.

Because this situation was way outside his wheelhouse.

His plan had been to dump Eliza—and yeah, he heard the coldness in the word—on her mother. She'd left him, after all. She wasn't his problem.

But her mother was gone. Phone disconnected. Off social media.

Weird enough, but when added to what they'd learned today, and then the attack...?

Something was going on, something dangerous.

Which left Sam with two choices. Leave Eliza against her will at the police station and go on with his life.

Or take responsibility for her.

He checked from mirror to mirror, window to window, searching for the van. No sign of it. They weren't being followed. Assuming the people in the white pickup weren't her enemies—and why would they have dropped her off if they were...?

Yeah, there really wasn't a choice.

He aimed the car toward home.

∼

Sam paced the length of the deck behind his house. Gray clouds hovered overhead, threatening rain, and the ocean breeze had kicked up, chilling his skin. But he barely noticed.

Daniel had been examining Eliza for twenty minutes, Camilla acting as nurse. Sam had wanted to stay, but Daniel insisted he leave.

"I need to examine her, and you're getting on my nerves."

So Sam paced on the deck. And waited.

She'd fallen asleep on the way back to his house, and he hadn't been able to rouse her when they'd arrived. Propelled by panic, he'd carried her inside, calling for his brother.

Daniel had been as cool as ever, directing him to take her back to the guest room.

Had the second blow to her head done serious damage? Had her injuries the night before been worse than they'd thought? Was she bleeding internally? Slowly drowning in her own blood?

The thought had his gut churning.

The slider opened, and Camilla stepped outside, a blanket wrapped around her shoulders. Sam would probably be cold, too, if not for the fear.

"Daniel will be out in a minute."

"What did he say?"

Camilla's smile was patient. "That he'd be out in a minute."

"We should call 911. Right?"

"Let's wait and see what he—"

"What if he misses something? What if she needs tests? An MRI or..."

"Daniel knows what he's doing. He treated all manner of illness and injury in a mission hospital in Sudan—without MRIs and CT scans or even X-rays. He can handle a concussion." Her tone was soothing as she patted the seat beside her. "Come here and sit."

"I can't."

"Okay, then." She stood and approached him, grabbing his hand. And then she started praying, out loud, for Eliza. For her safety and protection. For her healing. For wisdom as they tried to figure out what was going on.

Sam didn't add anything. He was too worried to put his feelings into words. And anyway, she knew what to say.

He just stood there thinking, *Yes,* and *Please,* and *Amen.*

The slider opened. Camilla cut off the prayer, and they both turned as Daniel approached.

"Well?" Sam didn't mean to sound so demanding.

"She's very lucky," Daniel said. "Or, more likely, God protected her."

"What are you talking about?" He was in no mood for cryptic answers.

"She was hit in the head again?" Daniel asked, though it seemed he already knew the answer.

"She's awake?"

"Woke up while I was examining her." Dan's eyebrows lifted. "She said someone punched her—?"

"Long story." Sam hadn't told them about the attack at the house. He hadn't told them anything except that she needed medical attention.

"She's still recovering from her concussion, and getting another head injury on top of it... That could have been bad, but she seems all right. She passed all the cognitive tests, except she still has amnesia, of course."

"You're saying she's fine?"

Daniel squeezed Sam's arm. "She's tired. She has a headache, and she's resting. But she'll be fine."

Sam shook off his brother's hand, spun, and walked to the railing, looking out at the waves. They were churning, higher than usual, boats bobbing and swaying. There must've been a storm out there, somewhere. A storm just beyond the horizon. Was it coming their way?

He squeezed his eyes closed. Thank God she was all right. But she might not have been. Anything could've happened.

It hadn't, though. He'd gotten her home. She was safe, for now. Sam pulled in his first deep breath in hours.

Dan stood beside him. "You want to tell us the story?"

He turned and leaned against the railing, crossing his arms to ward off the cold. And the fear he didn't want to acknowledge.

Camilla, misunderstanding his pause, said, "I can go inside, let you two talk." She started for the door.

"No, it's fine."

She turned back. "If you're sure..." She settled on the wicker couch, and Daniel sat beside her.

But Sam was too keyed up to sit. He recounted everything that'd happened from the time they'd arrived at Eliza's mom's house until they headed home. "She was fine. Talking to me. I knew she was hurt, but I didn't realize..." He shoved a hand through his hair. "And then she fell asleep, and I thought it made sense that she'd sleep. She was tired and hurt. But when I couldn't rouse her... I wanted to take her to the hospital, but she's so scared, and I had just gotten through lecturing her about trusting her instincts, so I didn't. But..." He forced himself to shut up.

Camilla's face had paled, her eyes wide.

But Daniel was red-faced. "Who was it?"

"She didn't know. They must've been watching the house. Waiting for her to show up."

"Why?"

"How should I know?" He pushed off the railing and paced. "That's the problem. We know nothing. Nothing! Her mom knew she was going to be in town, at least that's what we think.

But if they were supposed to go to Florida together, then did her mom go alone? Or maybe... What if something happened to Linda?"

He hated to think that. Sam wasn't Linda's biggest fan, but she was the only family Eliza had left. No siblings. Her father gone. No cousins or aunts or uncles that Eliza had ever mentioned.

Where was Linda? If they were supposed to go somewhere together, then why would she go without her?

And if they were planning to go together, why would Eliza fly to Manchester? Why not just meet her mom in Florida?

"Did she recognize the men?" Camilla asked.

"She said she didn't, but I think maybe... She didn't seem sure."

Daniel pushed to his feet and walked closer. "You think it's safe to be here? Those guys probably got your license plate number. They can find the house."

"The car belongs to the business. Even if they had the ability to trace the plate, the address will direct them to the office in Portland." Though Sam did most of his work from home, he kept an office in the city. "It won't lead them here." He paced some more, then spun to them. "I'm going to call the York police and tell them what happened. Maybe if those goons go back to her house, they'll catch them. More importantly, we need to find out where she's been the last five years. I'm going to call Jon."

"Who?" Daniel asked.

"Grant's best friend—you remember. From the Army?"

"Oh, yeah. He came up to camp a few times."

Camp. That was what the family called the multi-level home his parents had built on an island off the coast of Maine when the boys were kids.

"Why would you call him?" Daniel sounded genuinely confused.

"He's a private investigator. Maybe he can figure out where Eliza's been the last five years." Sam grasped at the idea, the first decent one he'd had since the attack. "I'm calling right now."

CHAPTER EIGHT

ONLY FIVE O'CLOCK in the morning, but Eliza couldn't sleep anymore. She felt like she'd been in bed for days. She had no idea what time she'd climbed beneath the covers the day before—actually had no memory of doing that—but she did know the sun had still been out when she'd woken up to Daniel's soft, "Are you with me? I need you to open your eyes, Eliza."

All she'd wanted was to go back to sleep, but she'd answered all his questions and obeyed all his commands. Then, she'd taken some Tylenol and fallen asleep.

It wasn't shocking that she was wide awake at five a.m. She showered, washed her hair, blow-dried it, and dressed in the fresh clothes. There was a shopping bag full of them. Bras, underwear, socks, jeans, T-shirts, sweatshirts, sweaters, yoga pants, pajamas. There was even a pair of cushy slippers.

It was enough to last a week or longer.

Had Sam picked the things out? How weird would that be, him choosing her underwear? More likely, Camilla had done it. Eliza didn't recognize the name of the store—were there no Walmarts nearby?—and could find no receipt in the bag. The clothes were good quality, the jeans soft and stretchy when she pulled them on, the sweatshirt warm and cozy.

The house was quiet.

She followed the low lighting to the stairs and crept down, thankful for the slippers that whispered against the hardwood. Maybe she should wait for the house to wake up, but she was starving. Camilla had offered to get her some food when Daniel had finished examining her the afternoon before, but Eliza had felt too sick to swallow anything but small sips of water. She hadn't eaten since breakfast the day before, which she'd expelled in the parking lot after the attack.

She found the light switch in the kitchen, opened the over-size refrigerator, and snagged a piece of American cheese. The fridge was packed with food.

While she nibbled the cheese, she searched for bread or crackers and found both in the butler's pantry. A giant butler's pantry. It had a counter covered with every appliance imaginable and shelves stocked with everything a person could need. Did Sam cook for himself? Looked like he must, based on all the ingredients. Pasta and rice and potatoes and beans and tomatoes and soup and bread and crackers and nuts and...

So much food.

Her chest tightened, and she pressed her hand against it, considering what she was feeling that caused that reaction.

Guilt.

She let herself be in the moment, allowing the feeling to overtake her. Tried to assign memories to it. But all it wielded was a sense of foreboding.

Because she wanted to eat? Because of all the food? She remembered her odd comment at breakfast the morning before —asking for seconds, worrying about other people who needed to eat.

What did that mean?

No memories came, but her head pulsed with pain.

She popped two slices of wheat bread in the toaster, then figured out how the fancy coffee maker worked and got a pot started.

The food helped. The coffee might as well have come straight from...

The river of Your delights.

Whoa. She knew that phrase. From the Bible, wasn't it? How would she know that? She'd never been particularly religious, hadn't been raised in church. Dad had talked about Jesus occasionally but had only taken them to church on holidays. Mom never wanted him to get *"too carried away with all that foolishness."*

Yet she knew a Bible verse. Another mystery.

Eliza finished the toast, left the plate in the sink, and took her mug with her. She'd only seen the living room, kitchen, and dining room on this floor. She wanted to poke around the spaces Sam had reserved for himself.

The ones he'd probably never show her.

No, she shouldn't snoop. But...well, she wanted to, and this was her chance.

By the dim morning light coming in through the open blinds on the east side of the house, she made her way past the front door, down a hallway, and around a corner, where she found two doors, one on the right, one straight ahead. She opened the one on her right first and hit the light switch.

Her breath caught.

It was Sam's office, and it looked just like the one he'd had in his old house, in the life she remembered.

Only, not really. This office was considerably larger. It had more bookshelves. Two chairs opposite the desk instead of one. And, unlike the one in his last house, this room had a wall of windows facing the ocean and a door that opened to a deck that ran the length of the house.

But the desk was the same as the one he'd had when they'd started dating. And the area rug... She'd found that at an antique shop and called him to tell him about it.

He'd bought it, sight unseen, on her recommendation. And he still had it.

Everything in her wanted to step into the familiar space, let it wrap itself around her. But Sam promised his clients confidentiality, and she'd always been careful to respect his boundaries where work was concerned. She turned off the light, stepped out, and closed the door.

She half expected him to be standing there, arms crossed, brows lowered. He used to be happy. Not easygoing, exactly, but not so quick to anger. The last couple of days had shown her how much he'd changed. Except maybe it was her presence bringing out the anger in him. Maybe, if she weren't there, Sam would be his old genial self.

Either way, if he knew she'd gone into his office, he wouldn't take it well.

She opened the other door and stepped in, turning on the light.

It was a living area, though not nearly as elegant or formal as the living room. More like a den. Like the other rooms on this floor, one wall was windows. Drapes hung at the edges, ready to be pulled closed. A flat-screen TV was affixed to the wall over a long console table. Beside that, a stone fireplace rose to the ceiling. She recognized the sectional and coffee table from his other house.

This room reflected Sam. Framed photographs of his favorite teams hung on the walls, along with a giant motocross poster. More sports paraphernalia was displayed on narrow shelves, along with books he treasured. *The Lord of the Rings* trilogy, *The Hitchhiker's Guide to the Galaxy, Fahrenheit 451*. She ran her hands along the titles, remembering them. Remembering conversations about them.

There was an autographed baseball in a clear acrylic box. A tiny replica of Gillette Stadium, complete with the Patriots logo at the fifty-yard line. A few photographs of Sam in a helmet and protective gear riding a dirt bike. A pocket watch. An old Swiss Army knife that had belonged to his grandfather. A painted ceramic eagle.

And photographs everywhere. His parents, his brothers, his niece and nephew. Friends, grandparents. They were on boats and ski lifts, in living rooms and backyards, fishing and swimming and laughing.

These were Sam's treasures. Why did he hide them away?

An easy chair near the windows faced the fireplace and the view, not the television. On the table beside it, a thick book lay open.

She crossed the space and peered at the pages.

A Bible?

Sam read the Bible?

Since when?

His parents were religious, and his brothers, but he'd never talked to her about God. That must've happened after they'd broken up.

She set her coffee on the side table, settled in his chair, lifted the footrest, and then slid the Bible onto her lap.

Not only was it open, but he'd marked under a bunch of words, and there was writing in the margins. She read the verse beside it.

"Take hold of my words with all your heart; keep my commands, and you will live."

Beside that, he'd written, *"But how?"*

Eliza kept her finger there and flipped the pages. He'd underlined a lot of passages. And written more notes.

Was this really Sam's Bible? Maybe he'd borrowed it.

She turned to the front, looking for an inscription. Sure enough...

Dear Sam,

May the words penetrate your heart and cause your eyes to seek your Savior. In Him, you'll find peace.

Love, Mom and Dad

Wow. It was Sam's Bible, and he was reading it. Studying it. It obviously mattered to him.

"Comfortable?"

She startled, barely keeping the thick book from landing on the floor.

Sam stood in the entryway. Arms crossed. Brows lowered over angry eyes. Just like she'd imagined him a few minutes earlier.

She swallowed the fear that jumped to her throat. "Hey. Uh..." She closed the book, cringing as she did. She'd lost his place.

After setting it on the side table, she pressed the button to lower the footrest, cursing the time it took to go down.

Sam hadn't moved.

"I shouldn't have... Sorry. I just wanted to see. You mentioned yesterday that you'd had places—"

"Private places."

"You're right. I'm sorry." Her heart was thumping, her hands shaking. She stood on unsteady legs, itching to bolt from the room. Afraid of...

What?

Sam wouldn't hurt her. She squeezed her hands into fists and took a deep breath. Then another. "I didn't know you read the Bible."

"Yeah, well..." He dropped his arms. "Why are you here?"

She didn't think he'd appreciate the real answer—she'd been curious and nosy. And anyway, he could guess those.

She was trying to come up with a suitable response when her gaze snagged on a photograph. She crossed to it and lifted it from the end table.

Mountains in the background. A white railing in the foreground. And a woman, hand shielding her eyes, staring at the view.

The photo'd been taken from the side. A snapshot. Of her.

She ran her fingertips over the cool glass, imagining him standing behind her. Watching her take in the vista. Snapping a photo without telling her.

They'd been at the Mount Washington Hotel for a wedding. It was early in their relationship, and he'd come as her date. He hadn't known a soul, but he'd charmed everybody that day, just like he always did.

Charming. Hiding his true self.

She set the photograph down, unsure what to make of it. Wanting to scour the room for pictures of other women.

But he was watching her. If anything, he looked even more angry than before. "What do you want?" No charm in his tone this morning.

"Why do you hide the best parts of yourself?"

His Adam's apple worked. "I keep my private life private."

"You entertain a lot?"

His gaze hit the floor, the back wall. "Sometimes."

"Strangers? Business associates?"

"I have a right to privacy."

"You shouldn't need privacy in your own home. This is the one place you should be able to be yourself."

"And yet here you are, in my *private* room."

She ignored the dig. "This is what you've always done. Put

up barriers, walls to keep people out. You let people just so close, but never let them see the real you."

"You don't know me, Eliza."

"You haven't changed a bit. Charming, easy on the eyes."

That lifted his brows, but she wasn't finished.

"But don't let anybody get too close. Don't let anybody in."

"I let you in."

"Did you?" The words were a challenge, revealing nothing of her fear.

Had he, really? Had he finally let her in, and she'd left him?

Or was he lying to her? To himself?

If only she could remember.

"I did my best." At least his tone lost some of the anger. "It doesn't matter now."

"What happened between us?"

"Grab your coffee." He shifted away from the door. "Let's go."

She was tempted to refuse. She needed an answer. But this was his space, his house. He'd been nothing but good to her since she'd barreled back into his life.

"I never said... Thank you, Sam, for all you've done for me. And are doing for me. For taking me in. For the clothes." She rubbed the soft material of her sweater.

"Let's go." He gestured for her to precede him.

She grabbed her mug and walked past him, down the hall and around the corner toward the kitchen, feeling his presence behind her. "Did you buy them? The clothes?"

"Camilla picked them out."

"You paid, I guess." In the kitchen, she turned to face him. "I'll pay you back."

"With what?" He flipped on the overhead lights, revealing an almost smile on his face. "I have plenty, Eliza. I'm happy to do it."

The kindness in his expression stole her words. She cleared her throat. "Thank you."

"You're feeling better?"

"The headache is still there, but it only pounds when I try to remember something."

"You slept all right?"

"Are you going to answer my question? From before?"

He rounded the corner into the butler's pantry and came back with a cup of coffee. "I have work to do."

Apparently, that was a no. "It's"—she checked the clock on the oven—"five thirty in the morning. And...Sunday, right?"

"Unless we figure out what's going on with you today, I need to get ahead. We're leaving here at ten o'clock."

"Where are we—?"

"I looked up Jeanette on Facebook. She's a children's pastor at a church outside of Portsmouth."

"That can't be right. A pastor? Are you sure you have the right—?"

"It's her. I don't know where she lives, but according to her profile, she doesn't live in York anymore. I assume you don't know where she moved to?"

Eliza was still wrapping her head around the fact that her best friend was a pastor. At a church.

"Didn't think so," Sam said. "Rather than try to dig up her address, I think we should just meet her at the church. And anyway, if your friends are watching her—"

"Why would they be?" Panic had her pulse spiking. "How would they know about her?"

"I have no idea. I don't know who they are or what they know. Until you remember...something, we should assume they know everything about you. Maybe Jeanette will be able to shed some light on what you've been up to."

That seemed like a good idea.

"Will that make you miss your church service?" She tossed the question out, an obvious ploy for information.

"It's fine."

Oh. Apparently, he was taking the whole religion thing seriously.

"I'm going to read my Bible and pray, and then I'm going to get some work done. Can you entertain yourself for a little while? There's a TV in your room. There're books—"

"Do what you need to do. I can take care of myself."

By his grunt, he disagreed, but he didn't say so. He walked out of the kitchen and down the hall. A moment later, she heard the faint thud of a door closing.

Shutting her out completely.

Apparently, not everything had changed.

Jeanette's church was nothing like Eliza had imagined—not that she knew much about churches in general. But where was the white siding, the tall steeple with the church bell? Except for the sign out front, this building could be a private school or a YMCA.

Eliza directed them to the door with a sign that read *Children's Worship Center*. According to the website, the service had begun at ten thirty, and it was nearly eleven, so the lot was full of cars but mostly empty of people.

Sam parked and killed the engine on his truck. He'd let Daniel and Camilla take the Audi, since they planned to pick up Sam and Daniel's parents to go house shopping with them. The pickup was too high for Mom and Dad to climb in and out of easily.

At least that was Daniel's reasoning, but Sam had laughed

and punched him in the shoulder. "You just want to get the Audi on the open road."

Daniel hadn't disagreed.

Sam didn't seem to find any humor in the current situation as his gaze darted around the rows of cars. "This was stupid. We should have come when there were more people around."

"You really think those guys are watching the church?"

His lips quirked at the corner like he was attempting a smile. He'd been much less belligerent after the Bible reading and praying that morning, so maybe there was something to the habit. If she wasn't mistaken, he was making an effort to be nice to her, an effort she appreciated.

"What do you think? Any bad feelings about being here?"

She took the question seriously, closing her eyes to let it resonate. "I think we're okay."

"All right, then. I trust your judgment." He climbed out of the truck, and she did the same, thankful for the step that kept her from having to jump. She met him by the tailgate, and they walked beneath the thick clouds to the entrance.

She stepped across the threshold and stopped to take it in. She couldn't remember the last time she'd been inside a church. Certainly before Dad's death, and she'd never felt anything but impatient.

But this felt different. Comfortable, like an old friend.

The small foyer was all bright colors and happiness, filled with the sound of children squealing, crying, and laughing from nearby rooms. A rainbow was painted on the wall straight ahead above a little cartoony ark with animals sticking out from every window. A tall desk was flanked by hallways that led deeper into the building.

Behind the desk, a redheaded grandmotherly type talked to a teenage boy, who was nodding and yes-ma'aming her. "On it." He disappeared down a hall, and the redhead turned to them.

"You must be the Smarts. Do you need to stay together, or is it all right if I split you up? We could use one of you in the toddler room, but the four-year-olds need another helper."

"Actually," Sam said, "we're here to see Jeanette. Is she around?"

"Oh. Uh... Yeah." She looked from him to Eliza. "You're not here to volunteer?"

"Sorry," she said.

"Don't worry. Jeanette'll suck you in. It's her superpower. Names?"

Sam spoke before she could answer. "Sam Wright."

If the woman was surprised he didn't offer Eliza's, she didn't say so, just picked up a walkie-talkie and pressed the button. "Jeanette?" She turned and walked a few feet away.

Thanks to the noise of all the children, Eliza didn't hear the rest of what the woman said. She stood beside Sam near the door and turned a questioning gaze on him.

He leaned close and lowered his voice. "If your friendly neighborhood attackers are here, the last thing we want is your name being repeated all over this building."

"Good thinking."

The redhead came back. "She's coming. It might be a sec, though. We're short on help."

They pretended they didn't hear the pleading in the woman's voice. What did Eliza know about taking care of kids?

A line of little ones walked past, all holding onto a strap following the grown-up leading the way.

"Now, there's a trick," Sam said. "I guess it keeps them together."

Eliza barely heard him.

The kids—she guessed they were three years old—wore dresses and slacks and jeans. One boy had donned a Superman T-shirt—and cape.

She'd never seen any of them before in her life.

And yet, her eyes stung.

A longing she'd never experienced rolled over her as she watched the last one pass.

It was a painful gnawing in her gut. A...need. A visceral need. She wanted to follow them. To stay with them. To hold them close.

"Eliza? What is it?"

Sam moved into her line of vision, worry and compassion on his face. "What happened?"

"I don't..." She blinked, felt moisture in her eyes.

Felt the pressure of her fists against her stomach where she was pushing, pushing against the yearning.

He gently took her hands and wrapped them in his. "Did you remember something?"

It was right there. On the edge of her consciousness. The Something she couldn't remember. The Important Something that mattered more than anything else.

She closed her eyes and tried to move toward it, through the darkness, the thick fog in her mind.

Oh. Her head.

She pulled her hands from Sam's and squeezed her temples until the pain passed.

The Something dissipated like mist.

She opened her eyes to Sam watching. Waiting for some revelation. But nothing came.

"Are you all right?"

"Yes. I don't..."

"Eliza? Oh, thank God!"

She turned just in time to see a fast-moving blur. And then she was wrapped in a hug. She picked up the floral scent of her best friend's perfume, the frizzy hair that would never cooperate itching her nose. Jeanette's sobs racked Eliza's chest. "Thank God. Thank God you're all right."

To her, it felt like they'd seen each other a couple of days before, maybe a week or two. But tears streamed from Eliza's eyes anyway, a reaction to her friend's emotions.

Finally, Jeanette leaned back and gripped her shoulders. The bruises hurt, but Eliza didn't say so.

"Where have you been?" And then, seeing her face, her eyes widened. "What happened to you?"

Eliza didn't know how to answer that.

Sam cleared his throat. "Can we go somewhere private please?"

Jeanette turned to him. "Sam." No friendliness in her voice. "Are you responsible for that?"

"Of course not," Eliza said. "Why would you even...?"

"An office?" He ignored Jeanette's question. "Broom closet?"

"Sure. Right." She wiped her eyes and took Eliza's hand as if she might disappear, pulling her down a hall past doors that were closed on the bottom, open on top. Inside, children played and bounced and laughed and cried.

Jeanette led them around a corner and down another long hall, this one dark and deserted, leaving the kids' classrooms behind. She unlocked a door and pushed it open, then turned on the light.

Eliza stepped into an office. Utilitarian desk. Shelves over-flowing with brightly colored books, tubs of crayons, paints, and craft supplies.

Jeanette looked the same. Blond curly hair trying its best to escape a ponytail. Scant makeup. Bright blue eyes that missed nothing. Jeans and a sweater and leather boots with a short, stacked heel. Maybe she had a few more wrinkles than Eliza remembered, but they didn't detract from her looks. She'd always been naturally beautiful.

She sat in one of the guest chairs, pulling Eliza down into the other. "Where have you been?"

"It's a very long story. Are you really a pastor? How did that happen?"

"Also a very long story. After you left—"

"We know you're busy." Sam gave Jeanette an apologetic look as he closed the door and leaned against it. "Maybe you two should catch up another time. Sorry to interrupt you at work."

She barely spared him a glance, aiming her words at Eliza. "What's going on?"

"When was the last time we saw each other?"

Those blue eyes narrowed. "What do you mean?"

"My memory's a little..." She was groping for a way to explain, but Sam didn't have any trouble.

"She has amnesia." When Jeanette looked up at him, he added, "She's lost about five years. Anything you can fill in would be really helpful."

Jeanette blinked. "Five *years?*"

"Crazy, huh?" Eliza tried to sound flippant. "But I figured, if anybody knew where I'd been—"

"I know nothing. You just... You took off. Said you were taking a job with some clients and moving."

"What clients?" Sam asked. "What were their names?"

She glared at him. "I don't know. Somebody she was working with."

Seemed Jeanette was holding a grudge. Eliza was about to try to diffuse her friend, but Sam beat her to it.

"I love your protectiveness." His tone was calm, measured. "I'm sure I deserve your wrath. It would really help Eliza if you'd try to remember."

Jeanette turned away from him almost dismissively. "You

worked with them for a while. Do you remember any of your clients?"

"A few, yeah."

"It was a married couple. You told me they were starting some kind of a home for young women—a drug rehab or something?"

It sounded right. Felt right. She closed her eyes, tried to probe that memory. Pushed through the throbbing in her head. Pressed her hands to her temples. She had to remember. She had to.

But the pain was overwhelming.

"Hey, it's okay." Sam's hand slid over her hair, a gentle touch that felt so familiar it made her want to cry. "You'll remember. Don't try to force it."

She was still breathing through the pain when Sam said, "Jeanette, do you remember when that was?"

"It was early summer, five years ago." Jeanette's cool fingers brushed Eliza's scalp. "Are you all right?"

She nodded, not quite ready to speak.

"The pain usually passes after a few moments," Sam said. "Did Eliza say why she was going with them?"

"You didn't tell me much, Eliza. Just said it was a good opportunity, and you needed to get away."

She couldn't see but imagined, by the hardness in those last words, that her friend was shooting Sam another look. But then her tone softened again. "You promised you'd keep in touch. But I never heard from you again."

How could she have done that? Abandoned her best friend? What kind of person would do that?

"And then I got the letter yesterday," Jeanette added. "Mailed overnight express."

Eliza's eyes snapped open.

Sam asked, "What letter?"

She looked up at him, then back at Eliza. "You broke up with him. Do you remember that? Did he tell you—?"

"He told me. I don't remember."

"He tell you why?"

"She'll remember on her own." His words were measured. Not defensive. Not angry.

But hope blossomed in Eliza's chest. Maybe she could at least get one question answered. "Jeanette, tell me what happened. Surely you know."

"Nope." Jeanette's lips popped on the P. "You wouldn't say. But by your reaction, he hurt you. Badly."

Eliza's gaze flicked to Sam, expecting to see the angry mask he donned so much these days. But she only saw sadness. He caught her looking and schooled his expression. "Tell us about the letter."

Again, Jeanette spoke to Eliza. "You don't remember?"

"Nothing for five years until Friday night."

Her friend stood and rounded the desk, where she opened a drawer and grabbed a huge floppy purse. From it, she pulled a white overnight envelope with familiar orange and purple text on the side. Jeanette handed it toward her.

Eliza could feel Sam itching to grab it, but he restrained himself.

"You carry it with you?" Eliza took it.

"Read it. You'll understand."

She took a single sheet of note paper from inside and unfolded it. It had the Hyatt Hotels logo on the top.

Dear Jeanette,

I have so many things to say to you, things I'll explain in person soon. I hope you can forgive me for disappearing, for not keeping my promise. Until I have a

*chance to explain, please know one thing: I should have
listened to you. I'm sorry.*

*There's nobody I trust more to take care of this for
me. I'll be there soon. Until then, keep it somewhere safe.
My future depends on it.*

I love you.

Eliza

She read the words again, trying to make sense of them.
Trying to remember writing them. Folding the letter. Putting it
in the mail.

"Listened to you about what?" Eliza asked.

"I didn't want you to go. It felt like a knee-jerk reaction to"—
her head tipped toward Sam—"whatever he did. I didn't think
you should make any impulsive decisions."

"I'm not impulsive, as a rule."

"You're not. That's why I was so worried. You didn't usually
just discard our advice."

"Yours and...?"

"Your mom's, of course. She didn't want you to go either."

Huh. Why would Eliza have ignored her best friend and her
mother to go off with strangers?

"What was it?" Sam asked. "In the letter?"

Eliza tipped the envelope up and dropped the contents into
her palm.

A key.

A simple gold key.

"Does it have any markings on it?"

She didn't miss the hope in his voice, but there was nothing
but a number.

"May I?" He held out his hand.

She dropped the key into it, and he studied it. "It's small, too small for a house key. Maybe a locker? A safe deposit box?"

"Right," Eliza said. "In some bank. Somewhere in the world."

"The postmark is from Denver, if that helps."

"Oh." Had she been in Denver? How could she not remember?

A squawk filled the silence.

Jeanette pulled a walkie-talkie from her waistband. "Yes?"

The redheaded grandmother's voice came through. "You'd better hurry. They're plotting mutiny."

"Five minutes." She put the device back, sighing. "I have to go."

"Sorry for this." Eliza stood. "For...all of it."

Jeanette rounded the desk and pulled her into another rib-cracking hug. "I'm glad you're here and...safe."

Eliza imagined her shooting Sam another one of those looks over her shoulder.

"Why don't you come stay with me?" Jeanette backed away. "I'll help you figure this out."

"Oh, um—" Eliza didn't want to look at Sam. Didn't want to see the relief on his face. But could she put her friend in danger? How could she keep them both safe and figure out what was going on when she couldn't remember anything?

Sam wanted to be rid of her, and she couldn't blame him. "If you don't mind," she said, "but I should tell you—"

"She's staying with me for the time being." By Sam's tone, the matter was settled. He was less confident when he added, "If that's all right, Eliza. It just seems like, with everything going on—"

"Yes, it's fine."

Jeanette's open expression closed. "He hurt you."

"We're not together," Sam said. "There's more happening than you understand."

Eliza added, "I don't want to put you in danger."

"What danger? What's going on?"

"I don't know," she said. "That's the problem."

The walkie-talkie squawked again.

"I have to go. You'll be all right? Keep in touch?"

"One more thing," Eliza said. "Do you have any idea where my mother is?"

A look of confusion crossed her face. "Should I?"

"No. I just hoped..." Eliza forced a smile. "I'll reach out when this is over. Can you write down your phone number?"

Jeanette pulled a business card from a container on her desk and handed it over. "My cell's on there."

Eliza hated to leave her friend, but she didn't want to put Jeanette in danger. And, despite what had happened between her and Sam, she wasn't ready to leave him.

They said their goodbyes, and Sam walked Eliza to the exit, staying right beside her, a hand on the small of her back. The slight pressure there felt protective. Maybe possessive.

Eliza was glad she wouldn't be putting Jeanette in danger, but what about Sam? He'd already been attacked once.

By staying with her, he was risking his safety. If anything happened to him, how could she live with it?

CHAPTER NINE

SAM'S STOMACH growled as they reached Shadow Cove. He had a fridge full of food, but he didn't feel like cooking. Or going home to an empty house with the woman he was trying very hard not to fall for again.

Eliza had been quiet for most of the drive. He wanted to question her about what they'd learned from Jeanette, but maybe she needed to process on her own.

"Are you hungry?"

"It's been a long time since breakfast." She was staring out the window at the little downtown area. "I can see why you chose this place. It's darling."

Darling. Not the word he'd have chosen. He tried to see it through her eyes, the little souvenir shops and restaurants and galleries and boutiques along both sides of the road. Most of the businesses were in old houses—or new structures built to look like old houses—all painted in bright colors. Flower boxes overflowed with mums in shades of yellow, orange, brick-red, and white. Pumpkins and potted plants decorated steps. Trees canopied the sidewalk and main street, their leaves already showing hints of the color that would burst in a couple of weeks.

Giant hydrangea bushes lined the front of a few structures, their blooms aging, beautiful in their own way. Just a couple hundred yards farther and they'd bump into the coastal road that lined the rocky shore.

Sam loved the town and the people he'd met here, workers in the restaurants he frequented, friends from church. Shadow Cove fit him a lot better than the oversize house he'd chosen. "It's not too far from the office."

"Which is...in Portland? Is that right?" At his nod, she said, "In the same building?"

"Yeah. My assistant works there all the time. I go in when I have meetings."

"Do I know your assistant?" Eliza asked.

"New guy. Hired him a couple years ago. He's good, sees things I miss."

"You miss things?" The humor in her voice had him glancing her way. "I can't imagine."

That wasn't true. She knew his flaws firsthand. He was good at what he did—finding buyers for business owners who wanted to sell and negotiating the terms—but he'd gotten better when he'd slowed down and started asking more questions rather than assuming he knew everything.

He'd learned that lesson the hard way when he'd negotiated the sale of Eliza's father's company. The beginning of the end of their relationship.

"There's a deli," he said, "or we could get burgers or... You still don't like seafood, I guess."

The scrunched-up face she made had him nearly laughing.

At least that hadn't changed. How did someone grow up on the coast of Maine and not like seafood?

"The deli sounds good."

He found a spot on the street a few doors down. The temperature was in the fifties, and the wind whipped off the water. Eliza wrapped her arms around herself for the short walk. Her thin jacket wasn't going to cut it. He'd need to buy her something more weather-appropriate.

He opened the door, and Eliza preceded him and stopped at the end of the short line. The place was only half-full, the low murmur of diners not quite drowning out the eighties music playing overhead. She studied the extensive menu on the wall behind the case and then looked up at him. "What do you recommend?"

"If you like horseradish, the French dip."

"Do you want to split it?"

"Uh, no. I'm a grown-up. I can eat my whole lunch. And so should you."

She turned back to the menu. "Ever had the salads?"

He wasn't exactly a salad-for-a-meal kind of guy. And she needed fat and protein to put on some of the weight she'd lost. But he ought to keep his thoughts about her figure to himself. "Everything here is fresh."

They placed their orders, grabbed their drinks, and found a table by the window. In the summer, tourists and locals meandered along the sidewalks, enjoying coffee or slushes or ice cream, carrying shopping bags or beach bags on their way to the small stretch of sand just down a ways. But today, though the clouds had broken up a little, the wind and temperature kept people inside.

"Had any thoughts about what we learned from Jeanette?" he asked.

"I think I know the couple she's referring to. At least, I remember their existence. But I can't picture them and don't know their names."

"You must have liked them, though, if you moved away with them. They were married, I guess?"

She nodded, though the movement was slow, tentative. "That feels right."

"A home for women?"

Again, that slow nod. She blinked a few times before closing her eyes. Then she squeezed them, her lips pinching.

"Don't do that." He reached out, nearly took Eliza's hand. But she lifted them both to rub her temples, keeping him from the bad decision.

Her eyes opened, and she sipped her water.

"That hasn't worked yet, you trying to remember," he said. "Maybe you'd be better off just letting the memories come when they come."

"And in the meantime, what? Am I supposed to just hide?"

He shrugged. "We follow the clues we have, I guess. Maybe Grant's friend will uncover something."

"I hope so. But... Are you sure about this? About me staying with you? Because we're not together. You're putting yourself in danger. I don't want anything to happen to you."

"Don't worry about me."

"Okay, but I don't want you to feel obligated. I mean, because of what Jeanette said, as if you hurt me. I don't know what happened, and... I'm just saying, you don't owe me anything." She looked away. Swallowed. "It's not that I don't appreciate it. Besides Jeanette, you're the only person I have, the only person I can trust."

As if the weight of responsibility hadn't been heavy enough.

She covered her face with her hands. "I shouldn't have said that. I'm sorry. What's wrong with me?" The words were muffled behind her fingers.

"There's nothing wrong with you, Eliza. You're scared, that's all."

She lowered her hands. "I should just go, leave you to—"

"We're staying together." No way he was letting her go, not as long as she was in danger. Still, he didn't mean the words to sound so harsh and regretted causing the flash of fear in her expression. She hadn't been so sensitive when they were together. "The thought of you trying to deal with this on your own..."

"I could go to Jeanette's."

"She's going to protect you? Fight off your enemies with crayons and blocks?"

"You're not wrong. But neither am I. You don't owe me anything."

"I'd rather you stay with me. Please."

Eliza's small smile lit her face. "Thank you. I'd prefer that too."

Good. At least that was settled.

"I can't imagine how Jeanette became a children's pastor," Eliza said. "She had one of those families that was at church all the time, but as far as I knew, she hadn't been in years. And you're religious now too. It's a weird coincidence."

"Maybe."

Sam had returned to church after the pain of losing Eliza had nearly done him in. He'd gone at first because his parents practically dragged him, worried when he started skipping family events and social events he normally would have enjoyed. He'd visited the family church the first time to placate them, but he'd continued going because they were right—there was peace in Christ. There was peace in being loved for who he was, forgiven for all his sins, and guided in his choices. He wasn't great at asking, but when he did, God was always there for him.

There was also peace in the knowledge that, though he hadn't known where Eliza was, God knew, and God cared.

Sam had been praying for her for years. Not that he'd ever thought he'd see her again.

"Maybe...what?" Eliza asked.

He was saved from explaining when one of the owners, the chef's wife, delivered their meals. She was short and plump, wearing a red apron with the deli's logo on it. "How you doing, Sam? It's been a while since you graced us with your presence."

"Hey, Molly. This is my friend Eliza."

Molly looked her way and smiled. "Glad to see he finally got himself a date."

Eliza looked about to set her straight, but Molly turned her attention to Sam. "Lemme know if you need anything."

"Will do."

Eliza waited until she was out of earshot. "She's a friend of yours?"

"When the tourists are gone, it's a pretty tight-knit community."

"I'm glad you're a part of it."

"I needed to be."

Again, Eliza seemed to wait for him to explain. When he didn't, she picked up her fork.

He cleared his throat. "I'll pray real quick."

"Oh."

She set the utensil down, and he uttered a short blessing over their meal, adding, "Bring Eliza's memories back, Lord, and keep us safe. We need Your help."

She echoed his amen, then tried the salad. "Mmm. It's good." She'd chosen one with lots of fruit, but also grilled chicken and feta cheese. A little protein, anyway.

He dipped his sandwich in the au jus and took a sizable bite. Salty and warm with enough horseradish to give it some zing. When he'd swallowed, he steered the conversation back to her past. "Could you call your old employers and get the couple's names?"

"Did I leave on good terms?"

He shrugged. She must've quit after she'd dumped him.

"Oh. Right."

"But I can't imagine you burning bridges," he said. "That's not your style."

"I'll call them tomorrow."

He dug into his meal. He was halfway through with his sandwich when she pushed her bowl away. She'd barely made a dent.

"Why don't you try finishing the chicken at least?"

"Gluttony's a sin."

He felt his eyebrows hike and worked to lower them. "Would that make you a glutton, eating your whole salad?"

"Don't you think I've had enough?"

"Do you?"

She shrugged, eyeing the food.

"Are you still hungry?"

"I've had all the bites I should." She shook her head. "I mean... What do I mean?"

"How many bites have you had?"

"Fifteen." She answered as if it made sense. Answered as if she'd expected the question.

Fifteen.

She'd counted her bites. Counted, as if there were a limit. As if she wasn't allowed to eat more.

Rage clawed up his throat, but he swallowed it back. Kept his mouth shut until he could speak levelly. Waited for her to explain. Or at least realize there was no reasonable explanation.

"I don't understand." Her words were barely audible.

"Me either."

"Why would I...?" She rubbed her lips, pressed them together until they turned white. "I must not have had enough food. Which explains why I've lost weight."

Sam tried Daniel's soothing voice. It'd worked before. "Do you still feel hungry?"

Her head bobbed, fast, like she was embarrassed about the answer.

"Will you try to eat a little more then?"

She slid the bowl closer and forked another bite.

He watched her chew and swallow.

Itched to punch the person who'd limited her food.

And frankly, to demand she explain why she'd allowed it.

"Would you just...talk?" she asked. "Please?" Her eyes were wide and filled with fear. "Distract me?"

He could do that.

He told her Daniel and Camilla's story, then updated her on his parents and the rest of his brothers and what they were doing—as much as he knew. Grant lived in New Hampshire now, working as a cop in Coventry. Michael traveled more than he was home, working in sales. Michael never shared much, and Sam hadn't been great about keeping up with him.

So different from when they were kids. Once upon a time, Sam and Michael had been best friends.

Bryan was a professor at Bowdoin and had just gotten tenure. Derrick, the baby of the family, flew a charter jet.

"That's great. I remember he wanted to learn to fly." It was the first time she'd spoken since he began the monologue. While he'd talked, she'd eaten, and he was glad to see it.

"It suits him," Sam said. "He always had his head in the clouds."

"Is his work seasonal? Mostly tourists, or business people?"

"He stays busy year round."

She gazed out the window toward a maple tree, its leaves hinting at the bright orange-red that would soon cover it "My favorite time of the year."

He remembered that, remembered how he and Eliza would

walk hand in hand through the woods so she could enjoy the foliage. Remembered how she'd stop and stare straight up, wonder in her eyes at the bright colors. Remembered how he used to be as mesmerized with her as she'd been with the foliage.

"Were the leaves pretty where you've been living?" He took a shot with the question. Maybe catching her off guard would jog a memory, elicit a response.

"It was too barren. Hardly any trees." She froze, fork halfway to her mouth.

He didn't speak. Just waited and hoped.

"There were mountains, or at least they called them mountains. In the summer, they just looked like big rocks." Though her eyes remained open, she seemed to be focused far away. "In the winter, they were snow-capped, even when we didn't have snow in the valley. I lived in a...compound of some kind. There were multiple buildings."

Sam swallowed all his questions, not wanting to push.

After a minute, she shook her head. "That's all."

"Did it seem like Colorado? Utah?"

"I don't know. I've never been to... Well, I don't remember ever going to either. It was barren and...dry. Like desert, but I don't remember it being hot."

"Okay. That's good." He'd been in Salt Lake City but not the rest of Utah, but wasn't much of it desert? Wasn't that where Moab and Zion were? He'd seen pictures of the national parks, and they looked arid.

Of course, Colorado had arid land too.

"It's not much." Her shoulders fell. "Why can't I remember?"

He reached across the table and took her hand, only then realizing what he'd done.

Her quick intake of breath matched his own shock as their palms met.

Her hand felt so perfect wrapped in his, as if it were made to be right there.

Somehow, he managed to keep his voice level. "Your memories will come, Eliza. Don't try to push it, and don't beat yourself up about something you can't control. It's okay."

Her answering smile was slight.

"Take the win." He squeezed her hand and let it go, leaning back in his chair, away from her. Needing to find his equilibrium again. "Every memory brings us closer to the answers."

In time, they'd all come back to her. She'd remember where she'd been, why she'd left. She'd remember why she'd broken up with him.

And then this reunion would be over.

~

"How did you know to do that?"

Eliza's question snapped Sam's focus to her. They were back in his truck, inching forward in traffic along the narrow coastal road that would take them to his house. To the left, ocean waves crashed into the rocky cliff. To the right, mom-and-pop businesses that'd been there for years—an ice cream shop, a swim and surf shop, a couple of restaurants. Behind those, the town rose on forested hills.

"The question you asked me about the foliage," she clarified. "The one that got me to remember. How did you know?"

He shrugged. "I didn't. Just thought, maybe if we came at it from a different direction..."

"Smart."

"You taught me the importance of asking the right question."

"I don't remember that."

"It wasn't like a class." He smiled at her, found her watching him, and turned his focus back to the road. "You were always so good about figuring out the right questions to ask, and you'd get information I would never have uncovered."

"I just ask what feels obvious."

"I guess that's your gift, because what was obvious to you definitely wasn't to me. You remember when I introduced you to some new clients—Marcus and Julie Russell? We went to—"

"That seafood place."

Sam grinned at the memory. Julia had picked the restaurant, and he hadn't wanted to balk while he was still trying to win their business. He could still picture Eliza trying to eat around the clams in her clam chowder. "I thought I had them all figured out, but within ten minutes, you'd uncovered their real goals for the sale of their business. That information helped me put together a deal that fit into their plans. I never could have done that without you."

"Really?"

"It's taken me years to learn what comes so naturally to you, and I'm not there yet. But I practice. I listen. And I try to figure out questions that lead to honest answers. I don't know why people don't just say what they want."

"I think sometimes they don't know."

He considered that. "Maybe. Or maybe they're worried about being judged. Or...I don't know. That if they tell the truth about their goals, maybe they'll jinx it. Anyway, all I did today was practice what you always modeled."

She was quiet beside him, and though the traffic had picked up speed, he risked a look. She seemed pensive.

"What is it?"

"When you talk about me," she said, "it feels like you're

talking about someone I used to know, an old friend I haven't seen in years."

"It doesn't feel like it's five years ago? It doesn't feel like no time has passed?"

"It did at first. Or maybe... I was hurt and confused and... I don't know, Sam. It's a strange feeling."

"You're handling it very well."

"Speaking of special gifts."

He had no idea what she was talking about.

"You've always been good at recognizing people's strengths. More than that, you tell people when you see their talents. You're a natural encourager."

He couldn't help but laugh. "I don't know about that."

"I do. You just did it with me. Not only noticed something I do well but told me about it. Most people don't do that."

"I try to use my powers for good."

She chuckled beside him, but as he considered her words, a niggling of guilt bubbled in his stomach. Because, yeah, he could be an encourager. But he'd been known to use that particular gift to his own advantage—to get people to trust him, to get people to want to help him. To build his business and make a lot of money.

He was pretty sure that, if God had given him that gift, he hadn't been using it properly. He'd have to think about that. And pray about it.

They reached the marina in the small cove, where sailboats and motorboats pitched this way and that in the growing waves. Clouds had moved in, along with the heavy scent of rain.

He turned and wound up the hill toward his house. Daniel and Camilla should be back by now. Not that Sam was eager to lose Eliza's company, or share her with his brother and sister-in-law. That was the problem, though. The more time they spent together, the more he remembered why he'd fallen in love with her.

And the more he forgot how she'd ripped his heart out and stomped on it.

"I haven't gotten to your house from this direction," she said. "It's so pretty."

The road was narrow and lined on both sides with newer homes on large lots, all sporting windows that faced the ocean. Manicured front yards and perfectly landscaped flower beds made the street feel bright and cheerful despite the gray clouds overhead. Beyond his house, the hill continued up another few hundred feet, mostly forest, though a few structures peeked through the thick trees. Sam hadn't wanted to live any higher, though. He liked his spot, close enough to watch the boats in the cove but far enough away that he had privacy from all the summer visitors.

"I fell in love with the neighborhood long before I saw the house. It's too big for me, of course, but I hoped..." Was he really going to tell her how he'd longed for a wife, a family? Not a chance.

"Have you met your neighbors? I bet they're..."

Her voice trailed as they rounded the last corner.

Police cars. Two...no, three of them. Two on the street.

One in Sam's driveway.

"What's going on?"

He didn't even try to answer Eliza's question as he stopped behind one of the cars and threw the truck into park. "I'll come around."

"I can..." The rest of her words were lost when he slammed the door and hurried to her side. She was halfway down by the time he got there. He grabbed her around the waist and lifted her to the ground, gaze flicking behind them.

Just in case.

He wrapped an arm around her waist and stayed glued to her side. Because something was going on, and he had a very bad idea what it might be.

"Where have you been?" Daniel's voice was uncharacteristically loud—and angry—as he stormed down the driveway toward them.

Behind him, a uniformed police officer was talking to Camilla, who was wrapped in a blanket, sitting sideways in the back seat of the cruiser, her feet on the asphalt.

More cops were crouched near the bushes on the edge of his property.

"I called you," Daniel said. "Twice."

"Phone's on silent. What happened?"

"You said they wouldn't be able to track you! You were certain of it."

"Tell me what happened."

"They were here, that's what happened. Your two attackers." His gaze shifted to Eliza, and he took a breath.

Eliza's skin was white, her eyes wide and filling. A hand covered her mouth in horror.

Sam shifted closer and squeezed her to his side.

When Dan spoke again, his voice was calmer. "Sorry." He raked a hand through his hair. "I was already inside, but Cammie left a bag in the car and went to grab it. I heard her screaming. By the time I got out, they were dragging her away."

Sam's gaze flicked to Camilla. She was standing now, pointing toward the bushes. Whole and healthy.

Thank God. Thank God she hadn't been hurt.

"How did you get her away?" Sam asked.

"I called her name." Daniel swallowed. "I was chasing them down, hoping to...I don't know. Give her a chance to escape. But when I called her name, they let her go."

They'd realized she wasn't Eliza. Which meant her

attackers didn't know her that well, though they'd just seen her the day before. Maybe these were different attackers?

Because Eliza and Camilla didn't look alike. Camilla had twenty years—and probably twenty pounds—on her. She was gorgeous, but in a totally different way than Eliza. Her hair was darker, and where Eliza's eyes were hazel, Camilla's were bright blue.

But if you didn't look that closely, if you assumed...

Eliza sucked in a breath, then another. "I'm sorry. I'm so sorry."

Daniel's eyes, furious seconds before, shifted to compassion. He squeezed her arm. "It wasn't your fault." Then, he flicked an angry glare at Sam. "We didn't know they'd be able to track you down here."

"Maybe it was the people who dropped you off the other night," Sam said. "But why would they have left you if they were the ones who were after you?"

Eliza couldn't seem to come up with an answer.

"That doesn't make sense," Daniel snapped. "They must've tracked the Audi."

Sam wasn't so sure. "The car's registered to the company."

"And the company's registered to you," Daniel said.

"But it's not like my address is publicly listed. I mean, how would they have found it?"

"Real estate records." Eliza's words were flat but confident. "It's not that hard to look up names in property databases."

"You've done that?"

She shrugged, nodded.

He wanted to probe that memory, see if they could discover anything else. But a gray-haired uniformed police officer ambled down the driveway and stopped in front of him, hitching his pants higher under his expansive middle. "Your brother and sister-in-law seem to think you might know something about what happened here today."

"And yesterday," Sam said. "You can coordinate with the York Police Department."

"You called them?" Eliza asked.

"After the attack yesterday."

The cop's eyebrows rose. "This is the second attack?"

"We'll tell you everything we know," Sam said.

Except they didn't know enough. Not nearly enough.

CHAPTER TEN

AN HOUR LATER, Eliza descended the stairs with the shopping bag she'd found in her room that morning. It was filled with her new clothes, her dirty clothes, and the toiletries she'd used since she'd been here. Everything she owned—and there was space to spare.

Sam and Daniel were in the middle of an intense conversation in the entryway below.

"You know I would never—"

"I know." Daniel ran a hand down his face. "She's all right. That's all that matters."

"If I'd had any inkling they'd be able to track her here, you know I'd never have stayed. I certainly wouldn't have had you two borrowing my car."

Eliza should have realized. She should have said something.

"It scared me," Daniel said. "I just got her back. I can't imagine..."

When Daniel didn't finish, Sam asked, "She's okay?" His voice was filled with compassion and care.

"She's been through worse."

Eliza had heard just enough about the *worse* that her

stomach turned over at the thought. After what Camilla and her family had been through—believing Daniel dead, a car accident that nearly killed their son, then a kidnapping... The last thing Camilla needed was more trauma. Eliza cleared her throat, and the men looked up at her. "I didn't mean to interrupt."

Sam climbed the stairs toward her and held out his hand as if she needed help carrying her suitcase. She handed him the shopping bag.

"This is it?"

"My designer luggage."

He lifted it like he was weighing it. "You let me know what else you need, okay?"

The look in his eyes... She couldn't name it. Or maybe just shouldn't, because the word *affection* came to mind.

"Yeah, sure. I will." She continued her descent. Sam beside her.

Daniel seemed to be waiting. "I owe you an apology, too," he said when she reached him. "I'm sorry I yelled. I was—"

"You owe me nothing." She squeezed his arm. "I'm sorry I brought this to your doorstep."

The corner of his mouth ticked up. "Technically, Sam's doorstep." He looked past her and up the stairs, and his expression shifted, becoming similar to the concern she'd just seen in Sam's face. "You all right?"

"Quit worrying. I'm fine." Camilla joined them. "You made a plan?"

"Dad's on his way. We'll stay with him." To Sam, he said, "You two should go to the camp."

"The other Wrights are there," Sam said. Eliza almost asked who he meant, and then he added, "They're having a girls' weekend." And she remembered Sam's cousins—four, maybe five girls. Women now, she supposed.

"There's plenty of room," Daniel said. "I'm sure they wouldn't mind."

"We're going somewhere nobody will find us. Away from anybody who could get hurt."

"Yeah. Probably not a bad idea." Daniel's lips pressed in a grim line. Then he shifted to his wife, wrapped his arm around her, and led her to the living room. "You need anything? Tea?"

"Stop doting. I'm fine."

Eliza watched them, this couple in love. The way they looked at each other. The way they took care of each other. She'd seen it in Camilla's behavior as she'd acted as Daniel's nurse—the respect, the affection.

Now she saw it in Daniel, how he wanted to serve her. How he worried for her. How he loved her.

They settled side by side on the couch, speaking too low for her to hear. Meeting each other's eyes. Reaching out for gentle touches as if to assure themselves the other was still there.

They weren't overly polite or putting on a show. This was true. Two people who'd nearly lost each other and who understood what they had. Understood that the other wasn't replaceable.

She thought of her own parents.

Mom demanded.

Dad acquiesced.

There hadn't been peace in her home, not for many years before Dad's death. More like a tenuous cease-fire.

Every once in a while, Dad would kick up his heels, and war would break out all over again.

Her parents' marriage wasn't what she wanted.

What she was witnessing right now...that was what she longed for.

She might not remember where she'd been for the last five years, or what she'd been doing, but deep down, what she yearned for hadn't changed. She wanted to be with a man she could count on. She wanted to be with a man who cherished her. She wanted to be free to live and love and sometimes even make mistakes without them blowing up in her face.

She wanted a family, a home of her own.

"She's okay."

Eliza startled at Sam's low words. Had he seen longing in her face? Heat warmed her cheeks.

He settled a hand on Eliza's back and steered her toward the kitchen. "Let's just give them a minute."

Right. Because she'd been spying on a private moment. How embarrassing.

She rounded the corner into the kitchen, where a cardboard box sat on the island. She looked inside. Empty.

"I had an idea," Sam said, "but I don't think it's going to work."

She turned to face him, leaning back against the granite countertop. "What idea?"

"We're going to need food, and obviously I have plenty, but I don't want to put it in a box. Assuming we're being watched, we don't want—"

"You think we're being watched?"

His shoulders lifted and fell. "Don't you? They know where you are now. The woods are thick farther up the hill. They could be anywhere."

"That's comforting. Thanks."

His mouth quirked at the corner. "Obviously, we're not staying."

That much she'd put together when he'd told her to pack. "What's the plan?"

"You remember my friend Colton?"

"You went to college with him, right?"

A quick nod. "He's got a place we can borrow. And a car.

We just have to get from here to there without being followed. Which is where it gets complicated."

～

Twenty minutes later, they said goodbye to Daniel and Camilla and climbed into an Uber. Sam had ordered the car to take them to a bed-and-breakfast in downtown Shadow Cove, where he'd made a reservation.

But when they got there, they walked inside and then through the lobby and out the back door.

They'd decided a box—or even a suitcase—full of food would be too hard to maneuver, especially if they had to move quickly. Sam hadn't wanted anything that might slow them down. He'd swapped her shopping bag for a backpack similar to the one he wore.

They hurried through the rear parking lot, around a corner, and through a skinny alley between two red-brick buildings. Crossed a quiet street, then went straight into another alley.

"I feel like Jason Bourne."

Sam quirked a smile her way. "Bond. James Bond."

She giggled. Honestly, James Bond had nothing on Sam Wright.

He stopped at the end and sent a text.

A moment later, a bright red sports car raced up and slammed on its brakes.

Sam opened the door and levered the front seat up. "Your chariot."

That elicited a laugh. This day couldn't get any stranger. She handed her backpack to him and slid into a backseat that had barely enough room for her legs. No way could Sam sit back there. Or really, any normal-sized human being, not comfortably, anyway.

Sam pushed the front seat back up, forcing her to bend her legs to the side. "You all right?" he asked.

"It'll work."

While Sam took their bags to the trunk, the man in the driver's seat wrapped his arm around the passenger headrest and faced her. "Been a long time."

"Thanks for doing this." She took in the fancy auto. "Based on the ride, I'm guessing business is good."

"This old thing? It's my spare." Colton Gray winked. He'd always been overly friendly, but she'd never felt anything but safe with him.

The trunk slammed, and Sam climbed into the passenger seat. "Let's go."

Colton hit the gas, and Eliza was slammed back against her seat.

"We're okay," Sam said. "You don't have to fly."

"Who said I did?" He whipped through town and out the other side in a matter of seconds. She worried they'd be pulled over, except who'd see anything but a blur as they passed?

Eliza remembered her last conversation with Colton. "You still in the bullion business?"

"And loving it."

"Market's been good lately," she said. "Volatile."

"That's the key," Colton agreed. "Whether it's going up or down, the more trades the better. As long as you buy low and sell high."

"And hedge," she added. "You do that yourself or you pay someone?"

"I don't trust anybody else to do it right." Colton aimed the car toward Portland. "You can lose your shirt if someone screws up the hedge."

"No kidding. And even if you do it right, you have to be careful not to deplete your cash with too much inventory. You have to know what'll move and what won't. I try to take advantage of the arbitrage as much as possible. Sell, then buy, take the profit in the middle."

Colton glanced at her in the rearview. "You've obviously been busy since we last talked. You working for a bullion retailer? Or doing it on your own?"

She blinked. "Uh..."

Sam, she realized, had stayed very still for the entire conversation. Not interrupting. Just letting her talk. She wished she could see his face.

"Remember the last time I saw you two?" Colton seemed oblivious to the sudden tension. "You grilled me about what I did, how it worked. You remember that, Sam?"

Sam nodded.

"You kept asking me to explain. I remember thinking you should just take notes for as many questions as you asked. Sounds like you figured it out."

"I guess so," she said, though she couldn't explain it.

She'd always had an innate understanding of how money worked. She'd studied finance in college, and after she'd sold Dad's business and lost her job, she'd gone to work as an investment adviser. She'd dealt with mutual funds, retirement accounts, that sort of thing. There was a big difference between a financial planner and a bullion trader. A big difference between paper stocks and gold and silver coins and bars.

It seemed she'd learned a lot in the last five years. But where? And why?

Was that related to the couple she'd moved away with? Maybe she'd left with them and then struck out on her own. That must've been the case, because what could bullion trading possibly have to do with a drug rehab center?

She tried to remember. Tried to put it together. All that gave her was a fresh headache that had her closing her eyes.

She didn't open them again until Colton turned into a parking lot behind a long row of townhouses. Between the buildings, she caught a view of the water. That had to be Portland Harbor.

He whipped into a parking spot. "This is where I leave you. Sam, you need instructions on how to handle a machine like this?"

"I think I can manage."

"Not sure you're acquainted with quite so much power under the hood."

"Idiot." But the word held humor.

The men both climbed out, and Sam pushed the seat up. He reached to help her. "Sorry you got stuck back there. Still got your legs?"

She slipped her hand into his. "My legs and I survived."

Sam's gaze flicked down as she swung them out of the car and stood. He licked his lips. The slightest tinge of pink colored his cheeks, and he wouldn't meet her eyes.

At least she knew the sparks between them weren't all being generated on her side.

Colton came around. He was taller than Eliza remembered, though not as tall as Sam, and he didn't have Sam's broad shoulders. He gave her a quick side hug. "It sounds like I should be offering you a job. We'll talk when you get back. Whenever... whatever this is has passed."

"All right." She would need a job, eventually. Probably. Assuming...well, a lot of things. "Thanks for the ride. And the car."

"For you, anytime." He shifted to Sam. "Use it as long as you want. And the cottage. It's just sitting empty."

Sam gave his friend a back-slapping hug. "I appreciate this."

"You'd do it for me."

"In a heartbeat." He backed away. "We'll be in touch."

Sam held the passenger door for her, and she settled into the butter-soft leather seat.

After thanking Colton one more time, Sam sat beside her and shifted into gear. "Guy's an overgrown toddler."

"But he's your best friend."

He hit the gas and maneuvered through the parking lot at a much more reasonable speed. "That he is, though I rarely have to endure his driving." He flicked the windshield wipers on as the first spattering of rain fell. "His childhood dream was to be a racecar driver."

"Exciting, those races." She put false enthusiasm into her voice. "Look, he's making a left turn!"

Sam chuckled.

"I appreciate that he's letting us use this...what is it?"

"Porsche 911."

"It isn't exactly incognito."

"The other option was a Hummer."

She laughed. "Real low-key kind of fellow."

"You picked right up on that, savvy girl that you are. Don't worry about the car. We weren't followed."

"So we're safe, for now."

He nodded. A few seconds passed before he spoke again. "So...gold and silver?"

"Apparently."

"You think you've been trading, or just learning about it?"

Based on the conversation they'd had—the one that had felt so natural to her that she hadn't realized how strange it was—she said, "I've been trading. I'm sure of it."

"Hmm." He stopped at a light. "Another...clue."

"Suddenly, you're less James Bond and more Jacques Clouseau."

"'The Pink Panther'?" He smacked his chest as if she'd wounded him. "At least give me Sherlock Holmes."

"Hercule Poirot—with the mustache."

"You're killing me, Watson." But it wasn't any of those fictional detectives gazing her way. It was all Sam. Humor and affection and...attraction.

Desire skimmed over her, warm and tingly.

The moment stretched between them, a million memories from when they were together.

And then he snapped his gaze forward. Squeezed the steering wheel with one hand. Shifted into first and sped through the green light.

Maybe trying to leave that moment in the Porsche's dust.

And maybe for him, he had. But Eliza's feelings weren't so easily forgotten.

~

Eliza stared up at the so-called cottage.

The two-story log home sat on a giant lot at the end of a long driveway that meandered through the forest. It wasn't visible from the road, but the area around it had been cleared, giving visitors a great view of the peaked roof with its river-rock chimney in the center, flanked by windows on both sides.

After Sam got out to open the garage door, he settled back in the car and caught her staring. "Wait till you see the inside." He parked the Porsche in the garage, and they climbed out into a tidy two-car garage lined with skis, fishing rods, snow shoes, and winter coats. With their backpacks in hand, he opened the door leading to the house, and she stepped into a kitchen and gazed at the great room.

Wood beams, wood floors, wood trim. But because the walls were painted soft white, it wasn't dark or overpowering. There was very little color, aside from the natural tones, but huge windows overlooked the forest, adding a thousand shades of green and, at this high altitude, hints of the yellows and oranges and reds that would explode in the next couple of weeks. The rain had stopped, and the clouds parted, allowing the last hint of sunlight through. She stepped deeper inside and caught a view out the back windows of snow-capped mountains in the distance.

Not a bad place to hide.

Beyond the kitchen, a long dining room table separated this area from the cozy sectional that faced the fireplace, which seemed even more grand from the inside. A plush white area rug in front of the hearth had her wanting to take off her shoes and squish her toes in. Except it was way too cold to take off her shoes. Or her jacket.

Behind her, Sam dropped the sacks of groceries they'd picked up in town on the granite countertop.

"Oh, sorry. I can help." She pulled items out of the bags, unsure where to put them. She gave up trying to find a pantry and just stacked them near the oven. "Why don't I get started on the soup?"

He turned from where he was loading things into the refrigerator. "Are you hungry?"

"It's better if it simmers a little while."

"And you don't need a recipe? Because I have my laptop."

"It's not that hard." Why she could remember how to make taco soup—and trade bullion—but couldn't remember where she'd spent the previous Sunday, she had no idea.

"I'll just put this in your room and find the thermostat." He carried the backpack with her things up the stairs while she searched cabinets. She should have thought this through better. Her recipe would make enough soup for a crowd. The two of them would barely make a dent. Maybe they could put the leftovers in the freezer for Colton to enjoy after skiing this winter.

She found a heavy cast iron pot—one of those uber-expensive ones they sold at Williams Sonoma—and lit the stovetop, then started searching again.

"Whatcha looking for?"

"Cutting board?"

He snatched a wooden one leaning against the tile back-splash. "Will this work?"

No idea how she'd missed that. She reached for it, but he held it to himself. "What am I cutting?"

Oh. He wanted to help? She tossed him the onion, and he snatched it out of the air. "Dice it please."

While he did that, she started the ground beef browning, then added the onions when he was finished. "You chopped them small."

"You said diced." He looked confused. "Isn't that diced?"

"It's perfect."

He turned away, but not fast enough for her to miss the satisfied smile, and started opening cans of chili beans, tomatoes, corn, and beef broth. "All these, I guess?"

"Yup."

When he took one to the sink, she stopped him. "Don't drain it. We need the liquid."

"You're the boss."

She'd slept much of the hour-and-a-half drive from Portland to North Conway, New Hampshire. She felt refreshed, better than she had since...well, as long as she could remember, in this decade, anyway. The headache that had throbbed incessantly was mostly gone. Her wrist, while still a little sore, only really pained her when she tried to lift something heavy—like the pot in front of her. The bruises still hurt if she thought about them, but for the most part she didn't.

"You haven't seen a strainer, have you?" she asked.

"I'll find one." The sound of cabinets opening and closing, then, "Got it."

"In the sink please." She pulled her sweatshirt sleeves over her hands in case the handles were hot and started to lift the pot. She'd gotten it there, after all. But with the meat and onions...

"Let me." Sam nudged her out of the way and dumped the contents into the strainer, letting the fat dribble down the drain. "Back in the pot?"

"Yup."

He did that and set it on the stove again, watching her as she added some water and the taco seasoning packet. She stirred, waiting for the water to evaporate away.

"What's next?"

"We dump the cans in and stir." She started with the beans.

Right beside her, Sam added the corn and broth. They got the rest of the ingredients in, and she reached past him to grab a wooden spoon from a container near the stove.

He grabbed it and handed it over. His fingers brushed hers, leaving a trail of heat on her skin. He didn't seem to notice. Or maybe he just hid it better than she did.

Could she blame her red cheeks on the hot stovetop?

"That's it. Now it simmers."

He spun to the sink and started washing dishes.

"I can do that."

"You cooked. I clean."

They'd cooked together, but she didn't say so as she tossed the cans and wiped the countertop.

It felt strange having a man in the kitchen with her. Cooking with her. Cleaning with her. It wasn't the cooking that felt strange—she felt like she'd done a lot of that. But doing it with another person—a tall, strong, broad-chested man who didn't ask anything of her.

Or criticize her. Or snap at her to hurry up.

Anxiety pooled in her middle as a memory niggled.

She closed her eyes and let it come. She could see no faces, hear no voices, but it was right there, rising and disappearing like the steam coming off the soup.

A touch on her shoulder, and she jumped.

"Whoa." Sam lifted his hands, wide eyes narrowing fast. "Tell me. What did you remember?"

"I don't know. Nothing really. Just a sense. Cooking."

But his suspicion didn't fall away. "Remembering cooking made you jump out of your skin?"

She lifted her shoulders and dropped them, going for casual.

He turned away, muttering under his breath. All she caught was, "...have to hurt somebody."

Seemed a little drastic, but the words soothed a tender place in her heart, a place that felt starved for protection. For more than just protection.

Another room ran along the back of the great room, a sunroom with a wall of bookshelves. It would be lovely in the morning, watching the sun rise over the valley.

Now the sun was setting behind her, darkness encroaching. She wanted to turn on a lamp. But that would make the space a fishbowl. Anybody would be able to see in.

Nobody would, of course, not with the house hidden so far from the road. But still...

She crossed her arms, chilly again now that the cooking was finished, and watched darkness slide across the valley below.

Sam flicked on a dim lamp behind her. "Just texted Colton. He said the upstairs gets toasty, but it takes a long time for the downstairs to heat up. It's the cathedral ceilings, all the windows."

"That's fine."

"I'm going to light a fire. Meanwhile"—he snatched a blanket from the back of a chair and draped it over her shoulders—"you'll just have to cuddle up."

She wrapped it around herself. "Thanks." It helped. But the problem was, she wasn't in the mood to cuddle up, at least not all by herself.

But Sam had already moved away. He knelt in front of the hearth, tearing newspaper into strips.

She watched, mesmerized as he teepeed narrow logs, then lit the paper. Sparks crackled, disappearing up the chimney.

Sam nudged paper and logs this way and that with a poker, urging the wood to catch. It did, and flames rose, illuminating his face and that intent expression he always wore when he was focused on a project.

Wandering closer, she held out her hands to let the flames warm her skin.

He stood and backed up, stopping just inches from her. He looked down at her and smiled.

Her whole body responded. It took everything in her not to open the blanket and pull him in. Not to rise on her tiptoes and kiss those lips.

He blinked, shifted away. "That'll warm us up."

"Hmm." She felt warm enough, and the heat had nothing to do with the blaze.

"There's a TV room upstairs," Sam said, "if you want to watch something. It's already warmer up there."

TV? Some dumb movie or sporting event? She stifled the sigh that tried to escape. All these things she was feeling... Obviously, he was feeling none of them.

Which was fine. They'd broken up. According to Jeanette, he'd hurt her. According to him, she'd been the one to end it. He'd moved on. He had five years of moving on behind him, whereas her wound felt fresh and raw.

She couldn't let herself fall for him again. But the problem was, she'd never—in her memory, anyway—stopped loving him.

Her feelings weren't exactly well-trained soldiers, eager to do her bidding. Right now, they felt like toddlers let loose on a playground. Running, swinging, sliding. Laughing, screaming, crying. Total chaos.

Completely uncontrollable.

When she didn't respond to his suggestion, he added, "Or we can watch the fire for a little while."

She settled on the sectional. He took a seat catty-corner to her, because heaven forbid they get too close.

"You know what this reminds me of?" His voice was low in the dimly lit room, his face glowing as he stared at the flames. "That weekend we went skiing with my brothers. You remember?"

"Sunday River, right?" The ski resort with, in her opinion, the best trails in Maine. "All the brothers except Daniel."

"Right. We got that condo. Spent two days on the slopes."

"Wasn't the best conditions, if I remember. More ice than snow."

"You nearly killed me." He laughed, the sound rumbly and gorgeous. "You and—I don't know, one of the girls—had stopped to take pictures, so I beat you to the bottom. I'd looked back to watch you. You were always so...elegant." His Adam's apple bobbed, and he glanced away. Then his grin returned. "The moguls you handled like a pro, but then you lost control on the straightaway."

She laughed with him. "It was icy."

"Typical. Swooshing down the mountain, making the rest of us look bad. Then falling over in line."

"Hey, I only did that once."

His eyebrows hiked over that slow smile.

Okay, so she'd done the standing-still-fall more than once, but she wasn't about to cop to it.

She remembered well trying to get to know Sam's brothers' dates. Sweet Christian girls who slipped in remarks about God between fashion and food as if He fit right there.

And though she hadn't joined in the talk, had barely understood half of what they were talking about, they'd been kind to her. They'd laughed and joked and teased, but she remembered some deep conversations too. One of the women—Eliza thought she'd been Michael's girlfriend—had exuded such a sense of peace that left Eliza longing for what she had.

"That was the place with the game room, right?" Sam asked.

"What I remember is you and Michael in an epic foosball battle. I thought you two were going to break that thing."

"I beat him."

"What was it, best of thirteen by the time you were done? You two were pretty evenly matched." And competitive. And though it'd seemed all in good fun on the surface, something darker had hummed beneath.

"The point is, I won." Sam grinned at the memory.

She reflected his expression, but another memory was nudging its way in.

"I remember the fire pit." Humor no longer infused his words.

Maybe Sam was a mind reader because she'd gone to exactly the same place.

Michael had picked the condo and had ensured there were enough beds for everyone. Boys in one room, girls in the two others. She'd thought how silly it was that the couples weren't sleeping together, but apparently the other brothers didn't do that.

At the time, she'd thought it was weird. But that wasn't the sense she had of it now. Now, it seemed...sweet.

Late the second night in the condo, Sam had started a fire in the pit outside, and the two of them had escaped to be alone. They'd cuddled up on a bench together. The temperature had dipped into the low twenties, but between the subzero sleeping bag Sam had draped around them and the fire—and their closeness—she hadn't been cold.

She could still see Sam's face, glowing in the reflection, gazing at her.

She could still feel his arms around her, his lips on hers.

She could still hear his tender words of promise and forever.

The night hadn't gone the way she'd expected. There'd been no physical intimacy beyond the kissing. Yet, they had been intimate. They'd been in love.

Her eyes burned.

She was surprised when she caught Sam watching her. Their eyes held, his reflecting her own sadness.

"What happened between us?"

He shook his head, looked away.

"I need to know."

"You'll remember soon enough." He pushed to his feet and headed for the kitchen. "Think this is ready?"

She followed. "I need to know, Sam."

He stirred the soup, ignoring her. She was about to demand answers when he set the spoon down and faced her. "I can't tell you because I don't really know. I mean, I know what happened, but I don't know why it led to you leaving me. Disappearing for five years. You never even let me..." He swallowed hard. "You need to remember so you can tell me."

"How can you not know?"

He held her gaze but said nothing else.

"I don't understand. Are you saying I just left. I didn't talk to you?"

"I'm saying you didn't explain."

"Why would I do that?"

"If I knew, I'd tell you."

No. That didn't make sense. What could he have done that

would cause her to walk away? How could she ever have walked away from him?

He found bowls and spoons.

She turned to the fridge and grabbed the small container of sour cream and the shredded cheddar, then opened a bag of tortilla chips.

Apparently, they were going to eat dinner and spend the evening together, all while pretending there wasn't a giant question between them.

Maybe he could do that. She couldn't.

He grabbed a ladle and handed it to her. "Ladies first."

She spooned soup into her bowl, then added a sprinkling of cheddar. "Maybe you could... Like you did before, with the questions you asked. Can you think of another way to approach what happened? Help me remember?"

"No." He was following her, though he'd taken twice as much soup and piled it high with cheese and sour cream. "Kitchen or living room?"

It was still so chilly. "By the fire, I think."

He tucked two bottles of water under his arm, snatched the bag of chips, and headed that way. She followed with her own bowl and sat in front of the fire on the inviting area rug. It was as soft and cozy as she'd guessed it would be.

As soon as she settled, he said, "Thanks for the food, God. Please bless it." And then he dug in. Not exactly the eloquent prayer he'd offered at other meals.

"I don't believe you," she said, picking up the conversation he'd probably hoped to end. "You could help me remember if you wanted to."

"Let me expand my answer." He opened both bottles of water and took a long drink from his. "Yes, I could help. No, I won't."

Frustration had her voice rising. "Why not?"

"Because I don't want you to remember. Because when you do, you'll leave me again."

Her breath caught, but he hurried on.

"You're in danger, and I'm trying to keep you alive. Until we figure out what's going on, we need to stay together."

"And then what?"

His mouth opened. But rather than speak, he filled it with a spoonful of soup.

But, by the stubborn set of his shoulders, the hard look on his face, he wasn't going to answer her question. Or budge on his decision.

Maybe it was the anger she felt wafting from him, as tangible as the heat from the fireplace, that brought back the niggling. She closed her eyes, leaned into it.

Saw a man in a kitchen. A man standing at the edge, crossed arms, a scowl on his face. Fear rose in her throat, scratchy like acid, as she hurried to get food on the table.

People waited for her. Adults and children. No faces. Just tension, thick and bitter.

She gasped and opened her eyes.

Sam's gaze was on her. He said nothing, just waited.

"I remember him. The guy from Mom's house. His name is Gil. Gilbert C. Lyle."

"Which one was he?"

"With the goatee." The big one who'd attacked Sam.

"Tell me what you remembered."

"He was watching me cook. Impatiently."

Sam's eyes tightened at the corners. "Were you...with him?"

Was she? Surely not.

Closing her eyes again, she considered his question, just letting it float around her.

Had she been with that man? Married to him, or dating him?

She examined the feelings racing in her head. Fear. Anxiety. Distaste. Distrust.

No affection. No friendliness. No regret.

"He wasn't a boyfriend. He was just...in charge."

"Of what?" Sam sounded angry, and she agreed entirely.

"I don't know. Me, maybe. But not just me. There were others." Sam opened his mouth, but she hurried on. "I don't know who. His is the only face I see. The only name I remember."

Sam's lips rubbed together, and he nodded. "Okay. Good. That's good. Weird that you know his middle initial, but..." He pulled his phone from his pocket and typed a text. "I'll let the police and Jon know. And google his name."

"Okay."

After a moment he said, "Nothing helpful is coming up on his name." He dropped the cell on the coffee table, then nodded to her soup. She hadn't taken a bite. "Aren't you hungry?"

She was. And she wasn't going to pretend otherwise. Or count her bites. She was going to eat as much as she wanted. Nobody, not Gilbert C. Lyle or anybody else, was going to control her, ever again.

CHAPTER ELEVEN

BECAUSE WHEN YOU DO, *you'll leave me again.*

Had he really said that? Out loud? Sam shoved food into his mouth, wishing there were a TV in this room. Anything to distract him from the woman by the fire. The way the flickering light danced on her sable-colored hair. The way her eyes, flashing in anger just a few minutes before, now held determination as she ate her dinner. As if she had to fight for every spoonful.

He wanted to fight for her. Fight like he'd never fought for anything. But he knew how that story ended. He might be willing to fight for her, but as soon as he didn't measure up...

She'd be gone.

Easier to focus on things that couldn't hurt him. Business associates. Casual girlfriends. Money, money, money. If business associates chose to work with someone else, who cared? If a casual girlfriend met the man of her dreams? *Happy for you and have a nice life.* Money was always there. Always the right size, always the right color.

Didn't love him back, though.

All his pursuit of success and pleasure and money, and he

was still alone. He'd even convinced himself he liked being alone.

And then Eliza had barreled back into his life and messed everything up.

And then what?

Her question hung in the air between them. He knew the answer. She'd leave again. Assuming they both survived this... quest, for lack of a better word, she'd thank him profusely and then go back to wherever—and whoever—she'd run to before.

Eliza wasn't a go-it-alone kind of person. Unlike Sam, who managed his own life with very little input from others, Eliza had always needed people around her, counselors and friends. So there'd been someone, maybe a whole community of some-ones. She'd return to them and never look back.

Which was why he needed to keep his feelings to himself. This was going to hurt badly enough when it was over.

And then he'd return to his former life. Working sixty hours a week just to fill the time, attending business events and every fancy party in Portland with a beautiful woman on his arm, a woman he'd kiss on the cheek before leaving her on her doorstep.

He'd liked that life, hadn't he?

Yup. And if he needed love, he'd get a dog.

When his phone rang, he was glad for the distraction.

Eliza looked up from her soup.

"It's Grant." He answered with, "Hey, bro."

"Eliza's back? You guys were attacked, and you didn't tell me?" Grant's words were low and angry.

"So much for Jon's confidentiality agreement."

"Jon? *My friend*, Jon? What does he have to do with this?"

"Uh..." Sam had obviously jumped to the wrong conclusion. "I hired him."

"You hired *Jon*!"

Sam held the phone away from his ear at Grant's raised voice.

"Geez, man," Grant said. "I'm your brother. I heard about this from Dad, but you asked my best friend for help? And not me?"

"Why would I have called you?"

"Gee, I don't know. Because I was a Green Beret. A bodyguard. Now I'm a cop."

"With a job. A full-time job. You're not a detective."

"As a matter of fact, I *am* a detective."

Oh. Sam probably should have known that.

"And Summer was a bodyguard too. She could've—"

"Yeah, I'm really gonna hire my sister-in-law to protect me."

"Not you, idiot. Your girlfriend. Summer can keep her safe."

Sam met Eliza's eyes, wondering how much she could hear. Maybe he should hire bodyguards. Maybe that was the smart play.

"We're safe for now."

"Thank God for that." Grant's anger seemed to have drained. "Where are you?"

Sam hadn't told Daniel or his father where they were going. Not that he didn't trust them, but...well, it seemed wiser to keep their whereabouts secret.

He didn't want to think about his reasoning. If the people after Eliza attacked Sam's family, he didn't want them to be able to tell where they were.

Keep them safe, God.

Sam couldn't protect everyone. His family had each other, and Dad and Daniel could protect Mom and Camilla. Eliza had nobody. "We're in the mountains."

"Near me?" Was that hope in Grant's voice?

"Sort of, I think." Sam wasn't sure exactly where Coventry was. He'd only visited once, when Grant proposed to Summer, and he certainly hadn't come through the mountains to get there.

"Tell me everything," Grant said.

Sam did, starting with Eliza's late-night arrival at his house and ending when he and Eliza arrived at Colton's rental property.

When he was finished, Grant said, "Wow. Thank God you're safe. How can I help?"

"I just texted a name to your friend. He's one of the guys who attacked us on Saturday. Maybe you can help track him down."

"I hear she has amnesia. Is she getting her memory back?"

Eliza was watching, so he offered a smile. "A little at a time."

"Okay, good. Let Jon know, would you, that you want me to help? He can be a stickler about his rules."

"I'll text him right now. And, uh...I really appreciate your help, Grant."

"You should have asked me from the start."

Yeah, he probably should have. "Next time."

"Let's hope there isn't one of those."

Sam chuckled. "No kidding."

"I'll be in touch." Grant ended the call, and Sam texted a heads-up to Jon before tossing his cell on the coffee table.

"He sounded...annoyed," she said.

That was one way to put it. "He's going to work with Jon to help us figure this out."

"I always liked him." She'd finished her soup—every bite—and carried the bowl to the kitchen. "Out of curiosity, why didn't you call him to begin with?"

Fair question. He followed with his own bowl, and they set to work cleaning. "I didn't want to bother him. And Jon's a private investigator, so he won't balk when I pay him. Grant would do it out of obligation."

Eliza turned from loading the dishwasher. "You don't think Grant would help because he loves you and wants you to be safe?"

"I guess, yeah. That's the obligation part."

"Is that what love is to you? Obligation?"

Whoa. How'd she end up there?

He turned away, searching for a plastic container. He didn't find anything even close to large enough for the vat of soup. Giving up, he covered the pot with its lid and shoved the whole thing into the nearly empty refrigerator.

She resumed loading the dishwasher.

As he put away the rest of the food, her question lingered. Was that how he saw love? As obligation? Not on his part. When he'd been in love with Eliza, he'd have done anything for her. And not because he had to but because of an overwhelming desire to make her happy. To protect her. To care for her. To provide for her.

And he felt exactly the same way about his parents and his brothers and Colton. Well, not *exactly* the same way, but if they needed him, he'd be there. He wanted to help them. He'd felt honored the few times any one of them had called on him.

Like when Derrick had asked him for help financing his private charter business. Buying a jet was no small thing, but Derrick's business plan was solid. And Sam had the resources to help.

Like when Mom had asked him to get Wi-Fi at the camp—actually a beautiful home on a private island, one all the brothers had helped build. He'd been thankful that she trusted him with the task and knew he'd take it seriously. It was a little thing, but that she'd reached out—it mattered to him.

He'd sacrifice anything for the people he loved.

He just didn't think they felt that way about him.

Eliza certainly hadn't. He hadn't expected much from her

that disastrous day—just that she'd listen, let him explain. But she wouldn't even give him that. All the love she'd professed, gone in an instant.

How deep could it have run?

Not as deeply as his.

And that was the crux of it. Not just with Eliza but with everyone. The more he loved, the more quickly he was tossed away.

And there was a happy thought.

When the kitchen was clean, he said, "I'm going upstairs to get some work done and catch the Patriots game. You're welcome to join me."

Maybe his words hadn't been very welcoming because she shook her head. "That's okay. I think I'll grab a book and go to bed."

While she perused the bookshelves in the sunroom, he double-checked that all the doors and windows were locked, then added another log to the fire.

With a couple of books in each hand, she headed for the stairs.

"If you leave your laundry outside your door," he said, "I'll start a load tonight."

"I can do it in the morning."

"I'll take care of it. Just get some sleep."

She smiled that pretty, natural smile that had the power to derail him. "Thanks. Good night."

Three hours later, the volume of a commercial roused him out of sleep. He'd worked on his laptop for much of the game, trying to get ahead on the week's tasks, then drifted off in the fourth quarter, not sorry at all to have missed the end of a blowout loss.

He clicked off the TV and the light as he left the den. It was quiet and dark aside from the glowing coals he could see in the fireplace from the second-floor walkway that overlooked the great room. No light shone beneath Eliza's door, though she'd left her dirty clothes there, as he'd asked.

He grabbed them and took them downstairs. He'd start a load in the morning.

After changing into his flannel pajamas—not his normal sleepwear, but he figured he'd better don more than his boxer shorts—and brushing his teeth, he headed for the living room. He put his handgun, taken from his safe that afternoon, beneath the cushions, where he could grab it quickly. Then, he tugged the blanket Eliza had used earlier over himself, stretching out on the sofa in front of the fire. Not that he thought Eliza's pursuers would find them, but if they did, Sam would be ready.

His worries led to nightmares. But those morphed to dreams. To one dream.

The gentlest brush of Eliza's hair across his cheek. Her sweet breath on his skin. Her soft lips on his mouth. So tender, her touch. Barely there. It wasn't enough.

He needed more.

He dug into her hair, loving the feel of her soft strands tangling in his fingers. He pulled her closer and dove in. Tasting her. Wanting her.

But it still wasn't enough. He wrapped his arm around her, pressed her body against his. Ran his hand down her side, enjoying the silky fabric against his palm. Feeling her smooth curves.

And then she issued a soft moan of pleasure. It sounded so real.

Don't wake up. Not yet.

But he was waking up. He knew it. And yet, Eliza was still there.

Still in his arms. Still kissing him.

He opened his eyes. Yanked his hands off her.

Pushed her away.

Sucked in a breath. "What the...?"

"Sorry. I'm sorry." She scrambled off him, off the couch, and stood in front of the low flames in the hearth, the only light in the room.

The sight of her in silhouette, combined with the memory already replaying, didn't help cool the fire inside him.

"I didn't mean... I just wanted... I didn't think you'd wake up. I thought I'd just... A little kiss because I missed you and I couldn't sleep. That was all. And then I was going to leave you alone."

He was still trying to wake up, still processing.

"But then you kissed me back." She covered her face with her hands. "I thought you knew..."

Everything in him wanted to cross the room and make her feel better.

And then his wiser self shut that moron up.

"I shouldn't have—"

"You're right! You shouldn't have!" He tried to throw his blanket off, but it was tangled in his legs. He finally got it free and tossed it. "Imagine if I did that to you. Accosted you in the middle of the night, in your sleep! You'd have me arrested!"

"I wouldn't." Her words were low behind her fingers.

"Well, you could!" He was angry. No. Furious. The nerve of her. He should feel violated. He should feel...

He had no idea how he *should* feel.

He knew how he *did* feel, though. Like he wanted to curse himself for waking up. Like he wanted to cross the space between them and wrap her in his arms and kiss her senseless. And then take her upstairs, and...

And yeah.

No.

He didn't do that anymore. Definitely not with Eliza.

How did he feel? He had an answer for that. And it was going to require a long walk in the frigid mountain air to overcome. Or maybe he should just head straight for the cold shower.

"Go to bed, Eliza." He tried to temper the rage still humming in his tone. With no memory of the previous five years, their breakup was fresh and painful for her.

He understood that. He was trying to be kind, trying to be patient.

But right now, he needed her to leave before he lost his thin hold on self-control. "I'll see you in the morning."

And not before.

God help him, he wouldn't survive round two.

CHAPTER TWELVE

ELIZA WOKE up to sunlight streaming in through the window, her eyes scratchy from lack of sleep—and probably dehydration, considering how many tears she'd shed the night before.

Not that she hadn't deserved Sam's wrath. That was her reward for breaking the rules.

He'd been sound asleep when she'd gone downstairs for a bottle of water, so she'd crept closer, just to see his beautiful face without the guarded look she didn't want to get used to. He lay on his back, one arm dangling off the edge of the narrow couch, the other tucked beneath the blanket that covered him to his waist. His face was relaxed, peaceful. A tiny smile played at the corner of his mouth. His strong jaw, roughened with a day's growth, didn't hold the frustration she usually saw there. He looked softer, kinder.

This was *her* Sam, the Sam she'd fallen in love with, who was so different from the angry, standoffish man who'd been by her side for days. He wore red-and-black checkered pajamas with a reindeer embroidered on the front. She could imagine his brothers and parents in those same pajamas on Christmas morning, since obviously, Sam hadn't bought them for himself. No, they had Peggy Wright written all over them. Eliza loved that Sam and his brothers would dress in matching pj's to make their mom happy.

That was the kind of family they were.

The kind of man he was.

She'd moved in close, drawn by pink lips in their almost smile.

Just one little kiss.

He'd never know.

Don't do it.

Her mother's voice rang in her head, but she ignored it. One little kiss wouldn't hurt anybody.

She kneeled beside the couch. Leaned in. Brushed her lips against his.

Let herself linger there, reveling in the closeness, pretending it was real.

About to back away.

But his hands came around her. Pulled her closer. He'd deepened the kiss, and all the love she felt for him exploded inside. Her fears dissipated. Everything would be okay because *her* Sam was back. Holding her. Loving her.

And then he'd pushed her away.

Even after, as she'd stood in front of the fireplace, heat burning her face like the glowing embers warmed her backside, even then she'd thought, *But you wanted me.*

She'd felt it. She'd known it to her core.

Only later, lying in bed and replaying the moment on a loop, did it occur to her that he probably hadn't been dreaming of her at all.

He'd probably been dreaming of someone else.

That was when the tears started.

In the bright light of morning, the *somebody else* took shape in her mind, not just a phantom female but a woman with long blond hair, a perfect face, and a figure to make a monk swoon.

Images of Sam with the blonde flipped through Eliza's brain like a slideshow. Posing for a camera. Caught in a laugh. Dancing. One of the pictures felt like a gut-punch.

And the memory supplied a name.

Kayla. No, not that. Cadence? Kaylee?

Kylee.

Kylee Trubridge. Of *the* Trubridges.

Sam had introduced her as a friend at one of the events Eliza attended with him—a dance, a fundraiser. Who knew? But whenever Eliza and Sam went to anything, Kylee was there.

Always laughing a little too loudly at Sam's jokes. Touching him a little more than was appropriate—but not enough that Eliza wouldn't look like a jealous shrew if she said something.

Though Sam had laughed off her concern—*we've been friends for years*—Eliza had sensed that Kylee wanted more than friendship.

Eliza didn't remember exactly why she and Sam had broken up, but Kylee had played a part. That felt heartbreakingly true.

Kylee was the woman Sam had been dreaming about the night before. No wonder he'd pushed Eliza away. She'd never stood a chance next to the rich, model-gorgeous blonde.

Now Eliza covered her face as shame burned her skin.

This was what she got for disobeying. She should have listened to her conscience, even if it sounded like Mom's voice in her head. She should have followed the rules. Every time she broke them, the world fell apart.

Mom had told her not to hire Sam to consult on the sale of the business. *"You need someone older. Someone with more experience."* She'd offered her choice, of course, a sixty-something friend from the club. But Sam's proposal had blown the other man's away. Sam had courted Eliza's business—and he'd courted her. And in the end, he'd made good on his promise, finding a buyer who paid more than she'd ever dreamed for Dad's business. A seven-figure deal that set Eliza and her mother up for life.

Even Mom had agreed to the sale—at the time—though she conveniently forgot that part when the new owners fired all of the company's employees, Eliza included.

Sam had warned her it might happen. The new owner had refused to sign a deal contingent on keeping the current staff but had assured them both that he had no plans to make any changes on that front.

Sam had trusted the buyer, and Eliza had trusted Sam.

Mom's *"I told you so"* still rang in her ears.

As did her constant insistence that Eliza not get involved with Sam. *"Men like that'll break your heart."*

Men like that. Meaning handsome and successful, with the reputation of a playboy. The most-eligible-bachelor type. What would a man like that want with boring Eliza?

Eliza had been sure Sam wasn't the man Mom thought. That he'd be strong and steady like Dad had been. Like Sam's dad still was.

Turned out Mom was right about that one too. Though Eliza had no memory of it, she could imagine the speech Mom had given her heartbroken daughter after the breakup.

Every time Eliza defied her mother, her world blew up.

And sometimes people got hurt. Not just Eliza, but people she loved.

Sometimes, people died.

What had she done to cause the mess she was in now? Something Mom had warned her against, and Jeanette too. She might not know the details, but she figured it was her fault.

Like last night's kiss.

If only she could lie in bed all day. Avoid Sam for the rest of her life. How could she face him after what had happened? After he'd so thoroughly rejected her?

But it was after eight, and he was moving around downstairs. Putting it off wasn't going to help.

She showered, letting the warmth soothe her still-sore body, and tried to wash away the evidence of her tears. Then she took her time fixing her hair with the blow dryer she'd found beneath the sink. Her hair was longer than she'd ever worn it, falling to halfway down her back, and took forever to get dry. The long, straight hair, combined with her gaunt, sunken cheeks, was not attractive. Maybe if she could curl it, but Colton hadn't stocked the place with curling irons.

When all this was over, she'd cut it back to the medium-length style she'd worn before. Meanwhile, she needed to put on some weight.

At least she could restore something of what she'd lost.

An hour after she'd opened her eyes, she took a deep breath for courage and walked downstairs.

Standing on the far side of the kitchen island, Sam looked up from his laptop. "Morning."

"Hey." She didn't walk all the way into the room but froze near the dining room table. "I want to apologize again for—"

"It's fine." He lifted a hand to punctuate his words. "Let's not."

"Can I just explain?"

His lips slid into a smirk, but he leaned a hip against the bar and crossed his arms. "This ought to be good."

She flinched at his sarcasm and fought the urge to flee. "I know it's been five years for you. But for me, it feels like we're still together. Or should be. And...I guess it's not as easy for me to get past our breakup as it was for you."

"You think it was easy?"

His volume had her taking a step back.

"It wasn't *easy*, Eliza. It was..." He pulled in a deep breath. Blew it out. "I get your point." The flash of emotion he'd shown was shuttered behind the cold expression he'd worn for days. "It's fine. I forgive you. Please just...don't do anything like that again."

As if she hadn't learned her lesson.

He headed for the stove. "Eggs?"

"I'm not that hungry. You didn't have to wait for me."

He turned back. "I yelled at you last night. You shouldn't have kissed me—don't misunderstand what I'm saying—but the way I responded wasn't your fault. So...sorry about that." He started the gas stove. "Consider these apology eggs."

"I've never had that flavor."

That earned a look and a tiny smile.

They were moving on from her blunder. And it hadn't hurt that much.

She needed to ask him about Kylee, though. Would their truce end when she did?

He swirled a pat of butter in a pan and added the eggs he'd already whisked, then pulled cheese and a little bowl of chopped veggies out of the refrigerator. He seemed engrossed in the task. He'd always made breakfast when they were together. "Start the toast, would you?"

She did, then poured herself a cup of coffee. She set plates, utensils, salt, and pepper on the bar. When the toast popped, she buttered the pieces.

Sam slid the giant omelet onto one of the plates, cut it in half, and then shimmied half onto the other. "Do you need anything else?"

"Nope." They both sat.

She salted her omelet and tried a bite. Melted cheese, onions and crunchy peppers, fluffy eggs. "Delicious." She almost added *as always,* as if she'd eaten one of his omelets the week before.

"Thanks." He forked a huge bite.

"It was Kylee, wasn't it?"

When he turned to her, he looked almost...nervous. "You remembered."

She started to speak, stopped. "Wait. Remembered what?" Because all those images that'd flashed through her mind were only pictures. Nothing she'd witnessed firsthand.

Sam shook his head quickly. "What about Kylee?"

"What did you mean?"

"Forget it. It doesn't matter."

She had a very strong suspicion it did matter. A lot. But he shoved in another bite of eggs.

"Have you ever been married?"

He spluttered, swallowed, sipped from a glass of water. "What? No. Why would you ask me that?"

His words *sounded* true, but the images in her head didn't lie. "I saw photographs of you and...I'm pretty sure it was Kylee. Lots of photos."

"We're friends, Eliza."

"She was wearing a wedding gown. You were wearing a tuxedo."

"Where did you see these...? Were you stalking me?" Anger hummed on his words. "I never found you on social media, so what did you do? Make up some kind of dummy account? And somehow fooled me into accepting a friend request. All so you could stalk me? What the heck?"

She kept her voice calm, refusing to respond to his anger. "I didn't do that."

"You don't remember anything, but you remember *not doing* that? I don't think so."

"I didn't see the pictures online. I saw them..." She closed her eyes, imagined them. On paper. In her hands. Folded together. "Somebody printed them out for me." When she opened her eyes, Sam was glaring at her.

"Your mother, of course." Bitterness tinged his words. "She and I remained friends on Facebook until recently. Though *friends* was never the right word for it. She probably wanted to..." He shook his head. Shoved a bite of food into his mouth. Swallowed and said, "Eat, Eliza."

"Don't tell me what to do."

"Right. That's what your mother is for."

"I defied my mother to be with you."

"Defied her? You were a grown woman. You didn't need her permission."

An old argument she didn't want to have. "You're saying you didn't get married, because I saw the photo."

He stood abruptly, his chair scraping against the tile, and rounded the island to grab his phone. He scrolled silently.

She bit into her toast. Then had another bite of omelet and sipped her coffee, wondering what in the world he was looking for.

Finally, he returned to her side and handed her the cell.

The image stabbed her.

Kylee looked impossibly beautiful in her wedding gown, much prettier in color than she'd been in black-and-white. She was beaming at Sam, who was smiling just as wide back at her. They looked deliriously happy.

Just what Eliza had wanted to see.

"Thanks for that." She handed him the phone back and turned her focus to the food. As if she'd be able to eat another bite.

"Now look at this one."

Was he *trying* to hurt her?

"I get it. You moved on." She cut another bite of the omelet.

"Look at it, Eliza." He set the phone right beside her plate.

She couldn't help it. She looked.

Kylee in the arms of a different man. He'd dipped her, and they were kissing.

The man had blond hair.

"He was a fraternity brother," Sam said. "I took her to an alumni gathering, and they hit it off immediately."

Eliza looked from the photo to Sam. "She cheated on you with one of your friends, and you went to their wedding?"

"We were never together." He slid his phone off the table and shoved it in his pocket.

But that wasn't right. "I saw the pictures, Sam. More than just that one. Maybe you didn't marry her—"

"I didn't marry her." He sounded equally incredulous and annoyed.

"But you two were together."

He huffed a breath. Leaned back into his chair and faced her. "After you left... Fine. Yeah, we dated. You know how many events I attended for business. Charity balls and dinners and... The point is, I never liked to go to those things alone. Kylee was available."

"I told you she had a thing for you."

His eyes darkened. "You have a lot of nerve, you know that? You. Left. Me. When I wanted to talk to you about it, you disappeared. The time for explanations is long gone."

He dove back into his eggs.

She picked at her toast. Something wasn't right. Something didn't add up. Because she could hear a voice, a man's voice she couldn't place. *I'm sorry, sweetheart, but Sam moved on. He's married.*

The memory was suddenly as clear as the conversation she was having right now.

Who would tell her that? Especially if it wasn't true?

"You're saying you didn't marry her?" Eliza asked. "Or...was there somebody else?"

He rounded the island and shoved his empty plate in the dishwasher. Then he looked up to meet her eyes. "There was only one woman I ever considered marrying." His voice was low, not filled with anger but pain. "Bought the ring and everything. But she dumped me and disappeared for five years."

Eliza's breath caught.

He'd bought a ring?

And she'd left him? Why?

Unless... What had she said?

It was Kylee, wasn't it?

His response... *You remembered.*

And then she did.

CHAPTER THIRTEEN

THE DRYER BUZZED in another room, and Sam wasn't sorry for the excuse to walk out. He gathered the warm clothes in a basket and carried them to the dining room table.

Eliza was staring off into space, maybe trying to make sense of everything they'd talked about.

She wasn't rubbing her temples, though. So that was something. Whether it was something good or bad, he didn't know.

He pulled out the ugly plaid button-down she'd been wearing when she got to his house Friday night and draped it over the back of a chair so it wouldn't wrinkle, then dug through the clothes for his items. She could fold her own.

"I remember."

He froze, then resumed folding his T-shirt.

He'd known it was coming. It was just a matter of time.

"I saw you with her. At the restaurant that day."

He'd been with Kylee when Eliza had walked in and... caught them. As if he'd been doing something wrong. Which, okay, he had been.

They'd been shoulder to shoulder, laughing over something she'd said.

He remembered in exquisite detail the look on Eliza's face when she spotted them. Horror and heartbreak—an instant before she swiveled and ran.

"You lied to me."

His gaze flicked up. "Did I?"

"You were seeing her." She stood from the barstool, her voice tremulous.

"I wasn't."

"Right. So I just imagined the whole thing? Is that what you're saying? That she wasn't there with you?"

He lowered the pants he'd grabbed. Her pants.

She crossed the space and took them out of his hand. "Well?"

"I'm not saying you imagined it. I'm saying I wasn't seeing her."

"You sure saw her that day."

He grabbed another garment and folded it, thankful for something to focus on besides Eliza.

"You don't have anything to say to me?"

He set the folded T-shirt on the table. "You remember what happened after that?"

She blinked. "I walked out."

"You ran out without a word. It's just lucky I saw you or I would never have known you were there. I followed you. I left Kylee sitting there, alone, and I chased you."

"What, do you want a medal? You cheated on me."

"I didn't." But he couldn't manage to hold her gaze. Because, yeah, he might not have cheated, but he couldn't pretend it'd been nothing.

"Liar."

He squared his shoulders. This was a conversation he'd had in his head a million times. It was good he was finally getting to have it for real. Even if it ended everything. "I never lied to you. Never. Was I having lunch with Kylee? Yes."

"A *business* lunch. That's what you told me."

"And that's what it was. A business lunch in the same restaurant where I had all my business lunches. If it'd been some clandestine meeting, would I have told you where I was going?" Not that he'd ever expected Eliza to show up, but the point was, it hadn't been a secret. "She asked me to lunch because she wanted to talk about selling a division of her family's corporation. Her brother was supposed to join us."

"Convenient how you left out who you were meeting with. A potential client, you said."

"You'd have been okay with me having lunch with Kylee?"

"You think I should have been?" Eliza's voice was shrill. She took a breath, tempered it. "I saw you two together."

"Fine. You were right. She had a thing for me. I never realized... The point is, that lunch was supposed to be with her and her brother, but Ken didn't make it, and fine, she flirted with me."

"She kissed you. And you kissed her back."

He winced. He hadn't realized Eliza had seen that. Hated that she had.

It hadn't been anything. Certainly hadn't *meant* anything. He'd been shocked when Kylee's lips had met his and her hand had landed on his thigh. And yeah, he'd kissed her back. Because...she was beautiful. And she obviously had a thing for him. And yeah, he didn't always think with his brain.

So he'd kissed her. For like a second. And then he'd backed away and tried to make a joke out of it. They were friends, and he didn't want to ruin that. And he'd wanted her business. He'd still been hungry back then, trying to build his career. He'd wanted to laugh it off, get them past it, get to the close.

In retrospect, he should've reacted differently. Obviously.

"I did." Sam took a few steps toward Eliza. He needed her to hear him now. He needed her to know the truth. He breathed through his frustration and lowered his voice, tried to make it gentle and warm. Believable. Because he wasn't lying, but that might not matter to her. "That's what I was guilty of, Eliza. Flirting and that one kiss, which I ended after a couple of seconds. That's all it was. I shouldn't have done it. I'm not making excuses, and it wasn't okay. But that's all it was."

"And I was supposed to be okay with that?"

"You could've let me explain." He spoke slowly, enunciating the words he'd been rehearsing for five years. "You could have cared about me enough to give me five minutes of your time. But you saw what you chose to see, and it was your excuse to leave. You were gone so fast there was nothing but swirling dust in your wake."

"Don't act like it was nothing, Sam."

"I'm not saying it was nothing, Eliza." He emphasized her name like she had his. "I'm saying it wasn't everything. Or it didn't have to be. I'm saying, if you'd given me time—"

"How could you possibly have defended your behavior?"

Anger churned, bubbled up. He spun, walked away. Clenched his fists. Tried to remember all the words he'd said in this phantom conversation in the past. That speech had been eloquent. Now, he ground out the raw truth. "You were going to leave me."

"I loved you." She sounded incredulous, which just made him angrier.

"Not that much, obviously." On the other side of the table, he turned. Picked up a garment—a pair of silky underwear—and dropped it like it'd scorched his fingers.

"I have no idea what you're talking about."

"Do you remember your company's New Year's Eve party?"

Even as she shook her head, he saw the faraway look in her

eyes that told him the memories were returning.

She'd planned it as a grand celebration after the sale of the company. But earlier that day, the new owner had called to give her a heads-up that, though he'd promised not to, there would be layoffs. Rather than waste his time telling her the names of those who'd lose their jobs, he gave her the three names of those who wouldn't. Eliza's name was on that list, along with two low-level employees.

Everyone else got the axe January second. Eliza's friends. Her second family. Of course she'd resigned in solidarity.

Sam could understand why the jerk had wanted to warn her, probably trying to avoid a big ugly scene at the office. Why it couldn't have waited until after the holidays, though... That was the part that burned him.

It was bad enough the buyer had lied to Sam about his intentions. But if he'd waited one day, everything would have been different.

Maybe not better, though. Maybe he should feel thankful the jerk had ruined his plans.

Eliza attended the party that night with the horrible secret tucked inside. Sam's heart had ached for her, knowing how much she loved and respected her coworkers, most of whom her late father had hired and trained. He'd trusted her with his company, and from her perspective, she'd blown it.

Meaning, Sam had blown it.

Her lips tightened at the corners.

"You blamed me," he said.

"You said I could trust them."

"No. I said it was a great deal, that nobody else would pay you nearly what they were offering, and if it was about getting as much as you could for your father's company, then you should take it. But I made it very clear that the new owners wouldn't commit to keeping all the staff."

"But you said—"

"I said you needed to make your own decision. That I was only there to advise you."

"You advised me to take the deal."

He blew out a breath. Grabbed a sweatshirt out of the basket. Folded it carefully and set it on the T-shirt. Trying to rein in his emotions. "I can't see into the future, Eliza. It's not fair that you expected me to. That you expected me to make the decision for you and then blamed me when it didn't work out the way you wanted."

"What does that have to do with our breakup? The day I ran out of that restaurant, I distinctly remember daffodils blooming. We were still together in the spring, so we got past that night."

"Did we?" He waited for her to speak, but she clearly didn't know what he was talking about. "Three times at that party, I overheard you asking people what they thought of me. Wondering if you were making a mistake to trust me. Three people, none of whom knew anything about me except what you'd told them and what they'd gleaned in brief introductions. You and I had been together almost a year, Eliza. A year! I loved you. I *adored* you. I felt terrible when that jerk laid off your staff. Obviously, I don't understand how you felt. But after that night, I was afraid I was going to lose you. I hoped you'd be able to..."

"I forgave you."

"I didn't need your forgiveness." His words were cold, but he couldn't help it. "I didn't do anything wrong. I did the job you hired me to do. I told you all the options. I told you what might happen. You made the final decision. And then you got that terrible news." He cut off her retort with, "I get it, okay? I get that you were disappointed. But three times at that party— three times—you sought relationship advice from practical strangers. 'Is Sam a mistake?' That's what you asked your administrative assistant. And then that plaid-pants geek from software development and some kid who worked in shipping. You can blame my stupid lunch with Kylee for our breakup, but you were looking for reasons to end it."

Her mouth opened. Closed. He waited for her to deny it, but she didn't. Just blinked a couple of times. Swallowed. Obviously, she remembered enough.

"I was going to ask you that night," he said. "To marry me. But then you got the news about the layoffs, and it wasn't the right time. For the next four months, I tried to hold it together. Hold *us* together. You grieved the loss of the business and your job, and maybe your father all over again. When you got angry, you took it out on me. Still, I stayed. I let myself be your punching bag. And your mother's punching bag, and believe me, she never passed up an opportunity to take a shot at me. But I loved you. I thought...I thought you'd get past it."

Like the idiot he'd been.

Hadn't he learned his lesson? He always loved too much. Loved more than other people did.

His brother Michael had taught him that, taught him that nobody would stand by him. But he kept falling for it, over and over. Like a chump.

How much was she remembering? How much of this was news to her? And what emotion had tears tracking down her cheeks?

He didn't know. Didn't really want to know.

Which was a lie, but whatever.

"Easter Sunday." He found one of his handkerchiefs and held it out to her. "You remember?"

She took it and cleared away her tears.

"We attended church with your mother, even though she hated church. But Linda Pelletier is all about appearances. Why you wanted to go with her when my family had invited us to join them, I have no idea. Felt sorry for her, I guess, thinking she'd be all alone. I wanted to be with you, so I put up with her glares and underhanded comments."

He'd gotten them reservations at the club for lunch. Right after they were seated, an acquaintance waved him over from across the room. He left the ladies with their menus and talked to the guy. He was gone five minutes, tops. Neither Eliza nor Linda saw him coming back.

"You know what I heard?" When Eliza shook her head, he continued. "Your mother telling you for the millionth time that you should end things with me. That I was a playboy, which was so far from the truth... And you knew that. Or at least I thought you did. But she'd upped her game. This time, she suggested I'd probably taken a kickback on the sale of your company." His jaw felt so tight with anger that it ached. "She told you I didn't love you—couldn't possibly. Those were the words she used. Your cruel, shrill mother." He pressed his lips closed, though he'd already shared more of his opinion than he should have. "She said that I was going to meet somebody 'more suited' to me. That'd I'd move on from you and leave you heart-broken. You know what you said?"

Eliza shook her head, eyes wide and watery.

"'I know.' That's what you said to her. You *agreed* with her."

"I'm sure I didn't. I just—"

"Couldn't stand up to her. Ever. I knew then that our relationship was doomed. It would always be doomed because your mother hated me. Eventually, she'd convince you to leave me."

"I don't... I don't remember that."

"Yeah, well, I do." He returned his attention to the laundry. Pulled a pair of his jeans out of the basket and folded them. Something for his hands to do while his heart nearly beat out of his chest.

"Did you ever ask me about it?"

He slapped the stupid jeans on the table. "So you could

deny it? Or explain it away?"

"Why not just break up with me?"

"Because I loved you. I wanted it to work. I was willing to risk..."

"You cheated on me."

Anger spiked, quick and dangerous. "I shared one two-second kiss with another woman, one who thought I hung the moon, because my girlfriend was working up the nerve to dump me. If that makes this all my fault then...whatever. Everything else was my fault."

"I don't understand." Her voice was small. "Did we ever talk about it? Did you explain all that?"

"When? After the kiss? You wouldn't talk to me. Practically screamed at me to leave you alone. So I let you go. I thought I'd talk to you when you calmed down. But you blocked my number. When I went to your apartment, you were gone. I reached out to your mother, but the only time she answered the phone was to give me a piece of her mind. I endured the whole high-pitched accusation in order to try to explain to her what happened, how I felt. To see if she'd... Well, I was an idiot, obviously. Jeanette took my call long enough to ream me out, so apparently you'd told her just enough. I never saw you again. Believe me, I looked. I went to your office. Hung out at your favorite coffee shop. Even watched your mother's house, thinking you'd show up there. But you were just...gone."

"That fast?"

"It took me a week or two to get past my own anger and realize..." What he'd lost. That he wasn't willing to lose it. That he wanted to fight for it. "It never occurred to me that you'd leave. I thought I had time to fix it." He dug through the now cool and wrinkled laundry, then pushed the basket across the table toward her. "The rest is yours."

She barely gave it a glance. "I don't understand. Why would

I do that?"

"Because I didn't matter to you as much as you mattered to me."

"That's not it."

"You don't know. You don't remember—"

"The things you said... They all feel right. As awful as it sounds, I can see myself agreeing with Mom to get her to shut up before you came back. Not because I thought she was right but because it wasn't worth fighting with her. And, I mean, we were in public, and you were there. What would have been the point?"

"Standing up for the man you claim you loved? Not point enough for you?"

She seemed to shrink, her shoulders hunching. "I could never stand up to her. And every time I did, I regretted it. I was still with you, so I was trying." She dabbed at the tears on her cheeks. "But the thing is, I did love you. Desperately. I never doubted you. I certainly never thought you'd done anything underhanded with the sale. Sam, I loved you. I adored you. I lived in fear of you leaving me."

Her words threatened to soothe the raw and broken places in his heart. He couldn't let that happen. "You were the one who left."

"But why?"

He threw up his hands. "If you ever figure it out, let me know, will you? Because I wasn't perfect, but I didn't deserve how you treated me." He grabbed his folded clothes and headed up the stairs. He stopped halfway to the top. "Don't leave without telling me. I don't want to spend the rest of my life worrying that somebody kidnapped you. Okay?"

At her nod, he climbed to the second floor, refusing to worry that she'd be gone when he came back down. But knowing, deep down, that it was only a matter of time.

CHAPTER FOURTEEN

ELIZA STARED after Sam a long time, but he didn't return.

Not that she knew what she'd say to him. The idea that she'd broken up with him—had been looking for an excuse—sounded so bizarre that she couldn't wrap her mind around it.

But the things he'd said felt right. And anyway, he wouldn't lie to her. She needed the rest of her memories to return if she was ever going to make sense of it.

She was halfway through folding her laundry when something lying on the dark wood floor beneath one of the dining room chairs caught her eye. She swiped the strip of plastic, barely glancing at it on her way to throw it away.

Her foot pressed the lever to lift the lid of the trash can, but her gaze caught, and she froze.

The plastic thing was maybe two inches long, a quarter inch wide, and pointed at one end. A long number was written on one side. She flipped it over. The other side had an email address—a string of seemingly random numbers and letters followed by the familiar *@gmail.com.*

Where had it come from? But even as the question occurred to her, so did the answer.

She lifted her plaid shirt from the chair where Sam had draped it and checked the collars. Sure enough, one was stiff with a plastic...she had no idea what to call it, but it was the thing that went into the collars of shirts—men's shirts—to keep them stiff.

The plastic piece in her hand had to have come out of the other, which was floppy.

Maybe this was the reason she'd been wearing a man's shirt when she showed up at Sam's on Friday night.

"Sam." When he didn't respond, she tried again, louder. "Sam!"

Footsteps sounded above. "What?" He hurried down the stairs. "What's wrong?"

"I found this." She held it out to him.

He took it from her. "What is it?"

"It came out of my shirt." She showed him the floppy collar.

"Huh." He studied the thing in his hand. "It's your handwriting."

It was.

"What does it mean?" he asked.

She shrugged. "A login and password, I assume."

"But to what?" Not waiting for an answer she couldn't give, he set it down, tapped his phone, and took a picture of both sides. "Just in case." And then he ran up the stairs, returning seconds later with his laptop.

"Top three sites," he said. "Where should I check?"

"I don't know."

"Don't think, just talk. What comes to mind?"

"It's a Google email address, so maybe a Google drive?"

"Great." He clicked. Typed. "Nope. What else?"

"Dropbox?"

A second later, "Strike two."

"We get more than three, right?"

"This is a different kind of game." He looked up, gave her a quick smile.

It did feel nice to have a clue.

And what had she done to her life that she was reduced to trying to solve a mystery like some sort of inept PI?

"Maybe it's related to money? Maybe a bank?" She named as many as came to mind, but the email and password combination didn't get them access anywhere.

"What else could it be?" Sam paced across the kitchen. "Let's try the places I have accounts." He started rattling off names. She sat at his laptop and typed.

PayPal, Venmo, CashApp. No, no, and no.

More banks.

Nothing.

"You were in Denver," he said. "Let's look up—"

His phone rang.

"It's Jon." He answered and put it on speaker. "This is Sam. Eliza's here too."

"I have some information."

"Great." Sam slid the laptop back to himself and opened a note. "Go."

"We need to meet." The man's voice was deep.

The confusion on Sam's face probably matched her own. "Why?"

"Grant wants to see you," Jon said. "You're in the mountains, right? How far are you from North Conway?"

"About thirty minutes."

"Could you meet us there?"

Sam met her eyes, clearly waiting for her to weigh in.

"Whatever you think," she said.

His gaze darkened. "Hold on, Jon." And he muted the phone. "Is it a good idea or not?"

"I don't know. What do you think?"

"I'm not making all the decisions, Eliza. This one's on you."

Oh. She hated choices, especially when nobody would give her counsel. Her life's motto—what would anybody else do? Because her decisions always blew up in her face.

But Sam had that stubborn set to his jaw. He'd wait her out if it took all day.

"Yeah, okay. We need to know what they learned. We should trust their judgment."

He tapped the phone to unmute it. "Just tell us where and when."

Eliza stepped into the old-house-turned-business in North Conway, her sneakers loud on the wood floors. Behind her, Sam pulled the door closed against the chilly wind.

There was a shop to the right that seemed to carry everything from souvenir mugs to ski parkas. And plenty of souvenirs that sported the name of this place on it.

She and Sam had spent the rest of the morning trying to figure out what website the hidden password would open up to them—to no avail. She'd remembered to call her former employer at the investment firm where she used to work, but he'd been out of the office. The assistant, a woman whose voice Eliza didn't recognize, promised to have him call her back. When he did, she might get the name of the couple she'd moved to Utah with.

It was just past one o'clock, and she was ready for lunch. Maybe, if she quit trying to remember what the password went to, the answer would come to her. She found it worked like that sometimes—just letting the information simmer, not forcing it.

The foyer had old wood floors worn from years of wear, pale green walls, and dark wood trim. Straight ahead, a stairway led upstairs, guarded by a simple chain with a sign hanging from it, telling her the upstairs dining room was closed. The restaurant was to the left, where a host stood behind a wooden stand.

"Four for lunch," Sam said behind her.

The host grabbed four menus. "Follow me."

There was no protective hand on her back today as Eliza preceded Sam across the dining room. In fact, he'd been very careful not to touch her since their discussion earlier.

She was being very careful not to care. It wasn't working very well.

They were seated near rear windows that looked out over a patio—outdoor dining, though it was too cold for that today. But the view—a grassy field in the foreground, mountains in the background—would be a beautiful backdrop for a romantic meal.

Which this definitely wasn't.

They'd barely glanced at the menus when heavy footsteps drew her attention. Sure enough, Grant was crossing the half-empty restaurant toward them. He looked older, of course, but also happier than the last time she'd seen him. Like Sam, Grant had dark hair and eyes. But, as muscular as Sam was, Grant was bigger. Not just taller but broader with a barrel chest and arms thicker than her calves.

Sam stood and stuck out his hand to his brother, who ignored it and wrapped him in a back-slapping hug before stepping back. "Glad to see you in one piece." Grant turned to Eliza and smiled. "It's good to see you again."

"You too. I hear you tied the knot."

He grinned, the look almost boyish.

The man behind him was even bigger than Grant, at least six-four and built like a tractor-trailer. Light-brown hair and intense gray eyes. He greeted Sam—apparently, they'd met before—and then turned to her and stuck out his hand. "Jon Donley."

"Eliza Pelletier. Thanks for doing this."

His only answer was a quick nod.

The men sat at the round table, one on each side of her. They were all three so big that she felt like a little girl at a table full of grown-ups.

She'd sort of expected them to dive right into business, but they didn't. They caught up with each other. Joked and teased, directing a lot of their comments to her. Jon told stories about Grant from the Army, and he reciprocated with his own tales, which had her laughing so hard tears streamed from her eyes. There were stories about Sam and Grant and the rest of the brothers from childhood, stories about Jon's childhood and his favorite cousin, Grant's wife, which made the tough guy's expression soften. Jon shared a few stories about his own wife. She was a movie star so famous that even Eliza had heard of her, but Jon made her sound down-to-earth. Funny and kind.

"I'd like to meet her someday," Eliza said.

Jon's expression dimmed the slightest bit. "She'd like to meet you. Eventually."

Eliza had the very strong impression Jon didn't want her anywhere near his wife. Which, considering the danger she was in, made sense.

"We dropped her and Summer off at the Christmas store down the street before we got here," Grant explained. "We're happy to have an excuse to miss that."

The group ate and talked and laughed as if all were right with the world. And nobody said a word about what was going on with Eliza. About her amnesia. About the fact that somebody had attacked her and Sam—and then Camilla.

It all felt so normal—like life ought to be. Safe and secure and relaxed. No undercurrent of tension. Nobody demanding anything. Nobody sending cruel jabs.

No angry guard in the corner, glaring at her. Daring her to *try it.*

The thought brought her up short. Try what? What did Gil think she was going to do?

She closed her eyes and tried to remember.

But for the first time that day, her head protested by throbbing.

Gentle fingers slid around her wrist, and she realized she was massaging her temples. She looked up to see Sam's concerned expression.

"You remember something?"

"Nothing new."

"Don't push it. The memories will come." His words were kind, but he pulled his hand back.

Jon and Grant were watching.

"Sorry."

"You all right?" Grant asked.

"Just trying to remember. I'm fine." She forked a bite of salad and popped it into her mouth. Crisp lettuce, warm chicken, and a cool, sweet strawberries, all covered in a raspberry vinaigrette. But as much as she enjoyed it, her appetite was gone.

The lighthearted mood had lifted, leaving behind heaviness and fear.

Sam paid the check, refusing to let Grant or Jon contribute. After he added the tip and signed it, he said, "What have you got for us?"

"Gilbert C. Lyle," Jon said. "Thirty-one. Born in Duluth, Minnesota. Enlisted at eighteen. Never saw combat—except what he caused. Got kicked out of the Army at twenty-three for getting into a bar fight with a fellow soldier."

"Sounds like a piece of work." Sam's gaze flicked to Eliza, his eyes stormy. "Not exactly your type."

"I'm sure we weren't together."

He didn't seem as sure but said nothing.

"No record of employment after his dishonorable discharge," Jon said. "Only record is his rap sheet. Assault, assault with a deadly weapon, and sexual assault."

Sexual assault? She let the words float around for a minute, but they didn't land. She'd interacted with this guy, but not in *that* way. So that was something.

"How is he not in prison?" This from Grant.

Jon shrugged. "Charges are all in different states, so maybe that played a part. Anyway, things went quiet for him about three years ago. No employment. But he does have one more arrest about a year ago for assault in Utah. I looked up the address he gave the cops. A halfway house in Salt Lake that claims he never stayed there. Unfortunately, the cops never followed up because the victim refused to press charges." He glanced at his notes. "Victim was Nicole—"

"Moore." The name popped out before Eliza even realized she knew it.

Jon pulled a pen from his shirt pocket. "What do you know about her?"

"Um..." She closed her eyes, trying to remember. Her head started to throb.

"Don't force it, Eliza," Sam said. "Just relax. We're not in any hurry."

Right. Because she could relax while they were all watching.

But Sam smiled at her, sipped his soda. "You guys catch the game last night?"

The men started chatting about football.

Giving her a moment to think.

She closed her eyes. Nicole Moore. She considered the name. Nicole Moore. It didn't bring anxiety but peace. Nicole was an ally.

An image came. Tall, sandy-blond hair that needed a trim. High cheekbones and gray-green eyes. Smiling.

Her laugh. The way she took her coffee—three creams, no sugar.

Eliza could picture Nicole's eyes widened in fear, could hear her voice lowered, sharing a secret. Not a fun secret.

They ate together, but not always. It was a treat when they did. Even though they lived near each other, just across the grass. Down the hill.

"Nicole lived in the dorm."

The men's conversation stopped, but Eliza didn't open her eyes as she related what she remembered. "She was a resident, but also the house manager. She'd been there a long time—one of the longest residents. We were..." Her eyes opened, and she found Grant and Sam watching her.

Jon was jotting notes.

"We were friends. *Are* friends. She was on my side."

Jon looked up "Of what? What sides?"

"I don't...I don't know."

"No problem," Jon said. "I didn't look into her because I figured she was a girlfriend or something. But now that I know you're connected to her, I'll do a deep dive. See what I can learn. Tell me about this place, this...dorm, did you say?"

"Yeah. I think it's a home for women, like a rehab center. But...I don't think it's for addicts. Or *only* for addicts. It was more like a place where troubled young women could come, learn to live on their own. Mature a little, I think. They lived in dorms." As she spoke, the pale sketch in her mind filled in with dark lines and colors. "There was only one dorm at first, big enough for just a handful of women. But they expanded that building, then added another. Another structure held the kitchen, dining room, rec room, and nursery. It's a farm. I remember horses, chickens, goats. The girls worked the land and learned how to take care of themselves and the children."

Nobody said anything, but Eliza knew they were itching to question her.

"Some of the women had children. Others were pregnant when they got there. There was a medical facility—a doctor on staff, I think. So nobody ever got to leave."

Beside her, Sam's eager expression darkened.

What had she said?

She closed her eyes, replayed it. "Not *got* to leave. *Had* to leave, maybe. But..."

That didn't feel true. Had Nicole been trapped? A prisoner?

Had Eliza?

The answer was right there, but she couldn't...

Her head throbbed, a wave of pain that had her stomach roiling. She heard a groan—her own, but she couldn't stop it.

"Hey, it's okay." Sam scooted closer, rubbed her neck. "Just let it go. Take a breath and let it go."

She did, releasing her grip on the memory that had been so close she could taste its bitterness. Her headache receded, and she opened her eyes and looked at Sam.

He dropped his hand. "Better."

"It's so frustrating."

Across from her, Jon tapped his pen on his notepad. "That was great information. That's really going to help us track these people down."

"Okay, good. But, didn't you look me up? I lived there too. Not in the dorms, but somewhere on the property. I'd think my address would show exactly where it is."

"Unfortunately," Jon said, "there's no record of you in Utah or anywhere else for the last five years."

"What? That can't be right."

"The only driver's license I found for you was issued in Maine. It looks like you renewed it—probably by mail."

"I don't understand. Didn't I have a job? A lease or something?"

"It's unusual," Jon said. "But the pieces are coming together. With the name you gave me, and now that I know what I'm looking for, I'll be able to figure out where you've been and who you've been with." He leaned toward her. His smile turned him from fierce warrior to friend. "This is good news. We're closing in on it."

They were. The answers were coming.

Hope crept in around the ragged edges of her memory.

A few minutes later, the guys stood, stepping aside to let Eliza lead the way back to the foyer. She was eager to get on the road and talk through everything she'd learned with Sam. The memories were close now. A little prompting, and they'd come back.

"Can I talk to you privately for a second?" Jon's voice came from right behind her, and she turned, but he was addressing Sam. Holding his gaze like he was trying to tell him something.

Sam noticed it too. "Sure. We can talk outside."

"Wait." She moved in front of the door. "Is this about me?"

Jon's expression gave nothing away.

Sam said, "I'll find out and let you know."

She focused on Jon. "I want to hear what you learned."

His gaze flicked from her to Sam. "Just give us a minute, okay?" He reached past her for the door.

Sam followed, but she grabbed his arm, feeling the strength there as he turned back. "This is my story. I have a right to hear."

"And I'll tell you. I promise." He followed Jon outside.

Grant was standing beside her.

"Do you know what they're talking about?"

"Nope."

"He didn't tell you?"

"Everything I knew, Jon just told you both. So whatever that is...?" He shrugged. "I wouldn't worry about it. Maybe he thinks it'll upset you."

"You don't think this is upsetting? Being left alone?"

Grant pressed his hands against his chest and stepped back. "I'm wounded."

She wasn't ready to let go of her anger, but she couldn't help the amusement that tipped her lips up.

He nodded to the store. "Let's see what they have."

"Big fan of shopping, are you?"

His only answer was a low chuckle, but he held out his arm in an *after you* gesture.

Like she was in the mood to shop. But she stepped into the place. It was bigger than she'd first guessed. She walked among the displays but barely registered the offerings. Coffee cups. T-shirts. Keychains. Magnets. In the back hung a small selection of ski apparel.

Why hadn't Jon told her what he'd learned? What was the secret?

She was drawn to a rack of baby clothes. Tiny T-shirts, sweatshirts, bibs, socks, all New Hampshire themed. She fingered a baby-soft moose with a little blanket attached. She imagined an infant cuddled up with it. She'd always wanted children, a family.

Where had that dream gone?

What had she been doing for the last five years?

She slid around the display and saw Grant staring at a pink T-shirt that read, *Daddy's Little Girl.*

Huh.

"I don't think that'll fit you," she said.

When he saw her, his eyes widened. His cheeks turned pink.

She took a guess and said, "Congratulations."

He looked around, lowered his voice. "We haven't told anybody. We thought we'd share the news at Mom and Dad's anniversary party."

"I won't spoil the surprise, I promise."

"Hopefully, you'll be there too."

She couldn't bring herself to hope. "Where is it?"

"Sam's. He likes to host."

She could imagine the scene. Sam in his element, serving the family he loved so much.

She lifted a pair of pink baby shoes and slid her finger along the sparkly side. "It's a girl?"

Grant shrugged. "Too soon to tell." But obviously he'd be happy if it were.

She could imagine a tiny girl nestled in those muscular arms, gazing up at her father. The thought had her stupid eyes prickling.

Grant squeezed her arm and turned away, giving her plenty of privacy for her breakdown.

Sam had bought her a ring. She hadn't had a moment to process that since he'd confessed it that morning.

If only she hadn't run away. What could possibly have propelled her to do something so stupid, so reckless?

"Hey." Grant's voice, not directed at her.

"Where is she?" Sam didn't sound happy.

"Uh..."

Eliza brushed her tears away and stepped out from behind a display. "What's going on?"

He stepped up to her. Right in her face. A muscle ticked in his jaw. "Apparently, you were with a man."

The words were low and angry.

"Dude, calm down." Grant gripped his arm, but Sam shook him off.

"You flew to Denver with him. Spent the night with him. Then the two of you flew to Manchester."

She blinked, stepped back. A man? No, that didn't feel right at all. She shook her head. "I don't—"

"Don't lie to me, Eliza. And don't pretend you don't know. It's fine for you to do...whatever with whoever you want. I don't care. But then you ran to *my* house, into *my* arms, as if you couldn't survive without me. All the while, there was Levi."

He hurled the name like a grenade.

And it hit its mark. And exploded.

Levi.

Levi!

Oh.

She couldn't...

How could she have...?

What kind of person...?

What kind of *mother*...?

She stepped back, bumped into a display. Sucked in a breath. Another.

Levi.

Where was he? What had she done?

"Eliza. Hey." Sam gripped her arms. "What is it?"

She couldn't get enough air. Couldn't breathe.

Lost her footing. Was swooped up. Carried, but she didn't know where. Didn't care. Because...

Levi.

She was set down, lowered to a seat.

"Exhale, Eliza. We need a...a paper bag or something."

Darkness was pressing in. There was no oxygen. Her lungs exploded with need of it.

Someone shook her shoulders. "Open your eyes. Open your eyes, Eliza."

She did, and Sam was right there, his expression no longer angry but afraid.

"You need to exhale. Come on." He inhaled then blew the air out. "With me, sweetheart. Breathe with me."

She tried, blew as hard as she could. And sucked in more air. Sweet oxygen.

"Again. Focus on my voice. Nothing else." He blew out a breath, and she did too.

Someone held out a bag to him, but he ignored it. "Again. Blow out really hard."

She matched her breathing to his. Over and over until the dizziness passed. The black receded.

Sam sat back on his heels and ran his handkerchief across his sweating forehead, a million questions in his gaze.

What was she going to tell him?

How could she possibly explain?

"Are you all right?" The concern in his expression had her eyes filling.

She might be breathing again, but she was far from all right.

Because memories were crashing over her like waves in a storm, sweeping her legs out from under her, pulling her into deep, deep water.

She might never take a full breath again.

CHAPTER FIFTEEN

SAM FORCED HIS MOUTH SHUT, trying to give Eliza all the space she needed for...for whatever was happening.

And maybe he shouldn't have come at her with such anger.

No *maybe* about it.

But the thought of her traveling with, spending the night with, waking up with some guy...just a few hours before she threw herself into his arms.

Yeah, jealousy was ugly. And sticky like sap. He'd need a lot of soap to wash it off.

He'd deal with that—and whoever *Levi* was—later. He needed to get Eliza calmed down or he'd be taking her to the hospital, despite her protests.

Her eyes were closed but scrunched up. Her fingertips pressed against her temples.

She'd been like that for a couple of minutes now, giving nothing away.

Then she opened her eyes and saw him. And if he weren't mistaken, recoiled a little.

Great.

Apparently, his wasn't the face she was longing for.

Which wasn't supposed to hurt because he wasn't supposed to care.

But he did.

He couldn't help it, even if this ended in his delivering her to *Levi* and walking away.

She looked above him, and he glanced at the backs of Jon and Grant, who'd positioned themselves between her and the people moving through the small foyer, keeping prying eyes away.

He turned back to her. "Anything I can do?" There. That sounded kind, not jealous and petty, though those emotions were still close to the surface.

She shook her head, winced.

"Headache?"

"A little."

He waited for more. An explanation would be nice. Like, who in the heck was Levi? And why did his name cause that reaction? They'd traveled to Manchester together, so where was he now?

And then he realized...

Was Levi the one who'd given her those bruises?

If so, Sam was going to find him...and hurt him.

Her voice was low, almost frightened. "Is there anything else Jon needs to tell us?"

Sam felt the men shift behind him.

"I'm sorry that happened," Jon said. "I thought Sam might be able to shed some light... Well, anyway, I was trying to find a way to bring it up without upsetting you. I thought he would help." He glared down at Sam, who suddenly found himself wishing he were standing, not crouched, head about knee-high to Jon, who looked like he wanted to rip it off.

Which...yeah. That was fair. Jon had taken him aside to ask if Eliza had mentioned a Levi or traveling with anyone. He'd thought the information might upset her because it was closer to home, more personal. Jon had been trying to protect her.

Sam hadn't listened to his warnings as he'd stormed back into the building.

Eliza addressed Jon. "Thanks for trying, anyway."

The man grunted. "You guys know everything I know." He took a breath, almost smiled. "You've given me new leads. I'll get going on them."

Eliza looked at Sam then. "Can we go back to the cabin?"

"Are you okay to walk?"

"Yeah. Thank you for... I don't know what happened."

Panic attack, he figured. He'd worked with a client who had one every time they discussed the sale of his business. One time, the guy ended up curled on the floor in Sam's office. Scared him to death.

But he'd learned what to do.

He pushed to his feet and held his hand out to her. When she slipped hers into it, he pulled her to her feet.

"Need a ride to your car?" Grant's gaze flicked to Eliza but landed on Sam. "We're right out front."

Sam tossed the question to her. "What do you think?"

"We can walk. It's not far."

They stepped out into the sunshine and said goodbye to the guys. "Thanks for everything," Sam shook Jon's hand, adding, "Sorry about that. I uh... I got a little worked up."

Jon's eyes crinkled at the corners, a hint of amusement. "I get it."

Sam turned to Grant. "I owe you one."

"I don't think that's how it's supposed to work, bro." Grant pulled him in for a quick hug, then wrapped an arm around Eliza's shoulders. "It's going to be okay. God's got you."

She smiled up at him, blinking rapidly as if she were trying to stop tears. "It was good to see you again."

"It won't be the last time, I'm sure."

The guys jogged to a shiny black pickup truck that had probably cost more than Sam's had—which was to say, stupid expensive. But Jon was married to a movie star, so money wasn't an issue.

Eliza gave one last wave, then she and Sam walked down the sidewalk toward the narrow street where they'd parked. She hugged herself against the cold.

"You need my jacket?"

"I'm fine."

They turned at the corner, away from the busy street, and the traffic sounds faded. The cars that had lined the road earlier were mostly gone now, and the red Porsche stood out.

"Are you going to tell me who—?"

"I will. Soon." Her words were flat and emotionless. He suspected it was taking all her energy to hold herself together.

He could wait. At least she wasn't demanding to be taken to an airport or a bus station so she could go in search of Levi.

The way she'd reacted when he'd first said the name, it was as if she'd misplaced the guy. At least Sam wasn't the only man Eliza had forgotten about.

Not fair. Amnesia was strange, and from what he'd read, it could last for weeks, sometimes months. It was good her memories were coming back. Not her fault he happened to hate her memories.

The pounding of footsteps, then...

Something crashed into him from behind. He lurched forward, landed hard on the asphalt. A fist pummeled the side of his head.

Eliza screamed. "Sam!"

He elbowed the guy on top of him, felt flesh and bone, and elbowed harder.

"Oomph."

The guy shifted to protect himself, and Sam bucked him off, spun to his knees, and jabbed the heel of his hand toward the guy's nose. But he dodged, and Sam's blow glanced off his cheek.

Sam managed to get to his feet.

Got a look at the guy. Spiked blond hair—same one who'd come after them at Eliza's mom's house. Which meant the big one was here too.

He wanted to look for Eliza, but Spike charged.

Sam aimed a kick at his head.

Spike stumbled, landed on his back and flipped over.

"Sam!" Her voice came from farther away.

Spike was about to launch himself forward.

Sam yanked the gun from its holster beneath his shirt. Didn't have time to aim as Spike came toward him.

Hopped out of the way, whacked the butt of it hard on Spike's head.

The guy went down to his hands and knees, started to rise again.

Sam whacked him again, hard.

The attacker collapsed

Sam turned, scanned the street.

Eliza was seventy, eighty yards away, being carried. Feet kicking. Fighting with everything in her. To no avail.

He had the gun but couldn't risk a bullet hitting her. He ran that direction.

But a trunk opened. Goatee—Gil—tossed her inside. Slammed the lid. Ran to the driver's door.

Sam stopped to aim but didn't have time to get a shot off before Gil dove into the sedan.

Gil pulled out of the spot. Hit the gas, gunned it in the opposite direction.

CHAPTER SIXTEEN

ELIZA GROPED IN DARKNESS. There had to be a safety latch, right? Somewhere?

She had to get out of this trunk.

Because if they got her, they'd get the information out of her. And once they did that...

They'd kill her.

They'd kill her and bury her body. Nobody would ever find her.

But there was no latch. Only darkness and hopelessness as Gil hit the gas. The man was ruthless. The thought of being his captive...

Dear God, help!

What had Grant said to her? That God had her? But it felt like nobody had anything. The world was spinning out of control like the wheels beneath the car.

But...but words filled her mind, her heart. Words she had no memory of, and yet...

"Trust in the Lord with all your heart."

She did. She did trust Him. She didn't know why or when or how, but she felt a deep faith in her heart that she couldn't explain.

"Help me!" She shouted the words as if He wouldn't be able to hear through the trunk. "I need You. You promised me it would be okay. You promised!"

He had. The memories were coming back. She'd done this horrible, scary, risky thing because God had told her to. He'd whispered in her ear every step of the way. *Trust Me.*

He wouldn't abandon her. She had to believe.

And then...

A bang.

The sedan lurched, and she slammed against the back.

The screeching sound of metal against metal.

The car was still moving, slowly. And then...

"Put it in park!"

"Working on it!"

The words were muffled, but familiar. Still, she was afraid to hope.

The car slammed to a stop.

A car door slammed.

And the trunk opened, pouring in sunshine and cool air.

A man looked down at her. Not Gil.

Sam.

He reached in, scooped her out. Held her close, burying his head against her neck. "Thank You. Thank You, Jesus. Thank God I got you." They stayed like that a long, long time. "I've got you, Eliza." He said it over and over, maybe trying to convince himself as much as her.

She held on tight. Held on for all she was worth.

Slowly, Sam let up his grip enough for her to slide down until her feet hit the ground. But she stayed in his arms, her cheek pressed against his jacket. His heart was thumping wildly. He was breathing like he'd run a race. Maybe he had.

"Police are on their way."

She turned. Jon was kneeling on Gil's back. When he struggled, Jon shoved the man's face into the ground. "You keep fighting, you're gonna be out cold by the time they get here."

Gil, the man who'd bullied her so many times. Who'd loomed over her, frightened her, intimidated her. Who'd told her how much she could eat. Who'd taken food off her table and dared her to protest. Who'd practically starved her.

Now, he quit fighting. Just lay on the ground, flat on his face. Subdued.

"Where's Grant?" Sam shifted—keeping her in his arms—to look around. "He all right?"

"He's with the other one." Jon, who'd been so kind at lunch, looked fierce and terrifying. "We drove by just as you started sprinting. Grant jumped out—while the truck was still moving—and I banged a left and spun around the corner, thinking I'd ram him or, if nothing else, follow him."

"How'd they find us?"

"That's a good question." Jon wrapped his arm around Gil's head, hand in his face. Oh. His finger was at the man's eyeball.

Sam moved, blocking her view. All she heard was the low rumble of Jon's voice.

A moment later, he swore just loudly enough for her to hear, and she leaned away from Sam to see.

He looked furious.

"What?" Sam asked.

"I'll tell you in a minute. Good shot, by the way."

"Thanks."

She looked up at him. "You...shot him?"

"The tire. Caused the crash. I was running to get you when Jon came from"—he nodded to a cross street—"up there. Hopped out of his truck and..." Sam grinned, then laughed. "How did you do that?"

Jon shrugged.

"What?" she asked.

"I think Goatee was gonna keep going," Sam said, "tire or not. But Jon ran to the door, even though the car was moving, pulled the door open, and punched him. Then grabbed him out and tossed him on the ground."

"Yeah," Jon said, "but you slowed him down. And got the car stopped. And got the girl."

Sam looked down at her, and his amusement faded. He swallowed, hard. "Yeah. I got her."

CHAPTER SEVENTEEN

TWO MEN HAD BEEN BEATEN, and one was unconscious when the cops arrived.

The other started screaming that he'd been tortured.

Sam didn't know exactly what Jon had said to the guy, but Gil was still breathing, and he still had both his eyes. Sam figured the dipstick should shut up while he was ahead.

He shouldn't have been surprised when the police insisted that he, Eliza, Jon, and Grant go to the station with them and fill out a report.

Even Grant flashing his credentials hadn't helped.

So the four of them recounted to a detective at the police station everything that happened on the street in North Conway.

And then Sam and Eliza told him about Camilla's near kidnapping at Sam's house.

And the attack at Linda Pelletier's.

And then, the detective *suggested* they stay until a state investigator arrived.

When he did, they recounted the story again. Sam sat on one side of Eliza at a table in a small room—a break room, if the half-empty box of cookies on the counter was any indication. Jon sat on her other side. Grant excused himself after recounting all he knew—those police credentials were finally good for something.

When they finished, Detective Jones—silver hair, suit and tie—leaned back. "What I want to know is, why?" He directed the question to Eliza. "Why are"—he glanced at the paperwork in front of him—"Gilbert Lyle and Elliot Ramsey after you?"

Elliot Ramsey, a.k.a. Spike.

She looked to Sam for help.

"She has amnesia," he said. "She doesn't remember."

The man didn't even flick a gaze his way. "You can speak for yourself, Miss Pelletier."

"Right. Sorry. I was involved with these people in Utah. At least we think that's where it started. I think maybe they were doing something illegal. I think my plan was to expose them, but like Sam said"—she shrugged—"it's all really fuzzy."

"You have a lot of guesses for someone who claims to have amnesia."

"She does have—"

The cop lifted a *shut-up* hand toward Sam, still watching Eliza.

Sam would press his point, but he saw it too. It seemed at least some of Eliza's memories had returned.

Finally, Jones said, "Expose them how?"

She licked her lips. "Um, I think..." She looked toward Jon, but he added nothing. "I learned today that I was in Denver. I think maybe I left evidence there."

"Why Denver?"

She shrugged.

"You don't remember why you went to Denver?"

"I didn't remember any of this until lunch today. It's coming back, but I haven't put the pieces together."

Again, the man said nothing. No questions. No comments. Just...silence.

Sam was itching to defend Eliza. Or just stand up and leave. Those two thugs were lucky to be alive. Sam and Jon had done nothing wrong, and Eliza's only crime was nearly getting kidnapped.

But Jon said nothing.

Eliza said nothing.

And Sam wasn't about to be the jerk who stuck his foot in his mouth. He'd done enough of that today.

After what felt like ten minutes but was probably more like three, Jones sighed. "All right then." He pushed back in his chair and stood. "You're free to go. But Miss Pelletier?"

She was already standing, clearly as anxious to be out of there as Sam was. "Yes?"

"When you get your memory back, would you call me?" He handed her a business card. "You brought these people to my state. We need to know what's going on."

A single nod, and they filed out of the interview room.

Grant was leaning against a desk in the small police department. He pushed away when they approached. "I got the truck. Everything okay?"

"Yup." Sam kept walking until they were outside. It felt like they'd been in there for hours, but the sun was still poking through the clouds.

They climbed into the truck, Sam and Eliza in the roomy backseat of the cab. Jon started it up but didn't move. "That was fun."

"You can't blame them for wanting the story," Grant said. "That was the third incident in a couple of days."

"At least Gil and Elliot are in custody." Eliza clicked on her seatbelt. "I can breathe easier."

"They are in custody, but I wouldn't let my guard down." This from Jon, who met Sam's eyes in the rearview mirror.

"What?"

"Gil told me how they found us." He focused on Grant. "They were watching you. I thought I spotted a tail when we left Coventry this morning."

"I figured that out when you made all those quick turns." Grant didn't sound happy. "I assumed it was a reporter."

Right. That probably happened a lot when Denise Masters was involved.

"Me too," Jon said. "I lost him."

"Apparently not." Sam couldn't help the tone—or the volume. "You led them right to us."

Again, that steady gaze in the rearview. "I'm a professional. I know what I'm doing."

But his eye contact didn't hold. He looked down. A second later, he held his phone up.

Eliza leaned in to see the photo.

Sam didn't need to lean. It was a snapshot of Denise Masters and Grant's wife, Summer, surrounded by Christmas decorations. Posted on Instagram.

Jon took the phone back, showed it to Grant.

"Oh. A fan."

"One who doesn't give a"—his gaze flicked in the rearview— "whit about Denise's safety, obviously, broadcasting to the world exactly where she is."

"How did they find us, though?" Eliza asked.

Sam fielded that. "Jon's truck. It was parked outside the restaurant."

"Yup." Jon sounded furious. "I should have been more careful. It just never crossed my mind..."

"But why were they watching Grant?" Sam asked. "I mean, why not Dad or Daniel or—"

"They're all being watched," Jon said. "Your whole family."

"All of them?" Sam's heart thumped in his chest. He'd known it was possible, in theory, but... Were that many people after Eliza?

"That's what Gil told me," Jon said. "Your brothers. Your parents. Gil said they figured you'd eventually reach out to one of them. They put their money on Grant, which is what I would have done. Farthest away, a cop with military experience."

Grant turned to face Sam, face red, eyes hard. "We practically handed you guys to them."

"You didn't know." Eliza reached into the front seat and squeezed his shoulder. "You couldn't have known."

"Are Denise and Summer safe?" Sam asked.

Oh. That hadn't occurred to Eliza. "Did we put them in danger?"

"They're fine," Jon said. "I called them right after the attack and told them to get an Uber home."

"I'm sure Summer went from buddy to bodyguard in about three seconds," Grant added. "She can handle herself. She's always armed and ready. And on her guard when she's with Denise."

"I'm sorry." Tears wobbled Eliza's voice. "I never meant for any of this to happen. To pull you guys into this. It all just spun out of control."

Sam handed her his handkerchief, itching to hear what she remembered. "Take us back to Colton's car."

"We're going there, but you won't be driving it." Jon reversed out of his spot. "There weren't that many cars on that street, and only one with Maine plates. I assume you were in the Porsche?"

"Yeah."

"Even if they didn't get the license number, how many cherry red Porsche 911s do you think are registered in Maine?"

Grant said, "Seriously, bro. Could you have picked a *more* conspicuous car?"

"I didn't plan on them finding us."

"Plans go awry," Jon muttered.

No kidding. "So what are we doing?"

Grant said, "We're meeting Michael."

"What?" Sam couldn't help the anger in his voice. "Forget it. I'm not putting him in danger too. Besides, I'm sure he has better things to do than—"

"Don't be an idiot," Grant said. "He's your brother. He wants to help."

Sam seriously doubted that.

"He's been out of town, but he heard what happened from Dad and called me as soon as he landed."

"Why'd he call you?"

"I assume he called you first."

Sam had gotten a couple of calls while they were at the police station but hadn't checked. He did now, and sure enough, there was a message from Michael.

And four from his current client, along with an angry text.

> This is what you call concierge service? I need you to call me back. Pronto.

Sam had sent him the buyers' most recent offer the night before. Apparently, his client wasn't impressed with his advice that he should accept their terms.

He tapped out a quick response.

> Family emergency. I'll call you as soon as I can.

It was the rare moment when Sam put his clients off. Business had become paramount in his life.

But there were more important things than closing deals. He put his phone away.

"Michael rented a car at Logan," Grant was saying, "and he's on his way. We're meeting him in Concord. You'll take his rental, and he'll drive the Porsche back to Colton's."

"And make himself a target?"

"Chances they'll see him are slim. And he'll be alone in the car. They're not going to mess with him."

The last thing Sam wanted was help from Michael. And anyway... "It's not my car. I can't just let Michael—"

"Already talked to Colton," Grant said, "and he's fine with it."

"You've got this all figured out." Sam didn't mean to sound so...grouchy. But he didn't like needing his brothers' help. Or anyone's.

"You're welcome," Grant said, not a little sarcastically.

"Sorry. Thank you."

Beside him, Eliza crossed her arms as if she was barely holding herself together. Half of him wanted to pull her close and comfort her.

The other half couldn't stop thinking...*Levi*.

He wanted to go back to Colton's. To put his feet up and drink a beer and listen to her story and make a plan. But... "We can't go back to the cabin, can we?"

"Why not?" Eliza sounded heartbroken.

He knew how she felt.

"Colton's car," he said. "Colton's cabin."

"Then no," Grant said.

Eliza practically withered.

"I'll get you a safe house."

Sam wished he could tell Grant that he'd manage it. That he didn't need his little brother's help. But he was wrung out. Aching and bruised. And way, way out of his league.

CHAPTER EIGHTEEN

ELIZA OPENED her eyes when the truck slowed. She'd spent the nearly two-hour drive from North Conway to Concord letting the memories come. She didn't have them all, but it seemed just a matter of time.

The most important one she wouldn't let herself dwell on.

Levi.

If she did, she'd be useless. She needed to focus if she was going to get him back.

Her son was counting on her.

Jon parked at the back of the department store's lot. "Can you text Michael, tell him we're here?"

Sam pulled out his phone, but a black Ford sedan pulled up beside them.

"No need." Sam opened his door and climbed out, then walked around to help Eliza from the tall truck. Not that she couldn't get down by herself, but she didn't mind the way he took her hips and set her on the asphalt. "You all right?"

"Yeah." She tried a smile, but it felt as brittle as she did.

Michael was fast-walking toward them. Sam had barely turned his direction when his older brother wrapped him in a quick hug. He backed away but held Sam's shoulders, studying his face. "You all right? I heard you got jumped."

"I'm fine." Sam shrugged out of his grip and stepped back, straightening his jacket. "You remember Eliza?"

Michael squinted, frowned. He looked...hurt, though he masked it quickly. He was a little over six feet—about Sam's height. His hair was lighter than Sam's dark brown, maybe with some hints of red, though it was hard to tell under the glow of the bright parking lot lights. He had a day's worth of whiskers on his cheeks and wore jeans, a button-down open at the collar, and a sports coat. He aimed a tight smile at her. "Good to see you again. I hear you've had a rough couple of days."

"You could say that."

"Amnesia?"

"I'm starting to remember."

Michael was giving her a look she couldn't decipher. Like he was waiting for something, or...expecting something. But she couldn't figure out what.

"Thanks for doing this."

"Anything." To Sam, "Anything you need."

"Just the car. Sorry about the inconvenience. I wouldn't have called you."

And that remark brought a flinch from the older brother.

Eliza didn't blame him.

Michael looked beyond them, and she followed his gaze to where the Porsche approached. "I'm not complaining," he said. "I get to drive Colton's 911."

Grant parked the sports car and climbed out. The brothers greeted each other with a handshake and smiles. They seemed comfortable together, natural.

Not how Sam seemed with either of them. He opened the door to the Porsche and pulled his laptop bag from the floor of the backseat. He'd brought it that morning, just in case. One small favor.

Sam slammed the door and turned to Michael. "Be careful with the car. I'd rather not buy Colton a new one."

"Like I'm going to wreck it." To Eliza, Michael added, "But I will have some fun." He waggled his eyebrows, and she grinned.

"Where did you fly in from this morning?" she asked. Seemed a reasonable question.

"Europe. Work."

Vague, but she didn't push.

"We need to head inside and pick up a few things," Sam said, "since all our stuff's at the cabin."

"I'll find a safe house." Grant hugged Sam again, then squeezed Eliza's shoulders. "Try to stay out of trouble."

"Believe it or not, this is me trying."

He chuckled. "Scary thought."

Michael gave Sam a hug, then turned to her and opened his arms.

She barely knew the man but let him pull her close. When he did, he whispered in her ear. "I'm MC. Remember me." And then he let her go. "Be safe, you two."

Before she could respond or even think, Michael had climbed into the Porsche.

What in the world? Who was...?

Oh.

It was fuzzy, but the initials meant something. She wanted, needed to remember, but forcing memories didn't work. She let the question shift to the back of her mind.

After the guys left, she and Sam headed inside, where they split up to save time. She grabbed the cheapest pajamas she could find, a sweater for the next day, and undergarments. Sam caught up with her in the health and beauty section, where they grabbed necessities.

"Sorry there's so much. I'll pay you back when—"

"Just get what you need," he said. "Don't worry about it."

She couldn't keep up with Sam's moods. After he'd pulled her out of the trunk, he'd been tender. At the police station, he'd defended her. But before that, at the restaurant, his anger had shocked her. He'd been jealous.

Right now, he was abrupt.

But also generous, so she wouldn't complain.

Back in the car, Sam attached his phone to Bluetooth, and she studied the map that came up on the screen. "We're going to Boston?"

"Yup." He backed out and headed for the exit. "That okay?"

"It's just... I have a problem."

His gaze swung to her, amusement at the corner of his lips. "Just the one?"

"Ha-ha." But it wasn't really a laughing matter. "I need to get to Denver."

"I figured. That's why we're going to Boston. It's time for you to tell me what's going on." Maybe he heard his demanding tone, because he added, "Please."

That wasn't what he most wanted to talk about, but she wasn't ready to tell him about Levi. And this certainly wasn't the place.

But before they could get into any of that...

"I have no ID."

"Oh. Right. You've remembered a lot. Do you know what happened the night you showed up at my house?"

"Nope. Those last few days, maybe weeks, are still a blur. It's like I'm remembering from the past forward. The closer we get to the present, the murkier it feels."

MC—Michael—was still fuzzy.

How could she have had contact with Sam's brother? It didn't make sense.

"I've heard of people losing their wallets on vacation and explaining to the TSA agents what happened. They'll let you on."

"What if they have access to the information Jon got? He said there was no record of me anywhere in the last five years."

"Do you think they do have access to—?"

"I have no idea. Maybe, but I can't take the chance. I have to get there. Soon."

"What's the rush?"

"The sooner this is over, the sooner your family will be out of danger. And me and you."

"All right. You're right. I could ask Derrick to fly us."

"Didn't Grant say he was on a trip? Florida, right?" He'd made the comment offhandedly during lunch.

"Right. I forgot."

She hated to do this, especially considering they were in central New Hampshire, but... "My passport is at Mom's house."

Sam groaned. He said nothing for a stretched-out moment. Then... "We were almost killed there, Eliza."

"I know."

"If they're watching the house—"

"I don't know what else to do. I have to get to Denver. Even if I had a car—or a license—it would take days to drive to Colorado. My passport's still good, and I need an ID. You can drop me off at the end of the street, and I'll go myself."

"Right." The word dripped with sarcasm. "That's gonna happen." He was quiet for a moment, then, "At least Tweedledee and Tweedledum are in custody. It'll be nice to test out my fighting skills on fresh meat."

He was kidding. She knew that, but still...

This was a dangerous move.

He handed her his phone. "Put in your address."

She did and studied the map. An hour to York. Then another hour-plus to Boston. Add to that the time they'd spend at Mom's house. Best-case scenario, they'd get to the safe house around eight thirty.

Assuming they weren't killed or kidnapped between now and then.

"I have an idea," she said.

"Does it involve me driving to Vermont?" He was angling onto the interstate. "Maybe a pitstop in Montreal?"

"Are you always so grumpy?"

He flicked a gaze her way, a tiny smile on his lips. "Sorry. It's been a long day."

The understatement of the century. She hadn't slept well the night before, and she'd heard Sam awake a long time after she'd...what had he called it? Accosted him?

She didn't have mental energy for the shame that tried to consume her. At least now she remembered the truth. That she was forgiven. That God loved her anyway.

That thought wiggled a memory free. MC. She could hear his voice. He'd been all business on the phone, but she'd trusted him immediately. Now she knew why.

Michael sounded so much like Sam.

They'd messaged each other, and the messages had been more personal.

Romantic?

No. Not romantic. Spiritual. He was the one who'd told her about Christ. She could see the words on the page, words she'd heard over and over, all her life from her father and in church. But she'd never understood. She hadn't thought God would want her, but the way MC had talked about Him...

She'd been desperate enough, and lonely enough, to reach out to God. And God had reached right back.

MC had led her to the Lord. And...

There was more to it, and it wasn't related to the bullion business. At least, she didn't think it was.

"Why don't you ask Michael to meet us at Mom's?"

That earned another groan.

"He said he wanted to help, and he can't be that far in front of us. Unlike your other brothers, nobody knows where he is. Nobody's following him. You two can watch the doors, and I'll grab the passport. In and out in five minutes, maybe less. Assuming... Do you still have the key?"

"I mailed it to Mrs. Jensen Saturday afternoon. Figured she'd need it to check the house."

"Well, we'll have to figure out a way to get in, break a window if we have to." When Sam said nothing, she asked, "What's the deal with you and Michael? You've always been standoffish with him."

"We're just like that."

"But he wasn't standoffish. Only you."

"We're brothers." The undercurrent of his words—*don't push it.*

"Fine." She was sick of Sam's anger. "I have stuff too. Stuff you want to know, and I'm willing to tell you."

"Good. Let's hear it."

"You can answer this one question for me. Michael's the nearest to your age, isn't he? Seems you two should be close."

"Seriously?"

She said nothing, and after a few seconds, he blew out a breath. "It's stupid. I need to get over it."

"Over what?"

"Why do you care?"

She couldn't tell him the truth—that she needed to see Michael again, needed to find out how he was involved. Also, what they were about to do was dangerous. They could use his help. And Sam was so...cold to him. "He seems like a nice guy. He went way out of his way to help you—help us. I think you could have been nicer."

"Asking him to go to your house with me, that would be nice? 'Hey, bro, I know we're not close, but you wanna risk your neck for me?' That'll go over like a lead balloon."

"I bet he'd do it."

"He'd feel obligated."

"There's that word again. Love, obligation. They seem interchangeable to you."

"Who said anything about love?" He shot her a look, then barked a laugh. "You're a pain in the rear, you know that?"

She couldn't exactly argue that point.

"If I was rude to Michael, I'll apologize."

"Great."

Traffic slowed to a stop at the toll, and Sam gave her a long look. She held his gaze, not backing down. "Fine." He focused forward again. "When we were little, we were best friends. He never seemed to care that he was older or that he could do so much more than I could. We played ball. We rode bikes. We did everything together. When he turned thirteen, he started hanging out with a bunch of...cool kids, I guess.

"He brought his friends over one day. When I saw them shooting hoops, I put on my sneakers and ran out to play. Never occurred to me Michael wouldn't want me there." A few moments passed, and then, "His friends teased me. Called me names. Loser. Geek. Nothing awful but... Michael didn't...do anything. He just..."

"He didn't stick up for you." Eliza ached for the boy Sam had been—and the man still bearing those wounds. "Did he pick on you too? Or just stay silent?"

"Doesn't matter." That muscle ticked in his jaw. "I told you it was stupid. It was a million years ago."

"Still hurts, though, getting rejected." She could remember the horror in Sam's face the night before when he realized who was in his arms. Yeah, rejection was a knife to the heart. "You two never made up?"

"We're fine. We didn't talk about it or anything. Guys don't do that."

"No, guys sulk and carry grudges."

He glared at her, but he couldn't exactly argue.

"He was your best friend. What did you do after that? Start hanging out with...who's next in line? Grant?"

Sam shrugged. "Grant and I never had much in common. I used to ride my dirt bike. That was my thing, the only thing I could do that my brothers couldn't, not like *I* could, anyway."

Sam had shown her photos from those days—races and bumpy tracks with jumps and dips. Terrifying. "You were good, right?"

"Yeah. Won a lot of races. I planned to compete in the New England Motocross, but I wrecked my bike at another event, and my mom..." His lips pressed together in a sort of smirk-smile. "She saw the crash, and that was it. She put her foot down, and not even Dad could budge her."

Eliza couldn't imagine letting Levi do anything so dangerous. "I bet you were disappointed."

He shrugged like it didn't matter.

"Did Michael ever see you race?"

"Why would he have?"

"Um, because he's your brother?"

"He was busy with his friends."

Ah. So it wasn't just that one time. "You ever talk to him about it?"

"Right. I'm going to bring up a gripe from twenty years ago. How pathetic would that be?"

"No more pathetic than you continuing to punish him for it."

"I'm not—"

"What would it hurt to talk about it? Maybe you two could find resolution. You could get over your bitterness—"

"Thank you, Dr. Phil. Can we talk about your stuff now? Seems slightly more urgent."

"I'm just saying—"

"Eliza." A hint of pleading tinged the name.

"Sorry. Okay. But you should call him. See if he'll meet us. I don't want us to go to Mom's alone."

Sam tore his gaze from the road to glare at her. "You're getting on my nerves."

He'd made that crystal clear. "But I'm not wrong."

He grumbled. Then lifted his phone to unlock it. "Find his number. I'll call him. To keep you safe."

CHAPTER NINETEEN

SAM ENDED the call with his brother. As Eliza predicted, he was not only willing to help but seemed eager to.

"I'll get there first," Michael had said. "Stake it out. See if anybody's watching it."

Like he was some sort of super spy, but it seemed like a good idea. "Stay safe," Sam said. "And also...maybe think about how we can get in. We don't have a key."

"No problem," Michael said. "Call when you're close, and I'll meet you. No need to show the thugs what car you're driving."

Sam had no idea how they were going to hide the sedan—or the Porsche Michael was driving—but maybe Michael would figure it out by the time they got there.

"Feel better?" he asked Eliza.

"Strength in numbers. Hopefully, we can get in and out without any problems."

Only if their luck changed, and Sam wasn't counting on it.

And he needed to know what was going on. "Am I going to have to drag this story out of you?"

"Sorry. Just trying to figure out how to start. I know you

want me to tell you who Levi is, and I promise I will, soon. For now, I want you to know that he's not a boyfriend or a husband or anything like that."

"Oh." Sam tried not to let his relief show, but he could feel her watching him in the dark car. Not that he'd hidden his jealousy. Or had any plan to explain it away. "Okay."

"Some of it's still a little fuzzy, so bear with me. Five years ago, I had clients, a married couple. Jedediah and Lola Keller. He was a physician, and she was a psychologist. They had a good deal of money, and I talked them through their investment options. We'd only worked together a couple of months, but they were impressed with me and offered me a job in Utah, where they planned to open a home for troubled young women. I declined immediately. You and I were together, and I thought —hoped—we had a future."

He wasn't sure why she paused, but he nodded. Wanting her to keep going.

"That was a really hard winter. Selling Dad's business, losing my job, losing all Dad's friends and coworkers their jobs... It was like his death all over again. I'm sure that seems dumb to you—"

"It doesn't," he said. "I couldn't really understand what you were going through, but I work with a lot of grieving people in my job, people like you and your mom. I've learned that grief is...sneaky. You think it's gone, but it's just looking for a new way to attack."

"Interesting way to look at it. And insightful."

For all the good it'd done him with Eliza.

"Anyway," she said, "when I saw you with Kylee... It wasn't just that you were flirting. Or that you'd lied to me—which, I know you didn't. But from my perspective, that's what it looked like. Which made me question everything—your integrity, and your loyalty, and..."

"I get it. You made assumptions, which felt right at the time."

"My heart was broken."

"And you took the job the Kellers offered you, even though both your mom and Jeanette told you not to."

"Yeah."

"That wasn't like you."

"Let's just get through the facts. We'll come back to my reasoning later."

They seemed too closely linked to separate, but she was pressing on.

"The Kellers had already moved out there and bought the property. There was a house on it, and they let me live with them until my house—right next to theirs—was finished. They built a dorm, and a few months later, we welcomed the first women. Mostly girls, really. Late teens, early twenties. A couple of them were addicted to drugs. One was pregnant. I didn't know all of their issues, only that their families were willing to pay—no small amount—for the Kellers to help them learn how to manage their lives. It was rehab, in a sense, but not just from drugs. It was more like rehab from...from bad decisions. And trauma. All the women were in trouble in one way or another. And I guess, in a sense, they were all addicted. Drugs, alcohol, gambling, video games, pornography. Many were addicted to men and approval and love. Or what passes for love to those who don't know any better."

He knew the type, avoided the type, even back before he was walking with the Lord. Because those kinds of women were too easy to exploit, and he had enough to feel guilty about.

"More came over the years," Eliza continued. "A few had been abused—physically, sexually—some since childhood. They were angry, dangerously so. Or riddled with anxiety. Or depressed or despairing. The Kellers helped them."

"How?" Sam asked. "Did they develop some kind of a twelve-step program? Are they believers, or—?"

"No, not Christian. They didn't use the AA steps. Nothing like that. Lola counseled them. She and Jedediah provided plenty of places for the girls to work. Every year, they planted and harvested crops—vegetables and fruit. There were horses and cattle and chickens and goats, all of which needed to be cared for. It was a huge property covering acres of land, all surrounded by a security fence."

It sounded idyllic. He could see the draw for people trapped in chaos. When Sam's world felt out of control, he needed to get outside, take in fresh air, see the world. Something about the sheer size of the ocean, the grandeur of the mountains, reminded him how small he was. How big God was.

"Some women preferred woodworking or crafts," Eliza said, "focusing on things they could sell, like quilts or jewelry or benches or picnic tables. The goal was to teach them to work hard and make their own way, their own decisions. Good decisions."

"A lesson you needed to learn." Sam shouldn't have said that, but at least the words had been gentle, not accusatory.

She barked a humorless laugh. "True, but I wasn't in the program. I was an employee."

"And your job was...?"

"To manage the finances. And let me tell you, they were raking money in. The women came thinking they'd be there a month or two. But most stayed longer, some much longer. I'm talking years."

"Years? Who was paying for that?"

"Their families. The first three months were very expensive —tens of thousands of dollars. But then the price went down. After a year, it went down even more."

"So it was a good deal."

"I thought so at first, but the women were supposed to be learning how to live in the real world. Instead, a lot of them were hiding at The Ranch."

"Was that the name of it?"

"Keller Ranch, but we just called it The Ranch. Jed and Lola wanted me to keep my distance from the residents. Jed told me they were rough, not like me. So I spent most of my time with Jed and Lola and Miss Sharon—Lola's mother—who ran the office. Money was pouring in, much more than we needed to keep the place running. The Kellers were sort of...not as drastic as preppers, necessarily, but concerned about the economy failing. Which got us to talking about bullion."

"Ah. Which brings us to the conversation you had with Colton."

"Exactly. I remembered what Colton had told me about his job and suggested we start trading. They liked the idea and had a website designed, and suddenly, I was trading gold and silver online. I started small. I worked with suppliers and built relationships until I could sell a product, then buy it and have it drop-shipped to fill the order, taking the profit in the middle. That way there was little to no inventory to deal with."

Sam sent her a smile. "You're an impressive woman."

"We both know that's not true."

It was true, but Eliza had never seen herself the way he saw her.

"Money, financial matters," she said, "that I understand. I built a little empire, and I loved it. I felt competent and comfortable. And like a part of their family."

"You had a family, though. A mom, anyway."

"Yeah. A real family, as opposed to the Kellers. Their brand of family..."

The way her voice faded... They were finally getting to the meat of the story.

"It was all a lie," she said. "My mom was manipulative."

"Gosh, I never noticed."

She chuckled, but it died fast. "Compared to them, Mom was on the peewee team."

"Wow."

"And of course I fell for it."

"Don't do that, Eliza. You trusted them. It's not your fault they didn't deserve your trust."

"Hmm. Tell me how you feel in five minutes." She took a breath, blew it out. Plowed on. "About six months after I relocated, I decided to contact you. I *needed* to contact you."

He risked a glance, but Eliza's face was hard to make out in the dark car. "You didn't, though. Did you? Did I miss something?" The thought that she'd called and he'd missed it...

"They talked me out of it."

"Why?" Whoops. There was the demanding tone he'd been trying to hold at bay.

But Eliza continued as if she hadn't noticed. "They're the ones who printed those photos off social media. Jed told me you'd gotten married. That you'd moved on. That obviously, you never felt for me what I felt for you."

When Sam caught up with *Jed*, he was going to have to kill him.

But... "You believed him?" Sam tried to keep his tone even.

"I had no reason not to."

"You could have believed in me."

"But it was Kylee," she said, "and I'd seen you—"

"I loved you, Eliza. You really think I could marry another woman that soon? What kind of a man—?"

"But don't you see? From my perspective, you'd lied to me about having lunch with her. And it was the first time you'd gotten caught, but how did I know it was the first time you'd been out with her? Maybe you'd been seeing her for months. I believed a lot of things that weren't true. I can't blame the Kellers for most of it. I just...I always knew I wasn't good enough for you. I decided you wanted to break up with me. I mean, you'd been pulling away—"

"You were the one pulling away."

"So were you." She pressed on through his denial. "I remember now, the time after the New Year's Eve party. You claimed that you did everything you could to keep us together, but that's not true."

"What did you want me to do? You were the one planning to leave."

"After I learned about the layoffs, yeah. I was reeling. Questioning every decision I'd ever made. Not just you. Not just the sale of the business. Everything. But after I resigned and it was over... Mom and most of the employees blamed you. And the more they did, the more I realized the truth. You found a great buyer, and you warned Mom and me what could happen. You gave us all the information and let us make the decision."

"I did. I tried to make it clear what could happen." He hadn't thought it would, though. He was new to the business, and too trusting. He could see past people's lies now. See their motivations better. Sometimes see things they didn't know themselves. Lessons he'd learned the hard way.

"Mom and I took the deal because...well, it was a lot of money. A great price for what Dad had built. It felt like a way to honor him. And Mom was worried about how she was going to make ends meet. The money solved her problems. So we took the chance." She lifted her hands, palms up, and then let them drop in her lap. "It didn't work out."

"Not the way you wanted it to," Sam said. "But all those employees found other jobs. You and your mother split seven figures. It was a good deal."

"You're right. The point is, at the time, the more everyone

railed against you, the more I defended you. I knew, I *knew,* that you weren't to blame. Even so, things were different between us after that. It was like...like you were pulling away from me."

He flashed a look at her. "Eliza, *you* were pulling away from *me.*"

"I wasn't. That Easter, Mom was being her typical annoying self, and I was just trying to shut her up before you got back. When she said all that stuff about you, how you were a playboy, how you probably swindled us—"

"You agreed with her."

"No, I didn't. I didn't agree. I was saying, 'I know what you think, and I'm not having this argument again.'"

"I'm supposed to believe that."

"You could have asked me about it. You could have been honest with me."

"Why? So you could..." He clamped his lips closed.

"Reject you?" The words were soft and gentle. And ticked him off. "The point is," she said, "I felt you pulling away. I tried to talk to you about it. Do you remember? We were on the trails behind your old house. I asked you if there was something wrong? If you were upset with me about something. And you said no. You said everything was fine. But it wasn't fine."

Yeah, he remembered. "What was I supposed to say?"

"The truth, maybe?"

"The truth? Was that what you wanted? The truth was that you couldn't buy a pack of gum without getting someone's counsel. You were never looking for *my* advice, though."

"There was nobody I looked to more than you."

"Until the layoffs."

"That's not true. I asked—"

"You took that job in Portsmouth, and you didn't even tell me about it beforehand, much less ask me what I thought. But I'd put money on the fact that you asked your mother."

And...now she went quiet.

Because he was right, and she knew it.

So he pressed forward. "It was just a matter of time before your mother talked you into dumping me. You never could stand up to her for long."

"So you pulled away."

"What did you expect me to do?"

"Maybe not start dating other women."

"I didn't. I explained..." There was no point going over that again. "I should have talked to you about my worries. I should have been honest."

"And I shouldn't have left."

In the silence, the wheels rumbled down the highway, mile after mile. And there was no going back.

As much as he wanted to deny everything she'd said, he couldn't. In retrospect, he'd blamed everything on her, but she was right. He had been so afraid she was going to leave him that maybe, *probably,* he'd pulled away. Built his walls, as his father called it. Protected himself.

And in doing so, hurt her.

"Eliza."

"Yeah?"

"I'm sorry." Sorrier than he could ever express. Could all of this have been prevented by a simple conversation? The question burned like acid.

"Hey, Sam?"

"Yeah?"

"Me too."

"Okay, then." They needed to move on. "They told you I was married."

"I believed them because...well, because I'd always been jealous of Kylee."

He'd known that much.

"And I started thinking that maybe you'd been in love with her for a long time, and maybe you were only with me because you felt guilty about what happened at my company. And maybe you'd been biding your time until you could break up with me without looking like a total jerk."

"Why would you think those things?"

"Because you were too good for me. It was just a matter of time before you figured it out."

"That's your mother talking." He reached across the console and took her hand. "I hope, if nothing else, being apart has gotten her out of your head."

She didn't answer that. Which meant, probably not.

"Can I ask you a question?" She said nothing, but he saw her nod out of the corner of his eye. "Why didn't you check for yourself? Call me or look at my Instagram or Facebook?"

"I wasn't going to call you. I thought you were married. And we weren't allowed to get on social media."

"You weren't *allowed?*" He took his hand back. "What do you mean?"

"It's all so obvious in retrospect, Sam, but at the time, it made sense. Jed believed—and I think he's right—that half the women's problems were related to social media. It can be really damaging, so he banned all social media at The Ranch. And he monitored everything online. I didn't mind not being connected anymore. I felt at peace there. Like I'd left all my problems in Maine."

"Nice to know I was just some...problem you could walk away from." And there he went, right back to the bitter tone. "Sorry. I shouldn't—"

"I'm not defending myself. Just explaining."

He didn't like her explanation. In fact, he was getting angry all over again. Because maybe she'd quit letting her mother control her, but it sounded like she'd just found another master.

Oh, what did it matter? Wasn't he supposed to not care?

Just like that, he was back on the couch, Eliza in his arms. His mouth probing hers. His hands sliding across her silky pajamas. Pulling her closer. Wanting her with every cell in his body.

And outside the restaurant earlier, hearing Jon's question about Levi...and yeah. Sam had been furious. Furiously jealous. Ready to kill someone.

Not care? Right.

That lie wasn't flying anymore.

～

Hitting the drive-through in Manchester was partly about filling his empty stomach.

And partly about taking some time to pull himself together. He needed to hear the rest of her story, and he needed to keep his opinions to himself so she wouldn't clam up. Or edit her remarks to avoid his questions.

Okay, fine. His judgment.

He drove while they ate, chatting about nothing. She was taking her time with her burger, but he finished his. He wadded up the paper.

She took it and shoved it in the sack. "Nothing like a healthy dinner."

"At least you had a salad for lunch."

"That's right. You had a burger."

"But lunch was a thousand years ago, so it's fine." He took the exit onto the highway that led toward the coast. It was time to get back to her story. "You didn't contact me because you thought I'd gotten married. Then what happened?"

"I was heartbroken. I poured myself into...the things I had to do."

He heard evasiveness in the pause, then the hitch at the end of the sentence.

"About a year ago," she said, "Miss Sharon was out of town for a couple of days. As a rule, I wasn't supposed to answer the phone, even when she wasn't there. Jed told me to let it ring. But once, the same number called four times in a row, and I thought maybe it was an emergency. It was an irate mother who demanded that we let her daughter go—as if we'd been holding her prisoner. I explained that the residents were free to come and go as they pleased, but the lady was not listening. She threatened to call the police. I recognized her daughter's name and knew that she'd been with us for over a year. I told the mom I'd talk to her daughter, and if she wanted to leave, I'd walk her to the gate myself whenever the woman told us to be there. Turns out, the woman was at the gate and wanted her daughter brought right then."

"Were you supposed to do that?"

"It wasn't my job, but I was the only one around. It didn't occur to me that Jed and Lola would mind.

"I found the girl in the barn, mucking out a horse stall, and told her that her mother was there to pick her up. I told her that if she wanted to stay, she had to tell her mother the truth. She needed to learn to stand up for herself."

Sam didn't miss the way Eliza's glance cut to him at those words.

"She told me she wanted to leave, but... Oh, Sam, she looked terrified. At first, I thought she was afraid of her mother, and I could relate. But she was looking all around. She asked me where Jed was. I'd seen him out in the field, which was on the far side of the property. She didn't tell anybody goodbye, didn't stop to get her things. She just ran, flat out, to the gate. She'd climbed it and jumped down the other side before I reached the keypad to open it up. Her mother squealed away so fast that I barely got a look at the car."

Sam imagined the scene. "So she *escaped*?"

"That's what it looked like, but it didn't make sense. I mean, their families were paying us to keep them. Why would she need to escape? I got nervous, thinking I'd done something wrong. Maybe her mother wasn't trustworthy. Or maybe the woman on the phone hadn't been her mother at all. Maybe I'd been duped."

"Even so," Sam said, "she was an adult. She could go wherever she wanted, right?"

"Exactly. When I told Jed what happened..."

The long pause had Sam trying to read her expression. Not a good idea while he was driving.

"He wasn't happy," she finally said. "He tried to hide it, but... He said, 'Next time, come get me, okay? Let me handle it.'"

"By *handle* it, he meant *prevent* it."

"Yeah. From then on, I kept my eyes open. I started digging into the files. I looked at the women's applications. They were selective about who they let in. Jed said they'd only take women they were sure they could help. But the applications told me the criteria was based on one thing. Every young woman who checked the *needs financial aid* box got denied. But the women whose families could pay got in."

Okay, so they were greedy. But still... "I don't understand. Could the women not contact their families?"

"They could. They had access to phones at certain times."

"Then, if they wanted to leave, why didn't they just say so? And if they said so, why would the families keep paying?"

"That confused me too. As far as I could tell, all the women were there voluntarily, and all their parents were happy to pay for them to stay until they were"—she lifted her fingers for air quotes—"recovered. Obviously, I was missing something. I started hanging out with the girls, trying to figure out what was really going on. That's how I met Nicole. She's in her twenties, a big fan of Jed. She thinks his tactics are brilliant. She got me a copy of the curriculum Jed wrote, which I read. I listened to his teaching. But I saw it very differently than Nicole. He wasn't trying to make the women free and independent. He was manipulating them to make them dependent. It was like a...a—"

"A cult." His stomach cramped. And not because of the burger and fries.

Cults were dangerous, sometimes deadly. And Eliza had been in one.

No, not *in* one. Financially managing one. Which was...

Too disturbing to wrap his mind around.

"I don't like that word." She sighed. "But...yeah. I guess so. I mean, most of the girls loved him. No, they *worshipped* him. And he ate it up and wanted more.

"I would slip into gatherings and watch. It was masterful and horrifying the way he drew them in, acted like he was encouraging them but actually making them feel small and insignificant. It made me sick."

She was quiet a long moment. Sam wished he weren't driving so he could read her facial expressions.

"A lot of the women were pregnant." She blurted that like it was the worst news so far.

"You already told me that, that some were pregnant when they got there."

"I counted four in a group of fifty once. Four who were showing. But they weren't new to the community. They'd been there more than nine months."

"Whoa. What are you saying?"

"There weren't that many men around. Gilbert and Elliot, but they weren't allowed anywhere near the women. And it wasn't like they were handsome or even nice. Maybe Elliot could've seduced one of them, but four? No, I never thought they were the fathers. Which meant..." The long pause had him guessing, but he kept his lips clamped shut. "It was Jed," she finally said. "He was sleeping with them, fathering children with them. They built this huge nursery for kids early on, much bigger than I ever thought they'd need. But it was filling...with Jed's children."

"And you didn't realize any of that? For years?" How could she have missed so much?

"I always thought money was my superpower," she said. "Turns out, my gift is overlooking the obvious."

He reached across the console and took her hand. "Sorry. I don't mean to... I'm sure you were busy."

"I was. And until last year, I didn't pay attention. I did my job and figured they were doing theirs."

"Did the wife know what was going on?"

"I don't know. Lola was my closest friend there. My confidant. She helped me understand so many things about myself, about my relationship with my mother. I never sought out the young women because I had her. But she worships Jed. The way she talks about him... I used to think it was sweet. My mother was so demanding with my father, and he just did what she wanted. But Jed and Lola seemed to have a great marriage. There's a scripture that says women should respect their husbands, and she was a good example of that."

Eliza knew Bible verses? Interesting. They'd need to come back to that. "There's also a verse that says men should love their wives like Christ loves the church. Not sure ol' Jed was living up to that."

"Right. Maybe Lola knows about the women, maybe not. Either way, I don't think she has the courage to stand up to him."

"This woman's a psychiatrist?"

"Psychologist."

"Close enough. She should have known better. Did you notify the authorities?"

"We'd had investigators—even FBI—poking around more than once. They'd gotten tips that the place wasn't what it purported to be. But it never led to anything. Jed was good at deceiving people, starting with the women. They said what they had to say to protect him. The ones who hadn't drunk the Kool-Aid were conveniently absent when anyone came around asking questions. I needed hard evidence."

"No, you didn't!" The flash of anger surprised him, and he tempered his voice. "You needed to leave. Get somewhere safe. You could have told the authorities what you knew. It wasn't your job to...to take them down."

"You think I should have just abandoned those women?"

"Yes."

"Would you have done that?"

"It's different."

"Why, because you're a man and I'm a woman?"

"No. Because..." Because Eliza was vulnerable. And the thought of her putting herself in danger made him physically ill.

There was a protracted silence. Her voice was calm when she spoke again. "I did what I did. Do you want to hear about it or not?"

His hands were aching from squeezing the steering wheel so hard. Noticing his elevated speed, he eased his foot off the gas and set the cruise control. He took a breath and grounded himself in the surroundings. Still dark out there, nothing but trees on both sides of the highway now that they were well past Manchester. They passed a sign for a town called Nutfield. Sounded like a peaceful place. He doubted anything dangerous ever happened in Nutfield.

A glance her way told him she was waiting for him to answer her question.

Fine. She was here. She'd survived—so far. "Sorry. You're right. Go on."

"Jed only used paper records. Whenever the office was empty—which wasn't often—I scanned them and uploaded them to a private server. It took months to get them all."

"I thought you said Jed monitored your online activity."

"He did. But he trusted me with our bullion storefront. I told him I needed a safe space for financials and opened an encrypted account. I gave him the password and put a bunch of business-related stuff in there. I figured he'd glance at it a few times to be sure, but then he'd leave it be. After a few weeks, I just...changed the password. When he never asked me about it, I started putting the documents there. All the files, the applications, the financial records, and the medical records—which showed the births, of course."

"The babies were delivered on-site?"

"Jed's a physician. My friend Nicole is an RN, so she assisted. They were lucky there were no complications with the babies or the mothers. I got all those records uploaded and then backed them up onto a different cloud server—one of those automatic backup systems that stores your files in case your computer crashes."

"Oh. Smart."

He caught her quick smile.

"That's what the email address and password are for."

"The ones we found in your shirt? I'm glad you remembered."

"Me too. Then I put the boring business stuff back in that folder, in case Jed looked. He'd find nothing that hinted I was working against him."

"Diabolical."

"I needed to tread carefully. Not only was he getting the worship of all these women, which I think he felt he deserved, but he'd amassed millions—much of that because of what I'd done with the bullion business. He had every reason in the world to make sure I never told anybody what was going on. He didn't suspect anything, at first."

It was those two words that had his blood pressure rising again. *At first.*

"Then he started seeing me with Nicole and the other women. He asked me about it, acting as if he was worried about me. I told him I was just curious, like I was impressed with his results. But I've never been much of an actor. That's when he had Gil and Elliot start watching me, my security." She air-quoted that word. "Jed suggested I eat dinner with him and Lola every night, even asked me to cook a few nights a week at their place. He wanted to keep an eye on me. I didn't have the nerve to refuse. Gil would stand in the corner and stare, arms crossed, a glower on his face. Jed could make nice all he wanted, but Gil made sure I knew I wasn't safe."

That explained a few of her memories—and reminded him of that first breakfast together. "Food was scarce?"

"We were all given an allotment."

"Not enough, obviously."

"It was fine until Gil decided to help himself to my stores. I had the feeling if I reported him..."

She didn't finish the statement, but Sam got the gist.

"Were Gil and Elliot the ones who caught up with you Friday night?" Sam pressed. "Who gave you those bruises?"

"I don't know. I don't remember...a lot. What I'm telling you happened months ago. After Jed got suspicious, he had Gil and Elliot remove the copy machine from the office, claiming it was broken. But I had the evidence I needed at that point. I just had to figure out how to get out."

"They wouldn't let you leave?"

"Technically, I could leave the property whenever I wanted to. I'd borrowed cars to run errands many times. But I didn't own a car. I could have bought one, but—"

"That would have raised their suspicion," he guessed.

"Exactly. The day I ran into you in Salt Lake—"

"I knew you were in trouble." He slammed a hand on the steering wheel. He could still see the fear in her eyes. "I should have grabbed you and gotten you out of there."

"I wouldn't have gone with you." Her words were quiet.

"Why? You just said—"

"There was nothing, nothing I wanted more than to..." Her voice faded. "Anyway, that day, I'd just left the hospital and—"

"For what? Were you hurt?"

"Everything's fine. I had hoped to drive myself, but when I asked to use a car, Jed had Gil and Elliot drive me."

"But they weren't there when you came outside. You said they were circling the block. We could have disappeared."

"There were things I needed. I couldn't leave yet."

"What things? What could have been more important than getting away?"

"Evidence."

"You said—"

"There was more than what I put in that file, stuff I hadn't known about before. I learned later that not all of Jed's women had been willing participants."

"He was raping them?" This just got better and better.

"Or...manipulating them, but not all of them were happy to be having his children. He wouldn't let them leave once he got them pregnant."

"How'd you figure that out?"

"Some of it is speculation, I admit. But the files told me a lot. The girl I helped escape? Her family had quit paying months before she left. Jed was amassing followers. I think he bled them for everything they had, then just...kept them. I overheard one of the girls saying how glad she was that Jed had convinced her to stay, how lucky she was that he'd chosen her."

Lucky. Right.

"There was a hidden drawer in his office desk," Eliza said. "I walked in once when he was sliding something into it. The way he jumped—like I'd caught him in the act—had me wondering. He slammed it shut and locked it. It took me weeks to get access when nobody was looking and pick the lock to see what was inside."

He imagined her in there, looking over her shoulder, worried about getting caught. What would have happened if she had been? He reached across the space and took her hand again, needing the connection. A reminder that she was safe. "What was it?"

"DNA tests. Proof that he was the father of twenty-two babies."

Twenty-two.

Sam couldn't comprehend the mind of a man who'd do such a thing.

"That's how he was keeping the women there," Eliza said, "even those who wanted to leave. He told them they could leave, but the babies were his."

Sam wasn't proud of the words that came to mind.

"I had to get those records, Sam. I couldn't copy them. I had no camera or smart phone to take pictures of them, and the copy machine was gone. I couldn't leave without them."

"That's why you didn't come with me." He caught her nod out of the corner of his eye. "Is that what's in Denver?"

"I assume so."

"How'd you get away?"

"I don't...know." That pause in the middle...

"Do you remember something?"

"Yeah. Someone helped me. Someone from the outside." She rubbed her temples.

"Don't push it." No need to give herself a headache.

The GPS spoke. They'd crossed into Maine and were almost to the exit.

"Why not take the information straight to the authorities?" He hit his blinker, moved into the right lane to exit. "Did you come to Maine to see your mother?"

But if she had, how had she ended up miles away from York in Shadow Cove?

"You need to call Michael and tell him we're close."

He wanted her to finish her story. He wanted to know everything.

But if he guessed right, she wasn't sorry they'd arrived. Whatever else she had to say, she didn't seem eager to tell him.

He'd get the rest of the story after they got her passport. Hopefully, they wouldn't meet any of Keller's thugs along the way.

CHAPTER TWENTY

ELIZA FELT LIGHTER.

She'd told Sam the story—most of it, anyway—and he was still with her. Maybe not impressed, but then neither was she. How many poor decisions had she made to get herself into this mess?

She'd thought she was so strong when she ignored Mom and Jeanette's advice. Going her own way, making her own decisions. She'd never been good at that, but she'd been trying.

Stupidly, because she'd ignored two people who loved her and had chosen to listen to—and put her faith in—two people who'd only ever wanted to use her.

She'd given them decision-making power over her life.

But she'd taken it back. One photocopy, one hidden file at a time.

Sam parked around the side of the restaurant where Michael said he'd meet them. "Not sure why Michael thinks this car will be more conspicuous than a bright red Porsche."

"He sounded like he had a plan."

"Yeah. Weird."

"What does he do for a living again?"

"He sells machine parts to factories, mostly overseas." Sam climbed out, and she did the same as a car pulled up. Not the Porsche but a dark-colored sedan. Michael rolled down his window. "Hop in."

She appreciated the legroom in the backseat. "Hey."

He turned toward her, eyes squinted.

She nodded, then shrugged. Trying to tell him she remembered a little. Why they were keeping this from Sam, she didn't know, but she was certain that MC—Michael—had helped her, so she'd follow his lead.

Sam settled in the front seat. "Thanks for doing this."

"Glad you asked."

"Whose car?"

"Belongs to a friend. Colton met me at his house."

Michael drove toward Mom's house but parked on the street parallel to it. "There's a path."

She gazed at the house. "My friend used to live here. We went back and forth a lot."

Michael's only response was a quick nod. "I've been watching your house. No sign of bad guys, but that doesn't mean they're not here. We go in the back."

"We don't have a key," Sam said. "How are we going to get in."

"Don't worry about it. Sam, you and I will keep watch while Eliza retrieves the passport. We keep it dark." He handed them both flashlights. "In and out fast. Got it?"

Sam was looking at his brother, grinning. "Yes, sir, Inspector Gadget, sir."

Michael didn't smile. "You were almost murdered here, right?"

Sam's expression dimmed. "Just never seen you so—"

"Let's go." Michael pushed open the door and climbed out.

They did the same, then crept between the houses and into the woods, lighting the narrow path with the small flashlights.

It was surreal, being back here. She had no idea what she'd done a week before, but this path felt familiar, smelling of mud and dead leaves. Had it always been so dark at night? When she was a kid, she and her friend would run back and forth at all hours. She'd never been afraid before. Tonight, though, the air crackled with danger.

Sam held a skinny, leafless branch out of the way. "Go ahead. I don't want it to hit you."

She ducked under it as she passed, but he moved into the lead again. Michael was bringing up the rear, both of them acting like guards.

They crossed the backyard. The grass was overgrown—very un-Mom-like. But then, Mom wasn't here.

Where was she?

Eliza really needed to remember that, soon. Because when she found Mom, she'd find Levi.

Wouldn't she?

Please, God. Please let them both be safe.

She couldn't think about that or she'd fall apart.

One thing at a time.

Sam stopped at the bottom of the steps that led to the back door. "Should we break a window?"

Michael held something out. "Put these on."

She took what he offered. Gloves? "Why? This is my mother's house."

Sam said, "You always carry plastic gloves with you?"

"I'd prefer not to get arrested. Or questioned. Humor me."

They donned the thin, clear gloves. Then Michael crouched in front of the door and picked the lock.

As if it was something he did on a regular basis. As if it made perfect sense that he carried a lock-picking kit.

There was definitely more to Michael's story.

A few seconds later, he stood and pulled a handgun from a holster.

Sam took his out too.

The sight had her pulse racing.

Michael twisted the knob and pushed the door open. He turned, put a finger over his lips, and stepped inside.

Eliza followed but froze in the space between the back door and the basement door. And gasped.

The table by the back window had been knocked over. Four potted plants lay on their sides, pots broken, dirt and leaves and flowers scattered across the floor in the breakfast nook.

She swung her flashlight to the kitchen. Plates, silverware, glasses—everywhere. Shards of glass. Knives.

Mom's things. All the things Eliza had grown up with. The things that had made this house a home. Destroyed.

The rancid scent of rotting food had her wanting to step back.

"I don't under—"

A hand slid over her mouth. Not hard, but it silenced her.

"Just in case," Sam whispered. "Quiet."

She nodded, and he let her go.

"Stay here." Michael raised his gun—like they do on TV shows—and moved through the kitchen, into the dining room and then out of sight.

She and Sam stood silently. She barely dared to breathe.

Aside from the familiar creak of a step, Michael made no noise. A minute—maybe two—passed before he returned. "It's clear. They tossed the whole house. Find your passport as fast as you can."

Sam gripped her arm and walked her through the house to the stairs. "Go ahead. I'll be right here, watching the street."

She didn't want to go up alone, not in the dark, creepy space that had once been her home.

But she did. At least the stairs were clear of debris, as was the hallway. But her bedroom was wrecked.

How was she ever going to find it?

Her passport had been in a box, which she'd stored on the upper shelf in her closet before she'd moved to Utah. She shined the light that way, but the box wasn't there. She moved the flashlight beam through the room. Her mattress was bare, cut to shreds. Old stuffed animals, torn apart. Toys broken, a jewelry box on its side, surrounded by cheap trinkets. Makeup she hadn't worn since junior high crushed into the carpet.

"Hey."

She jumped.

"Sorry," Sam said. "I thought you heard me coming. Michael's keeping an eye out. He told me to come help you. Any idea where to start?"

"Look for a shoebox."

He did in one direction, so she searched the other.

"Is that it?" he asked.

She saw the bright red box at the end of her bed and crouched beside it. Empty, but maybe... She picked through the things nearby and... "Got it." She shoved the passport in her jacket pocket and zipped it up.

"Let's go."

At the bottom of the stairs, the rancid scent she'd picked up when she'd first walked in hit her, stronger than before. "What is that?" She covered her mouth and nose and crunched through the space to where Michael was looking down the stairs into the basement. When he saw her, he started to close the door.

She grabbed the edge. "What?"

Michael spoke to Sam behind her. "We should go."

"No," she said. "What's wrong? What's down there?"

"I'll tell you in the car." Again, he tried to tug the door out of her hand, but she held on and swung around.

Aimed her flashlight down the stairs. The beam landed on...

A woman.

A crumpled body.

Eyes open and lifeless.

She gasped. No! "Mom!" She started down, but arms grabbed her around the waist.

The basement light flicked on.

"It's not her," Sam said. "It's the neighbor. It's the neighbor, Eliza."

Gray hair. Wrinkles. Not Mom. *Not Mom.*

Michael uttered a curse. He'd moved to the front of the house, but now he was running toward them. "They're coming! Get her out of here."

Sam pulled Eliza out the back door. She tried to run, stumbled. Dropped the flashlight.

He dragged her into the woods. "Come on, Eliza. Run."

She was trying. She just couldn't see through the tears. Couldn't see anything but Mrs. Jensen's body lying on the basement floor.

"Faster." The voice came from behind. "Or carry her."

Suddenly, she was swept up in Sam's strong arms. "Tuck in." He held her against his chest and bolted through the forest.

She tried to be as small as she could, but trees and limbs still grabbed her feet, pulled her hair. Seconds later, they made it through the woods and past the house to the car.

Sam opened the back door and climbed in, her on his lap.

Michael got in the driver's seat, started the engine, and hit the gas. The force of it slammed the door shut.

Behind them, two men bolted from the woods onto the street and watched as they drove away.

CHAPTER TWENTY-ONE

THEY SHOULD BE WEARING SEATBELTS, especially considering the way Michael zoomed out of the neighborhood, whipping around corners and flooring it on short straightaways. He seemed to know what he was doing.

And Sam wasn't ready to let Eliza go.

She sat sideways on the seat, her legs draped over his lap, and gripped his sweatshirt in her fists, crying into his chest.

He held her close, rubbed her back, whispered in her ear. "It's okay. We're safe."

They were. By the grace of God. And Michael.

No way Sam could have gotten them out of there without help.

Michael hit the main drag, crossed to the opposite side, and pulled into the lot where they'd met, then parked around the back. "Let's go."

Sam opened the door and helped Eliza out, but she didn't go to the rental car. Instead, she stumbled a few steps and threw up in the bushes at the edge of the lot.

He stood behind her, rubbing her back and knowing exactly how she felt. Mrs. Jensen, that poor woman. Had she been there when the thugs came? Or had she let herself in, thinking Linda was home? Or had she thought she could thwart a burglary?

They might never know. She'd paid the price for being neighborly.

The people after Eliza were willing to kill to get what they wanted. The thought had Sam wanting to expel his own dinner.

"We need to go," Michael said.

Sam nodded to indicate he'd heard, then leaned down to whisper to Eliza, "You all right?"

Her head shook, but she straightened. He pulled her against his side and turned her toward the waiting sedan.

Michael was on the phone, standing by the trunk with his suitcase. Only then did Sam register what he'd said. "We?"

He held up a *just-a-second* finger and spoke into the phone. "A suite or adjoining rooms. Text me the details." He ended the call and held out his hand, palm up. "I'm driving. I got us a place."

It'd been...two minutes, maybe. How had he already done that? And anyway... "Grant got us a safe house. We can get there ourselves."

"The hotel is close to the airport. And not connected with anybody you know."

"Michael, you've done enough." Way more than Sam would have asked or expected. "Don't you have to work?"

Michael turned his gaze to Eliza. He said nothing, just looked at her, waiting.

"He should come with us." She looked up at Sam, eyes watery, skin pale as death. "He can help."

Sam wished he could argue that he didn't need his brother's help, but he hated to think what would have happened at Eliza's mom's house if he hadn't been there. "Okay. Thanks."

He settled Eliza in the backseat and then climbed in beside her. As long as Michael was willing to drive, Sam would cuddle with Eliza. She seemed to crave the connection as much as he did.

"I need a bathroom," she said.

"Okay." But Michael drove ten miles down the road before he exited the highway. They passed a couple of fast-food restaurants that would work, but Michael drove another mile before stopping at a gas station. "I'll watch the door. Make it quick."

Sam didn't love taking orders from his brother. He really didn't love that his brother knew exactly what to do. "You need anything?"

"Sparkling water," Michael said. "Something citrus, if they have it."

Sam walked Eliza to the ladies' room. "Wait inside until I knock, okay?"

She nodded and disappeared into the single-stall restroom, and the lock clicked.

He stepped into the men's room and splashed his face, then stared at his reflection. He took a deep breath, blew it out, and tried to rein in his emotions. They were ping-ponging.

Eliza could have been killed.

Mrs. Jensen had been, and he didn't think he'd ever get over the sight of her at the bottom of the stairs. The stench.

He hadn't vomited, but he could have. Easily. Yet Michael...

What the heck? He was acting like a pro. Like he picked locks, drove evasively, and saw dead bodies all the time.

Thank God Eliza had insisted they call him. And now she wanted him to stay close. Sam couldn't blame her for not counting on him to keep her safe, considering what could have happened tonight if not for Michael.

He went into the store, grabbed a LaCroix for his brother and a Coke for himself. Then, he knocked on the ladies' room door.

When she opened it, some of her color had returned.

"You all right?"

A quick nod. "Can I get some gum?"

"Anything you need, sweetheart."

A tiny smile graced her lips, gone in a moment. But it was there. Maybe she trusted Michael to protect her, but she *loved* Sam. She might not have said so, but he knew.

And God help him, he loved her. He'd never stopped, no matter the lies he'd told himself. Thinking of what could have happened to her today—on the street in North Conway and just now at her mother's house...

He couldn't lose her again. If that meant putting up with Michael, so be it.

Whatever it took to keep her safe.

After Michael checked them into connecting rooms at the airport Hilton, he disappeared into the bathroom of the smaller room with the two queen beds, leaving Sam in the attached sitting area of the king suite.

He called his client, who answered the phone with, "I'm not paying you to ignore me all day." Ernest Topp's voice was louder and stronger than Sam had ever heard from the eighty-something businessman. "If I wanted crappy service, I'd have gone with your competitor."

"I'm sorry for the delay getting back to you," Sam said. "It couldn't be helped."

"Why? What's so dad gum important you blew me off all day?"

Probably not the best idea to tell him he'd been trapped in a police interrogation room when he'd first called. "Like I said in my text, I had a family emergency."

"Thought you were a bachelor. That was your whole spiel, that you didn't have a family to distract you."

Yeah. That'd been Sam's life—and lie. "How can I help?"

He listened to Ernest rail against his business's potential buyers for ten minutes, asking questions to discover the true problem. As angry as the client was, it seemed his issue was pretty small, related not so much to the price the buyers had offered but the timeline.

"All right, I hear you," Sam said. "I'll contact them and straighten it out." The client was still miffed, but Sam managed to talk him down. For now.

He didn't want to lose this deal. But if he had to choose between money and Eliza, she'd win every time.

She returned from the bathroom, where she'd changed into cotton pajamas.

He patted the cushion beside him but spoke into the phone. "I'll get back to you tomorrow."

"You'd better," the man huffed.

He ended the call. Biggest deal of his life, and he was going to blow it if he didn't pay attention.

He kissed her on the forehead after she sat beside him. "One more minute," he said, and typed an email to the buyers, outlining Ernest's objections to their latest offer. He sent it, then tossed his phone on the coffee table. "Sorry about that."

"It's fine. You have to work."

He pulled her against his chest, where she cuddled as if she belonged. She did, and unlike him, she hadn't forgotten that.

He inhaled her fresh scent and tried to push aside the memories of the night. "Good idea, calling my brother."

"Mmm."

She'd hardly spoken on the ride to the city.

"I'm sorry about your neighbor."

"We should call the police." She looked up at him with red-rimmed eyes. "We can't just leave her there."

"Michael said he'd take care of it."

Michael seemed able to take care of a lot of things for a guy who claimed to be a salesman.

He had secrets, but he'd done nothing but help them. He'd do right by her neighbor.

"Her husband died when I was in college. They lived in that house as long as I can remember. Her kids..." Eliza's voice hitched. "What a horrible way to lose someone you love."

"Yeah." He rubbed her shoulders. "It's incredibly selfish to say, but thank God it wasn't you."

"Or my mom. But the house..."

"Can be replaced," Sam said. "And so can everything in it."

"I know. You're right. I just hate that I brought that on Mom. And Mrs. Jensen."

"It wasn't your fault." He held her close even as she tried to push away. "It wasn't, Eliza."

"Of course it was. Of course it was my fault."

She seemed to have cried all the tears she had for the day. Her voice was emotionless.

"You didn't do that to your house, sweetheart. You didn't kill Mrs. Jensen."

"They were there because of me."

"That doesn't make it your fault." He brushed his hands down her hair. He liked it long, liked the silky feeling between his fingers. So many things had changed between them, but she still fit perfectly in his arms.

"Did I ever tell you why we moved to Maine?"

The change of subject surprised him. "I don't think so."

"Back in Arkansas, we lived in the house Mom grew up in. Her parents left it to her when they died. Her closest friend since childhood lived next door. Miss Marianne. She was so funny and so kind. She could make Mom laugh until she cried. Mom was happy back then."

Sam couldn't imagine that. He didn't think he'd ever seen a genuine smile on Linda Pelletier's face.

"Marianne had a daughter who was my age. Kristen. We were best friends.

"When we were eight, we were playing in the woods at the edge of the property. We went farther than we usually did, all the way to the little creek. It was at the bottom of a steep hill, maybe ten, fifteen feet down."

"A long way for a little girl."

"Seemed like it. It was summer, hot and humid. The crickets were chirping, the tree frogs singing. Kristen started to climb down, but I stopped her. We weren't supposed to play down there."

"Why?"

Eliza's shoulder lifted and fell against his chest. "Mom said it was dangerous. But I'd gone down the path with Dad, and I hadn't seen anything dangerous. I figured Mom probably thought I'd drown. But Kristen and I had been taking swim lessons for years, and the creek was so shallow we could see the bottom. And I wanted to show Kristen the creek. I wanted to put my toes in the water and cool off. So I ignored Mom's warnings."

Sam could imagine the scene. Two little girls climbing down. Maybe it was the events of the day, or maybe the thought of the steep descent, but his chest tightened.

"We caught frogs, big fat slimy things that squished out of our fingers. We laughed and splashed each other. I knew that when I got home, Mom was going to kill me, but I was having too much fun to care. I was hopping from rock to rock, ruining my new shoes. And then Kristen screamed."

Yup. He'd known something was coming.

"She was on the shore, holding onto her ankle. That's when I saw the snake slithering away."

Oh, no.

Snakes could do damage. There were no venomous snakes in Maine, at least none so toxic they'd harm a human, but in Arkansas?

"Dad had told me all about rattlers and vipers. I didn't know what kind of snake it was. I stood there, shocked, for way too long. I should have started running immediately, but...I was scared."

"You were eight," he said. "A child."

She pushed up from his chest but didn't turn toward him, just stared at the wall. "Finally, I told Kristen to stay there—as if she could climb out—and ran to get help."

And there was an image, a little girl, brown hair flying behind her as she scrambled up the steep slope and ran to her mother. They'd gone far, she'd said. How long did that run take?

"As soon as I got close enough, I started yelling. Mom came out of the house, and I told her what happened. I was so emotional that it took Mom a few seconds to figure out what I was saying. More time lost.

"Mom called an ambulance and told me to get Miss Marianne. And then she took off running across the yard and into the woods."

Eliza brushed away the tears dripping down her cheeks.

He pulled his handkerchief from his back pocket, still damp from her last crying jag, and handed it to her.

"I told Kristen's mother what happened, and we ran to the creek." Eliza's voice was shaking now. "All the way, I was thinking we'd run into Mom carrying Kristen back. Because of course Mom could fix it. But we didn't.

"Miss Marianne got there before me. She scrambled down the slope. And started screaming and screaming."

Eliza covered her ears as if she could hear the sound even now.

He pulled her against his chest again, and she buried her head in his sweatshirt.

"She was dead." Eliza barely moved as she said the words. "Mom was doing CPR, but it was too late."

"What kind of a snake bite kills that fast?"

"It was a timber rattlesnake. Most people survive if they get the antidote in time, but Kristen had an allergic reaction."

"I'm so sorry. I can't imagine."

"It was awful. Kristen's mother never forgave me or Mom."

"It wasn't your—"

"Mom lost her best friend. And so did I." Eliza continued as if she hadn't heard him. "We moved away. Dad said the move had nothing to do with Kristen's death, but I know better. We left Arkansas, sold the house Mom had loved so much, because of me. Because of my defiance."

"No, sweetheart." He squeezed her against him, wanting to shield her from all this heartbreak. "It wasn't your fault."

"If we hadn't gone to the creek, if I hadn't—"

"You were a child."

"My best friend died and our family lost our home because I defied my mother. I learned the hard way to follow the rules. Every time I didn't..." She pushed away and met his eyes. "Every time, Sam, I get burned. Or somebody I love gets hurt."

"Your mother told you that." Knowing where those words came from, he couldn't help the hum of anger in his voice.

"She lost everything that day."

"No, she didn't." He brushed hair away from Eliza's face and rested his palm on her cheek. "She still had your father. She still had you. She had her health. But if I know her, she's used that childish mistake to manipulate you ever since."

Eliza stood and walked to the window. She peeked behind

the curtains, not that there was anything to see but airport traffic and runway lights. "That's not fair." But her words held no conviction.

"It's true, and you know it. She should have assured you that it wasn't your fault. That sometimes, bad things happen and they can't be blamed on anyone, certainly not an eight-year-old girl." He needed to keep the anger out of his voice. Knowing the source of Linda's power over Eliza only made him dislike the woman more. "I bet she never let you forget."

"As if I could have." But Eliza sighed, turning to face him again. "But you're not wrong. When I was young, if I disobeyed... Even now, I can hear her voice in my head. 'You'd better be careful, Eliza. You don't want anyone to get hurt.' It was always a reminder here, a jab there."

"That explains your fear of making decisions. The way you so often bow to her wishes and rely on the counsel of others." Like friends. Cult leaders...

"Yeah."

"Thank you for telling me." He stood and joined her, placing his hands on her hips. He lowered his forehead to rest against hers. "I'm sorry for what happened to you. Thank you for trusting me with it."

She gazed up, eyes red from emotion. What he saw wasn't sadness but hope.

"Can I tell you the truth?" he asked.

Worry crossed her features, so he pulled her close, wanting to reassure her. When she was nestled against his chest, he said what he was thinking. "It doesn't make me like your mother any more."

She didn't pull away. The sound she made was more humorless laugh than anything. "You would have loved my father, though." She leaned back, and her smile lifted her face. "He was a good man."

"I believe that." He took her hand and urged her back to the sofa.

Eliza nestled against his side again. "He told me a million times that Kristen's death wasn't my fault. And Mom's tactics, so effective when I was young, became obvious to me over the years. I recognized the manipulation. Dad encouraged me to make my own decisions, even if they were opposed to what she said. Even if they were mistakes. That's why he wanted me to work for him. He taught me to run things, to learn to make decisions and live with them, and realize wrong ones wouldn't kill me—or anybody else."

He sounded like a good man, a lot like Sam's father. "I wish I'd met him."

"When he died, I was shocked to find that he'd left the business to me. He said in his will that he trusted me to take care of Mom. But all that responsibility... It was the grief, and the weight of all those people depending on me, that had me backsliding. Leaning on Mom again."

"Is that why you sold the business?"

"No. Honestly, it wasn't my dream. I liked working for Dad, but when he was gone, it was time for me to move on. Dad had been my rock, which I realize now... Depending on Dad was no better than depending on Mom. And when I started to pull away from her, I turned to you. And then Jed and Lola." Her sigh brushed through his whiskers. "In the last year, I've learned not to lean on people but to depend on God."

Oh.

That was new. Sam had been praying for Eliza for so long—for her safety and her salvation. Seemed like God had listened.

"I hired you against her wishes," Eliza said. "And I started dating you against her wishes. So I was standing up for myself."

She shifted away to face him and took his hand. "I know you don't like my mother, and I don't blame you. But I came to realize it wasn't that Mom didn't like you. She didn't want me to marry anybody. It was a little—"

"Selfish?" He should shut up. But he added, "Hateful?"

Eliza smiled. "She's still my mom."

"Sorry." Why were they still talking about Linda? What did she have to do with anything? With the story she'd told him? With the mysterious Levi?

"Mom was terrified I was going to leave her," Eliza said. "After Dad's death, I think she was afraid of being alone. It doesn't make her behavior okay. I'm just saying that I saw it. I wasn't going to let her ruin my life." She stared down at their joined hands. "I loved you." She looked up, held his eye contact. "I loved you so much. You were pulling away from me, and maybe I did blame you a little for what happened to Dad's company. Maybe I was preparing for when you'd leave me."

"Never," he said.

She sighed. "The point is, I want you to know, I need you to know... If you'd proposed..."

He stilled. And suddenly, everything seemed very quiet, as if even the air waited for her to finish her sentence.

"I would have said yes."

CHAPTER TWENTY-TWO

ELIZA WANTED to dip her head again, to hide from Sam's reaction to her words.

Because he said nothing. For an agonizing moment, he just stared at her. And she knew all this kindness, his calling her sweetheart and holding her close... She knew it didn't mean what she wanted it to mean. He didn't love her anymore. He didn't want her.

But then he cradled her face in his palms and kissed her.

Softly at first, maybe waiting to see if she'd pull away. As if she had the strength. As if this wasn't what she'd been dreaming of, longing for, for five years.

She told herself not to expect too much. To give him time. But her hands weren't obeying her brain as they gripped his sweatshirt and pulled him closer.

He urged her lips open, probed her mouth. He tasted of toothpaste and smelled like pine and fear and...Sam. That unique scent that was his and only his.

Wrapping an arm around her, he shifted her against him, deepening the kiss, and passion exploded inside her. Not just desire, but love and tenderness and gratitude and a thousand other things she had no name for.

He ended the kiss with a groan, holding her close. "I've missed you so much."

"I've missed you."

He set her back, held her eyes. "I love you, Eliza. I can't lose you again."

Oh, stupid tears. She told herself they were tears of happiness. Joyful tears.

She wasn't going to think about the fear his words thrummed in her chest. Because she still hadn't told him about Levi. And when she did...

His eyes narrowed. Was he nervous? How could he not know her feelings?

"Oh, Sam." She couldn't help the slight chuckle. "I've loved you every second I've been gone. I'm sorry I left. I'm sorry for everything, all of it. I wish I could go back. I wish..."

He pulled her against his chest again. "Let's not do that. Let's just go forward from here." He stretched out his legs, and she lay beside him on the couch, resting her head on his biceps, loving the weight of his arm around her waist, the soft press of his lips against her temple.

"We should get some sleep." And maybe a tiny part of her wanted him to stay with her, even if she knew it was a bad idea.

"I just want to hold you for a few minutes."

She let herself relax and enjoy the moment. She had no idea what tomorrow would bring, but tonight Sam loved her. Maybe it would be enough.

CHAPTER TWENTY-THREE

SAM WAS VERY careful when he climbed out from behind Eliza on the couch. She made a little mewing sound that had his gaze flicking to the king-sized bed.

Yeah.

He needed to go. He turned the covers down, then lifted Eliza off the couch and settled her on the mattress.

Her eyes opened. And she smiled. Then frowned. "Um, I'm not sure this is a good idea."

"Just tucking you in, sweetheart." He pulled the covers over her, kissed her gently on the lips, and turned the lamp off.

The door to the adjoining room was open just enough to light his way there. When he stepped in, Michael was reclining on one of the beds.

He set his phone aside. "She okay?"

"She's sleeping."

"You two didn't...uh—"

"I don't do that anymore."

Michael's lip tipped up on one side. "Good idea, until you get married, which might happen sooner than you'd imagined." He gave the adjoining door a pointed look.

The words had Sam remembering the kiss, the feel of her body against his.

Yeah, that wasn't helpful. He grabbed the sack of stuff he'd bought in Concord and disappeared into the bathroom for a shower.

Ten minutes later, dressed in a too-small T-shirt and scratchy sleep pants, he exited the bathroom. He needed to book them on a flight to Denver. He should have done that in the car on the way down, but Eliza had felt so good tucked up against his side.

Michael was back to scrolling his phone.

Sam stood between the beds. "I think you have some 'splainin' to do, bro."

"About what?"

Sam crossed his arms and waited.

Finally, Michael lowered the cell and looked up.

"Do all machine parts salesmen have friends who can deal with a dead body?"

Sam had expected his brother to flinch or look away. To evade. But Michael held his eye contact. "It's possible I haven't been completely transparent about what I do for a living."

Huh. So Sam wasn't going to have to force the information out of him. "International jewel thief?"

That brought a smile. "I love that your first guess has me doing something illegal."

Sam shrugged one shoulder. "I guess that eliminates smuggler and arms dealer." Not that Sam would ever believe Michael could be involved in anything like that. He'd always been passionate about justice. About standing up for the innocent. Well, once he'd grown up, anyway.

"Which leaves..." The thought that came to mind was outlandish, but no more so than international jewel thief. "Spy?"

Now Michael did look away.

When Sam didn't say anything, he turned back, though it seemed to take effort. "I work for the CIA."

Oh. He'd been half kidding. "Like...like Jack Ryan and...and Robert Redford in...what was that movie Dad loved so much?"

"*Three Days of the Condor*?" At Sam's nod, Michael said, "They were analysts."

"And you're...?"

He rubbed his lips together, held Sam's eye contact.

"Not an agent," Sam said.

A tiny shrug.

Sam sat hard on the opposite bed. "Wow. Seriously?" He tried to process, then remembered something. "Back in college, you applied for a job with them. We all got interviewed. But you said you didn't take the job. But obviously... Have you worked for them since then?"

"Yeah. Right after graduation."

"Do Mom and Dad know? The guys?"

"It needs to stay between us."

"They made you *lie* to us?"

Michael blinked, focused on the bedspread. "It seemed easier—"

"To lie. To everybody? To your whole family?" Small comfort that Sam hadn't been the only one in the dark. But still... "Why would you do that?"

"I didn't want Mom and Dad to worry. But I hate keeping it secret, especially from you. I'll tell you about it sometime." Michael glanced at his watch. "But it's late, and our flight leaves early."

"I haven't even booked it..." Wait. "*Our* flight? You're going with us?"

"Unless you don't want me to come. But I think I can help."

"Obviously. We'd be dead if not for you."

"I doubt that." A small pause, and then... *"You'd* be dead, maybe. She'd just be gone."

Gone. And then dead. Or captive.

If she vanished again... No, Sam couldn't do it again.

"I'm glad you called me." Michael's words had Sam shaking off the horrifying images.

"Eliza's idea," Sam admitted, "but... Me too."

"I got us tickets on a nonstop. Leaves at nine."

"I'll pay you back."

At that, Michael smiled. "I'll let you. Government salary and all that."

"Right." And didn't that just open a whole world of questions? Questions he'd have to ask another time. He climbed under the covers, his head buzzing with new information—from Eliza, now from Michael. It was too much to comprehend. And he was so tired.

Michael clicked off the light. Then, in the darkness, "You still hate me?"

"What? I don't—?"

"For about thirty years."

Oh. Not thirty. Not quite, anyway.

"I was a jerk when we were kids." Michael's voice was low and sincere. "I exchanged you for a bunch of losers I haven't talked to since high school. I don't know why I never... I should have apologized a long time ago."

Sam wasn't sorry for the darkness that hid his face. Because he could feel some very unmanly emotions coming on.

"I treated you like crap." Michael said. "So I know I don't deserve anything different from you. And if you want to unload on me... Well, maybe not tonight, but I'll listen to whatever you have to say. I owe you that. Or...whatever you want. The thing is, I'd really like you to forgive me. I want us to be friends again."

The prickling in his eyes... He'd blame that on fatigue.

Could it be that simple? Could he just...forgive?

What had he said to Eliza? That she couldn't be blamed for something that happened when she was a kid?

Michael had been a kid too. A teenager, but still young and dumb. Yet grown-up Sam had held a grudge against that kid for a long, long time.

Which made Sam feel a little like an idiot. A *lot* like an idiot.

"One condition," Sam said.

"Anything."

"Forgive me too. For—"

"Done. Long time ago." The covers rustled, and Michael added, "Get some sleep, dweeb."

He smiled at the old game. "You too, goober."

Just like that, the past was cleared away. Just like that, Sam and Michael had a fresh start.

Sam couldn't figure out how, but in the space of...he did the math and almost laughed out loud. Eliza had shown up on his doorstep Friday night. How could it only be Monday? In seventy-two hours, Sam had gotten back the woman he'd dreamed of and his favorite brother.

Tomorrow, they'd take the evidence Eliza had collected to the authorities. Hopefully, her enemies would scatter and leave her alone. And then Sam would start building the rest of his life, a life with family. A life with the woman he loved.

CHAPTER TWENTY-FOUR

UNLIKE PRETTY MUCH everything else in Eliza's life for the previous four days, the nonstop flight was uneventful. Despite the bizarre events of the day before, she'd slept well. Maybe because she'd been so tired.

Maybe because she'd fallen asleep in Sam's arms.

Even so, she'd groaned at the knock on the door between the adjoining rooms.

Sam's voice followed it. "We have to leave here by seven to make our flight."

She'd forced herself out of bed, stretching her tired muscles and analyzing the latest scrapes and bruises, courtesy of Gorilla Gil dragging her to his car and the mad dash through the woods.

A quick shower and change of clothes, and she joined Michael and Sam for the shuttle to the airport.

She sat tucked between them on the plane. Michael, in the aisle seat, kept himself busy on his laptop while Eliza snuggled up beside Sam and peppered him with questions about the years she'd missed. He indulged her, telling her stories, updating her on his business.

While she'd been in Utah, he'd built an empire. "I'm impressed."

"Helped that I didn't have a life."

Michael, who'd mostly ignored them, popped in with, "It was pathetic." But the words were delivered with a smile.

They managed to get through the nearly five-hour flight without talking about what would happen next. Without Sam or Michael asking her where they were going when they landed. So far, all she knew was that she'd left the evidence in Denver. The key she'd mailed to Jeanette told her it was probably at a bank. Looked like a bank key, anyway. But she couldn't remember.

Now, she gazed past Sam out the window as they descended. It was a sunny day, the sky bright blue overhead. The Denver airport, with its strange white peaks—maybe intended to mimic the mountain range behind it, though it was a pale imitation—looked familiar. Yes, she'd been here. And as they landed and taxied, memories came.

A flight. A dash through the airport, tugging Levi behind her. A Lyft to the bank... She'd been sure she would recognize which bank by sight but figured they'd be driving all over Denver to find the right one.

Now, she pictured the national chain's logo and remembered the short drive.

As soon as the wheels touched down, Sam had taken out his phone.

"You must be so far behind at work."

He lowered it to his lap, smiled at her. "It'll wait."

"Do me a favor? There should be a Wells Fargo about a half hour from the airport."

His eyebrows shot up. "You remembered?"

"I think so."

He searched, then... "Yup." He leaned over and kissed her.

So natural, as if they'd been together all this time. As if nothing had changed.

But they were back on the ground now, not floating on the clouds of make-believe. There was a lot standing between here and their happily-ever-after. Not just Jedediah and Lola Keller and the men they employed.

There was Levi, her precious son. The closer she got to seeing him again, the more the memories came back to her, the more her heart yearned for him.

And the longer she put off telling Sam, the harder it was going to be. She dreaded the moment. Dreaded what she knew she'd see in Sam's expression.

She loved Sam desperately, but Levi was her child, her responsibility. Her heart. If she had to choose between them...

She wanted them both. Was it too much to ask?

The plane jerked to a stop at the gate, and the seatbelt sign dinged. All around them, people stood and stretched. Overhead bins were opened, carry-ons hefted down.

Michael turned to them, voice low. His face, so relaxed a moment before, was back in the zone.

She had no idea how a salesman knew the things—and people—he knew, and she had a feeling she shouldn't ask.

"I'm going to rush ahead and get the rental car," Michael said. "You two make your way to the main terminal, but stay on this side of security until I call you. Okay?"

"Good idea," Sam said. "I'll take your bag."

Michael stood and pulled it out of the overhead. They'd stuffed all their things in Michael's small suitcase and brought it along, even though she hoped to fly back to Boston as soon as they were finished. "I'll take it. I don't want it to slow you down, in case you're spotted."

"Do you think they'll be here?" She'd enjoyed the respite of the flight, but now her heart thumped.

"If I was looking for you, I'd be staking out this airport. I assume they figured out you came here before. So...yeah, I think they will."

"Always the optimist," Sam said.

"Just trying to keep you two alive."

"You could be spotted too."

"They won't be looking for me. Probably." Michael's gaze cut to Eliza. "I only have to protect myself."

A small part of her wished she could protest, tell them she didn't need their help. Ha. If the last four days had taught her nothing else...

Passengers started disembarking, and Michael followed them out.

"Guess we're in no hurry," she said.

Sam kept his eyes on his brother as he walked away.

"You two seem better," Eliza said.

At that, a smile tipped his lips. "We talked last night. He apologized for being a jerk when we were kids. I apologized for holding a grudge for decades. We're good."

"I'm glad." And she was.

But it only added another worry. Because Michael hadn't told Sam yet that he'd tracked her down at The Ranch, that he'd known where she was for months.

They were both keeping secrets from Sam, secrets that wouldn't stay that way much longer.

At the curb on the departures level, Eliza slid into the backseat of the rented SUV.

Sam closed the door behind her, then got in the front beside his brother.

"No problems?" Michael asked.

"Nope."

Far from being pleased, Michael pressed his lips together as he merged into airport traffic.

Clearly, Sam saw Michael's concern too. "That's good, right?"

"Good. Strange, though." He caught Eliza's gaze in the rearview. "They tracked you the last time you flew, right? They must've found you in Manchester."

"I don't remember..." Even as she said it, a memory surfaced.

Flying over the familiar tree-covered landscape.

Mom waiting at the gate.

Holding Levi's hand, Eliza spotted her and drank in the sight. She looked older, a few more wrinkles, and more gray hair showed at her roots. She wore jeans, something she rarely did, but she'd paired them with a red turtleneck under an off-white leather jacket. Stylish, as always. Mom had made some mistakes, no question. She wasn't perfect, but she'd made a home for Eliza and Dad. She'd done her best.

Eliza had missed her so much.

Finally, Mom caught sight of them. She smiled and dabbed a tissue beneath her eyes. Was she *crying?*

She opened her arms, and Eliza fell into them.

They hugged for a long, long time, then Mom held her shoulders and stepped back. "Thank God you're home."

"Not quite," Eliza said. "Almost."

Mom barely registered those words, dropping to her knees.

The smile she wore... Eliza hadn't seen that smile in years. Maybe not since before Kristen died. "And you must be Levi."

Eliza's little tow-headed boy nodded.

"I'm your grandmother, and I'm so excited to meet you." She opened her arms and held them wide, an invitation.

When Levi stepped in and Mom wrapped him in her arms, tears dripped down her cheeks and off her chin.

Eliza had expected...well, what she always expected with her mother. Censure. Disapproval. She'd expected to hear a lecture about everything she'd done wrong and lots and lots of advice about how she could fix her life. She'd been prepared for that, willing to endure it to restore this relationship.

But when Mom looked up at her, only joy shone on her face. From her purse, she pulled a stuffed blue-and-white toy with the UNH logo on the side and gave it to Levi. "It's a wildcat."

He grinned, showing all his baby teeth. "Thanks." He beamed at her, then at Eliza. "See, Mommy?"

She touched the soft fur, then ruffled her son's curly hair. "It's so soft."

He hugged the toy to his chest.

Mom stood and pulled Eliza into another hug. "He's beautiful. Perfect. And I...I've missed so much. But we can only go forward." Mom's smile was gone when she backed away. "You'll find us?"

"As soon as I can. You got a new phone?"

"Yes, and disconnected the old one, for now. And got off all social media this morning. Just in case. They probably can't track me if I'm not on the app, but better safe than sorry."

Mom was leaning toward paranoid, and Eliza didn't mind. Better that than cavalier. Mom gave her the new phone number, and Eliza programmed it into the disposable she'd bought in Denver.

"You're going to see Sam?"

"I have to," Eliza said. "I know you disapprove, but—"

"If you need his help, then go and get it. Get *him*." Her eyes...twinkled. Who was this woman? "You two were good together. I wish I could... I was wrong about him. About a lot of things."

Eliza had never heard her mother admit she was wrong about anything.

Her surprise must have shown on her face because Mom laughed. A real, honest-to-goodness laugh. "Shocked you, have I?" Her amusement faded as she took Eliza's hand. "I've spent the last few years trying to become the kind of mother you'd want to come home to."

"Oh, Mom." Eliza pulled her mother close again, wanting nothing more than to disappear with these two people she loved so much. But the past would catch up with her. She couldn't run away this time.

After Kristen's death, they'd run from Arkansas.

After the breakup with Sam, she'd run to Utah.

This time, she was going to face it. Deal with it. And then she could step into her future free of the past, not weighed down by it.

The memory dissipated, and Eliza blinked. They were on a highway surrounded by fields that went on for miles and miles. Mountains rose straight ahead of them, shocking in their grandeur against the flat, flat land.

Sam was twisted in his seat, watching her. "You remembered something."

"I know where my mom is." And Levi. "She's safe."

"In Florida?"

"At a friend's lake house on the Cape."

"You know how to get in touch with her?"

"She got a burner phone, but I don't have the number."

"It's a start." He faced forward again.

Michael's eyes found hers in the rearview. "Hey, Sam. Find a place where Eliza can get a new jacket."

"We're going shopping?" Sam said. "Now?"

"The jacket she has is too easy to pick out in a crowd."

He wasn't wrong. Bright red, way too big for her. "I'll just take it off." Eliza did, but Michael wasn't appeased.

"They'll expect that. They won't expect you in a different jacket. Also, you wear your hair like that a lot?"

She fingered the ponytail. "Yeah. It's easier, since it's so long."

"We need a way to disguise it. Maybe a bun?"

"Um...I think I've been wearing it in buns too. I can just..." She yanked the ponytail holder out and let her hair fall.

"Too distinctive," Michael said, then to Sam, "Did you find a place?"

"Yeah. Just stay on this road..."

Ten minutes later, Michael parked at the curb in front of a department store. Eliza reached for the handle, but he stopped her. "Eliza, stay here where it's safe. Sam can do it."

Sam gave his brother a long look. "You think someone followed us?"

"Better safe than sorry."

He shot a look her way, maybe asking if she was okay with the plan. She had a strong suspicion that this was about more than just shopping.

"Grab a jacket, small"—Michael's gaze flicked to her— "right?"

"Yeah."

"Nothing like that one. Different color, different style. Fitted, I think. Also, big sunglasses that'll hide her face, and a hat if they have any. Nothing that'll draw attention, though. A neutral-colored cap. And get yourself a hat too. And a new shirt, in case they saw you at the airport."

Sam looked down at the nondescript navy-blue sweater he'd bought the night before. "This doesn't exactly stand out."

"Right now they're looking for a woman in a red jacket and

a tall guy wearing a blue sweater. You change the obvious things, you throw people off."

"Aye, aye, Inspector Gadget." The playful words weren't delivered with a smile. To Eliza... "Anything else you need?"

A whole new wardrobe, one that hadn't come from a grocery store or the secondhand bin at The Ranch. "No, thanks."

He slammed the door a little too hard, and Michael drove to the back of the lot and parked. "Can you come up front?"

She did, fearing what was coming.

"I have to tell him that I found you." Michael faced her, jaw tight and strong. Sam had grown a beard since Eliza left him, but Michael's beard was trimmed close, the cleft in his chin pronounced with that intense look. "He's going to be ticked off that I didn't tell him right away."

"Why didn't you?"

"A couple of reasons. But one of them was Levi."

Levi.

Right.

Of course he knew about Levi. She would never have told Michael, Sam's brother, but MC, the stranger on the other end of all those messages... He'd known what was keeping her at The Ranch. Getting away by herself—that would have been one thing. But escaping with her son...

She hadn't been able to figure out how to do it.

"You rescued me, Michael. You got me out of there. Sam's going to be grateful."

"He'll get there, but he's not going to start there." His golden-brown eyes seemed to look right through her. "It would be easier if he knew about Levi. The longer you wait—"

"I know. I get it. And of course I'm going to tell him."

"Okay. Good. When he gets back, I'll go inside, give you guys a minute to—"

"No. Not now." The thought was a fist squeezing the air right out of her. "Now's not the time. In a car. On our way to...to do all this stuff. I'll tell him later."

Michael stared at her. Maybe *glared* was the word. "Then, when?"

"As soon as we're done with the FBI."

"They know about Levi."

Right. They'd interviewed her at The Ranch on one of their many visits.

"They'll ask where he is," Michael said. "He's with your mother?"

"Yeah. They're safe. Will Sam be with me when I talk to them?"

"You going to ask him to leave so you can keep your secrets? How do you think that'll go over?"

She crossed her arms, rocked in the seat. She needed Sam on her side. She knew she'd have to tell him eventually, but not yet.

"What are you afraid of, Eliza?" Michael's words were low and kind.

So many things. "It's just... Every time I do something wrong, somebody gets hurt. Every single time. And leaving Sam... That was wrong. Stupid and... I never planned to stay away. I just needed some time to figure out..." She sighed. "Levi is the greatest gift of my life. Despite how he came to be, despite all my mistakes. So I did a bad thing, and I got a gift, and I know it won't last." She gathered her courage to face Sam's brother. "I know it won't last, so I'm holding on to Sam as long as I can."

"He loves you, Eliza. What do you think he's going to do?"

"Leave me. Hate me. I don't know."

Michael watched her a long time before he spoke again. "Sam's a good guy. He's not going to hold a grudge."

"Really? He's held a grudge against you since he was eleven."

Michael's mouth opened, snapped shut. "But I apologized, and he got over it. And you're way more important to him than I am. I understand the position you're in. I understand you're afraid. And believe it or not, I even understand the need for keeping secrets. I'm good at secrets. Really good."

That, she didn't doubt.

"Which is how I know the damage they do," he said. "Secrets separate us. They're invisible walls that keep the people we love at a distance. And the thing is, those people, those loved ones? They don't get it. They don't know why they can't get close to us. They think it's them, that they've done something wrong. So they try harder. Or they pull away. You can't truly love people you're lying to."

"I'm not lying—"

"Every minute you don't tell him, Eliza, that wall gets thicker. Every minute you keep the secret, you make it harder for him to trust you. And forgive you."

"An hour or two, Michael. That's all I'm asking."

His phone dinged, and he glanced at it. Put the car in reverse and headed for the store entrance. "I just got my brother back. I'm telling him about MC, about how I found you. And when he asks why I couldn't get you out of there...I'll leave that to you to explain."

CHAPTER TWENTY-FIVE

SAM SPIED Eliza in the front seat and was about to slide into the back when she opened the door and hopped out.

"You're fine where you are," he said.

"That's okay." Her smile was tight, confirming the feeling he'd gotten when his brother had sent him on this errand.

That there was more to this stop than a new jacket.

He handed her the bag and opened the back door for her before settling in beside his brother.

Michael started the car moving. "Got everything she needs?"

"Yup. Eliza, you might try the jacket on, make sure it fits. It's heavier than the one you have." He pulled up the address for the bank, and the map showed on the screen.

The package rustled in the backseat. Then, "It's great. Thank you."

He turned to see and wasn't disappointed. He'd chosen a fitted black suede jacket similar to one she'd owned when they were dating, and as he'd thought it would, it looked great on her.

She stuffed her hair in the black ball cap, then slipped on the sunglasses. "Well?"

"Like a new woman."

Her lips curled at the corners, but her eyes darted toward Michael.

"What is it?" Sam directed the question at his brother. "What did I miss? Or, should I say, what did you make sure I missed?"

"You guys hungry?"

His stomach had been growling for an hour, but he could wait.

Michael turned into a restaurant parking lot and drove around to the back, where he squeezed the rented SUV between two trucks. "I need food." He opened his door and stepped out.

Sam and Eliza followed. Part of him wanted to weave his fingers with hers.

More of him wanted to know what they were keeping from him.

Though Michael gave nothing away, Eliza was visibly nervous.

"Why is this place safe but the store wasn't?" Sam asked.

In front of them, Michael's shoulders lifted and fell. "Call it instinct."

"Mmm-hmm."

After they stood in line and paid for their Mexican food, they headed for a booth in the back, far from the windows fronting the place. Michael slid into one side, Eliza and Sam the other. Sam plopped the little number pedestal in the middle of the table so the servers could find them.

All the while, suspicion hummed through Sam. He knew, he *knew*, his brother would never betray him. Never.

And hadn't Eliza told him she'd never stopped loving him?

So what was the big secret that had Michael sending him on errands to get alone with her? That had Eliza looking so guilty?

"I was surprised when you and Eliza broke up." Michael scanned the area. The diners nearby were paying them no attention. "She seemed so perfect for you, and you were obviously head-over-heels. When she disappeared... Bro, you were not okay."

"I survived. Some would say thrived."

Beside him, Eliza shifted.

He needed to shut up and let them talk.

"Thrived?" Michael smirked. "Only people who don't know you would say that."

"You have a point?"

"I decided to find her, to put your mind at ease." To Eliza, he said, "This is no reflection on your character, so please don't be offended."

"Don't say anything offensive," Sam warned.

Michael ignored him. "Taking off all by yourself, without your mother or your best friend? Without even their blessing?"

Sam asked, "How did you know—?"

"I'm good at ferreting out information."

Right. CIA.

Still speaking to Eliza, Michael said, "I thought you'd be back in a couple of weeks, a month at most. When you weren't back after three, I started looking for you."

"That long ago?" she asked.

Which was the wrong question. The wrong reaction to the news. She didn't seem surprised he'd been looking for her, only the duration he'd looked.

Michael addressed Sam again. "I put out feelers with my contacts. I have friends in some three-letter agencies that have access to things I don't. For years, I got nothing. And then last spring, after you went to Salt Lake City, Daniel said he saw you talking to a woman and described her. He told me he thought she looked scared. He also said how you looked a little... Well, Daniel didn't say desperate, but that was the sense I got."

Nice. Call him desperate in front of his...well, whatever Eliza was. "Girlfriend" didn't feel right.

I would have said yes.

Almost-fiancée, then. Assuming Michael didn't make him look so bad in the next few minutes that she ran screaming from his life.

Michael looked her direction. "I figured it was you and contacted a friend at the FBI in Salt Lake. He got back to me a week or so later. He said a woman named Elizabeth Pelletier had been questioned at the Keller Ranch—"

"You knew? For six months?" Sam's voice was too loud, and a couple of kids at an adjacent table turned to look. He leaned toward his brother and lowered his voice. "You knew she was trapped in that place, and you didn't get her out? You just left her there?"

"Sam." Eliza slid her cool hand over his forearm.

He forced himself not to shake her off. "She could have been killed." He continued in a vehement whisper. "Do you know what that guy was doing? He was...he was imprisoning those women. He raped them." The words had him swallowing a rise of fear. He looked at her, and she gave him a small smile— whatever the heck that meant. To Michael, he said, "Eliza could have been—"

"I know," Michael said.

"Do you?"

Eliza patted his arm. "He helped me, Sam. He saved me."

She was aware that Michael had known where she was. Apparently, they'd been working together for months. Sam took a breath and tried to blow out his frustration—and most of the questions he wanted answered. Mostly, why hadn't his brother told him? And why hadn't she?

As if Michael could read his mind, he said, "She didn't know it was me. I told her yesterday in the parking lot in Concord. And she had no idea what I was talking about."

"After he told me," Eliza said, "I remembered about the man who helped me, but I didn't know it was Michael until yesterday."

That made sense—a lot more sense than his misplaced anger. She had amnesia. Her life was confusing and full of information she couldn't process.

Still, he hated that Michael had found her when Sam had failed. Michael had rescued her while he'd been useless and impotent.

He turned back to his brother. "Were you just too busy with all your...*machine parts sales* to get her out sooner?"

"There were more factors at play—"

"You and your three-letter agencies needed their evidence."

Eliza said, "I started collecting evidence a year ago, Sam. Michael had nothing to do with that."

"The place was heavily guarded." Michael's voice was cool. "It wasn't easy to get people in and out. But there wasn't a single moment after I discovered where she was that I wasn't trying to figure out—"

"You should have told me."

"I didn't want you charging in there and getting yourself killed."

"I wouldn't have—"

"You might have. You were at her mom's house yesterday. You saw the body they left at the bottom of the stairs." Michael swallowed. "If that happened to you... I wasn't going to live with that. I wasn't going to tell Mom and Dad they'd lost you right after they got Daniel back. I wasn't going to live with the knowledge that I could have prevented it. Maybe that makes me a jerk. A selfish jerk, but you're my brother, and I wasn't going to put you in harm's way."

"You had no right—"

"You have no right."

At the vehemence in his voice, Sam shut his mouth. He needed to listen. To ask questions. To try to understand instead of tossing out accusations. He swallowed all the words that wanted release and breathed a prayer. "I'm just trying to understand."

Michael's voice was even when he spoke again. "Those guys coming after her right now? They were on the property. All of them. They would have killed you. And if you'd gotten to her, there's a good chance they'd have killed her too. Even if she'd survived, if she hadn't escaped... It would not have gone well for her."

Michael was probably right. Sam would have charged onto The Ranch, demanding to see her. Demanding to take her with him. He'd like to think he'd have been smart about it, but...but it was Eliza. So maybe not.

He caught Eliza's wide eyes. Was she afraid of him? The thought churned his empty stomach, and he took her hand and held it. He just needed to understand. "That girl, the one whose mom called you. She walked away. Why couldn't you?"

"By the time I knew I needed to leave, they were watching me."

"All those guards," Michael added.

"I didn't have a car, and The Ranch is in the middle of the desert, miles and miles from the closest town. I needed help. And then I got a message from a person who called himself MC. It came through the business email address—a customer." She looked across the table and smiled. "He'd bought a few thousand dollars' worth of coins."

"It needed to look authentic," Michael said.

Eliza's expression was open and trusting. "He told me he was a friend and asked if I was all right, that he'd heard about the Kellers and was worried for me. I had no idea who he was. Honestly..." She shrugged, her cheeks turning pink. "I hoped it was you." She smiled at Michael. "Not that I'm sorry it was you."

"I get it."

"He's the one who sent me the Bible."

Sam's head snapped to his brother. "You did that?"

His head dipped and rose.

"We messaged a lot while he was trying to work out how to get me free," Eliza said. "By that time, I'd told him about the evidence I had collected, so it was just a matter of him coming up with a plan."

"And finding help. I couldn't do it alone."

"But he checked on me every few days," Eliza said. "I came to trust him. I told him how stupid I felt for having fallen for all the Kellers' lies. And then he sent me a Bible in a box beneath a bunch of coins, just in case anybody looked. And he included a note about how I'm precious and loved, how God wanted to forgive me." Her eyes filled.

Eliza had turned to God, and Michael was the reason.

"And a lock-picking kit?" Eliza added, rather randomly. "I just remembered that."

"Uh...what?" Sam said.

Michael said, "It was in the box with the Bible. So she could get the papers Keller'd stored in a locked drawer."

Right. She'd told him about that drawer.

"You were there?" Sam asked his brother. "When she escaped?"

"I planned to be, but something came up. I have friends who were in Utah for a training exercise. Spec-ops guys. They rescued her. Got her to the airport."

"I don't remember any of that," she said.

"Then why...?" Sam raked a hand through his hair. "I don't understand. If she was with them, then how did she end up getting hurt? Why didn't they protect her?"

"It wasn't an official mission," Michael said. "They were doing me a favor—at great risk to themselves. Not just from the guards they had to face—though they managed them with little trouble. But if they'd been caught, they could've been court-marshaled. They needed to wrap it up fast. They rescued her, dropped her off at the airport, and went back to the base before anybody knew they were gone. I'd gotten her a ticket to Florida by way of Denver."

"You were going to Florida?"

"Um, no?" Eliza looked as confused as he felt.

"She was never going to Florida," Michael explained. "We were trying to throw Keller off her trail. She stayed in Denver." He looked around, seemed to remember that was where they were. "She ordered a car—"

"This part I do remember. Getting the Lyft to the bank, opening the safe deposit box. By the time I got all that done, it was too late to fly out that night, so I booked a flight to Manchester the next day."

Sam was trying to put it all together. "Why Manchester?" For that matter... "Why were you in Shadow Cove?"

"To see you. It took me a long time, too long, to understand Jed's tactics, but once I did, I questioned everything he'd ever told me. So in Denver, I looked you up and discovered you weren't married and never had been. He'd lied. And I needed... you." She laid her hand over his on the table. He flipped it over and weaved their fingers together.

She'd come to see him. The truth burrowed deep. She'd said she never stopped loving him, and it wasn't that he hadn't believed her so much as he'd thought maybe she'd exaggerated.

Or, with the amnesia, she'd forgotten how she really felt about him. But now it was real.

Still... "Not that I'm sorry you came," he said, "but wouldn't it have been safer to go straight to the FBI?"

She licked her lips, swallowed. Looked at Michael.

"What?" Sam asked.

Michael said nothing.

Eliza pulled her hand back and crossed her arms. "I needed to see you. It's...it was probably a stupid decision, but I needed to see you before I did anything else."

"Why?"

"I promise I'll explain everything." By the way her gaze flicked across the table, Sam guessed she wanted to talk to him without Michael listening. Fair enough. He could wait.

A server delivered their meals—steaming plates piled with tacos and enchiladas and burritos. When she walked away, Michael lifted his fork. "I searched for her because I knew how much she meant to you. I thought, if nothing else, you'd know what happened. Get...closure or whatever. When I figured out she was in trouble, I did my best to get her out of it. It hasn't worked out like we planned it. They must've guessed Florida was a ruse, or hedged their bets and sent a couple guys to Manchester, maybe even Boston and Portland, too, figuring she'd head toward home." Michael shook his head. "I should've been there. I'm sorry." He shifted to Eliza. "I'm sorry you got hurt. That you're dealing with—"

"I'd still be at The Ranch if not for you." She reached across the table and squeezed his wrist. "You don't owe me anything."

Michael pulled his arm away, his gaze on Sam. "You and me. Are we good?"

Sam swallowed the emotions jumbling in his throat. "Sorry for how I reacted."

"I made a judgment call, and I stand by it."

"You found her, which was better than I could do. I tried. I hired a PI once, not long after she left."

Eliza let out a quiet gasp.

Yeah, well...

He hadn't planned to tell her that. Hadn't wanted her to know just how desperate he'd been to get her back. But Sam wasn't nearly as good at secrets as some people at the table. "Apparently, your contacts are better than my PI's."

Michael's lips rose in a smile, but his eyes weren't on board. "So, are we...?"

"We're good. It seems like..." He swallowed a lump and glanced at Eliza, who gave him a shy smile. "I owe you everything."

"Nah. We're brothers. We don't keep score."

"Unless it's ping pong," Sam said.

"Or air hockey." Michael dug his fork into his enchiladas.

Sam understood why he'd done what he'd done. And he was glad to have a better understanding of what'd happened to land Eliza at his house on Friday night. The pieces were coming together, but he didn't have the whole picture.

Eliza was still keeping something from him. As soon as he got her alone, he'd figure out what it was.

CHAPTER TWENTY-SIX

ELIZA LEFT Michael and Sam in the bank lobby and followed the employee into the room with the safe deposit boxes. The woman inserted her key into the proper box.

Eliza added the other, which Sam had held onto since they'd gotten it from Jeanette. Eliza really needed to get herself a purse. And a wallet. And a phone.

They turned the keys. The woman pulled the covered box out of its spot and set it on a table in the center of the room. "Just slide it back in when you're done."

"Thanks." Eliza opened the lid. The only thing inside was a manila envelope, thick with papers. As she pulled it out, the memories came back.

It'd been dark.

She'd opened the door of her little house at two a.m., holding her sleeping boy to her chest, to find a man dressed in black from his skullcap to the soles of his boots. The soldier/marine/whatever was barely visible against the night sky, and she wouldn't have seen the second one if he hadn't moved. As the first man ushered her out, the second dragged a guard into her house. She must've gasped or something because the soldier beside her whispered, "He's alive. He'll be fine."

The exterior door leading to the offices was unlocked already, the night-shift guard usually posted there unconscious, tied and gagged in the lobby. The soldier crossed the small space and unlocked Jed's office door—he must've gotten the keys off the guard—and she stepped inside, trying to figure out how to break into the hidden drawer with a child in her arms.

The second soldier moved into the room and held out his arms. "I got two of 'em. I can do this."

As if she'd hesitate to trust him. As if she wasn't putting her son's life in these men's hands already.

She handed Levi over and crouched in front of the drawer. It felt like it took forever, but finally, she picked the lock and pulled the papers out, then searched the office for some way to bundle them.

The first soldier snagged a manila envelope off a shelf near the door and handed it to her. He even smiled the tiniest bit, lines crinkling the black paint on his face.

She shoved the papers in, and he hustled her out of there.

Levi, bless his little-boy heart, was sound asleep in the man's arms. Her boy could sleep through a bombing.

They hurried outside, past the parking area and down the hill past the dorms. They ran between rows of crops to the edge of the property. All the while, she waited for alarms to sound, but none did. The soldiers must've dealt with all the guards on duty.

They reached the high chain-link fence on the far side of the field, and the soldier hoisted her up and over a thick blanket. How had she never noticed the barbed wire that topped the fence before? How had that not been a clue that the barrier wasn't there just to keep bad guys out but to keep the women in?

She was halfway down the other side when another soldier grabbed her waist and lifted her down.

Levi was carried up and handed down to a soldier waiting for him. Her boy woke up, and the man shifted him into her arms. Levi's eyes were wide but trusting, his curly blond hair matted to his face.

"We're okay, sweetheart. It's okay."

He was old enough not to cry, but he wrapped his arms and legs around her squid-style.

They were shuffled into a Jeep, smushed between the two broad and burly men who'd rescued them. Another climbed in the passenger seat, and the driver took off.

Just like that, they were free.

She'd left everything behind. The few possessions she'd owned could burn, for all she cared. She had her precious son and evidence to prove Jedediah Keller's guilt, and that was enough.

Now, she blinked in the bright bank lights and slammed the metal lid shut. She'd already closed the account, so she stepped out of the room, thanked the woman standing at the door, and hurried to the exit. She held the papers out to Michael and slipped her hand into Sam's, and the three of them returned to the rented SUV.

When they were all belted in, she took the cap, which felt so confining with all her hair stuck inside it, off her head. "That was easy."

"Almost done." Michael pulled out of the space and onto a six-lane road. "We'll be at the FBI office in twenty minutes."

"You really think this'll do it?" she asked. "Shut The Ranch down?"

"Along with the files you stored on that server, which prove fraud. What you got today will back up the women's claims that the Kellers were threatening to keep their children from them."

"Have any made those claims?"

"Not yet, but once the FBI gets warrants and questions everybody on-site, at least a few should open up, don't you think?"

"There are a couple who haven't been sucked in by his lies."

Michael's eyes crinkled in the mirror. "You did good, Eliza. Your testimony will be the key that puts the Kellers away for a long time. Honestly, I wouldn't be surprised if they try to disappear."

"That's not going to be as easy as they might have thought," Eliza said.

Sam twisted to face her. "What do you mean?"

"Our business account is set up at that bank. I just wired the money out."

"You did what?" He practically shouted at her.

Michael's eyebrows lifted in the rearview. "To where?"

"Another account. I'm not going to spend it. I just didn't want them to have access. I mean, they still have the operating budget for The Ranch—maybe ten or fifteen thousand. Nothing like what was in the bullion account. I have no idea how long it'll take for the FBI to freeze their assets—if they will—and even if they do, would they be able to freeze a corporate account, one not in the Kellers' names?"

"Whose name was it in?" Sam asked.

"The bullion business was mine. They didn't want it associated with them or The Ranch, and they figured they could trust me."

"Wow." Sam was nodding slowly.

"We started with their money, though. We had a contract. I got a share." She smiled at him. "I'm not as destitute as I look."

"I never thought—"

"Why didn't they clean it out already?" Michael asked. "Right after you disappeared?"

"I put a hold on it. I opened an account at a different bank from the airport last week. I planned to transfer the money out as soon as it was operational, but...amnesia."

"Right," Sam said. He didn't look happy. "Smart, except you gave them even more incentive to find you."

"They already had all the incentive they needed. I'm trying to destroy them."

"I see what you're saying." Sam was still facing her, his lips lifting.

Those little wrinkles around his eyes were new. She liked them.

"I'm impressed at everything you managed. The business and the evidence and... You're incredibly competent."

She shrugged, not able to hold back a smile.

Sam's phone rang, the sound loud through the speakers.

He glanced at the screen. "No idea." He rejected the call.

"It could be business," she said. "Shouldn't you answer it?"

"Probably." It rang again, almost immediately. "Huh. Same person." He lifted the phone and rejected it again.

But Eliza had seen just enough of the number. Area code 435...

Utah.

It rang again.

"Let me see." Her voice held a tremor, and Sam's easygoing expression was replaced with concern.

He lifted the phone so she could read the number.

She held out her hand, and maybe he noticed the way it trembled. He didn't give it to her.

She said, "Let me."

He answered the call. "Sam Wright."

A voice came over the speakers. "Hello, Sam Wright. I'd like to speak with Elizabeth, please."

Elizabeth.

Only one person would call her that.

Jedediah Keller. Her stomach dropped to her toes.

Michael hit the blinker, and its click-click, click-click filled the silence.

Sam was twisted to her, eyes questioning.

She held out her hand for the phone, wanting...needing this conversation to be private.

But he shook his head. And she didn't miss the anger in his expression.

"Now, please," Jed said. "Trust me. She'll want to know where I am. And who I'm with."

Michael turned into a lot. A car dealership. He headed toward the back, away from the street, and parked. As if it mattered now that they stay hidden.

As if anything mattered.

Sam was still watching her. Still not giving her the phone.

"She'll want to talk to me," Jed said. "Put her on. I really don't want to hurt anyone."

She swallowed a rise of nausea. "I'm here." Her voice cracked, and she cleared her throat. "What do you want?"

"Dear Elizabeth, you know what I want." His voice was reasonable, soothing. "I'm very disappointed in you."

A few seconds ticked by. Did he expect her to say something? To apologize? Beg for forgiveness?

He sighed. "This is not your fault, of course. You've been manipulated and lied to, made to question everything you believe. The men you worked with forced you to do what you did. I suspect they made you promises, which will prove disappointing, if they haven't already. I know you would never harm your family, the people who love you most in the world. Isn't that right, Elizabeth?"

Again, he paused. Again, she said nothing.

"I'm going to need the papers you stole from me, the money you stole from me, and whatever else they asked you to collect. When you bring me those things, I'm going to forget about this lapse of judgment and welcome you back into the family. Everything's going to be okay."

She couldn't speak. Couldn't think. Jed wouldn't call her to beg. He wouldn't call her unless he knew he could get what he asked for. Which meant...

"Where are you?" She squeezed her eyes closed, not willing to look at Sam and Michael, both of whom were twisted in their seats and watching her.

"I don't think I'll tell you that," Jed said. "But I will tell you where we were. A town on Cape Cod. Nice little house on a lake. I think Lola wants to buy it. Good place to hide out. Or, in your case, hide the people you love."

"Don't hurt them. Whatever you want—"

"Of course I won't hurt them, Elizabeth. You know I'm a man of peace."

"Let me talk to them."

The demand was met with silence that stretched a long moment. And then, "Here you go."

"Eliza?" Mom's voice was strong.

"Are you all right? Have they hurt you?"

"Levi and I are fine. And your friend, Nicole."

Nicole? Nicole was there?

"She's...going to be all right," Mom said. "Levi, you want to talk to your mother?"

A second passed, and then, "Hi, Mommy." His voice, so innocent, was a sunbeam in a dark cavern. "Grammy took me to the beach, and I picked up shells and I even saw a fish! The water goes on and on forever! I got my feet wet. It was so cold. And then Dad and Miss Lola came to surprise us."

"I'm..." She swallowed her tears and cleared her throat. "I'm glad you're having fun. I miss you."

"Are you coming soon? Gil's gonna let me walk in the woods, and then—"

"That's enough, Levi." Jed's voice was distant, but she heard the command in it.

"Yes, sir. I love you, Mommy."

"I love you, too, sweetheart."

She waited through another long silence, and then Jed's voice came back on the line. "This is going to be very simple. You—"

"Keep Gil and the rest of your thugs away from my son."

"Now, Elizabeth. If you hadn't betrayed me, I wouldn't have any need for the guards. But everything can go back to normal when you return what you stole. I'll release your mother, and you—"

"Both of them. All of them." She cursed the fear in her voice. "You get nothing unless you release all of them, safe and sound."

"Your mother will be released, and you and Levi will be with me, of course. And Nicole. That's the only way this works."

"No." There. That sounded strong. Sounded sure. "I'll give you whatever you want, but then we're walking away. I will not come back to you."

"Ah." The single syllable was low. Jed rarely got rattled. Never raised his voice.

She'd liked that about him when she'd first met him and Lola. She'd liked how calm and sure he was, a shelter in a storm. Now, she cursed his confidence borne of...insanity.

"Levi is *my* son," Jed said. "And he belongs with his father."

She closed her eyes, but not before she saw the shock on Sam's face. The horror.

Too late. She was too late to tell him the truth. And it didn't matter because if she lost Levi... She lost everything.

CHAPTER TWENTY-SEVEN

HER SON?

Her *son!*

Eliza had a child. Eliza had *Jedediah Keller's child?*

Now she was hiding her face in the back seat, practically folding in on herself.

Sam should be kind. He should be patient and helpful and...

He needed out of that car. Just a minute to pull himself together. He reached for the door handle.

Michael grabbed his forearm, grip strong. He lifted his phone in his other hand, and Sam saw the note he'd typed. *Write down the guy's number.*

A task. He could do that. He pulled a business card from his back pocket and jotted the phone number down.

Jed Keller spoke through the speaker. "You'll come back to us by tomorrow."

Michael was typing something into his phone furiously.

"Hopefully," Keller continued, "if you haven't made too big a mess of things, we'll all be able to go home after that. Will we, Eliza? Or will we have to move on?"

"I...I don't know."

"Have you turned over evidence?"

She looked at Sam, then Michael, who was shaking his head.

"No. I haven't turned anything over yet."

"Good, good. Then I think we can salvage this and get things back to normal."

Michael lifted his phone, and Sam leaned over to see what he was showing Eliza.

Where is he?

She shrugged, but he nodded to her to speak.

"I need to know where you are. I'm in..." At Michael's nod, she said, "Denver. I'll have to get a flight. Where should I go? Boston?"

"What are you doing in Denver?"

Michael shook his head.

"Doesn't matter now," she said. "Do you want to come here?"

Michael gave her a thumbs-up, but his focus was on his phone. Then, he looked at Sam, tapped the card he still held in his hand.

"You'll need to come here," Keller said.

Sam started to hand it over.

Michael shook his head, mouthed, *Give me more.*

Michael grabbed the business cards Sam held out, then took the pen out of his hand and started writing.

"Then you'll need to tell me where." Eliza's voice sounded stronger.

Sam craned to see what his brother was writing.

"Fly into Manchester," Keller said. "I'll send someone to pick you up."

Michael shook his head vehemently.

Sam couldn't agree more.

"No," she said. "I'll fly in, and then we'll figure out a place to meet."

Michael held the card to her, and Sam glimpsed it a second before she grabbed it.

No money for 5 days. Wire transfer out of the country.

"The thing is, Jed." Yes, she definitely sounded stronger. If she was faking it, she was doing a good job. "I wired the money today, but it won't be at my bank for five days."

"Now, Eliza." The man's patronizing tone made Sam want to punch him. Well, more than punch him. "We both know wire transfers only take twenty-four hours. You do wire transfers every day in my business."

His business.

Seemed Jed had forgotten who actually owned it.

"It's in an overseas account," Eliza said.

"You're lying." The man's voice held a threat for the first time in the conversation.

"You always said the American banking system was on the verge of collapse. With everything in the news lately, it seemed wise to get the money out of the country."

Michael gripped Sam's arm and handed him a business card. It had a phone number and a few other words. Michael mouthed, *Now.*

Oh-kay. Sam would figure it out. He climbed out of the car but didn't slam the door. No need to remind Keller that their conversation wasn't private. He moved into the next aisle of shiny new automobiles, carrying Michael's phone and two business cards in his hand. He dialed the number Michael had written.

A woman answered with, "If you're calling for another favor, I'm hanging up." Her voice was familiar, but he couldn't place it.

"My name is Sam Wright. I'm Michael's brother."

A slight gasp. "Is he okay?" Her lighthearted tone was all business now. "What's wrong?"

"He's fine." Sam read the notes on the card. Michael hadn't bothered with things like instructions or explanations. Aside from the phone number, all it said was,

Hostage negotiation. Location of phone ASAP.

"He's involved in a hostage negotiation," Sam said. "Two people have been kidnapped, and the kidnapper's demanding—"

"I don't need the details," the woman said. "He needs a location?"

"Of a cell."

"Europe? Asia?"

"Uh, probably somewhere in New England, actually."

"Okay, give it to me."

Sam read Keller's phone number, and she said, "I'll get back to you. Hang tight." She ended the call.

As he returned to the SUV, he prayed the woman would be able to find Keller.

Eliza was crying in the backseat. "Jed, Nicole hasn't done anything wrong. Just leave her be. Leave them all—"

"This is on you, Elizabeth. Whatever happens to her at this point is entirely dependent on what you do. You come back to your family and she'll be fine. As will your mother and our son."

Michael wasn't giving instructions now, just watching with his lips pressed into a thin line.

"Nicole had nothing to do with anything," she said. "She had no idea what was going on."

"I doubt that very much." The man's smug, arrogant voice had Sam's hands fisting. "But even if it's true, it's too late now. She's here, she's involved. You've endangered your mother, your best friend, and my son."

"He's mine." But Eliza's voice was small. Gone was the

confidence from a few moments before. She was practically begging.

Why were they still talking to this guy? She had her marching orders, right? Get on a plane, get back to New England.

But Eliza continued. "I never meant to hurt anyone, but what you're doing is wrong. Those women have the right to leave without being threatened or coerced. Don't you want followers who are truly devoted to you?"

"They are devoted!" The shout rang in Sam's ears and had Eliza wincing. She looked at Michael, who shook his head.

What did that mean?

"They love me, and why wouldn't they? I saved them, all of them. Just like I saved you."

"You're right." Eliza went back to staring at her knees. "You're right. I just...I forgot how desperate I was back then. I forgot, and I screwed up. I'll...I'll fix it, Jed. I promise. As soon as I get the money, I'll return it to you. I'll return everything. Just don't hurt them."

Sam's fury was rising. What was she saying? Why would she...?

But Michael was nodding his encouragement, despite the fact that Eliza wasn't looking.

Keller said, "Just do what you promise, and everything will be all right."

The phone in Sam's hand vibrated, but a glance at the screen reminded him it wasn't his. He handed it to Michael, who read the text, then gave Eliza a thumbs-up.

"I will," she said. "I promise. I'll be there with the money as soon as I can."

"Good girl. I'll be in touch."

The line went dead.

"We got it," Michael said. "Not a precise location, but a cell tower close enough to find them. You did great, Eliza. That was perfect."

"Made me want to vomit." She crumpled the business card in her fist.

Sam held his hand out, and she handed it over. On the back, it read, *Beg, plead, and gush. Whatever you have to say to keep him on the phone.*

"But it kept the line open," Michael said. "You could practically feel him puffing up."

She sat back against the seat. Tears streamed from her eyes, but she seemed to have given up trying to wipe them away.

Sam climbed out of the car and opened her door and took her hand. "Come on."

Her eyes were wide with worry, but she placed her palm in his and allowed him to tug her from the car. As soon as she was out, he closed her door and held her. "It's going to be okay."

She clung to him. "The thing is, he's right," she whispered. "This is my fault."

"Don't do that." Sam leaned back to face her. "You took a chance. It hasn't worked like you planned, but that doesn't make his decisions your fault. You didn't create that guy. You didn't make him do the things he did."

"I know, but—"

"Would it be better if you were still at The Ranch, doing his bidding. A prisoner?"

"At least my son would be safe."

"Safe? Living in the shadow of guards is safe?" He brushed a tear from her cheek. "Being trapped on a compound in the middle of nowhere with a madman? That's not safe, Eliza. You did the right thing." He pulled her close again, relishing in the warmth of her, the nearness. He needed the answer to the next question, and maybe she needed to talk about it. He took a breath and leaned away again, holding her eye contact. "Eliza, did he...force himself on you?"

She shook her head. "No. He never..."

The rest of her words were drowned out by rage that rolled over him like a storm surge. He'd expected her to say yes. He'd been prepared for that.

But Keller hadn't forced her. She'd gone to his bed willingly.

It took all his self-control not to let his anger and jealousy win. He continued to hold her, not voicing any of the thoughts racing through his mind.

She'd had a child with him, with that...that disgusting Jesus-wannabe.

No wonder she hadn't wanted Sam to know.

I've loved you every second I've been gone.

How could that be true? And if it wasn't, then had anything she'd said been true? Did she really love him, or did she just need his money and his help to get her kid back?

When they recovered Levi, would she leave again?

Maybe she cared about him, a little, but her feelings were nothing compared to his. Nobody's feelings were ever as deep as his. Which was why he was always the one getting left. Rejected. Laughed at.

He stepped away from her. Though he hadn't voiced any of his thoughts, it was clear by her wide, fearful eyes that she saw them in his expression. "You don't understand."

"You're right. I don't." He opened her door. "Get in."

Eliza crossed her arms and... Was she glaring at *him?* As if *he'd* done something wrong?

"Don't talk to me that way. It's not okay."

He wanted to be kind, but he didn't have it in him. He needed a few minutes to process.

Michael climbed out and rounded the SUV.

Eliza never shifted her focus from Sam. "I saw all the

pictures of you. You and Kylee dancing. Laughing. Kissing. Are you telling me nothing happened between you?"

And...yeah.

He was the one to break eye contact, because in an attempt to salve the wound Eliza had left, he'd slept with Kylee. And woken up feeling worse than before. Not only had he betrayed Eliza—and even though she'd left him, that was how he'd felt—he'd also led Kylee to believe he had feelings for her. Which made him a first-class jerk. "She wasn't married. Or the leader of a cult."

"Don't judge me, Sam. You have no idea what it was like."

"You're right. I'll never understand." *Shut up.* He had to shut up. But the next words escaped against his will. "I'd never spend my time and talents empowering and enriching and enabling a man like Keller."

Eliza reared back as if he'd punched her.

"Bro."

Sam barely registered his brother's warning tone. It was too late. His fury had won. "You took it a step further and shared his bed. Gave him a son. You should be very proud."

It was almost slow motion, the way Eliza's hand lifted, palm out. The way it came toward him and connected with his cheek. He welcomed the sting. He deserved it. He knew that.

It was a fine point on the end of this conversation.

Michael stepped between them, his focus on her. "Get in, please." His voice was low and kind. "It'll be all right."

Yeah.

Fine.

Everything would be just fine.

Sam swiveled and marched away, dodging rows and rows of perfect cars. He couldn't stay and listen to Eliza cry for a child she'd had with that monster.

He paced between a sea of sedans and SUVs and sports

cars. He shouldn't have said those things. Obviously, she'd been pulled into the cult. All that crap about how she hadn't known what was going on, how she'd been focused on the business and not paying attention to what the Kellers were doing with those girls. Lies. They had to be.

No wonder she hadn't told Sam about Levi. She was embarrassed she'd fallen for Keller's trap. Embarrassed she'd fallen for him.

It was a cult. Jed was a master manipulator, and Eliza had been vulnerable. Vulnerable because she'd seen Sam with Kylee. This was as much his fault as hers. It was just a lot easier to be mad at her than to deal with his own issues.

"Bro!"

He spun, and as Michael marched up to him, Sam said, "I know—"

"What is wrong with you?" His brother's words were laced with rage. "The woman you love is falling apart, and you walk away?"

"I know. I just need—"

"This isn't about you. Two of the people she loves most in the world are in the hands of a lunatic, and you're out here sulking because—"

"Did you know?"

He saw it, the truth on Michael's face.

"That's what you were talking about when I was shopping."

"I didn't know anything about the kid except that she had one."

"And you didn't think I needed to know that?"

His eyebrows shot up. "Really? I'm supposed to tell you that she has a child? How is that my business?"

"How is any of this your business?" He turned away, took a breath. Lifted a hand when Michael started to speak. "I know. I know you rescued her. I know all you've done for her—for me.

But a warning would have helped. I'm just trying to..." Process. Figure out how to live with it.

"You have a choice here." Michael's tone was measured. "You can get back in the car and work with us, or you can hightail it back to your life. Then I'll be the hero who saves her—again—and you'll be the jerk with all the money and nobody to share it with."

Sam could do that. He could go back to his safe, pathetic life. His lonely, lonely life.

"What's it gonna be?" Michael asked. "You gonna abandon her because of something that happened after you two broke up? Because she needs you, and I can't do this by myself." Michael stepped closer and dropped a hand on Sam's shoulder. "I love you, bro, but get your head on straight. Focus on what matters right now. You'll figure out the rest as you go."

Michael was right. Sam was being a jerk—again. All his anger was just masking how he really felt. Sad and heartbroken and betrayed.

Sam started for the car, but Michael stopped him and wrapped him in a bear hug. "This doesn't change how she feels about you. When she needed help, she ran to you. When I insisted she go straight to the FBI, she refused. She had no idea who I was, but she told me she needed to make things right with you first. She loves you." He slapped Sam's back a couple of times, then stepped away. "Try not to screw it up."

"That's not as easy as it looks."

Michael chuckled, but Sam didn't think anything was funny.

He marched toward the rental, praying with every step. He had no idea how to rescue three people surrounded by guards and keep the woman he loved safe at the same time.

And he had to do all that while not getting sidetracked by the fact that she had a kid...a kid whose father was a psychopath.

CHAPTER TWENTY-EIGHT

ELIZA SHOULD HAVE LISTENED to Michael. Now, her secret was out, and Sam wouldn't even look at her. She couldn't blame him.

And that didn't even matter because her mother and her son were in danger.

"Take the next left." Sam was directing Michael, but she had no idea where they were going.

Jed wouldn't hurt Levi. He doted on him, adored him. But he had no such feelings for Mom. And Nicole was there, too, sucked into his madness simply because she'd befriended Eliza.

Please, Father, keep them safe. Please.

She'd trade anything, do anything, as long as the ones she loved were safe. If that meant losing Sam...

She'd already lost him. Somehow, she'd learn to live with that.

But she couldn't survive if Mom or Nicole were hurt because of her. Or killed.

She couldn't live with it if Levi spent his life with that monster and his doting wife, raised to believe lies upon lies upon lies.

The car stopped, and Michael shifted into park. "Can you access the server?"

It took her a moment to figure out what he was talking about. "Yeah. I should be able to. Sam, we have that plastic thing, right?"

"Uh-huh." He pulled the white strip—the collar tab thing—from his pocket and handed it back.

The men stepped out of the SUV, so she did the same, then walked between them toward the little business center/copy shop ahead.

"What are we doing?" Eliza asked.

"Protecting the evidence." Michael lifted the manila envelope she'd taken from the bank. "Keller wants it back, but we need to keep a copy. If we can transfer what's in the server to a thumb drive—"

"But...wait." She froze in front of the door. "We're not going to turn it over? Shouldn't we just give this to the police and let them handle it?"

"We'll do that next, right?" Sam looked from her to Michael. "The FBI deals with this sort of thing all the time."

But Michael wasn't nodding. In fact, his lips were set in a grim line.

A couple of people stepped out of the copy shop, and Michael marched away from the door and foot traffic and cars, rounding the corner at the edge of the building.

Eliza and Sam followed. Sam was still a few yards away when he said, "What's going on?"

When they reached him, Michael focused on her. "The thing is, the FBI has their standard operating procedure. They can probably find them faster than I can. But I *can* find them, Eliza. I will find them."

"And then what?" Sam asked. "Are we supposed to rescue them? Go in, guns blazing?"

The question was ridiculous, but Michael didn't laugh. "Not exactly, but we'll figure out how—"

"I don't understand." Eliza's heart raced. "Why aren't we calling the police?"

"The professionals," Sam added.

At least she and Sam agreed on this one thing. That was something.

A muscle ticked in Michael's jaw. "The FBI will find them, surround the place, and then contact Keller. They'll try to negotiate, get him to release Levi and your mother and whoever else he's holding. You know him, Eliza. What do you think he'll do?"

She tried to imagine Jed backed into a corner, admitting defeat, and coming out with his hands up.

The picture wouldn't come.

"I've never met him," Michael said, "but from what you've told us and the conversation we just overheard—he's a narcissist, probably a megalomaniac, right?" The description fit. Michael turned to Sam. "You agree?"

"I'm no psychologist, but yeah. He's a Jesus-wannabe."

With a nod, Michael turned back to her. "He has a messiah complex, and maybe other mental illnesses. The point is, he doesn't seem like the type to negotiate a peace deal."

"But the FBI are trained to handle that kind of thing, aren't they?" She looked from one brother to the other. "I mean, they're better trained than we are."

"Better at negotiations, yeah." Michael's words were slow, measured. "I watched negotiators try to talk down a religious fanatic once. They assumed they could appeal to his common sense or morality or greed. But not everyone has the capacity for common sense. And some people's only moral code is their own desires—or delusions. And their greed can't be satisfied with anything any sane person would offer. And that can end..." He looked away, and in that moment, she had the sense that he wasn't seeing the drab parking lot or the neighboring businesses.

"What happened?" Eliza asked.

He shook his head. "Didn't end well." And then he met her eyes again. "I don't believe Keller will stand down. We have no idea how many men he has, how many guns. We have no idea how far he's willing to go to get what he wants."

"It'll be like Waco," Sam said.

"We don't want to get into a standoff," Michael said. "That's all I'm saying. And I think we can rescue them ourselves."

Sam was nodding. "I see what you mean." To Eliza, "I think he has a point. The messiah complex... Well, think about the difference between the true Savior and all the false saviors in history. Jesus died for His followers—died for everyone, even the people who nailed him to the cross. But false saviors..." He trailed his words, but Eliza saw where he was going.

"They expect their followers to die for them." Her words were a whisper because, God help her, she could picture that. She could picture Jed using Mom and Nicole as shields to protect himself. Even Lola, if he had to. And maybe Levi.

Sam's hand lifted toward her, and she wanted more than anything to take it, to feel his warmth and strength. But he stepped back. When she looked up at him, his eyes were cold.

His words rolled through her mind. *I'd never allow myself to be lied to and manipulated and dragged around like a puppy on a leash...spend my time and talents empowering and enriching and enabling a man like Keller.*

She wanted to hate him for those cruel words. If only they weren't true.

"This is your decision, Eliza," Sam said. "Your mother, your friend, your son. If you want to call the FBI, then that's what we'll do."

She focused on Michael. "If we don't, then what?"

A storm brewed in his eyes. "We rescue them."

"How?"

"Same way we got you. With help. But first..." He nodded toward the front of the store. "We secure the evidence. Unless... What do you want to do?"

The brothers were watching her, waiting for her to make the decision. If she made the wrong one, they could die.

Either way, they could die. Maybe there was no right decision. Maybe the situation was hopeless.

No. God promised His protection. Before she did all of this, He'd promised. She wouldn't doubt Him now.

Lead me, Lord.

No solid answer came, but she was filled with confidence in these men who'd already done so much for her. Their argument was sound. Even so...

"How do you know so much, Michael?" she asked. "I thought you were in sales."

His gaze flicked to Sam. "I have sort of a side gig."

She let her raised eyebrows ask the question. She was trusting him with the lives of people she loved. She needed to know.

"I can't say. I can tell you I'm one of the good guys. Not a"— his gaze flicked to Sam, and his lip quirked—"terrorist or international arms dealer."

"I guessed jewel thief," Sam said.

Michael almost smiled, but it faded. "You can either trust me or not, Eliza."

There was a tiny breath of peace in her heart, God saying the same thing.

You can either trust Me or not.

I trust You, Lord.

"Okay." She started toward the copy shop. "Let's make two copies. Better safe than sorry."

Inside, Michael headed for the shipping area.

Sam stopped at a copy machine with the envelope while Eliza approached the counter and spoke to the girl behind it. "Do you sell thumb drives?"

The girl pointed them out, and she chose a couple, which Sam gave her cash to pay for.

"Is there a computer I can use?"

"Yup." The cashier rounded the counter. "Follow me."

When Eliza was set up at the desktop on the far end of the store, she navigated to the secure server and keyed in the login and password she'd hidden in the collar of her shirt.

The information filled the screen, and Eliza let out a whoosh of breath. Because she'd known it was there, or should be. But so many things had gone wrong.

She started the process of copying onto the first thumb drive, then sat back and waited.

The waiting was the worst. When she had something to do, to occupy her mind and hands, she could drown out all the what-ifs. But stillness was torture. She closed her eyes and tried to breathe through her fear and focus on the here and now. Everyday sounds—the bell over the door, the chatter of customers, the rhythmic whush and whirr of the copy machine behind her.

Her father's voice found her. *All you can do is your best. You can't make it work. You can't control anybody else. You can't see into the future. You make choices, and you trust that God's got you, no matter what the outcome.*

And God had told her to trust Him.

But had she made one misstep too many? Was He really going to save her family—or was He going to let her live with the consequences of her bad decisions?

Please, Lord. Don't let anyone else pay the price for my mistakes.

She felt Sam's presence when he walked up behind her.

She needed to tell him.

She needed to tell him everything. Soon.

He pulled a chair up and sat. "You all right?" At least his voice was a little warmer.

"Sorry I slapped you."

"I deserved it. I deserved worse. I'm so sorry I said those things."

"Why? You were right. I was manipulated. I did use my talents to make him rich."

"You didn't know. And when you figured it out, you did the right thing. That took amazing courage and strength. I was just...jealous and petty. And I'm sorry. Can you forgive me?"

"If you can forgive me."

"Always." He reached over and squeezed her hand. "We're going to get them back."

She didn't know if that was true, but the words calmed her.

Michael approached her other side, and Sam said, "What's up?"

"I'm trying to think who we should send these to," Michael said.

Sam stood, and Eliza swiveled the chair and looked up at the brothers. "Why not the FBI? Don't we want them to have it?"

"We do." Michael's answer came slowly.

"But we don't want them acting on the information until we get Levi and Linda back, right?" Sam clarified. "That would tip our hand. Unless you could get them to hold off."

"I don't have that kind of pull. I don't think they'd go in that fast, but—"

"A couple more days shouldn't matter," Eliza said. "If the

women are still at The Ranch, they're safe. He doesn't want to hurt his followers."

"How sure are you?" Michael asked.

Sam was watching her, too, waiting.

"I mean, I don't... Whatever you two think we should—"

"Eliza." There was Sam's anger, peeking through.

But how would they know?

She considered the question.

The women would keep doing what they'd been trained to do. They'd harvest crops and muck out stalls and collect eggs. They'd build and weave and quilt and take care of the children. They didn't need to be guarded, though she didn't doubt a few guards remained. But most wouldn't try to leave, and if a few did... Well, maybe they'd get away. But in that respect, nothing had changed. The women had no reason to believe anything was wrong, at least as far as Eliza knew. Of course, something could've changed.

Everything could have changed. But...but she had to make a decision. Again, her father's words echoed in her mind. *You make choices, and you trust that God's got you.*

"I think they're safe, for now."

Sam squeezed her shoulder. It was nothing, really, just a slight touch. He'd probably forgotten for a moment that he hated her.

Michael said, "Good. So maybe..." He looked at Sam. "Mom and Dad?"

"I don't want to pull them into this."

The download completed, and Eliza swiveled back to the desk. She ejected one thumb drive, inserted the other, and started the process over.

"They're only pulled in if Keller knows we did it," Michael was saying. "And how would he?"

There was a pause, and Eliza looked up in time to see Sam cut his gaze to her.

Oh.

"You have a lot to lose." He sounded apologetic. "I know you'd never put anyone in jeopardy on purpose, but if your mom's life is in danger, or your son's—"

"I'd tell him anything, no question about it." Eliza turned her focus back to the screen. "You guys decide where to send the information, and don't tell me. Then, no matter what..." She closed her eyes against an onslaught of images. "I won't be able to tell."

The brothers moved away. She didn't look as they talked in low tones and couldn't make out what they were saying. She focused on the documents being transferred, the progress line inching across the screen.

Two more minutes. One more. And then it was done.

When she turned, Sam and Michael were both bent over envelopes, writing.

Five minutes later, the paperwork and flash drives were being overnighted to people the brothers trusted.

When they got to the car, Michael said, "Just so you know, we each chose somebody—not our parents—and filled out the forms. I don't know who he chose, and he doesn't know who I chose. Just in case."

Sam added, "Both packages have notes explaining what to do with it if we don't contact them in seven days. No matter what happens with you, Keller's going down."

She refused to dwell on the many things that could go wrong. "Smart."

The screen on the console showed directions back to the airport, and Michael headed that way.

Sam turned to face her. "Try not to worry. We'll keep you safe."

She loved the confidence in his words. The problem was, he said nothing about her mother or her son. Sam wanted to protect Eliza, and she was thankful for that, but she'd do anything to save Mom and Levi.

She needed to know he'd make the same choice.

CHAPTER TWENTY-NINE

SAM WAS TRYING to be nice, to make good on his promise of forgiveness. How could he hold a grudge after all he'd been forgiven?

But...Levi. The boy had changed everything. It wasn't fair of Sam to judge her for that, not when he'd hopped into bed with the first willing partner after Eliza had left him. Even so, he wasn't sure he'd be able to get over it. How could he? How could he love her son? If he married her, he'd have to raise the kid. Keller's kid.

Assuming they were able to put Keller behind bars. If not... What? Share custody with a crazy megalomaniac? Would she expect that of him?

Could he do it?

Thanks to Michael's friend, they'd put Keller's location somewhere in Maine northwest of Augusta. That part of the state wasn't exactly densely populated, which helped because it narrowed down the places Keller and his hostages could be. But the cell towers were far apart up there, meaning they had a much larger area to search.

Back in Denver, they'd debated which airport they should fly into. Not Manchester, of course. That was where Keller had told Eliza to go. Boston was the next most logical choice, which was why they'd discarded it. Providence could've worked, but if Keller and his people could figure out which flight she was on, then it was theoretically possible that they could get to Providence from Maine while she was in the air, especially if they were already guessing she'd land in Boston or Manchester. The last thing Sam wanted was to fight those guys off again. He had to be perfect every time. The goons only had to get it right once, and Eliza would be gone.

So, an hour before the nonstop to Burlington, Vermont, took off, Sam had purchased three first-class tickets. He couldn't tolerate another four-hour flight shoved against the window.

They got two seats together and one two rows back. Sam took that one, happy to be alone.

The flight landed just before midnight. They made it from the terminal to the rental car without incident. Sam drove, leaving the small city behind, while Michael tapped on his laptop in the passenger seat. In the back, Eliza stared out the window, not that she could see anything in the darkness except the blanket of stars overhead.

She hadn't spoken since they'd left Burlington.

They traveled over the river and through the woods—and coming 'round all sorts of mountains—for two hours. They were only halfway to Augusta, but they all needed to sleep.

"Is it a suite? Adjoining rooms?" Sam's voice sounded loud in the silence, only competing with the gentle rumble of tires on the highway.

"Couldn't find either." Michael had plugged his phone into the car, and the map showed that they were only twenty minutes from the hotel in Franconia, New Hampshire.

At least they had Michael's phone. He hadn't wanted Keller tracking Sam's phone the way Michael's friend had tracked Keller's, so he'd had Sam turn it off before they boarded the flight—right after he'd turned off the locator service and GPS and put it in airplane mode. Seemed like overkill, but Michael obviously knew a lot more about this stuff than he did. If not for the fact that it was the only way Keller could reach Eliza, Sam would've tossed it in the trash in Denver.

A few minutes later, he parked in the hotel parking lot and gazed at the place—two stories, white siding. "It's not exactly the Marriott."

"When did you turn into such a snob?" But Michael was smiling when he got out and opened Eliza's door.

The place was nice on the inside in a rustic-mountain-cabin sort of way. Lots of dark, warm wood. In the sunken living area just off the lobby, two deep, cushy sofas faced a huge stone fireplace, embers glowing within. A couple of workstations with computers filled the space beyond that, and then floor-to-ceiling windows that probably offered a great view in the daylight. Not so much at nearly three a.m.

Sam handed over his credit card and got the room keys.

"Second floor, right across the hall from each other." The white-haired woman spoke the words around a yawn. "Breakfast served seven to nine."

"Thanks for waiting up for us." Eliza flashed her a smile, then trudged up the wide staircase.

Behind her, Sam gave Michael their room key, then opened Eliza's door before handing hers over. He peeked inside—seemed fine—but stayed in the hall. "Let me know if you need anything."

"I need my clothes and—"

"Right." He turned for his room just as the door opened.

Michael tossed a plastic shopping bag to her. "I think that's everything."

She smiled at him. "Thanks."

"See you in the morning." She didn't wait for an answer, just went inside and closed the door.

Would things ever be normal between them again? Could they get past this? He had no idea, especially if it meant raising the son of a lunatic.

More likely, when this was over, she'd realize Sam wasn't the man she'd thought. When she did, she'd leave him again.

And he'd resume his life, go back to putting together deals and amassing his fortune.

Lonely and pathetic? Maybe. But money was always the right size, always the right color. And it never rejected him.

An hour later, Sam was still staring at the ceiling. So tired his eyelids felt like sandpaper, but he couldn't manage to keep them closed. Couldn't shut his stupid brain off.

It'd been a mistake to power up his laptop before bed.

The buyers had rejected Ernest's latest demand and threatened to take the deal off the table. Sam had forwarded their email to Ernest and told him he'd call him later today. And then he'd forgotten, wrapped up in Eliza's mess.

The email he'd read right before turning off the light churned like acid in his stomach. It was a short and terse letter from Ernest telling him his services were no longer needed.

Great. Just freaking fabulous.

He'd blown the deal.

And considering that Eliza had barely spoken to him in hours, he'd probably blown that too.

In the other queen bed, Michael had dropped off about

three seconds after his head hit the pillow. Just like Dad, who'd always joked about his ability to fall asleep fast.

The blessing of a clear conscience.

There was truth in that. Because Sam wrestled with all his shortcomings. The things he'd said to Eliza that day. The accusations. The cruelty in his words.

The way he'd treated Kylee. The morning she woke up in his bed, he'd been honest about his feelings—or lack thereof. Pretty lousy timing, that.

He'd made her cry. Now, she was happily married and well over her crush on Sam, but he still felt the shame.

Kylee had deserved better. So did Eliza.

And now he was messing up the only thing he'd ever done well—his business.

No wonder he couldn't get anybody to stick around.

And wasn't that a lovely thought to curl up and go to sleep with?

Lovely and petty and small, focusing on himself when a crazy person held Eliza's friend and mother and son captive. A person who'd harm at least two of them to get Eliza to do what he demanded. People were in danger, one of whom she loved more than her own life. Sam had to figure out how to protect them. This wasn't a problem money could solve, but money was the only thing Sam had to offer.

His thoughts churned and circled and churned until he wanted to pull his hair out.

Whatever. Sleep was overrated.

He dressed in his dirty jeans and his blue sweater, eschewing the ugly Colorado State sweatshirt he'd bought that day, shoved his feet into sneakers, and slid out the door, sticking the key into his back pocket. Maybe a walk would tire him out. If nothing else, he'd get a break from his brother's snoring for a few minutes.

He descended the stairs, thinking he'd look for food. They'd eaten on the flight, but that had been hours before. Maybe he'd sleep if he had a full stomach.

He was about to search for a snack bar or vending machine when he glanced into the dark living room. There was a figure on the couch in the light of the fire. Knees pulled up to her chest, blanket curled around her, gaze toward the hearth.

She must have added a couple of logs because flames danced, reflected on her beautiful face.

Not wanting to startle her—or talk to her—he crept, hoping to slip around the corner without alerting her to his presence.

But Eliza turned his way. "Oh."

So much for that. "I thought you'd be sleeping."

"Me too. We should both be."

Obviously, avoiding a discussion about her son wasn't bringing either of them peace.

He continued into the living area and settled beside her on the couch. She looked so small and vulnerable, and his mind flashed back to the previous Friday, the way she'd practically thrown herself into his arms. She hadn't trusted Daniel or Camilla that night, but she'd trusted him, completely.

Today, thanks to his cruel, callous words, he'd lost that trust. Or, more likely, she just remembered that he'd lost it a long time ago.

Without trust, what did they have? Bad memories and broken hearts.

Sheesh. He sounded like a country music song. Where was the twangy tune?

The only sound came from the crackling embers. The earthy scents of fresh pine and burning logs filled the room. The scent of home.

"Why can't you sleep?" He kept his voice low, barely above a whisper.

Her eyes flicked his direction but didn't hold. "You know why."

He wanted to take her hand. Instead, he clasped his together on his lap. "You want to talk about it?"

Eliza didn't speak for a long moment. Then, she pushed to her feet.

That would be a no.

He should just let her go. But..."I'm sorry." He caught her hand as she scooted by him. "We can just... We don't have to talk."

But she kept moving, gripping his hand and tugging him up behind her.

He followed, body hoping and brain fearing he knew what she was thinking. He'd have to reject her, and he wasn't sure he had it in him.

But she didn't aim for the staircase, for her bedroom. She crossed to a workstation and sat. A jiggle of the mouse, and the computer screen came to life.

He pulled a chair over. "What are we doing?"

"I'm sorry I didn't tell you about Levi." She opened a browser window and typed, not even glancing his way. "I just...I didn't know how. And I didn't want to say it in front of Michael. Or in public."

"We've spent a lot of time together."

"Not alone. Not since I remembered, when we were with Grant and Jon. And then Michael was with us."

There were a couple of hours in the car between Concord and York, but that was when she'd told him about the cult. Why she couldn't have slipped in the information then, he didn't bother to ask.

A website loaded, and she logged in.

Then, a list of file folders appeared. She clicked on Photos, which loaded more folders. They all seemed to be named by dates.

She clicked one, then scrolled. He was too far away to make out the tiny thumbnails.

And then, a little boy's image filled the screen. He had a round face and curly blond hair. He was grinning at the camera, showing a line of baby teeth and a little smudge of green on his nose. Frosting, Sam guessed, seeing the cake in front of him. A few slices had been cut out, but the words were mostly there. *Happy Birthday, Levi!*

Sam tried to find a resemblance to Eliza. But there was nothing. The kid had bright blue eyes where hers were hazel. He had curly hair where hers was straight. He had blond hair where hers was brown...though maybe it'd been blond when she was a kid. Sam's had been until he was six or seven.

And okay, maybe the *color* of his eyes was wrong, but he saw Eliza's in the shape. They were big and round and filled with wonder.

And, *wow.*

Levi was a beautiful child. Chubby cheeks tinged with pink, a chin that would grow stronger as he matured.

He was glad he didn't know what Keller looked like. Maybe if he never discovered similarities between the kid and his insane father it would be easier.

He felt Eliza's gaze.

"He's cute." Didn't exactly sum it up, but what did she expect from him?

"That was his birthday party."

"I actually put that together all by myself."

"He's four." When Sam said nothing, she spoke again. "You see what's in the background?"

He tore his eyes away from the little cherub and... "Christmas baby?" He looked at her for confirmation.

She was watching him with an intense gaze, as if trying to impart some valuable information.

"What? Is that important?"

She swiveled her chair to face Sam. "Did you ever wonder why I was at the restaurant that day?"

The change of subject had him scrambling. "Um..."

"The day you were with Kylee?"

"I never really... I guess I thought it was a coincidence. Or maybe you'd come to"—he shrugged, feeling stupid saying it—"spy on me. See if you could catch me... And, you did, I guess."

"I wasn't spying. I knew you'd be there. You always took clients there."

"Oh-kaaay."

She turned back to the screen and tapped the birthday cake. "He turned four last Christmas. Meaning, he'll be five this Christmas."

As if he didn't know what came after four. "Uh-huh." He was looking at the screen, seeking the clue she was not-so-clearly trying to lead him to.

And then he started doing the math.

Counting backward from December, five years ago.

And the truth slammed into him. Stole his breath.

He turned back to Eliza. "Are you saying...? What are you saying?" Because he was afraid to hope. Afraid to even think...

"I went to find you that day to tell you." She swallowed, straightened her shoulders as if preparing for a blow. "I was pregnant."

Whoa.

What?

After a few seconds, the starch went out of Eliza's spine. She leaned toward him, took his hand. Hers were cold as she squeezed his fingers. "It was just all too much. Dad's death, selling the business, then losing my job—everybody's jobs. And then I found out I was pregnant, and Mom had been telling me that you were going to leave me. Move on to someone else. She'd even told me to be careful, that if I turned up pregnant, you'd dump me like yesterday's trash. But I knew, I *knew* you'd be thrilled—as thrilled as I was that we were going to have a baby. I couldn't wait to tell you. That's why I was at the restaurant.

"And then I saw you with Kylee, and it...it wrecked me. And I thought Mom was right. You'd already moved on, and I couldn't face her. I was embarrassed and broken and I didn't want to tell anybody. I needed time. Time to get my feet under me, to figure out what I wanted without her harping on me with I-told-you-so's. I wasn't going to stay gone. I planned to get Jed and Lola set up with their finances and then come back. And then I stayed for months, until almost when the baby was due. And when I told them I was leaving, Jed told me you were married, and I...I didn't want to blow up your life. And I just...I had the baby, and..."

Her words were rattling around in his brain, trying to find a place to land.

But he was still processing that the child, the beautiful, cherubic child on the screen was...his?

Could it be true?

And just like that, he saw it.

The blond curly hair.

Sam's hair was curly if he let it grow too long. And it'd been blond when he was that age.

The boy's bottom lip, just a little fuller than the one on top. The cleft chin.

Features Sam had seen in the mirror all his life.

Levi did look like his father.

He looks like me.

And maybe it was because he hadn't slept that his eyes

prickled, that he had to clench his jaw to keep his chin from wobbling.

Or maybe it was because, for the first time, he was looking at...his son.

Eliza was still talking. He had no idea what she was saying, hadn't been able to focus on her words. Until...

"I'm so sorry, Sam. Can you ever forgive me?"

And that did it.

He stood suddenly. Stepped back.

Forgive her?

She thought he needed to forgive her? After all the cruel things he'd said to her? The terrible ways he'd treated her?

He didn't understand how she could have left. He didn't understand so much. But he did understand what mattered. That she'd had a child, on her own. That she'd done everything she could to protect that child.

His child.

Eliza didn't need Sam's forgiveness. He needed hers.

He pulled her to her feet, not missing the quiet gasp or the fear in her eyes.

As if he might hurt her.

Never.

He wrapped her in his arms and held her close. Overwhelmed with emotion. But it wasn't enough.

He backed up to look at her, this beautiful, beautiful woman. He pressed a palm on her cheek, into her hair.

She blinked, those wide eyes filled with confusion.

If he could speak, he would, but he didn't know how to put into words all the things he was feeling.

So he kissed her. He told himself to be gentle, to be tender. But his body was moving much faster than his brain. He urged her lips open and dove in, feeling her relief, tasting the salt in her tears. Or maybe those were his tears. And he didn't even care, couldn't have stopped them if he'd wanted to.

She melted against him, her arms snaking around his neck.

He wanted every single part of her. He backed her to the wall, braced one hand against it, the other behind her back, arching her closer. Feeling the warmth of her pressed against him.

He would never get enough of her. Never wanted to let her go.

He heard, or maybe felt, the little mew she made in her throat. The sound exploded desire in him, and he groaned.

Groaned and stopped and stepped away.

But he couldn't stand the distance.

He pulled her against his chest and held her there. Catching his breath. Breathing in her scent.

Slow down.

Because there was a right way to do this, and there was a wrong way. And he knew the pain in choosing the wrong way. He wasn't going to screw this up again. No way.

Eliza laid her hand against his heart. "I'm... I don't know what you're thinking. But...I'm sorry, for all of it."

He stepped back and took her shoulders in his hands.

She was staring at his neck.

"Look at me, sweetheart."

She did, and there was that fear again.

"I've been such a jerk." He swallowed, tried to keep his voice steady. "We both made bad decisions based on bad information. We both messed up. But one of our mess-ups created that precious..." He looked up, tried to blink the tears back. Decided it didn't matter and faced her again. "I love you. And I love him. And I will love him even more when I meet him."

And then, the rest of it slammed into him.

He'd known Keller was holding Levi. He just hadn't known...

His son. That lunatic had *his son*.

"I'll call Grant. He'll help, and Jon, too. I'll hire the bodyguards where he used to work. They were all special forces. We're going to figure this out. I swear to you, Eliza. We're going to get our son back."

CHAPTER THIRTY

ELIZA HURRIED through her shower and threw on the only clean outfit she had left, berating herself for sleeping so late. It was almost eleven o'clock. She and Sam had talked until dawn, only leaving when the foyer lights came on and the white-haired woman who'd checked them in spied them in the living area.

Sam had kissed her tenderly at her door and told her to rest. And she'd tried, but she hadn't been able to stop replaying the conversation. She hadn't fallen asleep until after sunrise.

Even so, how had she slept so late?

She still could hardly believe Sam's reaction to the news. She'd been sure he'd be angry at her for keeping his son from him. Sad at all he'd missed.

Instead, he'd held her, kissed her, and told her he loved her. And then he'd questioned her about Levi. *What is he like? What's his favorite food? Can he throw a ball?* He'd follow crazy tangents. *I can put a basketball hoop in the driveway. You think he'd like that?*

And a pool. Can he swim? He'd hardly balked when she said no. *Good! We'll teach him next summer.*

As if there were no question what the future held. As if she and Sam would be together, and Levi would be with them, and they'd live in his big house in Shadow Cove, and everything would be fine. Better than fine.

Perfect.

But the line that reverberated in her memories, what finally allowed her to fall asleep...

We're going to get our son back.

His absolute confidence.

Please, Lord. Her fear felt more acute this morning. Her future had always felt murky and muddled, but the image Sam painted—the three of them together, like a real family. She could see it, and she wanted it. She wanted it with every cell in her body.

It was so close, and she was terrified something was going to destroy it all. Her friend and her mother and her son were in danger. And so was the life she desperately wanted to build with Sam.

She felt like she was on a bus hanging over the edge of a cliff. One wrong move, and the whole thing would crash and burn.

Sam had slipped a note beneath her door, letting her know where he was. She took the stairs to the lobby, glancing into the living area where a few people sat on the sofas. She rounded the corner in the other direction and passed a gift shop. Inside, a couple of preteens were trying on hats and making faces in a mirror. The hotel had felt empty and lifeless the night before, but now it buzzed with activity.

She reached a door at the end of the hall and pushed it open. She'd barely stepped into the glass-enclosed sunroom when Sam headed her way. She sort of registered that other people were with him, but she couldn't take her eyes off the man coming toward her.

"Hey." He greeted her with a hug and a kiss on the forehead, then leaned back to meet her eyes. "Did you sleep?"

"Finally. And too long, obviously. You?"

"I didn't even try." He'd showered and trimmed his beard and, though there were dark smudges around his eyes, he looked wide awake and intense as he took her hand and led her across the thin carpet to a round table large enough for eight normal-sized humans. But the men seated there were anything but normal-sized.

Michael stood as she approached and wrapped an arm around her shoulder. "Morning. Get some rest?"

"Not much. Did you?"

He shrugged and shot Sam a look.

Before she could ask, Grant stood and gave her a side hug. "Glad you're safe."

Jon rose with the rest of them, but he didn't move from his spot on the far side of the table, just dipped his head. "Good to see you again, Eliza."

"How did you guys get up here so early?" she asked.

Sam chuckled. "It's not exactly early." He pulled out a chair for her, one facing the window and the spectacular view. Tree-covered mountains boasting every shade of green imaginable, broken up by hints of red, orange, and yellow.

Would she have her son back by autumn? Would she be with him to experience the spectacular New England foliage?

"You all right?" Sam asked.

"Yeah, yeah." She sat, and the rest of the men did as well. The table was covered with half-empty cups of coffee and glasses of water, not to mention stacks of paper and four laptops, all open.

While she'd slept, they'd been working on finding her mother and her son. The thought brought tears to her eyes.

She was so tired of crying. And being afraid. And being in pain. Her arm ached from where Gil had manhandled her two days before. Her hip throbbed from getting tossed into a trunk like a bag of bark mulch. Her wrist still ached from the previous Friday night.

But none of the physical pain rivaled the ache in her heart. She wanted her son back. And her mom safe. And everything to be okay.

Sam poured coffee from a carafe on the table into a clean cup and moved the bowls of sugar packets and creamer close. Then he slid a napkin-covered plate close. "I saved you a biscuit from breakfast."

"Thank you." She reached for a sugar packet and tore the top. "I'm in desperate need of caffeine, so maybe this is a dumb question." She focused on Grant. "How is it you're here already?"

Grant sent Sam a sardonic look. "He called me. About six hours ago."

She snapped her gaze to the man beside her. "You didn't."

He shrugged. "We needed to make plans."

"You told them about Levi?"

Before he could answer, Michael said, "Woke me before dawn. I think he'd have bought cigars if there'd been a store open."

Sam might've looked a little embarrassed, but he shrugged. "It's kind of big news. Haven't told anybody else yet, just these guys. I'm hoping to introduce him to everybody at the anniversary party. What a present that'll be."

She remembered her conversation with Grant and looked his way now. Sam's younger brother wore a slight smile. Apparently, he didn't mind that his and Summer's news might not be the biggest surprise of the day.

"We have to get him back first," Eliza said.

Sam's expression shifted to grim determination. "We're working on that."

"And?"

"We're still trying to narrow down where they might be. There're a lot of options in the area where his phone pinged. Houses and neighborhoods and strip malls. Not to mention vacation homes and—"

"Unless you can get a better location on him," Jon said, "we'll have to check them off one by one."

"But it would have to be a place he's connected with, right?" Eliza shifted her gaze from Jon to Sam. "Don't you think?"

"Why do you say that?" Sam asked.

"He didn't just randomly pick central Maine. There has to be a reason he went there and not...well, anywhere else."

"I've been trying to figure that out," Jon said. "From my research, Keller grew up in Massachusetts."

"But his father is from Maine," she said.

Jon squinted, tapped on his laptop. "His father's from Malden. His mother's from Revere. His father died when he was a kid."

"Right, but..." She nibbled a bite of the biscuit. Fluffy and soft and just salty enough from the butter that must've been brushed over the top. "His mom remarried."

"When Keller was"—Jon scrolled—"nine."

"The *stepfather's* from Maine," Eliza clarified. "Jed talked about him a lot. He respected him when he was young, but then he—"

"Arnold Cushing."

"Right. Arnold started making the family go to church, and Jed didn't like it. He lost respect for him then. I guess they fought a lot." She focused on Sam. "He told this story to explain about how weak people search for a higher power, but wise people follow guides who'll teach them to seek that higher power within themselves."

"Mmm." The low sound coming from Sam's mouth was

nearly a growl. "And he was one of those guides, I guess."

"The only one, as far as I could tell." She turned back to Jon. "His stepfather was an alcoholic, and he 'found God,' as Jed would say, at AA. According to Jed, he never conquered his addiction, and Jed believed it was because he leaned on a mythical God instead of on himself."

"Interesting theory," Grant said. "Except it goes against the millions of people who credit God with overcoming their addictions."

"Nobody ever challenged Jed. Wasn't worth the argument. The point is, they visited the stepfather's family a lot. I don't know where they lived, but Jed made it sound pretty remote. Also, Jed and Lola lived in Kennebunk when I met them. Maybe they own other property in the state?"

"Already checked that," Sam said. "Nothing in Maine."

"You're doing that?" Eliza asked. Because Jon was the private investigator, wasn't he?

"I do my homework when a buyer shows interest in a business I'm representing. This isn't so different from that." Sam tapped on his laptop. "I looked into properties owned by Keller's family and Lola's."

"Can you show me the area we're searching?" Eliza asked.

Sam clicked to a map. She leaned close and saw a satellite view. Forest. Miles and miles and miles of forest.

Levi and Mom could be anywhere. How would they ever find them?

⁓

After an hour of no results, the quiet tapping on keys was slowly driving Eliza insane. Probably because while the men worked, she had nothing to do. Nothing to add. She'd nibbled half the biscuit, but she craved something more substantial.

Maybe Sam could feel her frustration because he looked up from the screen. "I wish I had a laptop you could use. Maybe you could check on lunch? I asked earlier if they'd bring us something around noon." It was quarter past. "You guys hungry?"

"I could eat," Grant said.

"You can always eat." Then Michael winked at her. "I think it's a Wright family characteristic. Just wait till Levi gets big."

The idea that her son might grow up to be like these over-size men... She could hardly imagine it.

She pushed back in her chair and went in search of the dining room. After speaking to one of the waitstaff, who promised to deliver their lunches soon, she used the restroom and then headed toward the sunroom, glancing at the pictures hanging in the hallway. They displayed the hotel and property over the years. According to a plaque beside a black-and-white photo taken in the fifties, it'd started as a campground.

The thought niggled a memory free, and she hurried back to the sunroom. "I remembered something."

The men stopped what they were doing and looked at her, but she focused on Sam.

"After Jed's stepdad became a believer, he made Jed go to church camp every summer. The camp was in Maine."

"Okay, good." Jon shifted his gaze to his laptop and started typing. After a few seconds, he said, "Lots of options."

Of course there were. *Lord, a little help?*

"We should call his mom and stepfather." Sam looked up at her. "Do you think they'd help us?"

"They're dead."

Jon's gaze snapped up. "He told you that? That his parents are dead?"

Eliza was too excited to sit. This felt like it might lead to something. "Car accident when Jed was seventeen. His father'd had too much to drink and drove off the road. He talked about it a lot, how devastating it was when he got the news. How he was an only child who had to make his own way."

Sam was watching the private investigator over the top of his laptop, eyebrow quirked. "Not what happened?"

"Arthur and Marybeth Cushing are still alive," Jon said. "They live in Tennessee."

Eliza plopped in her chair. Why was she surprised? Jed would say anything to manipulate people, and what better way than to claim he was an orphan? That his alcoholic stepfather had killed his mother? It was a way to garner pity and respect all at the same time.

"Any chance you've dug up a number for them?" Michael asked.

"Hold up." Jon typed, and then Michael's phone dinged.

Michael started to stand but settled again, focusing on Sam and Eliza. "Do you guys want to call?"

Sam looked at her.

"I wouldn't know what to ask," she said.

Sam nodded to his brother. "I have a feeling you'll get more information than I could. What are you going to say?"

Michael shrugged. "I'll figure it out as I go."

He headed outside, then disappeared down a set of stairs that led to the yard below. It stretched a good fifty yards beyond the hotel, only interrupted by a covered pool and concrete patio.

Their lunches were delivered, and they ate while they searched for information, Eliza leaning in to read Sam's screen.

"Okay." Sam tapped his screen. "There are two camps on Cobbosseecontee Lake. I think one's a Christian camp. But I think... Is it too far east?"

"Yeah," Jon said. "And we have to find places that were open back then. This would've been... Keller's in his midforties, so thirty years ago."

"Wouldn't it have to be closed now?" Eliza asked. "Maybe not permanently, but for the season at least? Maybe we should find a place that rents in the off-season?"

"Great point, Eliza." Sam shot her a smile. "And we should look into abandoned camps too."

"Not as easy to find." Jon stood. "Gotta make a call." He headed out the way Eliza had come in.

Grant had been quiet through most of the conversation. Now, he looked at her. "I can't wait to meet my nephew."

"Oh." She smiled at the kindness in his eyes. "You're going to love him."

"Levi, right?" Grant asked.

"Yeah."

Sam bumped her shoulder. "I always liked the name Levi."

"That's why I chose it."

His eyes lit.

"Why Levi?" Grant asked his brother. "I mean, it's great, but—"

"Levi was Jacob's third son." Sam must've seen Eliza's confusion. "You know, tribe of Israel?"

Oh, right. She hadn't had much training in the Bible, but she knew what he was talking about.

"I guess he reminded me that third sons can matter. The Levites were sort of important." He nodded to his brother. "Fourth sons matter, too, I suppose."

Grant's eyebrows hiked. "You suppose?"

Sam chuckled. "No idea what the fourth son's name was."

"Judah." Grant seemed to be trying to hide a smile, but he failed, and it spread across his face. "As in, the Lion of Judah. As in, an ancestor of Christ."

"Whatever, idiot." Sam threw a napkin at him, which Grant snatched out of the air.

"You throw like a girl."

Eliza laughed. "I'm just glad there aren't twelve Wright brothers."

"You and Mom both." Sam kissed her temple. "So you chose the name for me?"

She nodded, shifting to watch his expression. "Levi Samuel."

"Really?" He blinked a couple of times, swallowed. "Not sure I deserve that honor."

"I wanted him to know you."

"Levi Samuel Wright. Well, I guess it's Pelletier, for now." Sam said. "LSP. Almost spells lisp."

"Fortunately, he doesn't have one," she said, "or those would be very unfortunate initials."

"He'll be a Wright soon enough." But Sam's cheer dimmed. "Wait... How did Jon not know he was your kid? His name had to be on the airline ticket when you flew in. How did Jon not notice Levi had your last name?"

Oh.

It wasn't that she didn't know the answer but that she didn't want to share it.

"Eliza?" Sam's expression morphed into that angry-intense look he'd worn so often in the last few days. "Explain."

"That *is* his name," she said. "His legal name. But Jed didn't want the state to start poking around at The Ranch, so he forged all the kids' birth certificates. The forged one—which was the only one I had access to—says his name is Levi Jedediah Keller."

"He forced you to give *my son* his name?" Sam's voice was too loud in the enclosed space, the words bouncing off the glass.

She sipped her coffee to give herself something to focus on. "He considers all the babies born on The Ranch his. He insists they call him Daddy and revere him like a father."

"Which is why he said on the phone that Levi is his."

"Exactly. But right after he was born, back when I still had some freedom, I got him an official birth certificate. I gave a false address, though, because I didn't want Jed to see when it came in the mail, but it's filed with the state. It's legal." In retrospect, she realized how twisted that was. At the time, she'd justified her decision by reminding herself how much Jed and Lola had done for her.

If only she'd seen through them sooner.

"He knows on some level that Jed isn't his father. I always call Jed Levi's pretend father—when Jed isn't around. Of course, I've made it clear to Levi that he shouldn't call Jed that. Fortunately, they don't spend that much time together."

"What would Keller say if he knew?"

She shrugged. "He never found out."

Sam watched her a long moment with something in his eyes she couldn't quite name. Maybe gratitude. Maybe hope? He didn't voice it, just returned his focus to his screen.

"I have an update on the woman found in your mother's basement." Grant's words sent acid to her stomach. "Her name was Carolyn Jensen. Widow, two kids. She lived—"

"Across the street," Eliza said. "I know."

"Cause of death was a head injury likely sustained when she hit the basement floor. Coroner said she had bruises on her body consistent with a struggle and a fall. They collected samples from under her fingernails for DNA testing. Those won't come back for a month at best."

"How awful." How many more people were going to get hurt before Jed was stopped?

"Somebody"—now Grant glared at the spot where Michael'd been sitting—"smoothed things over with the local police, but in the future, if you ever find a dead body, call the police right away."

"We were trying to stay alive." That from Sam, who didn't sound amused at his brother's lecture.

"Glad you did. Just saying, next time, go to the police."

"So we can be questioned for hours—again?" Sam sounded disgusted. "And then be released to deal with it ourselves?"

"They're doing their best, man."

"Yeah? Are the thugs still in custody?" By the challenge in his tone, Sam knew better.

Grant didn't look away. "They were released on bail."

"Too bad, considering now we know they killed that woman."

"We don't know that." Grant turned his focus to Eliza and softened his tone. "Coroner believes she was killed sometime Monday afternoon, when your attackers were in North Conway and then jail."

"Meaning someone else did it?" Her voice was too high. Even she could hear the terror in it. How many people were after them?

"Looks like it."

Sam squeezed her hand but offered no words of comfort.

The room was quiet for a few minutes as Sam and Grant returned to their research, and then Grant spoke again.

"I've been looking into Gil Lyle. Do you remember anything else about the assault charge? The one against Nicole Moore?"

Eliza hadn't thought about it, but now that she did, the details filled in. "Nicole was sick and had to see a doctor. Gil was telling her to get in the car, but she was distraught, begging Jed to go with her. He just patted her shoulder and told her Gil could handle it. Gil has all the compassion of a loaded shotgun, so I could see why she'd have preferred pretty much anyone else to drive her. I think she'd had a miscarriage."

"Gil's kid?" Grant asked.

"Keller's, probably." Sam's words sounded angry. He looked at her for confirmation. "Right?"

"That was before I knew Nicole and before I started

figuring out what was really going on, so..." She shrugged. "Gil drove her to the city. She was delivered back to The Ranch the next day in a police car. She scurried off to the dorm, but the officers came inside and asked Jed about Gil's employment. Jed downplayed it, saying Gil did some odd jobs sometimes. I was the one who made out his paychecks, so I knew he was employed full time. He and Elliot lived in a trailer on the property."

Sam asked, "They weren't guards at that point?"

"I never thought of them as guards, but in retrospect, maybe they were. The cops suggested that Gil didn't have the temperament to be around young, vulnerable women. I agreed wholeheartedly, even then. The guy was a creep."

"Did you tell the police that?" Grant asked.

"They didn't ask me."

"You could have offered the information," Grant said. "Keller lied to the police, and you thought it was—what? No big deal?"

"I figured he had his reasons."

Grant grunted. She could feel another *suggestion* coming on about how she should trust the police, but he seemed to think better of it, returning his focus to his laptop. "Police report says Gilbert Lyle and Nicole Moore got into an altercation at the hospital, and he was arrested."

"And the charges dropped, right?" At Grant's nod, Sam added, "I'm betting Keller made her drop them."

Eliza asked, "Why are you looking into that?"

"It's good to know your enemies. The more we know about the men we'll be facing, the better shot we'll have at defeating them. What about the other guy? Elliot Ramsey? What do you know about him?"

"As creepy as Gil was, Elliot was worse. Gil always had hatred in his eyes, which is scary, but at least you know what you're in for. Elliot was more..." She wasn't sure how to explain it. "While Gil looked like he wanted to kill, Elliot..." She crossed her arms and tucked her hands in, suddenly feeling a chill. "When I made the mistake of meeting his eyes, I saw hunger in them."

Sam growled beside her. "He ever hurt you?"

"Never came close to me. Gil would've killed him if Jed didn't fire him first."

"Did Elliot seem to be itching for a fight?" Grant asked.

"No, no. Not like Gil, anyway. Elliot's strong, though." She looked at Sam. "You fought him twice. What did you think?"

"He was capable."

Grant's lips twitched. "Not as capable as you, I guess."

"I was fighting for our lives. That's what we call motivation."

"You think...?" Eliza wasn't sure how to ask the question. Or maybe she just didn't want to. She directed her words at Grant. "You think you're going to have to fight them? Gil and Elliot and the rest of them?"

He didn't shake his head or smile or act like it was a silly question. "We're going to do whatever we have to do to rescue your son and your mother."

"And Nicole."

"Right. If that means battle, then yeah. That's what we'll do."

"And you don't have a problem with not calling the police?" Sam asked.

His lips slipped into a smirk. "It's not my first choice, but I understand the reasoning. Thing is, when it goes down, I think we should alert them. If anyone gets killed, we'll need the cover."

Her mind hitched on one word... *Killed.* She swallowed the terror it raised. "But...but how can you...? Wouldn't it be safer to have someone else go in? I don't want any of you to get hurt or..." She couldn't help but glance at Sam when she asked the question, but his focus was on his brother.

How could she live with it if Grant or Michael or Jon got hurt? How could she live with it if Sam did?

His arm slid around her, and he pulled her to his side. "We're just going to take one step at a time and pray the Lord guides us."

Grant smiled. "Jon and I've run some difficult ops. We got this."

The door opened, and Jon stepped into the sunroom. "Talked to a guy who works in parks and recreation. He gave me the name of three possibilities we can check out. One's closed, but the other two are operational."

Footsteps on the wooden staircase outside had them all turning as Michael reached the door. He stepped inside and hurried to his laptop. "I got a name. Birch Grove Christian Camp."

"That's one of the names I just got," Jon said. "It closed about thirty years ago."

Grant was already typing. "Found it. It's within the coordinates."

"Jed's parents told you that?" Sam's voice held a hint of skepticism. "Can we trust them?"

"The mother wouldn't talk to me," Michael said, "but his stepfather gave me an earful, starting with demanding to know how I found them. Apparently, Jed doesn't know where they live, and they don't want him showing up."

"What?" Eliza said. "Why?"

"Cushing said he threatened to kill them if they ever came near him again." Michael tapped on his screen. "Apparently, the last time Keller was at Birch Grove..." He read something, nodding slowly. "Yup, yup. This is it."

Sam leaned to see his screen. "It burned down?"

"Not the whole thing," Michael said. "One of the dorms caught fire, and it took out another one and a lot of trees. Fortunately, firemen got it stopped before it spread and took out the whole place." He looked up, gaze flicking to Eliza before it settled on Sam. "It was arson. The Cushings think Keller set it. The fire was started at lunchtime when the kids were at the mess hall. But one kid was sick and in his bed. He died of smoke inhalation."

Icy fingers trailed down Eliza's back. She wished she could protest, tell them the man she knew could never do such a thing. Five years earlier, she would have. But now...anything was possible.

"It was an accident?" Jon asked. "Not the fire, but the kid who died?"

Michael's head shook. "Can't know for sure, of course. But the victim and Keller didn't like each other. The night before, the guy had beaten him in a race or something. Keller was humiliated and angry."

"Was he arrested?" Grant asked. "Prosecuted? He'd have been a juvenile, but I can call—"

"Don't bother." Michael stood, pacing a minute before leaning his hands on the back of his chair. "That was the part that seemed to spook Cushing the most—the fact that Keller did it, and everybody knew he did it, but they couldn't prove it. He thought there were probably witnesses, but none of the kids spoke up. Cushing thinks they were all afraid of him. The camp closed that summer and never reopened."

"He's a psychopath." Sam's words, spoken under his breath, seemed to echo in the room. Or maybe just in her mind.

Her friend, her mother, and her son were in the hands of a psychopath.

A murderer.

CHAPTER THIRTY-ONE

SAM WOKE to find Michael's bed rumpled but empty. He had a vague memory of his brother returning sometime in the middle of the night. Sam had slept almost as late this morning as Eliza had the previous day. It was nearly nine o'clock. Considering he'd gone to bed at eleven... He couldn't remember the last time he'd conked out for so many hours.

The afternoon before, while Michael, Grant, and Jon headed to Maine to check out the campground where they believed Keller and his people were staying, Sam and Eliza drove to Concord. She'd needed to reach out to Keller, and they all decided it was better if she used a payphone far from their hotel, just in case.

She'd played her part perfectly, starting the conversation by asking to speak to her mother and her son. Sam's heart had nearly exploded at the little boy's voice as he'd listened in.

"I'm disappointed that you think I might hurt them," Keller said when he came back on the line. "Why haven't you answered my calls?"

Eliza's words pitched high and squeaky. "He left me. Sam left me."

"Well, now." Keller used a syrupy, manipulative tone. "We all knew that was going to end badly. That man never cared about you. That's why I tried to protect you from him."

"I know, you're right." Sam was leaning close to the handset to listen, his jaw clenched so tight that he was giving himself a headache.

"Let me know where you are," Keller said, "and I'll send someone to get you."

"I don't have your money yet, but soon—"

"We can wait for it together."

They'd anticipated that, and Eliza delivered her lines perfectly. "I don't want to come back until I've fixed the mess I made."

A long silence was followed by, "I'd prefer to have you safely back with your family."

By *family,* he didn't mean Levi and her mom. He meant himself and his sycophant wife. This guy was nuts.

Eliza's voice shook. "I know, but I'm just...I'm so embarrassed about all the trouble I've caused."

"You'll be forgiven as soon as you return everything you took."

"I have the paperwork with me."

"And where are you?"

"I'm at the bus station in Concord." Which was true. Better to stick as close to truth as possible, according to Michael. "We flew into Burlington last night, and Sam drove me as far as Lincoln and then dumped me. I sat in a gas station and waited for a bus. I wasn't sure where to go. Where are you? I can start heading your way. I'd rent a car, but I don't have my ID or my wallet. I'm just lucky Sam gave me some cash."

"Just sit tight. I'll send someone for you."

"No, Jed. I'm not staying here. It's creepy. Just tell me where to go."

"All right, then." He wasn't happy, but maybe he realized arguing wouldn't change her mind. "Get on the first bus to Augusta."

Augusta was the closest city to the campground. A good sign.

"I will. I'll reach out again as soon as I have your money." When Eliza hung up, she shuddered, then faced Sam. "I feel like I need a shower."

He guided her away from the strong diesel scent coming from idling buses. "That was perfect. I didn't realize what a good actor you are."

She gave him a sideways look. "The fear is genuine."

"You don't have to be afraid. That man is not getting anywhere near you."

That didn't change anything, of course. She worried for the people she loved.

Sam did too.

They'd continued south on the interstate to Hooksett, then took surface roads into Manchester and parked between the back of a dingy strip mall and a chain-link fence.

He texted a number Michael had given him when he'd directed them to this address. He knew a guy who could hook them up with equipment.

Thirty seconds later, an old man with gray hair and a beard Santa would envy walked out a rear door carrying a cardboard box. He peered both ways as if checking for enemies and then approached the sedan.

Or, more appropriately, the trunk. He knocked on the lid, Sam popped it open, and the guy dumped the box inside and returned to the door without a word.

"Uh, that was weird," Eliza said.

Weird indeed, making Sam wonder what was in the box. But at least they were done.

They'd returned to Franconia a little after six and ate in the hotel restaurant. The place was definitely date-worthy—tables with white linens, gold-trimmed stemware, and vases of fresh flowers, none of which held a candle to the vista the glass-fronted room overlooked.

He wasn't sorry the guys weren't back yet. He definitely wasn't sorry to be alone with Eliza. He peppered her with questions about Levi, gleaning as much information as she would share. They'd talked about the year they'd dated—lighthearted memories that made them both laugh.

Neither of them mentioned the future. He didn't know why Eliza avoided the subject, but he knew why he did.

Because the future felt like it was right there, so close he could almost touch it, this life with his son and the woman he loved. He could taste yummy meals shared around a table. He could hear the thump-thump of a basketball, the echo of childish laughter. He could smell the bonfire at the family camp and see the glow of the flames reflected in his little boy's face.

He was afraid to vocalize all of that, as if speaking it would jinx it. So they kept the conversation light, never getting close to the terror they both felt. After dinner, they cuddled by the fire in the living room. He'd had every intention of sitting there until the guys got back, but exhaustion caught up with him.

"All right, mister." Eliza stood after his third yawn in five minutes. "Off to bed with you."

"But I wanna stay up." His whine elicited a grin.

"Now I know where Levi gets it."

The thought that his son inherited anything from him—even an annoying whine—made him ache with longing. How could he miss somebody he'd never met?

How could he love somebody he'd never met? And yet he did. So much.

Eliza took his hand and tugged until he stood. "We both

need a good night's sleep." She led the way to the staircase. "We'll find out in the morning what they learned."

Sam rushed through his shower the next morning, eager to find out what Jon, Grant, and Michael had learned. Hair still wet, he hurried to the sunroom.

As he approached, the door opened, and one of the waitstaff stepped out carrying a tray of empty mugs and plates. He nodded at Sam, who smiled and grabbed the door before it closed.

"...make sure you're safe," Jon was saying. "We'll be listening to everything through the earpiece and watching the video feed. That way we'll know what we're stepping into."

"What would I have to do exactly?" Eliza asked.

Sam didn't hide, but he didn't announce his presence, either, just stood at the door. Because...what were they talking about? Eliza's and Michael's backs were to him. Neither Grant nor Jon seemed to notice him.

"You'll just move through the space, and we'll see the video." That from Grant.

"That'll give us information about the layout and how many people are there," Jon said. "And when we come in, you can get innocents down."

Wait.

Who were they talking about going in?

Not Eliza, surely.

Michael said, "I wish there were another way."

"We've gone over it and over it," Grant said. "The more we know, the less chance someone gets hurt."

"Yeah, but..." Michael's lips pressed together. "Who knows what that man'll do to her."

Grant said, "I think it's worth the—"

"Absolutely not!"

Eliza visibly jumped. When she turned to face Sam, her eyes were wide as if he'd caught her doing something wrong.

Michael swiveled, hands going up. "You just need to listen."

Neither Jon nor Grant seemed surprised he was there. Hard to sneak up on a Green Beret. Apparently, neither felt guilty for the reckless plan they were hatching.

"Sit," Grant said. "We'll tell you—"

"There's nothing you can say that's going to change my mind." He marched close. "She's not going in there."

At that, Eliza's eyebrows hiked. "It's not your decision."

Grant kicked out the chair beside Eliza with his foot. "Sit."

Sam was tempted to stay standing on principle.

"Fine. Don't." Grant poured a cup of coffee from a carafe. "You need this?"

Not anymore, now that his heart was racing. He was tempted to grab Eliza and run, get her away from these *brothers* who wanted to risk her life.

Was it not enough that Keller had three hostages? They wanted to give him a fourth?

Grant pushed the cup across the table toward him.

But it was Jon who spoke. "We think we found them."

"You *think*?"

"Why don't you close that door so the whole hotel doesn't hear us." Grant's suggestion held no smirk. No irritation.

Sam sent his little brother a look before he whipped the door closed. Stupid thing had soft-close hinges, robbing him of a satisfying slam.

Jon, cool as ever, spoke as if nothing were amiss. "Most of the camp's structures are dilapidated, but the main lodge is sound, the area around it cleared of debris. The windows are covered with thick cloth or paper, and maybe something more substantial behind that. We can't tell."

"So we know where they are," Sam said. "What's the problem?"

"We *think* we know," Jon said. "But not a soul went in or out while we watched. We couldn't get a look inside. It's possible the place is being rented, but—"

"So call the owners and find out."

Grant's voice was as patient as Jon's when he spoke. "Keller is the owner."

"That's impossible. I looked for properties in his name myself."

"It was purchased by a trust," Jon said, "so his name didn't come up in the records search. A little digging reveals that he's the owner of the trust."

Great. And Sam had missed it.

He approached the chair beside Eliza but didn't sit, just snatched the coffee and gulped it, scalding his tongue. He barely felt it. "So you found him. If he owns the place, then obviously he's there." He plopped the cup down, spilling liquid onto the white tablecloth. "What's the problem? You guys were special forces. You went into situations like that all the time, right?"

"We always had *some* intelligence," Grant said. "We were never sent in blind. If nothing else, blueprints and—"

"I can get blueprints," Sam said.

"Already tried." This from Michael. "The ones at the court-house are old. The structure's been remodeled and added on to since then."

"Usually, we'd have an idea how many people we'd be up against," Grant continued, "or where weapons were being stored, or where hostages were being held, assuming we were on a rescue mission."

"Even if we didn't know all that," Jon said, "we went in armed and prepared to take out targets. In other words, kill them. This isn't Afghanistan. We can't just shoot our way onto private property and start killing people. I'd rather not end up in prison."

Prison. Right. Sam would go to prison to keep Eliza and Levi safe. But yeah, that wasn't his first choice. And he didn't want his brothers or Jon to end up there either.

Jon added, "And none of that would stop us if not for the sheer number of vehicles."

"Four SUVs," Grant supplied. "Four eight-seater SUVs. Meaning there could be as many as thirty-two people in that lodge."

At that news, Sam sat heavily in the chair.

Thirty-two?

Even accounting for Nicole, Linda, and Levi, that left twenty-nine. How many of those would be armed and ready for a fight?

"Is the place big enough to hold that many?"

"Not comfortably," Grant said, "but for a few days. Probably four thousand square feet."

"Thirty-two assumes there aren't two vehicles in the garage," Jon added. "We tried to get a look, but its windows are covered as well. We have to assume there're more."

How could there be so many?

Sam turned to Eliza. "Did he employ that many guards?"

"There were ten, last I knew."

"He could have hired them." Jon's tone was patient. Sam figured they'd gone over this all night long. "They don't have to be mercenaries, soldiers. They can be bodyguards—like we were. If bad guys come in with guns, they're going to shoot. And then we'll end up having to kill innocent people."

"They're not innocent if they're working for Keller."

"It's not like Keller's going to introduce himself as a cult leader," Grant said. "They won't know."

"Fine." Sam stood and paced, thankful that they were at least giving him a minute to consider the problem. "We have to call the FBI. That'll give the good guys a chance to walk away. Assuming there are any in there." He looked from man to man, willing each to disagree. He was too angry to look at Eliza. The fact that she'd even consider walking into Keller's hands again...

But she was the one who spoke. "If he came with that many, he's prepared for a fight, maybe even itching for one."

"That's them talking." Sam tipped his head toward his brothers and Jon. "Don't let them scare you into doing something stupid."

"It's me talking." Eliza's voice didn't shake or tremble or even pitch higher. She sounded eerily confident. "I know him. He used to talk about how he'd handle it if anyone tried to get on his land, how he'd fight them off. How he'd take a stand. I always thought it was crazy talk. Now I think...I think maybe he wants it. Maybe he's trying to prove something."

"What? That he can get people killed?" He stood over her, arms crossed, doing a lousy job of hiding his anger. "All you're doing is proving my point. He's dangerous and volatile. There's no way..." He forced a calm tone and crouched in front of her. He took her hand, kissed her knuckles. "I can't lose you. I can't let you do this."

"I'm not asking your permission. My son is in there. *Your* son is in there."

It would have stung less if she'd slapped him again.

Michael had been quiet for most of the conversation. Sam stood and swiveled to face him. "You aren't on board with this."

"It's not ideal, but—"

"Don't." Sam heard the warning in his tone. He needed his brother now. He needed him to be the voice of reason. "Mikey."

He didn't miss the way his brother winced at the old nickname.

Sam swallowed a lump in his throat. "Help me protect her. Please. I need you to be on my side."

Michael looked away. Shook his head. When he turned back to Sam, his expression was softer. Like maybe he was listening. "Two mornings ago... Thirty hours ago, you woke me up from a dead sleep, bursting with news."

Sam remembered. He hadn't been able to wait.

"Bro, wake up."

Michael's eyes had popped wide. *"What? What's wrong?"*

"He's mine. He has my curly blond hair and Eliza's wide eyes, and he's the cutest kid that ever lived."

Michael had blinked a few times, slow to process. *"Levi? He's yours?"*

Sam had plopped on the opposite bed, nodding, swallowing all the emotions he was still trying to get under control. And then the strongest one rose to the surface.

Terror.

Michael watched him now. "You remember what you said? 'You have to help me get him back.'"

Of course Sam remembered.

"That's what I'm doing," Michael said. "I'm helping you—"

"Not at the expense of the woman I love!"

Eliza's hand slipped around his biceps, but he shook her off and stormed out of reach.

"He's not going to kill her," Jon said. "She's his only link to the money, and she won't have it. They'll have to keep her alive."

"They could hurt her. They could torture her. They could..." The images were strobing on the walls of his mind. "There has to be another way."

"I reached out to a contact at ATF." Michael stood, took a

step toward Sam but stopped a few feet away. Maybe warned off by the fury radiating from him. "They have Keller on a watch list. He's been amassing weapons."

"In Utah! We're in Maine."

"It's a two-day drive." Michael's voice was far too calm. "Eliza disappeared on Friday. Five days ago. The SUVs have Utah license plates. They drove here. The question is, what were they hauling? Men? Guns?"

Was this supposed to be convincing him to send Eliza in?

"I'll go." He looked at Michael, then at Grant and Jon. "I'll... I'll just walk up to the door. I'll get myself captured. They'll bring me inside, and I can get whatever information you need."

"Sam." Eliza reached for him, but he couldn't handle her touch right now, those soft fingers on his skin while she was choosing to walk to her death. He couldn't even look at her.

"That'll work." Sam's gaze flicked from man to man. "That'll get me inside and—"

"Killed," Michael said. "That'll get you killed, maybe before you set foot in the door."

"Better me than her!"

Michael flinched.

"And then they'll know we're there," Jon said.

"They'll be armed and ready for us," Michael added. "And a lot more people will die, maybe even your son."

Those words were a punch to the gut. "You guys have thought of everything, haven't you?"

He was furious, but Michael didn't react to his anger, just nodded.

Grant and Jon held his eye contact.

"We've done nothing but try to figure out another plan," Michael said. "All night long. Any other plan."

"This is it." Grant looked like the warrior he was, not the

little brother Sam had known all his life. "It's this or we call the FBI and take our chances."

"Fine." Thank God, a voice of reason. "Let's call them now."

"No." Eliza pushed her chair back and stood. "Keller will risk everybody to protect himself. He might die in the end, but he'll take as many people with him as he can. He's not going to negotiate or back down. This will be Waco take two."

Sam had been a kid when the Branch Davidian compound was surrounded by ATF agents. The people inside hadn't come out with their hands up or whatever the agents had demanded. The siege lasted days. And then...he could still picture the flames rising from the buildings that horrible day.

"I'm telling you," Eliza said. "He'll shoot his way out, or..."

"Burn it to the ground." Sam was horrified by the words, mostly because they came from his own mouth.

The maniac would probably think it poetic, starting a second fire at the scene of his first.

Going down in a literal blaze of glory.

And taking Levi and Eliza with him.

CHAPTER THIRTY-TWO

ELIZA WAS DOING her best to hide her fear.

When Sam finally admitted defeat, slumping in his chair and dropping his elbows to his knees, she realized she'd held a little spark of hope that he'd come up with another way.

Any other way.

But the brave part of her, the part that had agreed to this crazy plan, wanted to be with Levi. Because once these men started pounding down doors, once gunshots sounded, Levi would be terrified. He'd need her.

And if she could help keep Sam and his brothers and Jon safe as they tried to rescue her family, then it would be worth it.

"Let's do this."

Jon's words snapped her gaze to him. "Now?"

"Either that or wait another day. I've already got guys en route."

She expected Sam to protest, but he didn't even lift his head.

"We need to leave now?" At least her voice didn't betray her fear.

"Soon." Michael checked the time on his phone. "The bus leaves from Portland a little after six. From there, it's only an hour to Augusta. Your story will be that you took a bus from Concord to South Station in Boston and then switched to the one for Augusta."

"How will I get to Portland?"

"Sam'll drive you."

"No." He looked right past her and glared at his brother. "I won't."

His words were a knife, slicing through her false bravado. She blinked to keep tears at bay. She hadn't cried once today, and she wasn't going to start now.

Michael gave one short nod at his brother and focused on her again. "I'll drive you. That way, if Keller has somebody watching the bus stop in Augusta, he'll see you get off. It'll make for a long day, and I'm sorry about that, but it seems like the best option."

"A bus ride won't kill me."

Sam flinched. Poor choice of words.

Grant had stepped out a few minutes earlier. Now, he carried the box she and Sam had gotten the day before into the sunroom and set it on the table.

Michael dug into it. "Here we go." He took something out, something so small she couldn't even see it. "Any chance you have a button-down shirt?"

"I did, but it's at Colton's."

Grant swiped something off the floor on the far side of the table and tossed it to her. The plastic bag of clothes Camilla had bought for her last weekend. "Stopped by Colton's on my way to grab your things."

"Thank you. I'll go change."

In the restroom on the first floor, she slipped into the plaid shirt and the ugly canvas pants that Jed preferred for the women to wear. If she was going back, she might as well play her part well.

When she pushed back into the sunroom, the conversation she'd heard as she approached stopped.

Michael and Sam were staring at each other.

And then Sam swiveled and walked past her, not even meeting her eyes.

She turned and watched him disappear down the hall, fighting the urge to follow, to try to explain herself.

No. She was going to do what she had to do to protect Levi, and she wasn't going to let Sam make her feel guilty for that.

She sat, and Michael studied the buttons on her shirt. "Those are perfect. Is it okay if I...?" He reached toward her, and she scooted closer so he could reach them. He slipped something small and mostly clear over one of them, then looked over her head. "Can you see it?"

Both Grant and Jon moved in. Nothing like having a bunch of men stare at her chest. After a long study, they both moved away. "Gotta really want to see it," Jon said.

"I never did find it," Grant added.

"And he was looking for it." Michael's tone was soothing as he leaned back. "I've used these before. Even if they search you, there're no wires. You shouldn't have any trouble."

Grant was pulling things out of the box. Holsters and handguns and some sort of eyewear. This would be a rough time for a hotel staff member to step in. "What about metal detectors?"

"I've worn the camera through airport security," Michael said.

Nobody seemed to question why that would be, and maybe now wasn't the time. But eventually, she wanted to know more about the man's "side gig."

"Here we go." Grant took a case from the box, opened it up, and handed it to Michael, who took out a little clear...thing.

"This goes in your ear." Michael held it out for her to see. It was tiny, soft, probably silicone, much smaller than ear buds. "It's a speaker and a microphone, so we'll be able to hear everything you say. Like the camera, there're no wires. We'll control it from our end. You need to be within range, so it won't work when you're on the bus. Once you get on the property, we'll be able to hear everything you say and almost everything you hear. We'll only turn it on for you to hear us if there's something you need to know. That way you won't be distracted by our voices."

She nodded but couldn't seem to make herself speak. This was all getting too real.

Michael's hands were cold as he slid the tiny thing into her ear. "There. That's hidden. Is it okay?"

It felt weird, but it didn't hurt. "It's fine. Will other people be able to hear when you guys talk?"

"No. Not even if they're really close." They tested it, and it worked perfectly.

"What do I have to do, exactly?"

Michael stood and moved away, and Jon settled in the chair. He leaned forward and held her eye contact. "It's very simple. You go in. You do what's natural, what's expected of you. We're not asking you to do anything dangerous or risky. Just be there, look around. The camera and microphone will do the work. Whatever information you can get into conversation we'll take, but don't do anything to give yourself away. Don't tell anybody we're out there, not even your mother, not until we give you the signal. Your ear'll be off unless there's something you need to know. If you hear one of us, don't react."

"You said there'll be a signal?"

"I'll give you some notice, usually thirty seconds. And then I'll count down. 'Three. Two. One. Go.' On *go*, you get down. Stay near Levi so you can make sure he's down. The plan is to take them off guard and use stun guns to take them out. We don't want to kill anybody. We don't want bullets to fly. But we can't control what the enemy does. And they're armed. If they shoot, we'll shoot back."

"What if I can't stay near Levi? What if he's in another room and they won't let me see him?" Panic had built as she tried to imagine the scene. Now it bubbled over. Her heart pounded, her feet itched to run. This was too much responsibility. What if she screwed up? What if she made a mistake? She could get everybody killed.

"Then you'll tell us." If anything, Jon's voice was calmer and lower.

"How will I—?"

"You'll ask about him. You'll say, 'I want to see Levi. Where is he?' and we'll hear the answer. We'll be listening. We'll know if you're with him or if you're not."

"Right." She pressed a hand to her heart, breathing heavily. "But what if he's with Jed? What if he's in the line of fire?"

"We can only do what we can do, Eliza." Grant crouched beside her and squeezed her arm. "After that, we have to trust God. There's a verse in Isaiah where God promises to rescue children from tyrants. Do you know it?"

She shook her head, wishing she'd had more time to study the Bible, to know Him.

"It says, "Even the captives of the mighty shall be taken, and the prey of the tyrant be rescued, for I will contend with those who contend with you, and I will save your children.'"

I will save your children.

"Hang onto that promise," Grant said. "God's got this."

She nodded, trying to get her emotions under control. "Is there anything else I need to know?"

Grant stood and propped a hip on the table behind Jon. "If you get into a room, if you have some privacy, try to let us know where you are. The windows are covered, but we're hoping you'll be able to uncover one from inside. Move the fabric back or tear the paper. We don't need you to take the whole thing down. Just let a little bit of light out, if you can."

"What if I can't?"

"That's okay," Jon said. "You do what you can and trust us—and God—to do the rest. Even if you can let us know, don't take so much down that they figure out what you're up to. Understand?" She nodded. "When you get to the bus station, you'll call Keller from a payphone. You have his number?"

"Sam has it."

Michael held out a slip of paper. "I got it from him."

"Thanks." She shoved it into her pocket.

Michael checked his watch. "We'd better go if you're going to make the four o'clock bus."

Was she really going to do this, walk right into the enemy camp?

Where her friend and her mother and her son were being held.

Yes, yes she was.

She pushed to her feet. "I'll get my things and meet you at the door in ten minutes."

CHAPTER THIRTY-THREE

SAM WAS OUT OF TIME.

Eliza didn't see him in the gift shop when she passed, shoulders back, ready for battle. Except she was going into battle with no weapons. No way to defend herself. No way to fight a psychopath.

She was walking away from Sam, right back into Keller's life, and she'd probably get herself killed.

She was leaving him. Again.

To save her son. *Their* son. What kind of a mother would she be if she didn't?

Even so, the snide little voice in Sam's head told him she didn't love him. She'd never loved him. How could she really love him if she was so willing to get herself killed? She'd only come back to Sam because she needed help, and what a brilliant play. He and his brothers were about to put their lives on the line for her.

Of course. His son, their nephew, was in danger. Of course they were.

He was being ridiculous.

He'd been battling irrational thoughts since the moment he'd walked into the sunroom. Most were the same irrational thoughts that'd kept him alone for so long. They were the reason he had few friends, rarely saw his family, and almost never left the house except to meet clients.

He'd told himself a million times how much he liked to be alone. How he worked all the time because nothing gave him greater pleasure. It was a lie.

Eliza. She gave him greater pleasure. And if he were honest, spending time with his family did too. And friends. All the things he pretended he didn't need.

"Sir?" The checkout girl in the gift shop held out the receipt. "You need a bag?"

"No. Thanks."

Purchases in hand, he headed out of the gift shop, wrestling with himself. He was terrified, no question. All this anger was just hiding what lay behind it. Fear.

Pure, deep-seated fear.

Fear of rejection. Fear of being left alone.

And how stupid was that, to spend his life alone because he was afraid of being alone?

Amazing how pervasive and, frankly, effective the enemy's lies had been.

But Sam was done with all that. Sure, people would reject him sometimes. Maybe even Eliza, but was Sam really going to walk away from her because he feared she'd someday walk away from him?

No.

Sam was accepted and loved by the One who mattered. He could love others because God loved him. And if people didn't, that was okay. He'd survive because God's love would never fail.

Sam had missed too much of life by keeping people at bay.

His fear of rejection, of being unloved and left alone, had nearly destroyed the life he craved. But he had a chance to fix it.

He prayed he wasn't too late.

CHAPTER THIRTY-FOUR

SHE WASN'T GOING to cry.

Eliza splashed water on her face and stared in the mirror. "You can do this."

Her reflection didn't seem sure.

It was hard enough to face what was coming, but to do it without Sam's blessing? How could she leave things like this? How could he?

She grabbed her plastic shopping bags, filled with the collection of clothes and toiletries she'd gathered in the last few days, and opened the hotel room door.

Sam was there.

She barely had a moment to register the agony on his face before he took her into his arms and kissed her. Deep and desperate, he wrapped his arm around her back, arching her closer.

He smelled like soap and tasted of mint and was everything she wanted. She dropped the bags and slid her hands around his neck, holding on as if he were her only link to safety.

And in a way, he was. He'd keep her safe. If it were up to Sam, she'd stay tucked right here in this hotel and let everybody else risk their lives to save the people she loved. He'd be her shield.

How she wished she could let him.

But she had to go.

She pushed her palms against his chest, trying to force herself to end the kiss, to lean away.

After a moment, he pulled back just enough. Then pressed kisses on her cheek. The corner of her mouth. Her forehead. He held her against his soft sweatshirt, and she felt his rapid heartbeat, the rise and fall of his chest.

"I was a jerk." His words rumbled against her ear. "I know that, and... The thought of you being in danger, it wrecks me. I just got you back, and I don't want to lose you." He leaned away to look down at her. "Can you forgive me?"

"If you can forgive me. I know you don't want me to do this."

He squinted, studying her face. "No chance you'll let me lock you in a box until it's over?"

"You know I can't."

"I would do anything to protect you from this." He trailed a finger down her cheek, brushing a lock of hair away and leaving a trail of tingles. "You're so brave. And you're going to protect our son, and I'm going to do everything in my power to get you out of there unharmed. We all will."

"That's why I can do it, because I know you'll be there."

His gaze held hers, intent and serious. "When it's over, when you and Levi are safe and all the dust settles..." He looked up, giving her a view of his beautiful neck, his whiskers, his Adam's apple. When he lowered his face again, a tiny smile played at the corner of his lips.

He dropped to one knee.

Oh.

He looked up at her with those kind, kind eyes. "It's only

been five days. Well, five years and five days. Plus the year we dated, so... It's enough time for me. Too much, and I can't wait any longer. Because I love you, and I want to spend the rest of my life with you. I want to be your husband and Levi's father. I want to wake up beside you and make you breakfast and let you make me look bad on the slopes and teach Levi to swim and..." He chuckled, shook his head. "Will you marry me?"

And here she'd sworn she wasn't going to cry today.

He wanted her. Forever. She didn't know why a man like Sam would choose a woman like her. She didn't know why he'd forgiven her for keeping his son from him. She didn't know anything except that there was nothing she wanted more.

She dropped to her knees and slid a hand over his dark beard. "Yes. I will. But we have to wait until Levi's ready, which might be—"

He cut off her words with a kiss, this one sweeter than before, filled with not desperation but promise. When he ended it, she leaned away.

"Did you hear the *but*?"

"I heard the *yes*." He grinned. "When Levi's ready, when you're ready... I'd marry you right this second, but I can wait. Whatever you and Levi need." He lifted his hand between them, holding a ring. Sort of. It was blue and silicone, she guessed.

"It was all they had in the gift shop. The real one's at home."

"You still have it?"

"I never had the heart to get rid of it." He slid the temporary ring onto her finger, then held her hands. "I know it's cheap and ugly, but I feel like it's a link, a promise that you'll come back to me."

"I will. We will." She leaned in and kissed him.

Footsteps sounded at the end of the hall, then Michael said, "Oh."

"Go away." Sam didn't even glance at his brother.

But she did, and Michael met her eyes, and she knew the reprieve was over.

After Michael disappeared down the stairs, Sam sighed and reached toward the wall beside her, coming back with a duffel bag. Dark blue with an outline of the Old Man on the Mountain in white. "It's not luggage, but it beats plastic bags."

"Thanks." She opened it, seeing that he'd already added the manila envelope with the evidence they'd collected. She shoved her scant belongings inside.

"It's high quality," he said. "It cost more than your engagement ring."

She held the silicone band against the bag. "They match."

"Every woman wants her engagement ring to match her luggage."

She grinned, zipping the duffel, then pressed her palms against Sam's cheeks. "I love you."

"I love you."

"You still won't drive me to Portland?"

The joy in his expression faded. "I can't, Eliza." He lowered his forehead to hers. "I can't deliver you into danger. But I'll be there to get you back out. I promise."

"It's a deal."

He stood and pulled her to her feet, then walked her down the hall, down the stairs, and out the front door.

Michael was leaning against the porch railing, twirling the keys, Grant and Jon beside him.

Eliza looked up into Sam's face and smiled. "I'll see you soon, and introduce you to your son."

CHAPTER THIRTY-FIVE

THE WORLD PASSED by in a blur. Sam couldn't concentrate on where they were going. He was too focused on what he'd left behind.

Back at the hotel, standing on the front porch and holding Eliza's hand, he'd been almost too choked up to speak when Michael suggested they ask for the Lord's blessing and protection. They'd all prayed, and then Grant had spoken a scripture about God's promise to rescue children from tyrants. Sam had been meditating on that verse for most of the drive from Franconia to the campground, asking that God not only save Levi but Eliza as well.

Only prayer and God's promises were keeping him sane.

Grant's phone buzzed. He was driving, so Sam keyed in the code Grant had given him earlier and read the text, which sent a fresh spike of fear to his middle.

"News?" Grant asked.

"Bryan's coming. Are you sure that's a good idea?"

"He can handle it." Grant had said as much already. "He's got great aim, could've been a sharpshooter. He's quick-thinking under pressure. Not sure if I'd be here—or if Summer would—if not for him." Grant gave Sam a quick smile. "Trust me, you want him on your side. We'll position him high where he can alert us to threats and..."

"Take them out." The words left a sour taste Sam tried to swallow back. All of his brothers would be there. It was one thing to ask Grant and Michael to help. They were both trained. But Daniel had just overcome his own nightmare. He didn't need another one, and his wife and kids didn't need to lose the man they'd just gotten back.

Bryan was a college professor, and not the *Indiana Jones* type. And Derrick, the baby of the family, was more familiar with pulling pranks than pulling triggers.

But they'd all agreed to come. They were willing to risk their lives, possibly their freedom—if this went sideways—all to rescue his son and his...bride.

When Sam called Derrick to ask for his help, he'd been surprised at Derrick's quick, "Dude, I'm in."

"Really? Are you sure?"

That had only annoyed the carefree youngest in the family. "You'd do the same for me, right?"

"In a heartbeat." Because Derrick was his brother. But...no. That made it sound like he felt obligated. He'd be there for Derrick—for any of them—because he loved them.

And they loved him back. Why had he let himself doubt that? His brothers loved him enough to risk their lives.

"We're going to keep them out of harm's way, right?" Sam asked.

Grant shot him a look, annoyance in the set of his mouth. "What do you think, I'm gonna suit 'em up and send them into battle?"

"Well, no, but—"

"Bryan'll be high on the ridge with his rifle, watching the road and the front of the lodge. Daniel will be at our staging area, prepared to deal with injuries. He'll also call the police when the time is right. And Derrick'll be lookout on the opposite side of the property." Grant turned onto a narrow road barely wide enough for his pickup. "We know what we're doing."

"I'm going in, though. You're not putting me in some lookout position."

Grant's jaw tightened, but he nodded. "If it were Summer, nothing would sideline me, so yeah, that's the plan."

Grant parked behind Jon's huge pickup. He'd left the hotel minutes after Michael and Eliza. Sam and Grant had followed after Sam had packed his things and checked out.

In front of Jon's truck, there was a black Lincoln Navigator.

"Whose is that?" Sam asked.

"Belongs to GBPS." Right. The protection company Grant had worked at for years. "Hughes drove it up. He's been here since early morning."

Outside the truck, Grant and Sam shoved in ear pieces and tested them, strapped on double holsters, and checked their weapons. Pistols on the right, tasers on the left.

"You ready?" Grant asked.

"Lead the way."

There was no trail, so they picked their way over downed trees and prickly bushes. The day before, Grant had tied thin strips of red plastic around narrow tree trunks so they only had to walk from one to the next. It took twenty minutes to traverse the half mile to the hill above the campground, where Jon was lying on the ground, watching through the dense forest.

Sam dropped on one side of him and got his first glimpse of the lodge.

It was a one-story wood-sided structure with a red brick chimney on one end. Windows lined the long side facing them, each blocked by dark fabric or paper. The front and side of the property had been cleared of bushes and debris ten or fifteen feet out from the building. Meaning there was no cover if somebody wanted to get close.

On Jon's other side, Grant asked, "Hughes?"

Jon nodded toward a small building in the woods on the far side of the lodge. "He's watching through the attic window."

"What is it?" Sam asked.

"Equipment shed." Nobody would ever accuse Jon of being loquacious.

"Anything in it?"

"A four-wheeler and a dirt bike."

"That's weird, right? Hasn't this place been abandoned for years?"

Jon didn't respond, but another voice spoke in his ear. "They're as old as the hills. Doubt they even run." Must be Hughes on comm.

"Any sign of Keller or...anybody?" Sam asked.

"One man left around nine a.m., hasn't come back." Hughes again.

Eliza wouldn't even be in Augusta yet. If there wasn't someone at the bus stop waiting for her, it could be after nine before she reached the lodge. It was barely four.

"You have a layout of the campground?"

Jon backed up, stood, and walked away. Maybe Sam had asked one too many questions. But he came back a minute later, resumed his prone position, and handed a tablet to him. The screen showed an overhead view of the property.

"Thanks." Sam spent the next few minutes studying the layout. They were pretty high on a mountain, and the slope must've been fairly steep, considering how the road wound back and forth, turning a half mile as the crow flies into a two-or-more-mile drive. No quick exit—but no quick entry for police and other first responders, either.

Smaller structures were interspersed beyond the lodge all the way across the valley to a small lake.

"Cabins," Jon supplied.

Except one was so tiny, Sam couldn't imagine it was large enough for even a cot. "What's that?"

"Pump house."

"Ah." Beyond that... Sam spread the image to get a better look. "Is that a road?"

Jon glanced at the screen. "We checked it out yesterday. It's an overgrown trail. Leads up that far slope." Jon tipped his head, and Sam looked that way. Another tree-covered mountain hemmed this valley in on the far side. "Too narrow for an SUV. There's only one way out, and we're going to block it after Eliza gets here. Don't worry." The corner of his lip tipped up—the beginning of a smile, or maybe a smirk. "We got this. Nobody's going anywhere."

Over the next few hours, three more bodyguards showed up. Jon went over the plan with everyone. "Obviously, this is subject to change after we get a look inside."

The men, all as fierce as Jon and Grant, wore solemn faces as they geared up with bulletproof vests and weapons and night-vision goggles. They donned camouflage jackets and smeared black on their faces before heading to their posts in different spots surrounding the lodge.

Sam suited up as well, feeling like a little kid playing dress-up surrounded by all these warriors. But this wasn't a game. And he wasn't sitting on the sidelines.

After Daniel, Bryan, and Derrick fought their way through the forest, Sam shimmied back from the ridge and greeted them with hugs.

"Looking good, man." Derrick eyed him from head to toe. "I should get a picture."

"Try it and find out how it feels to be tased."

Derrick lifted his hands, a big grin on his face. "Take a joke, bro."

The smiles faded when Jon joined them, handing out night-vision goggles and bulletproof vests and jackets. "Keep these on. This is our uniform, how we'll know good guys from bad. You see someone in camo, don't shoot." He gave Derrick and Daniel pistols and tasers, then handed Bryan, who'd brought his own rifle, a taser.

"For now, we're just watching." Jon gave them a quick rundown on the plan, then focused on Daniel and Derrick. "You two find a place out of sight to hunker down." Then to Bryan, "I'll show you where we want you."

Rifle slung over his back and leaning on his cane, Bryan followed Jon higher up the hill, where he'd have a view of the front and the side of the building.

They disappeared into the trees.

Until they got the video feed from Eliza, there was nothing to do but wait. And pray.

CHAPTER THIRTY-SIX

ELIZA HAD PLANNED on having time. But the ride from Portland to Augusta passed too quickly. Even so, she figured she'd get to Augusta and call Jed, then wait for someone to come pick her up.

But she hadn't stepped ten feet from the grumbling bus when a sweaty hand gripped her upper arm. "Took you long enough."

She held her duffel bag close and tried to keep up with Gil as he dragged her toward the parking lot, ignoring the other passengers who disembarked, not that any of them were paying attention to her.

Gil wore a brace on one arm and had a scrape across his face and bruises beneath both eyes. The scuffles with Sam and Jon had left their marks. Unfortunately, he was still standing, still much stronger than she was.

"I'm here voluntarily," she said. "You don't have to abduct me."

The rage in the look he sent her could've sparked a house fire. He shoved her into the backseat of a black SUV and slammed the door.

She had to fight the urge to open it and run. This was what she wanted. This was her way back to Levi, her way to rescue her mother and Nicole.

Even so, terror squeezed her tight, nearly choking her.

Gil drove for twenty minutes, away from the congestion of the city. Though she couldn't see his face from her spot in the backseat, she didn't miss how his meaty hands gripped the steering wheel.

Then he turned down a country road lined with forest on both sides and braked hard.

This couldn't be the campground. Michael had told her it was an hour's drive at least. "What are we doing?"

He climbed out of the SUV and slammed the door.

Panic had her trying the handle. She had to get out of there, to run before he hurt her. But the door wouldn't open from the inside.

Gil opened it and reached past her for the duffel bag. He opened it, rifled through it, and pulled out the manila envelope, which he dropped on the front seat before pitching the duffel into the woods behind him.

Then, he yanked her out.

Before she could protest, he slammed her against the side of the car and rubbed his meaty paws over her neck, her shoulders. "Where is it?"

A scream tried to claw its way out, but she couldn't make her throat work. Couldn't do anything but stand there and take it, dreading the worst, especially as his hands slid down her front and beneath her shirt, his calloused palms scratching her skin.

But they didn't linger. They slid around her back, then down her hips and both legs. He lifted her foot, levered off her sneaker. Looked inside it and all around the outside and then tossed it into the woods. "Where is it? If I find it before you confess, you'll be sorry."

What was he talking about?

He let her foot go, and she put it down, feeling moisture seep through the sock while he removed her other shoe, jerking it so hard she had to hop to keep her balance. "Where is it?"

"Where is what?"

"The tracker. The wire." He tossed that shoe into the woods, then knocked her other foot out from under her.

She fell sideways, hard, on the gravelly ground, pain shooting up her shoulder, her wrist, her back.

He pulled off her sock, tossed it away. Then he crawled over her, straddled her, and held her arms against the ground. "Tell me where it is. Now."

"I swear, I don't—"

"The tracker. The wire. The listening device. I know you're wearing something."

"I'm not wearing a—"

"Don't lie to me." He lowered himself, got in her face. His breath stank of onions and rotten fish. "If it were up to me, you'd be naked and tied like a pig. I have half a mind to do it anyway. Jed'll get over it if it keeps him safe."

No, no, no. The horror of the picture he painted had her squeezing her eyes closed, begging God for help.

Gil went for round two, pressing his hands against every inch of her. He searched the breast pocket of her shirt, then the pockets of her pants. She didn't move, didn't fight. Just lay still, eyes closed, praying. Praying he wouldn't look in her ear. Praying he wouldn't find the button camera.

Thank God Sam wasn't seeing this. Thank God the camera only worked within a certain range.

Gil climbed off her to check her legs again, then flipped her and searched her back side as well.

"Ha!" He grabbed her hand and bent it up against her back,

shooting pain up her arm. "What's this." His fingers pinched the silicone ring Sam had given her.

"It's just a cheap ring. It's nothing."

"You didn't have it the other day. Meaning pretty boy gave it to you." He released her arm, flipped her over, then grabbed her wrist as if she might try to escape. Watching her closely, an evil glint in his eye, he slipped the silicone ring off her finger and studied it. "Maybe it's a newfangled listening device or a tracker. Or maybe it's some sort of symbol of your boyfriend's undying love. Either way..." He reared his arm back, and she flinched, expecting a blow. But he launched the ring into the woods. "It's gone now."

Gone.

Sam believed the ring signified the promise that she would return to him. She knew it wasn't a sign, not really. But somehow, without it, her hope faltered.

The plan was already falling apart.

The promise was gone.

Eliza tried to be as small as possible for the rest of the drive. She didn't speak, didn't dare open her eyes, and didn't stop the stream of prayers. And maybe God heard her, but it felt like the prayers went no higher than the roof of the SUV.

She should have listened to Sam. She should never have agreed to this. How could she possibly help? Every decision she ever made ended up hurting people.

The choice to follow the Kellers to Utah.

The sale of Dad's business.

The deadly visit to the creek back in Arkansas.

Like that one, this decision would get someone killed. Would it be Jon? Michael or Grant or one of Sam's other brothers? Nicole? Mom? She didn't even want to think about the other possibilities, but their faces swam before her eyes, the man and the little boy she couldn't bear to lose.

Please, God. Please.

It was dark by the time the car slowed and turned, switchbacking its way up a steep slope on a crumbling and bumpy road. And then a voice spoke in her ear. "That you, Eliza?"

Oh, Sam.

Thank heavens she was still looking down or she might've given the earpiece away with her surprise. As it was, she had to bite back tears.

"Can you let me know you hear me?"

She cleared her throat.

"Good. We see you."

His voice was reassurance. Her fears were still there, but she wasn't alone.

"Don't look for us, but we're all around. We're watching."

She longed for him to keep talking, but he quieted as Gil parked the SUV. He came around and opened her door, this time letting her climb out on her own. Her back ached, and when she stepped on the gravel driveway, pain stabbed the soles of her bare feet.

Gil didn't touch her, just walked beside her toward the building, carrying the manila envelope.

In her ear, she heard, "Where are your shoes?" Sam's voice was a low growl. "You're hurt. What did he do?"

"Okay," Jon said, voice as calm as ever. "We're muting our end. Remember, just because you can't hear us doesn't mean we can't hear you. The camera's broadcasting fine. You're doing great."

Didn't feel like it as she hobbled toward a porch outside a wooden structure nearly invisible in the dark. They'd been calling it a lodge, and she could see why as she approached, the way lit by a dim moon. Everything about it screamed rustic, a low building dwarfed by higher slopes and towering forest all around.

Three wooden steps led to a wide porch. She hung on the stairway's railing, hoping to make the climb a little less painful on her back and hip, which hadn't quit hurting since Gil had knocked her over. She was on the second step when the door opened and her gaze snapped up.

Jedediah Keller, barely a silhouette with the light shining behind him like some sort of angel of darkness. How had she not noticed how long his beard had grown? Was it always so unkempt, or had he neglected trimming and shaping it since she escaped? And maybe it was because she was a couple steps down from him, but he looked taller than she remembered. Wider. More powerful.

Or maybe that was her fear talking.

Jed looked from her to Gil and back. "What happened?"

The only thing the guard had said to her on the drive was, "If you tell him I searched you, I'll kill you."

Maybe it was reckless and stupid, but she couldn't stop the words as they exited her mouth. "Ask Gil."

Because really, he'd kill her anyway, first chance he got. He was itching to do it, payback for all the times he'd come after her and been thwarted.

Jed stepped down beside her and took her arm. "Come on, honey. Let's get you inside." Over his shoulder, he added, "I'll deal with you later."

And even though Jed was being nice to her and Gil was plotting her murder, she preferred Gil's company. At least she knew where she stood with him.

She made it up the steps and across the porch, then stepped over the threshold into a dim room. It was filled with people.

They were everywhere.

Men with guns leaning against fake-wood-paneled walls next to windows that had been boarded up. She could make out black fabric through the slats, hiding the barriers from the outside.

She was glad the guys could see that. But those boards... How would they get in?

Women and children huddled on rotting furniture and worn linoleum floors. The men glared or leered. The women wore wide, frightened expressions, so different from the adoring looks she was accustomed to seeing on the faces of Jed's followers.

Was it the guns that scared them? Or had Jed done something to reveal himself as the madman he was?

Remembering the camera, she turned to the right, scanning the faces a second time. Then to the left, taking in each one and recognizing most of them. Lola was watching from the far side of the room, eyes narrowed. In fury? Or suspicion?

There weren't as many people as she'd first thought. Four men on the right side, five on the left. Two against the back wall. Including Gil, that made twelve men all together, thirteen if she counted Jed.

Eight women, eleven children. Nicole wasn't there, and neither were the two Eliza longed most to see.

"The prodigal has returned." Jed made his announcement as if he expected a response, but nobody said anything. In fact, a few dropped their gazes. "Well, let's welcome her back."

That elicited a random clap and a few hellos and good-to-see-yous. She couldn't muster a smile but managed a slight nod before shifting to face Jed. "Where's Levi? Where's my mother?"

He leaned in, voice low when he answered. "Where are the papers you stole from me?"

Before she could respond, Gil handed them over. "This was all she had with her."

She didn't bother to point out that she'd had shoes and socks and a bag full of clothes.

Jed peeked into the envelope, then gave her a tight smile. "When I get my money, you'll get to see Levi."

"I need to see him now."

His eyebrows hiked. "What did you say?" She didn't miss the warning in his nearly whispered question.

She swallowed hard. "You told me if I came home"—the word tasted like sand—"all would be forgiven." She made sure to speak loudly enough that everyone would hear. She also knew the best way to get what she wanted was to appeal to his ego. "I trust you to do what you promised. I know I messed up. I know I caused you, caused our family, a lot of trouble. But I also know you'd never go back on your word. You can be trusted, Jed. I've always known that. Please, be true to your word. Please let me see my son and my mother."

His gaze flicked to the people watching the scene. His smile was tight when he focused on her. In his eyes, she saw warning. *Watch yourself.*

She swallowed hard but didn't look away. She wasn't fooling him. And he wasn't fooling her. As soon as she got the money— or, more accurately, as soon as he realized she was never going to give him back the money—he'd make her pay for everything she'd done.

God willing, she'd be safely away from him long before then.

Finally, he turned to the room, and the frozen smile he'd worn morphed into something that looked genuine, even warm. "Elizabeth has come back to us and begged forgiveness, and I am willing to grant it." He wrapped his arm around her back and tugged her close, like an old friend offering support. "I'll allow you to see Levi. Our son has missed you." Again to the room. "Go back to what you were doing. Let's give our Elizabeth some space."

The women started talking in low tones, the children, who'd been unnaturally quiet during the scene, returned to their play.

Arm still around her, Jed led her past ugly plaid sofas and a round wooden table surrounded by chairs where a group of women played Monopoly. Nobody looked up when she passed.

They reached the back of the room, and Jed urged her through a door and into a hallway. At the far end, more horizontal boards covered what she assumed was the rear exit.

One way in. One way out.

The sounds of chattering faded as the door to the common room closed behind them. Maybe Jed was taking her to see Levi and Mom. Or maybe that was all an act for the sake of the women and children.

Moving along the long, dark corridor that seemed to go on forever, doors on both sides, her enemy propelling her forward, she wondered if there was any end to the nightmare. Or if this was only the beginning.

They were nearly to the end of the hall when Jed stopped at a doorway, pulled out a set of keys, and stuck one into the keyhole on the knob. "You wanted to see them. So here you go." He pushed the door open and shoved Eliza inside.

She stumbled and would have fallen if a hand hadn't caught her and held her up. "You all right?"

Before she could register the voice—

"Mommy!" Levi launched himself off a low twin bed and into her arms.

Oh.

Thank You, God.

She held her son tightly, dropping her face into his neck to breathe in his little boy smell—sweat and dirt and a hint of spoiled milk, and it was the most wonderful scent in the world. "My sweet darling. I'm so happy to see you."

She expected him to back away. He'd never been one to allow long hugs, but he wrapped his legs around her torso and hung on as if he'd never let her go. She leaned her head away so she could see him, taking in his chubby cheeks, his matted blond hair, his sapphire blue eyes. He was dirty and in dire need of a bath, but he seemed unhurt. "I missed you so much."

"I missed you too. Pretend Daddy's being mean."

"What did he do?"

But Levi didn't answer with more than a tiny shrug of his narrow shoulders.

At the feel of a hand on her back, she turned, and her mother pulled her close. "Oh, sweetheart. I'm so sorry."

"None of this is your fault." Eliza gave her a one-armed hug, not willing to put her son down. "Are you okay? Did they hurt you?"

"Not much," Mom said, which didn't make Eliza feel better.

"How did they find you? Do you know?"

"I think from my planner. I saw one of the men with it, and the cabin's address on the Cape was in there. I meant to bring it with me."

The planner. Sam had had it in his hands when he and Eliza had been attacked at Mom's house the weekend before. All this could have been avoided if only they'd taken it that day. As it was, they'd been lucky to get out alive.

Something on the second bed shifted. The room was dim, and it took her a moment to understand what she was seeing.

"Nicole?"

Eliza's friend was huddled in the corner, arms wrapped

around her bent knees. She wore the canvas pants all the women wore, along with a ratty T-shirt under a worn windbreaker. Nicole had always been the most put-together of the women in the dorms, her confidence and, frankly, tall and slender shape making even the ugliest clothes look fashionable. But not now. She had a black eye, her cheek swollen beneath it.

"Oh, Nicki." Eliza sat beside her, shifting Levi to one side so she could get closer.

And give the camera a good look.

Eliza reached toward her, but Nicole flinched. "Who did this to you?"

Nicole shook her head.

"It's okay. I won't say anything. Did Jed do that?"

Again, she shook her head.

"Gil?"

At that, her friend flicked her gaze up, though it dropped again immediately.

Of course it was Gil. He'd probably enjoyed it, too. Eliza was just lucky Jed had told him not to hurt her or she'd look worse. She held out her hand, and after a moment, Nicole slid hers into it.

"I'm so sorry," Eliza said. "I didn't tell you my plan because I didn't want anything bad to happen to you."

Mom sat on the opposite bed, the springs squeaking. "She hasn't said a word since they tossed her in here earlier today."

Not a word? That was unlike her spirited friend, but this was what Jed did to people. He sucked the life out of them.

It was a sparse room with the same wood-paneled walls she'd seen in the common area, bare mattresses on two narrow beds, and a closet without a door. An overhead bulb gave off very little light.

"Wow. He even nailed boards over the window," she said, in case the camera wasn't picking it up in the dimness. "And what's that behind them?" She stuck her fingers through a gap in the rough wood. "Is it a curtain?"

"They stapled black wool to cover it," Mom said. "He's paranoid."

Paranoid probably wasn't the word, considering the men outside. But it was a good opening. "No kidding. Boarding up all the windows and even the back door. What if there were a fire?"

"He's been keeping everybody inside," Mom added, "not even letting the children out. It's nuts. It's like he's sure we're being watched."

Nicole hiccuped or...was she crying?

Eliza brushed her friend's hair away from her face. "You okay?"

"Nobody's watching. Nobody's coming for us." Her friend's voice was flat, emotionless, but at least she was talking. "Nobody knows where we are. We're going to be shoved back in those SUVs and hauled back to Utah, and nobody will ever see us again. That's if he doesn't kill us first." The pain in her eyes had Eliza's stomach churning. "I hope they do. I'd rather die than go back there."

"Oh, sweetie. We're going to be all right."

"How can you say that?" She looked around the dingy room. "We're trapped here in the middle of nowhere. Nobody cares." Her voice lowered as if she were talking to herself. "Nobody's ever cared."

"I care." Eliza patted her knee. "And I promise, I'm not the only one."

Mom gripped her sleeve. "What do you mean?"

Jon had told her not to tell them anything, so Eliza ignored the question and moved to the window, her arms aching from holding Levi. "Hey, buddy. Can I put you down for a minute? I need to do something."

"Come on, now," Mom said. "Come to Grammy."

It took Levi a moment, but he shifted out of Eliza's arms and into Mom's.

Eliza stuck her fingers through the wooden slats, trying to find a way to make a gap in the wool behind it.

"What are you doing?" The question came from Nicole.

"Maybe we can get out this way."

"We can't." Nicole sobbed into her knees. "We're trapped, and we're never getting out. You know what he's going to do, don't you? He's going to light the whole thing on fire. We're going to burn to death."

Eliza's head snapped around. "Why do you say that?"

A shrug. "I just keep seeing that place in Texas, the one where everyone was trapped inside."

Hadn't Eliza had the same irrational fear?

"That's not going to happen. We're getting out of here. Mom, see if you can find me something long and hard. Like... Oh! Get up, move over with Nicole."

Mom did, taking Levi with her, and Eliza flipped the mattress back to reveal a crisscross of metal springs and wires holding it up. Maybe something could be worked loose. She searched along the edges where the springs met the frame. Nothing, nothing.

And then she found one that might work. She unhooked the end attached to the frame. The other end of the spring was connected to the long wire that reached to the opposite edge of the bed. But there was a small gap in the eye. If she could just wiggle it free...

She pulled and twisted and tried to make it work, but it was too tight, thanks to the adjoining wires.

A voice in her ear startled her. "Unhook it from the other side."

"Goo—" Oops.

"Shh," Sam said.

"What did you say?" Mom asked.

"I scraped my finger. 'Gosh' is better than the alternative, right?" She twisted to face her mother and winked. "Pelletier ladies don't swear."

"Good save," Sam said.

She did what he suggested, unhooking the opposite side of the wire attached to the spring she was trying to work loose.

"No." Nicole's voice was stronger now. "You said 'Good.' Who are you talking to?"

"You're hearing things." Now that it was disconnected, Eliza had more leeway with the spring. She wiggled and cajoled this way and that, and then it came free. "Yes!"

"What did you do?" Nicole asked.

She turned and lifted the metal piece like a trophy. "I just want to see if I can peek outside. Maybe, if we can lever the boards away, we can get out of here." She dropped the mattress back down in case someone came in.

"Brilliant." Sam's word was kind in her ear.

She turned to the window and stuck the metal through the slats. It caught on the wool, but all the shoving and tugging she could manage didn't tear it.

"I didn't mean to startle you." She heard a smile in Sam's voice and wondered if it was genuine or if he was trying to keep her calm.

How in the world were Sam and the rest of them going to get in? She backed up to give the camera a view of what she'd been attempting—and so far failed—to do. "This is harder than it looks."

"What exactly are you trying to do?" Mom asked.

"Get us out of here." She jabbed at the wool, but it had almost no give.

"Our plan's in place, Eliza." Now it was Jon's voice. "If you can let some light out your window, then we'll know where you are. And show us how those boards are attached. We might have to pull you four out that way. We're muting again."

The voices in her ear went silent.

The voices behind her, not so much.

"I'm telling you," Nicole said, "she has a plan."

"If she does, then she'll tell us when the time is right." Mom's confident tone was so surprising, Eliza paused to take it in. Mom really had changed.

She prayed her mother's confidence was well founded.

The window covering refused to tear, despite the fact that Eliza was working up a sweat in the chilly air.

Think.

The wool was stapled down, and most of the staples were behind the boards. But maybe she could get access to one between the wood. It was too dark to see much, so she pressed the metal piece between the boards at the edge of the window, moving from gap to gap, praying for the telltale catch of metal.

Finally, standing on the bed to reach high on the window, she caught one.

She shoved the end of the spring against it and dug into the wood. It took a long time—a *long* time—but then, the staple gave way. She worked it out, then pushed the tool behind the fabric and pulled.

And got the slightest glimpse of window.

"Did you get it?" Nicole asked. "Are they coming? Please, tell me someone's coming." The hitch, the desperation, made Eliza's heart hurt.

She stared at the tiny space she'd made and waited.

After a moment, Sam said, "We're not seeing it."

Fine, then. She kept working at it. And working. And... there. A bigger opening. She angled so the camera could see.

In her ear, Jon said, "Move away from the window so the light can come through."

She did and was rewarded with Jon's soft, "Gotcha. I'll be back with a countdown. Muting again."

Thank God.

She turned her attention to the boards. Maybe she could pry them out. She shoved the tool beneath the end of one and levered with the opposite end of the spring. Did it move? She thought maybe...

"Please, Eliza," Nicole said. "Tell us what's going on."

"Quiet." And there was Mom's disapproving voice. Eliza was glad it wasn't directed at her. "Eliza's working on something. Leave her be."

"Why, though?" Nicole's voice rose, nearly a shout. "What's the point? If there's nobody out there, even if we get the window open, we won't make it fifty feet before they shoot us in the back."

"Keep your voice down," Eliza snapped,

"Why?" If anything, she got louder. "The sooner they kill us the better."

"Stop it!" Eliza swiveled and got in her friend's face. "You might be ready to die, but I'm not. My mom is not, and my son is not. So stop it."

"Doesn't matter." Tears streamed from Nicole's cheeks. "Nothing matters."

Levi looked up at her, blinking those big eyes. "I don't wanna die, Mommy. Are we gonna die?"

"No, sweetheart." She managed a smile for him, kissed him on the forehead. "We're going to be just fine. We're getting out of here."

"Don't lie to him," Nicole wailed. "It's cruel to give him false hope."

Eliza sighed. "It's not false hope." Jon had told her not to say anything, but it was either that or Nicole was going to be so loud that someone would come to check on them. And Eliza couldn't have that. "There're men here to rescue us. I just want to let them know where we are."

Nicole dropped her legs and scooted to the end of the bed. "I knew it. Thanks for the info." She knocked on the door and called, "It's me. Let me out."

What?

No, no, no! Eliza launched across the space and grabbed her friend's arm. "Don't. What are you doing?"

Nicole yanked away. "Don't touch me."

The door opened, and there was Jed, giving Nicole an expectant look.

"She said there are men here."

Jed dropped a kiss on her head. "Good girl. We'll be ready." He started to pull her out of the room, but Eliza grabbed a fistful of her shirt.

"How could you do this?"

Nicole turned back, peered down her nose like royalty at a beggar. "You're a brat who can't figure out where her loyalties lie."

Eliza stepped back. "This is what you call loyalty, letting a psychopath punch you in the face so you can betray a friend?"

"We were never friends." She turned to Jed. "She got a spring from the bed. She was trying to tear the wool. Oh, and check for an earpiece. She was definitely talking to somebody."

CHAPTER THIRTY-SEVEN

"NO!" Sam wanted to close his eyes and block out the sounds in his ear. But he had to know.

In the video, Keller glared down at Eliza, eyes filled with rage. "I knew you couldn't be trusted."

"Like you can? You're a liar and a fraud."

"Eliza, don't!" But she didn't hear Sam's warning.

A loud smack, and the video jumbled and jerked. He'd hit her. Knocked her down.

Levi screamed, "Mommy!"

"It's okay." Linda's voice, but Sam couldn't see her beyond the dusty floor where Eliza had landed.

"Jon, unmute!"

"Watch your volume." Jon's voice was calm, as always. "Everybody, prepare. We're going in two."

What was the point? Keller knew they were there. The plan Jon had put together depended on the element of surprise. It was over.

Eliza was hauled to her feet, pulled out of the bedroom. Behind her, Levi screamed, his cries of, "Mommy! Mommy!"

interrupted by Linda trying to calm him. A door slammed, and their voices muted, then faded altogether.

They were in the hall now, nearing the end.

Eliza hadn't said a word since Keller'd hit her.

"Unmute me," Sam said. "Now!"

"Stay calm, bro."

Michael's warning tone in his ear made Sam want to hit him.

A hand settled on Sam's shoulder, but he shook it off, barely glancing Grant's way.

"Unmuted," Jon said.

"Eliza, sweetheart. Let us know you're okay."

For a long moment, there was nothing but grunts and grumbling, those coming from Jed.

And then, finally, Eliza said, "Where are you taking me?"

Thank God. She was alive, conscious, coherent.

"Keep your mouth shut." The rage in Keller's voice lifted hot prickles on Sam's skin. He'd seemed arrogant and confident before. But this was the real man, bent on control at any cost. He pushed Eliza against the wall, moving so close that all the screen showed was darkness. "You'll do what I say, or I'll tear your mother limb from limb. Her screams will fill your nightmares for the rest of your short, pathetic life."

"Stay calm, sweetheart," Sam said. "We're not going to let that happen."

Beyond his tiny phone screen, men gathered, checking weapons.

"And then I'll kill you." Keller's voice hummed with fury and something else. Something that had Sam's blood running cold. Eagerness. The twisted desire to do just what he'd said. "If anyone tries to stop me, they'll die too. If everyone in this building has to die for your sins, so be it."

"I love you, Eliza." Sam couldn't help the emotion in his voice. "We're going to get you out of there."

"Levi." She spoke the name like a prayer. No. A request.

Sam closed his eyes. "Yes. I promise." A promise he had no idea how to keep.

"Levi's mine," Keller said. "You'll never see him again."

"Mom?"

"What happens to her now is on you," Keller said. "Everything that happens next, it's all on you."

Sam got the message. *Save them, not me.*

But he wasn't sacrificing anybody.

A door opened. Eliza was pushed inside a dark room, stumbled and fell. She was flipped to her back, and Sam got a glimpse of two men standing over her.

"I told you we should've stripped her."

Had to be Gil, the goon who'd brought her from the bus station.

A thump.

"Oomph." She jerked to the side.

He'd *kicked* her.

Sam was going to kill him. He was going to hunt him down and...

She was struggling, fighting. And then, "This must be it."

The video feed went dead.

More grunts. He had no idea what was happening. "We're coming. I love you, sweetheart."

"I love—"

Her audio cut off.

She was gone.

CHAPTER THIRTY-EIGHT

EVERYTHING WAS FALLING APART, and it was Eliza's fault.

All her fault.

Shouts came from far away, Jed issuing instructions. Men following his commands. Footsteps, a mountain of them.

She lay on the floor where they'd left her. Everything hurt. She pushed to a sitting position, then paused to breathe through a wave of pain.

She tried to see...something. Aside from a tiny bit of light coming from beneath the door, the room was completely dark. She wanted to stand, but she couldn't do it. Maybe if she had something to hang onto, but there was nothing. She crawled toward the light, tried the knob.

Locked. Of course.

She shifted to lean against the wall and dropped her face into her hands.

If only she'd followed Jon's instructions and kept her mouth shut.

If only she hadn't trusted Nicole.

If only she hadn't trusted Jed and Lola.

Regret filled her mind and lungs like toxic smoke until she could barely breathe. There was no escaping it now.

Lord, what have I done?

The whisper in her soul was a cool, clean breeze.

Trust Me.

Trust Him? After everything... After all the mistakes she'd made, could God really fix it?

There was no way.

He'd promised her that He would keep her and Levi safe. Back on The Ranch, after Michael had emailed his rescue plan, she'd gotten on her knees and prayed for guidance. And God had told her to do it.

He's My warrior. Go with him.

So she had. And if she'd obeyed what Michael and Jon told her, everything would have been fine. But she'd screwed up. She'd gone against their instructions.

So of course God owed her nothing. Of course she couldn't expect Him to fix her mess.

And yet, that breeze, that sense of His presence. *Trust Me.*

Was God still on her side? Even though she'd made horrible mistakes, could He still make it right?

Her father's voice found her. *All you can do is your best.*

Could she trust that God had her, even now, even after she'd made such a tragic blunder?

Maybe...maybe that was exactly what He expected. Not for her to be perfect or to always make the right choices, but to continue to trust Him, no matter what.

It was too easy. In theory. But now, locked in a dark room...it was impossible to escape. Impossible for her to believe God could fix this.

But He is the God of the impossible.

"Help me trust You. I want to. I want to believe You're here, You're listening, and You'll keep Your promises, no matter what." After the prayer, there was no fresh sense of peace. No lessening pain. Only...

Hope.

CHAPTER THIRTY-NINE

MAYBE ONLY SECONDS had passed when Sam felt a hand on his back. He didn't shrug it off this time.

"She's still alive," Grant said. "Join us when you're ready." He added, "Be ready now," and walked away.

Sam had to breathe. He had to shake it off and get up and do something.

"Come on."

Sam looked up and grabbed the hand Daniel held out, letting his big brother pull him to his feet.

They moved toward the gathered men, who were talking in low tones just a few trees away in the dense forest.

Jon turned as they approached. "Everybody set?"

Sam was about to respond when he heard voices in his ear again. Not Eliza but all the men chiming in. Derrick was at his post on the far side of the lodge, where he'd watch and report anybody coming or going. Bryan was up the hill. Michael was on the other side of the circle of men, watching Sam.

He nodded at his brother. He could do this. He had to do this.

"A couple of changes." Jon explained what the men would do differently now that they'd lost the element of surprise.

Sam stared through the trees at the little prick of light coming through the window. At least he knew where his son was, assuming Keller hadn't moved him.

Where was Eliza?

How hurt was she?

How much damage...?

"...and then Sam moves."

He turned his attention back.

"You with us?" Jon said. "You can sit out—"

"I'm with you."

"I want you in position in the woods"—he pointed to the back corner of the building—"as close to there as you can get without showing yourself."

"I remember."

But Jon repeated Sam's role anyway. "When we breach, cross to the building, stay low to the window and get them out. Bring them up here. Let me know when you're done."

"What if they're not there?"

"Then report it. Bryan?"

"Here," his brother said through comms.

"Cover us," Jon said. "You see anyone coming up the hill, sound a warning. If anyone aims to kill—"

"I'll take him out." Bryan sounded completely confident, as if the idea of killing a man barely fazed him.

"Daniel, you called the police?"

"They're on their way."

"Good. Everybody copy?" After a round of quick responses, Jon said, "God, be with us, get us to the hostages, and bring us out safe." After barely a pause... "Go."

Handgun out, night-vision goggles on, Sam ran down the hill, dodging tree trunks and hopping over brush. Just inside the tree line, he paused behind a thick trunk, breathing heavily, praying constantly, and watched as men converged on the windows near the front. They moved so stealthily that, without his goggles, Sam wasn't sure he'd have seen them.

In his ear, he heard a whisper. "Three, two, one. Go."

A loud thud.

Gunshots followed. And men's shouts.

Sam bent low and bolted across the clearing.

A bang, this one close. He ducked lower and told himself that breeze he'd felt by his ear hadn't been a bullet.

Then came a rifle shot. Bryan swore. "Missed. He's in the window on your side of the captives."

Other voices sounded in Sam's ear, but he blocked them out as he reached the building and started crouch-running toward his son. Up ahead, a flicker caught his eye, the glint of light off metal.

"If he shows himself," Bryan said, "I'll shoot."

Sam approached slowly, silently.

The glass was raised, only fluttering wool between Sam and the gunman inside the room.

Sam took a breath. *Here we go, God. Help me take him out. And not get shot.*

He stopped a foot away. Took out his taser and aimed toward where the gunman's hand should be.

But the gun shifted to aim at him.

Sam dove an instant before the gun fired. Beneath the window frame, he gripped the gunman's wrist. He yanked, bent forward, and levered the guy out the window and over his back. Dumped him on the ground.

The guy wrenched his wrist away and took aim.

Sam barely moved before a gunshot sounded an inch from his ear. Ignoring the ringing that blocked out everything else, he whacked the guy's forearm and punched him in the face. The man's head snapped to the side, and Sam reared back to punch him again.

But a knee jabbed him in the ribs. Sam moved to protect himself, got flipped off his feet and onto his back.

A fist came down hard toward his head. Sam knocked it out of the way just in time, kidney punched the gunman once, twice.

The guy leaned back, but not to protect himself.

He swung the weapon toward Sam's head.

And then, a gunshot.

Sam watched the shooter crumple. He collapsed to the side. What the...?

"Careful." Bryan's voice shook, but it was strong. "Not sure where that hit."

Sam scrambled out from under him, kicking his gun away, breathing hard.

The shooter wasn't moving.

Blood poured from a wound on his back. And when Sam looked, he saw it flowed from his chest too. The guy's eyes were open.

A quick feel at his neck, and... "You got him, Bryan. Thanks."

"Go get your son."

Sam had dropped the taser and the night-vision goggles. He grabbed the goggles and the shooter's gun, which he shoved in the holster where the taser had been.

These people were aiming to kill, and he would too.

The ringing in his ears faded, the sound of shooting filtering in. And shouts. And screams.

He ran to the next window, where light peeked through. "Linda?"

A gasp, and then, "Who's there?"

"Sam. Coming in." Hand covered with the sleeve of his

jacket, he broke the glass with the butt of his gun and cleared the edges. "I just gotta knock out these boards."

But as he said it, the bottom one was wrenched away, and Linda's face appeared. The wool was hanging loose, no longer stapled. She looked both terrified and determined. "I finished what Eliza started."

"Good job. Step out of the way. I'll get the next one."

She did, and he pounded on the board. It was as high as his head, and he didn't have a good angle. Sheer fury fueled him as he banged his fists against it.

Finally, it gave on one side. He grabbed it and pulled it out, getting a glimpse of the tiny dorm-style room.

Linda hurried forward from the back wall. "I don't know where Eliza is."

"I'll find her. Come on."

She held out her arms to the bed, and a little boy stepped into them. Linda turned to hand him through the window.

And Sam got his first look at his son.

A million emotions, but he pressed them all down.

"This nice man's going to get us somewhere safe." Linda's voice was kind. "Go ahead, sweetheart."

The little blond curls bounced, his eyes even bigger than his mom's.

Sam held out his arms. "Come on, son. Let's get you out of here."

Sam probably looked terrifying with the black on his face, the weapons and the goggles. But at the sound of his voice, the boy reached out and wrapped his tiny arms around Sam's neck. Linda shifted him into his arms. He wasn't heavy, but the weight of the moment pressed in.

Sam swallowed hard. Shifted Levi onto his back. "Hang on tight."

"Okay." A small, precious voice.

Sam held his hand out to Linda. "Careful of the glass."

"I need to find her."

"You need to take care of Levi. I'll get Eliza."

She looked from the door to him. He was about to threaten to come in after her when she finally took his hand. He helped her out the window and to the soft ground. "We're going straight to the woods. Stay low."

They bolted. No gunshots followed them. But an instant after they moved into the forest, an angry shout filled the air. The empty room had been discovered.

Linda and Levi were safe. Now, he just had to save Eliza.

CHAPTER FORTY

JED'S furious roar sounded from down the hall.

Eliza had searched the darkness for a window, hoping she could free herself, but this room didn't have one.

Were Levi and Mom safe? Had Sam gotten them out? *Please God. I'm trying to trust You. I do trust You.*

She had no idea what was going on, though fewer gunshots sounded now. Was it over? Were Jon and Grant and the rest of the men inside, freeing the women and children?

The door banged open, and she looked up, hoping to see a friendly face.

But Jed looked murderous. "Get up!"

Not waiting until she did, he gripped her arm in his huge hand and yanked her to her feet.

Pain stabbed her back, down her leg, and she stumbled.

He got in her face, jabbed something cold against her stomach. "Do not fight me or Levi pays."

Levi. He wasn't safe?

Oh, God. Help!

He pulled a roll of duct tape from a pocket, covered her mouth and bound her hands. Then, he propelled her into the hall and toward the door to the common area at the entrance. Two men stood guard there, weapons aimed and ready should anybody try to breach it.

But where were the women, the children? Had they been evacuated?

The doors on the right were all closed. Ahead, one on the left was open.

Jed stopped there, and she got a look inside.

Not evacuated. The women and children sat huddled in the middle of a room lined with dusty toys and cribs along the edges. There were fewer people than before, though. Jon and his men must have gotten some out. But not enough.

She scanned the faces. Nicole leaned against a wall, a smug expression when she caught Eliza's eyes.

Lola stood not far from her, but she seemed far from smug. She looked horrified.

Mom wasn't there. Levi wasn't there.

They were free. She had to believe that.

Guards stood at a door opposite the one where Jed and she stood.

"Is this everybody?" Jed asked.

"All that we could get back here," a guard said. "What's the plan, boss?"

"We negotiate. Don't have any choice."

Yes. That was the only viable option.

Except...except something wasn't right.

There'd been lights on in the living area and the bedroom.

But this room was lit by lanterns. Kerosene lanterns.

Jed held out his arm and did a *come on* gesture toward the wall.

Nicole started forward.

"Not you, Nicole. You fulfilled your purpose. Lola."

While Nicole blinked in shock and hurt, the older woman

approached. She looked afraid, but she didn't have it in her to fight him. Never had.

When she reached his side, Jed said, "I'm so proud of all of you. You've all done exactly what you were meant to do. We're going to get through this together."

So often, Eliza had witnessed rapturous looks on Jed's followers' faces. Not now. They looked wary and afraid.

Jed was going to get through this. Lola, and Eliza, too, but only because she was the key to him getting his money.

He wasn't leaving the rest to be rescued.

Did they see it, how he hadn't left the doorway, hadn't joined them in the room? How he'd called the one person he really cared about to his side? She tried to warn them with her eyes, flicking her gaze to the lanterns, but the women wouldn't look at her.

Jed whispered to Lola. "In the hallway."

She squeezed past Eliza, who dared not move, not with the gun still jabbed in her side.

"Be right back." Jed backed into the hallway, bringing Eliza with him. He snapped his fingers. When the guards at the door turned—Gil and Elliot, of course, his two most trusted thugs—he pointed to the room. "Inside." His voice was a whisper.

Elliot moved immediately.

Gil kept his post, shaking his head.

"Now." Jed's word was still a whisper, but there was power behind it.

With one last look at the door—Grant and Jon and the rest of the men must be on the other side—Gil approached.

"After you," Jed said.

Eliza saw the indecision on the man's face. But he did as he was told.

As soon as Gil cleared the door, Jed swung it closed. Checked to make sure it was locked—it was.

And then, he fished something from his pocket, leaned down.

Flicked a lighter.

No! She tried to stop him, to pull him away from whatever he was about to ignite.

Jed reared back and elbowed her in the head. Pain exploded.

Jed leaned down, then stood up.

He threw Eliza over his shoulder and ran.

Eliza's head bounced against his back, her bound hands dangling uselessly.

A loud pop sounded just as they reached the end of the corridor. Jed had removed the boards blocking the back door and now pushed through to the cool mountain air.

Screams followed them outside.

All those women. All those children.

And Eliza, flopping over the shoulder of a psychopath, on her way to an entirely different kind of hell.

CHAPTER FORTY-ONE

IN THE WOODS and climbing toward the staging area, Sam saw a figure in the eerie green-and-black night-vision world. He was about to aim the handgun when he got a glimpse of his face. Daniel.

His brother hurried down the hill, through the trees. "Figured you might need help."

Sam leaned away from Levi to see his face. The boy's eyes were wide as they flicked from Sam to Daniel.

"You did great, son. This is my brother, Daniel. He's going to get you two out of here."

Levi's arms tightened around Sam's neck like he didn't want to let go.

"I'm going to go get your mommy. I'll be right back."

Daniel pulled him away, then held out a hand to Linda. "Come on. Let's get you to safety." To Sam, he said, "Police'll be here any minute. Bryan just spotted them coming up the hill."

Sam turned and bolted down the hill, Daniel's soft, "Be careful" sounding in his earpiece. He was almost to the clearing when he smelled it.

Smoke.

And then heard the men's voices in his head.

"He's burning it down!"

"Get that door open!"

"Dear God, he's going to kill them all!"

Women and children and screams. So many screams.

"Derrick!" That was Jon's voice. "Get to the pump house. There's a hose—"

"Already on it." Derrick was out of breath when he answered.

All Sam could think was, *Eliza!*

He burst from the trees and was headed for the building when he saw something off to his left. Was that Derrick?

No.

A hundred yards away or more, there were two people. A man and a woman. Did the man have hair that went to his waist?

Then he realized what he was seeing. There was a person over the man's shoulder. And swinging down his back...

Eliza.

"They're getting away!" Sam shifted toward them. "Derrick, where are you? You have to stop them!"

"No." Jon was all commander now. "We need to get this fire out."

Sam wanted to argue, but he could hear the screams. All those women and children... Their lives mattered too.

Ahead, Keller and the woman disappeared into the trees.

Sam ran, flat out, desperate to catch up, paying no attention to the terrible noises in his ear.

Then sirens.

"Daniel." Sam was breathing hard. "Tell the police—"

"Already headed to meet them," his brother said.

Maybe the police could surround the place, head Keller off.

But up ahead, Sam heard an engine roaring to life.

And Sam remembered what Hughes had said he'd found in the storage shed.

The engine revved and then started to fade as it moved away. "They're on a four-wheeler," Sam shouted. Had to be.

Which meant, maybe...

He saw the shed, closed the distance. Inside, a rusty Honda dirt bike, probably twenty years old—very similar to the one Sam used to ride. Key, key...

Not in the ignition. He peered along the wall, on counters lining the edges of the room.

Come on. It had to be here. And then...yes!

He snagged a ring from a hook by the door, shoved the key in the ignition, and the bike roared to life.

"What's that?" Bryan's voice sounded above the rest.

"I'm going after them." He heeled the kickstand away, relieved to find the tires were sound.

"Be careful."

Sam wasn't sure which of his brothers had shouted that— maybe all of them—as he gunned the engine and roared out of the shed, following the fresh tracks to a path that led deeper into the woods. Ducking branches and skirting bushes, bouncing over tree roots that poked out of the ground, he thanked God for the goggles that helped him see and protected his eyes. Keller was doing this without that help. And on a slower vehicle, with two women in tow.

Maybe—*please, God*—Sam could catch up.

He had no idea where Keller was going, but the man had planned for this contingency. Why else keep the four-wheeler and dirt bike gassed up and ready if not to make a quick getaway? And if he'd gone to all that trouble, then did he have a car stashed somewhere?

Probably.

Sam had to catch him. And stop him. He'd figure out that second part when he completed the first.

The path switchbacked up a steep hill, then around to the opposite side.

The voices in his head faded. He'd moved out of range, and he was glad for it. His heart went out to all those innocents, and he prayed they'd be rescued. But he needed to focus.

He slowed at a fork. Which way? They were the same. Both wide enough for a four-wheeler. He searched for tracks.

There. Faint, but he was almost positive. He took the right fork and gunned the engine again.

He had to be moving faster than Keller. Why hadn't he caught up?

Had Sam gone the wrong way? Jon had said the paths wound all over this mountain. Keller and Eliza could be anywhere.

Please, God. Direct me.

He kept moving forward, hoping, praying he'd catch up to them.

The path started downward, winding back and forth to keep the descent from being too steep.

And then he saw it.

The glow of headlights bounced below Sam's position, probably only fifty yards or so, but on the twisty path, it was a much farther distance.

Below that, he spied another light. A road? A store?

A hidden getaway car?

Sam slowed, peering at the woods between himself and the four-wheeler.

If he followed the cut trail, he might reach them in time to stop Keller from escaping. But he might not.

It was a bad idea.

Maybe in the daylight, maybe on a mountain he was

familiar with, maybe on a gentler slope. But this...this was insane.

And the only way Sam was going to catch up.

He aimed the dirt bike toward the bottom. "Help me, Jesus. This is gonna hurt." And he gunned it.

Down. Straight down.

Branches whacked him in the face.

A tree root jutted ahead, and he barely got around it before it launched him off the bike.

Prickly bushes scraped him through his jeans.

He hit a hole, nearly lost it, barely kept the bike upright.

His heart dropped, and maybe he'd left it back there in the bracken.

Then he hit a rise, going too fast. His wheels came off the ground. He was headed straight for a tree. His life flashed. His mom and dad, his brothers. A thousand games of pickup basketball, football. The bonfire they lit every time they went to the family's little island off the coast.

Eliza.

Levi.

God, please...

The wheels hit.

Sam yanked the wheel to the side, barely avoided the wide trunk.

He slowed, breathing hard.

If he broke his back or killed himself, Keller would escape with Eliza.

He couldn't let that happen.

Where was the four-wheeler? No headlights ahead, but...

A road.

Sam sped to descend the last twenty yards, made it out of the woods, down a gully and up the other side.

The four-wheeler was across the street, headed into the

parking lot of a little store.

Sam considered trying to shoot a tire out, but he couldn't risk hitting Eliza.

If his guess was correct, they weren't going much farther anyway.

Praying he was right, he jumped off the bike, letting it fall on the asphalt, and bolted across the street. Maybe Keller hadn't heard him coming over the roar of his own vehicle. Maybe Sam could sneak up on him.

Beside the building, he paused, breathing hard, and texted his location to his brothers. At least they'd know where to look if this went south.

The four-wheeler's engine cut off.

Trading his phone for his handgun, Sam crept to the back corner of the building and spied around the back.

Barely glimpsed the gun in Keller's hand before he reared back.

A bullet hit the building right beside his head.

So much for the element of surprise.

And then the rest of what he'd seen registered.

Keller held Eliza in front of him with his other hand. She looked ragged, like she was barely able to keep her feet. Duct tape covered her mouth. Her hands were bound.

A second woman stood off to the side, same age as Keller, shorter than Eliza.

Behind them, a dark sedan.

"Drop the gun," Keller said, "and toss it where I can see it."

He pulled out his phone again, tapped out a text.

> Volkswagen. Blue or black, Massachusetts plates. Still here but not for long. Hurry!

He shoved the cell in his pocket. "Just let her go."

"Wish I could," Keller said, "but she has my money."

"Otherwise, you'd have let her burn with the rest of your hostages."

He heard the gasp. Eliza? No. Her mouth was covered.

Was it the other one? Lola, he guessed, Keller's wife, the woman Eliza had described as her friend and confidant.

Now, her kidnapper.

"Not hostages," the man said. "Devoted followers."

"So they all chose to burn to death?"

"I didn't want to do that." His voice was calm, almost conversational. "That's Eliza's fault. She left me no choice. The only way to get away was to make sure you and your friends had more important things to do than follow me."

Evil. The man was pure evil.

"I don't have to hurt Eliza." By the man's tone, he really wanted to. "But I will if you don't toss that gun where I can see it. Right now."

Sam didn't have a choice. He slid his gun onto the pavement, far from Keller.

"Come on out here," Keller said.

"So you can shoot me?"

"Can't exactly have you trying to stop us or telling anybody which way we headed."

The distinctive sound of tape being pulled from skin, and then Eliza spoke.

"Don't, Sam."

Keller muttered something Sam didn't make out. Probably telling Eliza what to say.

Her voice was weak when she spoke again. "I can't lose you too. I have to know you're still here. Even if Levi..." Her words hitched.

Sam heard a thump and an *oomph*.

"Don't hurt her!"

"Come out here where I can see you," Keller said.

He leaned against the side of the building, breathing hard, praying hard. He didn't want to get shot. He didn't want Eliza to get hurt.

He called, "Levi and your mother are safe."

"Oh. Oh, thank God." Her voice was stronger. "Go, Sam. Levi needs his father—"

"I'm his father!"

Sam ignored Jed, but Eliza's words were a stab to the gut. His son did need him.

So did the woman he loved.

What would Keller do if Sam refused? He might hurt Eliza, but he wouldn't kill her. He couldn't.

"Come on out," Keller said. "Now."

Sam didn't move.

A thud.

Another gasp, this one definitely Eliza.

Sam flinched, got low, peeked around the corner.

Eliza's arm was hanging at an unnatural angle from her shoulder. One hand covered her mouth like she was trying to hold in her reaction.

Trying to keep Sam from hearing, from knowing what that man was doing to her.

"Don't hurt her!"

"I'll keep hurting her until you show yourself."

The police were coming. Sam just needed to hold off another few minutes.

But Eliza screamed.

"Stop it!" That from Lola. "You're going to kill her."

Sam couldn't take it.

No matter what happened to him, the police would find the Kellers and stop them. They'd rescue Eliza.

Sam had to believe that.

Help me.

CHAPTER FORTY-TWO

ELIZA COULDN'T MOVE her arm. She'd had a moment of hope when Jed had unbound her hands and removed the tape on her face.

Then, he'd pulled her arm out of its socket. The pain was hot and sharp. But she'd managed to keep quiet.

Not so much when he whacked her on the head with the butt of his gun. That had sent her to her knees, the action so fast and shocking that the scream escaped before she could stop it.

She was on her feet again, only standing because Jed was holding her up. Using her as a shield.

Her head pounded. The pain in her arm stabbed even as she held it against her torso. She wasn't going to survive this. She knew that, and she could live with it. Levi was safe. Her mom was safe. All those women...

She had to believe Jon and Grant and Michael and the rest of the men were freeing them. Otherwise, they'd be here.

It wasn't the way she'd wanted it to work out. She'd dreamed of being with Sam and Levi, dreamed of being a family. She'd imagined them filling Sam's big house with love. More children. Laughter and peace.

But if the people she loved were safe...

She'd entrust them into God's hands.

Thank You, God. Thank You for protecting them, just like You promised. Be with them. Teach Levi the Truth.

"It's okay, Sam." She swallowed, tried to make her voice stronger. "Be with Levi. Raise him well." She couldn't keep the emotion out of her voice. "Don't let him forget me."

"He's not going to forget you because you're going to be with him." Sam stepped out from behind the building, hands raised.

"Sam, no!"

"I knew you'd do it." Jed's voice was filled with scorn. "Weak. You can never achieve greatness unless you're willing to fight for it."

"You seem to think strong means hurting innocent people to get what you want," Sam said. "But your definition is flawed. Strong men sacrifice themselves for the people they love. True strength comes from knowing there are worse things than death."

"You're wrong. Death is the end for people like you, small-minded and pathetic." To Lola, he said, "Open the trunk."

Eliza couldn't see her and was surprised when she didn't sense the woman's quick obedience.

"What are you going to do?" Lola asked.

"Obey me!"

A moment later, the car opened, and the trunk popped.

"Get in. You're driving." A moment later... "Are you in?" He didn't turn to check. "Close the door and start it up."

The engine roared to life and the door slammed, filling the air behind it with exhaust.

Maybe Jed didn't want his wife to see what he was going to do next. As if shooting a man in cold blood could be worse than trapping women and children in a room and setting it on fire.

He was insane.

"I guess this is it." Jed sounded eager.

The gun exploded.

At the same time, Sam dove to the side.

And Jed stumbled, letting up his grip on Eliza.

She hit the pavement, catching herself with her good arm, thank God.

But Jed kept his feet, kept ahold of the gun. Before he could take aim...

Sam pulled a handgun from a holster, aimed.

And fired.

Keller fell to his knees. Still alive. Shot but alive.

He roared with shock and fury.

His arm came up, aimed toward his wife.

Sam fired again. And again.

Keller fell forward, his head bouncing off the pavement.

CHAPTER FORTY-THREE

SAM CHECKED ON LOLA, who'd draped herself over Keller's body. As crazy as her husband.

He grabbed the gun he'd tossed and Keller's, unwilling to give Lola any chance to take revenge. Then he shut off the car and ran to Eliza.

She wasn't moving. "Sweetheart. Please be okay. Tell me you're okay."

She looked up at him, eyes wide. "Is it over?"

"Yes." Thank God.

He tried to help her up, but she winced in pain. No surprise, considering the separated shoulder and who knew what else.

So, ignoring the dead body and the woman weeping over it, he lay down beside Eliza and wrapped an arm around her, careful of her injuries. He relished in the warmth of her, her breath against his cheek. He brushed hair away so he could see her face. "What hurts?"

"Is Levi really okay?"

"He and your mom are fine. Our son is..." For the first time, he allowed himself to think about that sweet little curly-haired boy. The weight of him in Sam's arms. "He's amazing."

"Like his father."

Father. Sam could hardly comprehend it.

~

The next few hours were a blur. Sam's brothers showed up right after the police in the lot behind the little dollar store. Daniel, Michael, Grant, and Derrick arrived first. A few minutes later, Bryan joined them. All alive, most sporting injuries Daniel had already patched up. Hughes and the rest of the bodyguards who'd come to help were answering questions and tending the wounded at the campground.

Eliza and Sam rode to the hospital in the back of a squad car. They were ready to see Levi, but the cops wanted their statements first. While Eliza was treated for her injuries, Sam sat in a small conference room in the Augusta hospital and gave his statement, recounting the events.

Seeing Keller trying to escape.

The harrowing chase on the dirt bike.

And the realization that finding Eliza and freeing her were two very different things.

"You tossed your gun away and stepped around the building, even though you knew the guy was going to kill you?" The detective, a heavyset woman with a dirty-blond ponytail, sounded skeptical. She sat catty-corner to him at the small table. A uniformed cop was taking notes at her side.

"I had another gun." Sam explained about the man who'd tried to shoot him from the window and how he'd taken the man's pistol, just in case.

"So then what happened?"

Sam replayed the scene in his head.

Lola had done everything Keller demanded—except get in the car. She'd popped the trunk, started the engine, then slammed the door from the outside.

She'd crept close to her husband.

It'd taken everything in Sam not to look her direction and give her away.

Keller was just about to pull the trigger. Sam would've pulled his own gun and gotten off a shot, but Eliza was in front of him. He'd fully expected to die in that moment. His only regret, that he hadn't stalled longer and given the police more time to show up.

"Why did it take so long for you guys to get there?" he asked now.

"That store is a good distance from the camp," the detective said. "Not as the crow flies, but the roads go around the mountain, not over it. All our manpower was at the camp."

That made sense.

"So Keller's wife was creeping close...?" she prompted.

"She just...barreled into him."

Sam would probably replay that moment in his nightmares for years.

Keller firing, his shot going wide. He'd managed to keep his feet and not lose his grip on the gun, but he'd let go of Eliza. She fell away.

Keller pushed his wife off himself and swung the gun toward her.

But Sam fired first.

"You're saying the wife helped you?"

"Surprised me too." Lola Keller had saved their lives. And then Sam had saved hers.

"Any idea why?"

"Maybe she realized what he'd done, trying to kill all those women and children. Maybe she realized he was insane. Or...

Eliza had lived in a house right next to them for years. She worked closely with Lola. They were friends. Maybe she just wanted to save her friend."

"Hmm. Maybe." The detective asked a lot more questions, and sometimes the same questions in various ways. Apparently, Sam managed to answer them to her satisfaction because she finally pushed back in her chair. "We're done for now, but you're not off the hook."

"Meaning?"

"Meaning you guys shouldn't have been there in the first place. You should've called us the minute you knew something was wrong, not gone all SEAL Team Six."

Sam wasn't sure what their story was, so he kept his mouth shut, following the detective out the door.

He was ready to find Eliza, but in the corridor just down from the conference room, he spied Grant and Jon having a spirited conversation with an older cop who, judging by the way he carried himself, had some authority.

The detective who'd just questioned Sam turned to him, sardonic smile in place. "Good luck with that. The chief's fit to be tied." She headed the other direction, but Sam walked toward his brother.

"You should know better." The chief jabbed Grant in the chest. "You're a cop. Or you were. I'll have your badge. If it's up to me, you'll end up in jail for this."

Grant didn't say a word.

"Sir, I suggest you step back." Jon's voice was low, but he didn't need to shout for the strength in his voice to be heard.

The man blinked, then took a good look at Grant's face, then Jon's.

And took a step away.

"We called it in as soon as we knew what was going on," Jon

said. "You would have had us wait outside? Let all those people burn to death?"

"You shouldn't have been there in the first place," the older man said. "This isn't a war zone. And don't tell me you showed up with eight men armed to the teeth but you weren't planning something."

"Our plan was to save lives," Jon said. "And we didn't lose a single innocent. A couple of Keller's men were killed, but that couldn't be helped."

"You don't just give a bunch of overgrown boys guns and call them soldiers."

"Not boys." Anger hummed in Grant's words. "Former special operatives, SEALS and Green Berets. Trained and battle-tested. Which is why all the good guys are still alive—*and* all the hostages."

The chief saw Sam approaching. "You were a soldier?"

"Nope. I'm the father of one of the children who was held hostage and the fiancé of one of the women."

"You're going to prison. I hope it was worth it."

The words sent a fresh round of acid to his stomach.

Prison?

But then, the rest of what the chief said registered. "Worth it? To save their lives? All those lives?" Sam stepped closer. "What do you think?"

Before he could respond, a door opened and Michael walked in. "Phone call for you." He held out his cell to the chief.

The man reared back. "Who are you? What are you—?"

"You're gonna want to take that, sir."

He yanked the phone out of Michael's hand and barked into it. "Who is this?" And then, his spine straightened. "Sorry, sir. I didn't realize..."

Michael gestured to his brothers, and they moved toward the other end of the corridor.

"What's going on?" Sam asked.

"Called in a favor."

Behind him, the chief said, "But that's not what... No, I understand."

"What kind of favor?" Grant asked.

"The *get us all out of trouble with the local cops* kind. He won't like it, but he'll go along."

"Who is it?" Sam asked.

Michael just smiled.

A moment later, the chief said, "Yes, sir. I'll take care of it." And then, he stalked toward them, focused on Sam's brother. "Who are you?"

"Michael Wright, machine parts salesman."

The older man squinted, studying him. He was still red-faced as he handed over the phone. Then, he turned to the rest of them. "Apparently, your brother knows people in high places. I recommend you stay out of my jurisdiction. I catch you tapping a toe out of line, you'll end up in jail."

Sam nodded.

Jon didn't bother.

But Grant took a step closer. "I get where you're coming from, I do. If this had happened in my town, I'd feel the same way. But twenty women and children weren't burned to death in *your jurisdiction* because we prevented it. We risked our lives to rescue them. You didn't lose a single man, and if I'm not mistaken, you're going to get the credit for taking Keller down. So...you're welcome."

The man glowered a long moment. Then, he stalked away.

They were off the hook. And it was over.

Or it would be, as soon as he found Eliza and Levi.

CHAPTER FORTY-FOUR

ELIZA HAD BEEN TREATED for her injuries and released. Now, she hit the button to open the double doors and stepped into the waiting room. A few of Keller's *followers* rested in chairs looking shell-shocked. Where would they go now? What would they do?

Those women had gone to Keller for help. They'd gone to him to learn life skills and had instead learned to be dependent on a madman. What would the future look like for them?

Nicole approached, fury in her gaze. "I hope you're happy. You destroyed our lives. You killed a good man."

Eliza glanced beyond her, but none of the other women seemed inclined to get involved. Eliza kept her voice low. "He tried to burn you, your friends, and all those children to death."

"Don't be ridiculous. He had a plan to get us all out of there. You ruined everything."

Defensive words, angry words, filled Eliza's mouth, but she didn't let them release. Why spend a single moment trying to rationalize with an insane person? Instead, she gripped her former friend's arm, barely flinching when Nicole jerked back. "I'll be praying for you."

She turned her back on Nicole just as, from the other direction, Mom ran across the waiting room.

She grabbed Eliza and wrapped her in a hug. "Thank God. They told me you were injured, but they wouldn't let me back to see you."

She hugged her in return but was looking over her shoulder. "Where's—?"

"Mommy!"

Levi ran toward her, a man behind him, walking with the aid of a cane.

"I was so scared when Pretend Daddy took you away. I don't like him anymore. He's mean." Levi held his arms up, expecting her to pick him up. "Grammy said you were hurt but you're okay. They wouldn't let us come see you."

She took his hand and headed for a bank of chairs. "I got a little hurt, buddy. My arm." She showed him the sling. "I'm not supposed to pick anything up. But you can sit on my lap."

"Okay." When she sat, he crawled on and settled against her, causing pain in her ribs she worked to ignore.

Levi popped his thumb in his mouth—a habit he'd given up before they'd left The Ranch—then took it out. "I missed you. But Bryan was playing with me. He has to walk with that cane all the time, but he says his leg doesn't hurt much. Did you know he broke it falling off a giant cliff. Isn't that cool?" Levi stuck his thumb back in his mouth.

"So cool." Eliza couldn't help smiling at the man standing a few feet away.

He nodded. "Good to see you, Eliza."

"You too. Thanks for...everything."

"My pleasure." His gaze cut to Levi. "He's pretty awesome."

She kissed her son's head. "I think so. Where's Sam?"

"Right here."

She whipped her head toward the voice.

Sam was standing beside Mom, looking down at Eliza with so much tenderness in his gaze that tears pricked her eyes.

Levi took his thumb out of his mouth again. "You're the guy who saved us. Mommy, he came right up to the window and broke it and pulled me out and then helped Grammy and we ran through the woods to another guy. It was scary, but he carried me on his back."

"You were very brave." Sam knelt in front of them and smiled at his son. Then, he turned to her, brushing hair away from her face with his warm fingers. He held her eye contact a long moment, and she took in the sight of him. He had a few scrapes and bruises, but he was whole and well and...perfect.

Sam turned to Levi again. "You're just like your mom. Incredibly brave, incredibly strong."

She wasn't, not even close. She'd almost gotten them all killed. But also...

She'd done her part. She'd shown them how to find Levi and Mom.

Not perfectly, but God made up for all her flaws and some-how, miraculously, brought them through.

And maybe it wasn't the best time, but she didn't want to wait another moment. Bryan and Mom had moved away to give them some privacy. Nobody was paying them any attention.

She took Sam's hand but looked at Levi. "Hey, buddy."

His little eyes missed nothing, flicking from her to Sam.

"You know how Jed was your pretend daddy?"

He spoke around his thumb. "Uh-huh."

Sam's eyes widened as his gaze moved from Levi to her and back. Was he nervous?

She was too, a little, but something told her not to wait, that this was the right time. "Do you want to know who your real daddy is?"

Levi blinked. The thumb came out of his mouth. He stared at her with wide eyes and nodded.

She tipped her head toward the man she loved. "Levi, meet Sam Wright."

He sat up on her lap. Stared at Sam a long moment. Then he held his arms out.

Sam lifted him and held him close, breathing him in. Tears dripped from his eyes, but he didn't seem to notice.

Levi held on, his little shoulders shaking. Then he backed up, put his tiny hands on his father's face and studied him. "You're not a pretend daddy?"

Sam shook his head. "I'm your father, Levi." His voice cracked. "Your real father."

"Are you mean like Jed?"

"I promise, I'll never be like him."

Levi nodded as if the words were an unbreakable vow. He looked at Eliza, and he smiled. "I like my real daddy."

"Me, too," she said. "Very much."

Levi settled against Sam's chest and stuck his thumb back in his mouth as if it were all settled.

She'd thought Levi would be happy, even curious. But this reaction... This was...

Another miracle.

CHAPTER FORTY-FIVE

SAM CLOSED HIS LAPTOP. He'd added the final touches to the deal he'd spent months putting together. Ernest had decided that changing horses mid-stream wasn't the best idea. Or maybe he'd been convinced by the revised offer Sam had cajoled out of the buyers a week earlier.

If everything went according to plan, Sam would get it all wrapped up in the next week or so. And then...

And then nothing. At least not where work was concerned. Sure, there were clients clamoring to partner with him, but he'd put them off. He'd get back to that eventually, but...

"Daddy!" Levi skidded into his office in sock feet, fell down, popped back up, and launched himself into Sam's arms.

"Hey, buddy. When did you get here?"

"Right now!"

Eliza stepped into the doorway, and Sam stood and tossed Levi over his shoulder as he approached her.

"Well, hello, little lady." He leaned down and kissed her, speaking with a hokey cowboy accent. "Aren't you just as pretty as a field of bluebells."

Eliza laughed. "Goofball."

"Bagged myself a big old deer. Maybe you can cook him up for me."

Giggling, Levi pounded on his back with his little fists. "I'm not a deer, I'm your son."

Those words had emotion rising in Sam's throat. He wasn't sure he'd ever get accustomed to this.

His amazing, energetic, trusting little boy.

And the woman he loved.

She played along, peeking behind Sam's back. "Why, he sure does look tasty." Her accent was even worse than Sam's.

"Mommy! It's me."

"Oh, Levi? I thought you were a giant deer. Darn. Now what are we going to eat for lunch?"

While Levi recounted the menu for today's anniversary party, which he'd questioned them about multiple times—the kid did like his food—Sam kissed Eliza.

"I missed you."

"I missed you," she said.

She and Levi had been staying at the B and B in downtown Shadow Cove, but they'd spent the vast majority of every day in the weeks since the events at the campground by Sam's side. They'd gone for walks at the beach and along trails in the nearby state park. They'd shared meals. They'd watched movies. Sam had read countless books to his son and had even started tucking him in every night. And then he and Eliza would huddle on the little couch in her suite's sitting area and dream about their lives together.

They'd practically shut out the rest of the world.

That was going to change today.

The caterers were hard at work in the kitchen and on the deck. The rest of the family would arrive soon.

Sam put Levi down, and he ran upstairs to the bedroom that would soon be his. Thanks to the magic of online shopping, Sam had filled it with toys, some new since the last time Levi'd been there two days before.

"Did he ever learn to walk?" Sam asked. "Or did he go straight from crawling to running?"

"Maybe a few steps." She'd gotten her hair cut a few days earlier. It wasn't as short as it used to be, and he liked the extra length. He'd taken them shopping and bought them both new wardrobes. Today, Eliza wore a pretty silk blouse tucked into trim slacks. With the crisp jacket and new boots, she looked as fashionable as ever. Not that he cared. He'd take her in that ugly plaid shirt and those terrible work pants if those were the only option.

But he liked this version too. He loved every version of Eliza.

He tugged a lock between his fingers. "You're beautiful."

"*You're* beautiful."

"No." He tried to look stern. "I'm handsome and rugged."

"And gorgeous." She slid her arms around his back. He didn't miss her sigh against his chest.

"What's wrong?"

She leaned back to see his face. "Are you sure they're going to be happy?"

He kissed the top of her head. "Positive."

"They're not going to hate me for keeping their grandson from them all this time."

"Quit worrying. They already love you. And they'll fall head-over-heels with Levi in about five seconds. I promise."

When the doorbell rang, Eliza bolted upstairs to play with Levi—and hide.

Sam waited until she was out of sight, then opened the door to his parents. Dad was still tall and broad in his midsixties. Gray hair, but it made him look distinguished. Mom was downright short compared to her husband and boys. She claimed five-

five—nobody bought it—and had blond hair, though her roots were getting whiter all the time. She flashed a wide smile as she leaned in for a hug. "Good to see you."

Sam hugged her, then his father. Maybe he was a little nervous, but he did his best to hide it as he led them into the living room so they would have privacy from the caterers. Mom and Dad settled on the couch where, just a few weeks before, Eliza had barely been able to remember her name.

All her memories had come back since then, even those from that night.

Gil and Elliot had followed her from the airport, though she hadn't known it at the time. They'd caught up with her on a narrow highway that led to Shadow Cove, mostly deserted at that time of night. Gil had run her rented sedan off the road.

She'd crashed and bolted from the car, running toward light that turned out to be a campfire.

A lot of campfires, actually, surrounded by teenagers and deep in the woods.

Gil got ahold of Eliza before she reached them and tackled her. Knocked her down. She remembered a sharp pain to the back of her head.

And screaming.

The teenagers heard and came to her aid. Thanks to some quick thinking—and a couple of rifles—they ran Gil and Elliot off. When she couldn't remember anything, not even her name, one of them had offered to drive her to the address on the business card clutched in her hand. Adults would've taken Eliza straight to the hospital, but the kids were nervous about getting caught camping on private property, or so Sam assumed when he found Eliza's rental car. Her suitcase and purse were missing, of course, probably taken by Gil and Elliot that night. They'd been tasked not only with finding her but with finding out where she'd been and where she was going.

"Something wrong, son?" Dad looked up at Sam from the sofa, concern in his warm brown eyes.

Sam forced himself to sit, to be calm. He settled on an armchair beside his mother. "I have a surprise for you."

"Shouldn't we wait to open presents when everyone is here?"

"They'll understand," Sam said. "You remember Eliza?"

"Daniel told us she'd returned and was in a bit of trouble. We always liked her."

"Me, too," Sam said. "But I messed it up. Well, we both made mistakes, some pretty big ones. And...it's a long story. I promise to tell you everything, but right now..."

His parents both looked expectant. Hopeful.

"We're back together."

"Oh, good." Mom's smile was so natural as she glanced at Dad. "I'm so glad. We always thought you and Eliza made a good match."

"There's more, though." The words he'd rehearsed flew from his brain. He had no idea how to do this.

Suddenly, he understood why it'd taken Eliza so long to tell him the truth. How did you spring this news on someone?

He pushed to his feet and walked to the stairs, prepared to call her down.

But she was standing near the bottom, Levi's hands in hers. He looked as nervous as his mom.

Sam held out his arms, and Levi jumped into them. With his son propped on his hip, he took Eliza's hand, then kissed her on the head. "It's okay," he whispered. "I promise."

Together, they walked around the corner.

Mom gasped, a hand covering her mouth.

Dad stood, pulling her up beside him. They both stared.

And, if he wasn't mistaken, those were tears in Mom's eyes.

"Mom, Dad. You remember Eliza?"

They nodded, but they barely flicked their gazes to her. They couldn't seem to force their eyes away from Levi.

Clearly, they saw what Sam had missed the first time he'd looked at his son's picture. The resemblance was so obvious now.

Meaning they already knew. It made it easier for Sam to go on.

"This is Levi. Our son."

Sam had assumed Dad would be the first to react, but Mom skirted the coffee table and approached. She smiled at the little boy. "It's a pleasure to meet you, Levi. I'm..." She blinked tears back and swallowed. "I'm your Nana."

Dad was there now too. "And I'm Pops."

Levi's head was pressed against Sam's chest as if...as if he were the boy's safe place. But he said, "Hi."

Sam's parents grinned.

They hugged Eliza. There were tears and questions they didn't have time to answer, not yet. But it didn't matter. They had the rest of their lives to fill in the blanks.

Everyone else arrived. Daniel and Camilla had flown in for the occasion, timing it with the closing on their new house. Sam had invited Eliza's mother and her best friend. He was determined to mend fences with Jeanette, though she was turning out to be the bigger obstacle. Linda was different. Kind and generous. She'd even apologized to him for her behavior five years before. He'd been shocked speechless.

The group ate steak and lobster and fresh corn and all kinds of desserts. They toasted the anniversary couple. They talked and laughed and shared stories.

Grant and Summer announced her pregnancy, which led to more tears, more celebrations.

Later, standing on the deck, looking past the colorful foliage to the bright blue Atlantic, Sam watched his family. His five brothers, his two sisters-in-law, and the woman who would become his wife the following afternoon in a small ceremony after church.

Mostly, he watched the little boy whose last name would soon match his.

Eliza excused herself from her conversation and joined him at the deck railing. "What are you thinking?"

"I'm thinking that God must really, really love me."

She stepped into his arms. "God and I have something in common, then." She pressed a hand to the side of his face. "Because I really, really love you too."

The End.

...of this story, but Michael's story is just beginning. Because the woman he loves is missing...probably dead.

And it's all his fault.

Turn the page for more about *Rescuing You,* Book 2 of the Wright Heroes of Maine.

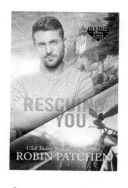

A heart-pounding tale of danger and devotion, the riveting second installment of the Wright Heroes of Maine series by a USA Today bestselling author.

CIA agent Michael Wright's world crumbles when his girlfriend, Leila, is snatched off the street and later seen in the grasp of a terrorist he's been tracking, Michael blames himself. Keeping his identity secret from her clearly didn't protect her. Now he must defy the Agency and fly to Iraq to rescue her.

Leila Amato escaped Iraq a decade earlier, only returning in her worst nightmares. But those nightmares have come true when she finds herself captive and all alone, or so she thought until she sees her identical twin sister.

Michael tracks Leila to a desert compound, but his rescue mission goes awry when he discovers her sister needs to escape as well. His detailed strategy can only ensure one woman's safety. Now they're on the run, trying to get out of the country before their enemies track them down.

But Leila's kidnapping is only one small part of a larger plot—one that endangers thousands of lives—and now he doesn't know who he can trust. Not even the woman who's stolen his heart. A woman who's been keeping secrets of her own...

A high-stakes international chase full of romantic suspense, spies, and a ticking time bomb that will keep you reading all night long.

ALSO BY ROBIN PATCHEN

The Wright Heroes of Maine

Running to You

Rescuing You

Finding You

The Coventry Saga

Glimmer in the Darkness

Tides of Duplicity

Betrayal of Genius

Traces of Virtue

Touch of Innocence

Inheritance of Secrets

Lineage of Corruption

Wreathed in Disgrace

Courage in the Shadows

Vengeance in the Mist

A Mountain Too Steep

The Nutfield Saga

Convenient Lies

Twisted Lies

Generous Lies

Innocent Lies

Beautiful Lies

Legacy Rejected

Legacy Restored

Legacy Reclaimed

Legacy Redeemed

Amanda Series

Chasing Amanda

Finding Amanda

ABOUT THE AUTHOR

Robin Patchen is a *USA Today* bestselling and award-winning author of Christian romantic suspense. She grew up in a small town in New Hampshire, the setting of her Nutfield Saga books, and then headed to Boston to earn a journalism degree. After college, working in marketing and public relations, she discovered how much she loathed the nine-to-five ball and chain. After relocating to the Southwest, she started writing her first novel while she homeschooled her three children. The novel was dreadful, but her passion for storytelling didn't wane. Thankfully, as her children grew, so did her writing ability. Now that her kids are adults, she has more time to play with the lives of fictional heroes and heroines, wreaking havoc and working magic to give her characters happy endings. When she's not writing, she's editing or reading, proving that most of her life revolves around the twenty-six letters of the alphabet. Visit robinpatchen.com/subscribe to receive a free book and stay informed about Robin's latest projects.

Printed in the USA
CPSIA information can be obtained
at www.ICGtesting.com
JSHW012051260923
49076JS00023B/227

9 781950 029372